Modern Irish-American Fiction

RICHARD FALLIS, SERIES EDITOR

Modern
Irish-American Fiction

A Reader

Edited by
DANIEL J. CASEY
and
ROBERT E. RHODES

Foreword by
SEAN O'HUIGINN

SYRACUSE UNIVERSITY PRESS

First Edition
94 93 92 91 90 89   6 5 4 3 2 1

The paper used in this publication meets the minimum requirements of American National Standard for Information Sciences—Permanence of Paper for Printed Library Materials, ANSI Z39.48–1984. ∞™

Library of Congress Cataloging-in-Publication Data

Modern Irish-American fiction : a reader / edited by Daniel J. Casey
and Robert E. Rhodes. — 1st ed.
    p. cm. — (Irish studies)
  Bibliography : p.
  ISBN 0–8156–2462–X (alk. paper). — ISBN 0–8156–0234–0 (pbk. :
alk. paper)
    1. American fiction—Irish-American authors. 2. American
fiction—20th century. 3. Irish Americans—Fiction. 4. Ireland—
Emigration and immigration—Fiction. 5. United States—Emigration
and immigration—Fiction. I. Casey, Daniel J., 1937–   .
II. Rhodes, Robert E., 1927–   .   III. Series : Irish studies
(Syracuse, N.Y.)
PS647.I74M64   1989
813′.5′08089162—dc19   88–32081
                                          CIP

MANUFACTURED IN THE UNITED STATES OF AMERICA

With love to
Dan, Tom, Mike, and Conor,
and
Tracy, Alison, Robin, Caitlin, and Nancy

DANIEL J. CASEY is Vice President for Academic Affairs and Academic Dean at the College of Our Lady of the Elms in Chicopee, Massachusetts. A four-time Fulbright recipient, he has founded and directed study-abroad programs in Ireland, Germany, and Japan. He has authored more than eighty books, articles, and reviews, including *Views of the Irish Peasantry, 1800–1916* and *Irish-American Fiction: Essays in Criticism*—both with Robert E. Rhodes. Casey is married and has four sons. He lives in Hadley, Massachusetts.

ROBERT E. RHODES is Emeritus Professor of Anglo-Irish Literature at SUNY, Cortland, where he taught Irish and Irish-American literature for thirty years. The author of scores of articles, reviews, and lectures, he has also co-edited two books. Immediate past president of the American Conference for Irish Studies, he is also a SUNY Faculty Exchange Scholar. Married, with five daughters, Rhodes lives in Cortland, New York.

CONTENTS

FOREWORD

Those of his Irish contemporaries who heard James Joyce proclaim his intention "to forge in the smithy of my soul the uncreated conscience of my race" marveled no doubt at the hubris of it. Many would have scorned the notion that after millenia of history the Irish conscience remained so much crude ore awaiting the furnace and anvil of the master wordsmith. However, the underlying premise of the conscience of a race, so problematic today, caused little difficulty then. Sympathetic Englishmen such as Matthew Arnold had discerned in the Celt certain spiritual qualities which the Anglo-Saxon, in his bluff if goodhearted way, had somehow lost in the rush to organize the world in a manner congenial to his simple tastes. The space thus cleared in the value system of the Anglo-Saxon world became the rallying-point for the Celtic revival in literature. The renascent forces of Irish nationalism, too, found the concept of the Irish race, regularly urged to manifest itself in a convention, a convenient vehicle to unite potentially divergent forces.

The history of the twentieth century and the modern Irish experience have taught us to be cautious about simplified concepts such as these. The definition of being Irish has happily defeated the efforts of friend and foe alike to squeeze it into preordained moulds and to this day retains some of the elusive properties which the nineteenth century so confidently pronounced to be an attribute of the Celtic mind. This is welcome and creative in real life, but it does pose problems of definition and demarcation for anyone who wishes to chronicle the Irish contribution to literature. The historian, or for that matter the anthologist, of Irish-American literature faces these problems in a particularly acute way. Is the criterion to be the Irish antecedents of the writer or the ethnic content of the work? Is Irish-

American fiction an artificial category or is it a distinct body of literature with characteristic traits and patterns of its own? Which writers are to be admitted to the canon of those who, in Joyce's sense, created the "conscience," or at least recorded the experience, of the Irish-American community?

In this collection Daniel J. Casey and Robert E. Rhodes have cast their net widely. The ethnic content of the works they have chosen varies widely, reflecting, as it naturally does, the different stages of assimilation of the Irish in the United States. The themes and concerns of the pieces are as much of general as of local relevance. Those good writers usually are. The use of language, the relationship between parents and children, the aspiration to status, the loss of tradition, the gap between the ideal and the real, the awesome mysteries of religion are all concerns which are no monopoly of the Irish, whether in Ireland or the United States. Yet it may be that the treatment of certain such recurring themes of Irish-American fiction are splinters of broken Irish traditions or carry echoes of Ireland in more ancient times. The pre-famine Irish world, for all its poverty and degradation, was also a society of great internal strength and social coherence with a highly developed oral tradition of literature in the Irish language. It is perhaps not entirely a coincidence that Finley Peter Dunne, the first significant Irish-American writer, is also an intensely oral one, even to the point of elaborating his own somewhat whimsical orthography to catch the living voices of Mr. Dooley and his cronies. Studs Lonigan's alienation is rooted in the circumstances of his youth and adolescence in Chicago, but his thwarted search for purpose and identity is also in poignant contrast to the old structured world of the clan or the village, where the young warrior or faction fighter had his allotted role. The experience of Catholicism, common to many of the Irish on both sides of the Atlantic, is of course another recurring theme in this anthology, whether as a source of mystery and consolation, a badge of singularity, or a stifling embrace to be broken. It is in this area that the parallels with fiction written in Ireland are perhaps most direct.

The story of the Irish in America is itself a compelling one. There can be few parallels in history for emigration so massive from one small island that today over forty million Americans trace at least part of their ancestry to Ireland. The Irish arrived for the most part in abject conditions, endowed only with their qualities that could be carried in the heart or in the head—courage, intelligence, a sense of loyalty, and a determination to succeed. These and their capacity for hard work and sacrifice established an active and creative presence at every level of achievement in American society. If there were faults and difficulties, it must also be said that they clung tenaciously to a vision of America which was more generous and far-seeing than many of their detractors. They pioneered the view that a sense of ethnic origin was something that complemented the American identity rather than subtracted from it. In politics they contributed outstandingly to the strength of democracy in America by establishing many of the conventions and structures that allowed successive ethnic groups to be integrated in a stable American polity.

This anthology at once mirrors the compelling story of the Irish in America and highlights another of their most significant achievements—the contribution which people of Irish origin made to American letters. That contribution is a significant one by any standards, and one that is still perhaps not sufficiently appreciated. It is one further area where the achievements of their friends and relations in the United States are a source of interest and pride for all Irish people and friends of Ireland.

Dublin, 1987   SEAN O'HUIGINN

Former Consul General of Ireland
and Assistant Secretary of Foreign Affairs

ACKNOWLEDGMENTS

The editors gratefully acknowledge the following: "Benediction," from *Flappers and Philosophers* by F. Scott Fitzgerald reprinted with permission of Charles Scribner's Sons, copyright 1920, an imprint of Macmillan Publishing Company, renewal copyright 1948 Zelda Fitzgerald; "Studs," reprinted from *Guillotine Party and Other Stories* by James T. Farrell by permission of the publisher, Vanguard Press, Inc. Copyright © 1935 by Vanguard Press, Inc. Renewed copyright © 1962 by James T. Farrell; and "Chapter 23" in *A Tree Grows in Brooklyn* by Betty Smith, copyright 1943 by Betty Smith, reprinted by permission of Harper & Row, Publishers Inc.

The selections, "Mort and Mary" (Copyright 1935 and renewed 1963 by John O'Hara. Reprinted from *The Doctor's Son and Other Stories* by John O'Hara), "Bill" (from *Look How the Fish Live* by J. F. Powers. Copyright © 1975 by J. F. Powers. Originally appeared in the *New Yorker*), and the passage from *The Gift* by Pete Hamill (Copyright © 1973 by Pete Hamill) appear by permission of Random House, Inc. and Alfred A. Knopf, Inc.

"Yonder Peasant, Who Is He?" copyright 1948, 1976 by Mary McCarthy, reprinted from her volume *Memories of a Catholic Girlhood* and first published in the *New Yorker*; "The Cemetery," copyright 1943, 1970 by Brendan Gill, reprinted from his volume *Ways of Loving* and first published in the *New Yorker*; and "A Temple of the Holy Ghost" from *A Good Man Is Hard to Find and Other Stories*, copyright 1954 by Flannery O'Connor, renewed 1982 by Mrs. Regina O'Connor, are reprinted here by permission of Harcourt Brace Jovanovich, Inc.

The following selections are reprinted by permission of Viking Penguin Inc.: From *Billy Phelan's Greatest Game* by William Ken-

Modern Irish-American Fiction

1

THE NEXT PARISH

An Introduction

Although Andrew Greeley's 1971 article, "The Last of the American Irish Fade Away," ends on the sanguine note that perhaps it really is not so, most of what he writes is to substantiate the claim of the title. Thus, as he would have it, with no clearly identifiable and sustained Irish-American community to write about and for, "The voice of the [Irish-American] storyteller is mute," and he adduces the deaths of the O'Connors, Flannery and Edwin; the pointless dreaming of J. F. Powers of a church dead, too; the relegation to scholarship of F. Scott Fitzgerald; and the lack of interest in what James T. Farrell has to say of life at the corner of Fifty-seventh Street and Indiana Avenue.[1] Greeley continues, "the storytellers have all vanished," and adds to his roster John O'Hara and Thomas Fleming, glad to have escaped their Irish heritage; Elizabeth Cullinan, whose depiction of the destructiveness of an Irish matriarch—in her novel, *House of Gold*— provokes little caring in us; and Farrell, who would not, we are told, have written at all if he had grown up in a different Chicago neighborhood.[2]

Even if we were to accept Greeley's dismissals—did his perception of a void at the heart of Irish-American fiction lead him to write his own series of Irish-American novels, works which many Irish Americans would deny are reflective of or written for them?—there is more to be said. While we might not blame Greeley for not knowing writers who were emerging in 1971—Pete Hamill, Mark Costello, Jimmy Breslin, and Joe Flaherty, for example—or for being unaware of writers who have come on the scene only in the last decade—Mary Gordon and William Kennedy, to name but two—he overlooks several writers who were and remained on the Irish-

American literary landscape, for instance, Mary McCarthy, Brendan Gill, J. P. Donleavy, Tom McHale, and Maureen Howard.

Interestingly, William Kennedy, who is assuredly today's premier Irish-American writer, in an interview appearing in the *Recorder*, the journal of the American Irish Historical Society, has paid his respects to some of the writers who have contributed to the body of what we can in fact call Irish-American literature: F. Scott Fitzgerald, John O'Hara, Eugene O'Neill, the O'Connors, and Finley Peter Dunne. And when asked about the existence of an "Irish-American literary tradition," Kennedy spoke of an "evolution" in the literature resulting from changes in Irish Americans' social, cultural, political, and religious positions; and he said of himself: "God knows where I am in all of this, in this evolution, but I *know* all that came before me. I know that those who came before helped to show me how to turn experience into literature. I know all that came before in the same way I know that the Irish ascended politically to become Jack Kennedy. After Jack Kennedy, anything was possible. Goddammit, *we've* been president, and you can't hold us back anymore."[3] The truth is, of course, that the Irish in America have not been held back for a long time, a condition that does much to explain developments and changes in Irish-American literature.

Charles Fanning's 1987 anthology of Irish-American fiction of the nineteenth century, *The Exiles of Erin*[4]—to which the present collection may serve as a companion piece—speaks of "the Irish-American tradition in fiction" and splendidly establishes three literary generations for the century: satiric voices before the Great Famine of the 1840s, practical fiction for immigrants of the famine generation, and literature for a new middle class. Like Kennedy, Fanning makes it clear that what changes were wrought in the literature came about in response to the social, political, religious, and cultural circumstances of the succeeding generations. Thus, for example, Fanning's third category, "literature for a new middle class," points to a degree of acculturation at the end of the nineteenth century that has only accelerated in the twentieth and has led, perhaps inevitably, to Greeley's—and others'— formulations about the untimely demise of Irish-American literature.

It just is not so, and perhaps Greeley knew it. In 1981, in a review of Greeley's *Irish Americans: The Rise to Money and Power* (1981), Daniel Casey cites Greeley's *New York Times* piece (mentioned above) and notes that in Greeley's book, *That Most Distressful Nation: The Taming of the American Irish* (1972), he had written:

"The Irish have finally proved to the WASPS that they could become respectable. But they have paid the price: they are no longer Irish." Casey adds: "In 1981 he tells us to forget all that: 'The Irish are wealthy, powerful, and still Irish.' Are we to believe Greeley now or Greeley then?"[5]

It is true that as Irish Americans move further into the mainstream there is less that can be specifically identified about their lives as "Irish" or "Irish-American" in ways meaningful in the not too distant past. Simultaneously, as Greeley observes in the *New York Times*, ethnicity is increasingly acceptable and is, indeed, an emblem of distinction. So in the normal course of events, older issues of politics and religion, for instance, are transmuted and find new manifestations in writing of matters and in ways that could not have been even imaginable or found acceptable in the nineteenth century or earlier twentieth century. Thus, Kennedy's correct perception of "evolution." Charles Fanning's *Exiles* provides us with a sense of that evolution through the nineteenth century—satire to practical fiction to literature for an emerging middle class—and with a means of gauging its branches in the twentieth.

While nineteenth-century satire gave way to immediate needs for a practical fiction, satire will be with us as long as there are topical targets and more persistent human follies. Thus, the objects of earlier satire—Fanning cites, among others, Yankee prejudice, political campaigns, and the American rags-to-riches tradition—have only yielded to newer versions of bias, political adventurism, and Irish Americans secure and smug in respectability.

The practical fiction of the famine generation grew from the needs of immigrants who were torn from their native soil—usually idealized in fiction then and later—were subjected to horrendous crossings, and then were faced with a disorienting new environment. As Fanning tells us, this literature, which featured a "programmatic, sentimental plot and idealized, exemplary characterization," had three major purposes.[6] First were efforts to counteract threats to the Catholic faith of the vast majority of the immigrants. While these menaces have largely disappeared in our time, religion in one form or another remains one of the major themes of twentieth-century Irish-American fiction. Second were illustrations of how to succeed and how to avoid failure in the New World. While the overt problem of not succeeding has doubtless diminished, it has only made way for moving beyond survival itself into the search for respectability for oneself and one's family. Additionally, it should be noted, the concept of family was and remains an important one in Irish-American literature. Third were works of nationalistic and political intention designed to aid efforts at home to free Ireland from British rule. While nationalistic views have not disappeared from relatively recent fiction—the current avatar of the Troubles in the North of Ireland has motivated some such fiction—the further Irish Americans have retreated from the homeland the less motivating nationalism became in the fiction. Instead, nationalistic fervor modulated into putting into practice the inordinate Irish ardor for practical politics to the extent that the Irish-American political novel is now a healthy if not always distinguished subgenre.

The third generation of nineteenth-century fiction, Fanning tells us, followed a larger American trend which pitted genteel romance against a new realism. Interestingly, Irish-American writers followed both routes, sometimes in the same work, the Studs Lonigan trilogy of James T. Farrell, for example, finding room for both the realism of urban fiction and the acquisition of bourgeois values, which, in turn, have found their place in fiction throughout this century.

In Eugene O'Neill's play, *A Touch of the Poet*, we are in Boston in 1828, where Con Melody, hard-drinking Irish immigrant, seeks to raise himself above the social level of the Irish he has left behind and the local shanty-Irish to that of the resident Yankees. To himself, one mark of his success is that he has managed to shed his brogue, though the sign of his ultimate failure and of his acceptance of his inability to achieve immediate acculturation is the return of the brogue at the end of the play when he shares drunken revelry with the local low-life Irish.

The two characteristics, the brogue and addiction to drink, are suggestive of how the Irish both lost and retained traits in life and in literature in the process of Americanization. Thus, Finley Peter Dunne's Mr. Dooley, transplanted Irishman, would not be Mr. Dooley without his brogue, which is no great handicap to him among the habitués of Chicago's Archey Road because his ambitions are more modest than Con Melody's. On the other hand, Con, who also runs a bar, would not be comfortable with the relatively decorous patrons of Dooley's establishment. He is the archetype—some would insist stereotype—of the blasphemous, hard-drinking Irishman who populates Irish-American fiction to this day, down to Jimmy Breslin's *Table Money* (1986), a novel about a Medal of Honor-winning Vietnam veteran, Owney Morrison. An examination of every facet and nuance of the Irish-American experience in fiction in the twentieth century, such as those intimated by the brogue and drink, is out of the question here—and the fiction can better tell its own story—but a brief survey of important issues of both the nineteenth and twentieth centuries including politics, religion, the family, and "making it," is appropriate, especially as shown in the works and writers represented in this anthology.

Perhaps because they were busy consolidating their gains in America and were immediately bound together by their predominantly Catholic faith, Irish Americans for much of the twentieth century, if we can judge by the lack of fiction on the topic, appear not to have been actively caught up in Irish nationalism. In more recent years, however, as the renewed Troubles in Northern Ireland have appeared endless and as the makeup of New York's Saint Patrick's Day parade, a sort of national emblem, has become more and more contentious, there have been a number of potboilers involving Americans in the Irish cause. Two examples will suffice. James Reid's *Offering* (1978) has as its protagonist Boston priest Thomas O'Neill, who, going to work for the IRA—"Oh Ireland, my first and only love, / Where Christ and Caesar are hand in glove," as James Joyce had it in "Gas from a Burner"—falls in love with IRA activist Mara MacRaimond. With terrorism from Belfast to Manhattan, Pete Hamill's *Guns of Heaven* (1983), was a very different book indeed from his sensitive, short novel about a father-son relationship, *The Gift* (1973), excerpted in this collection.

As suggested earlier, in the late nineteenth and twentieth centuries Irish-American ardor for the nationalist cause turned inward to American politics, a means of consolidating and advancing gains and perhaps a handy counterpart to nationalism. Ardor and determination, coupled with an uncanny instinct for the requirements of practical politics, resulted in the extraordinary success story told many times over when the American political story has been reprised. Though he declined to seek higher office, even Mr. Dooley, successful publican, was something of a politician: "His conduct of the important office of captain of his precinct (1873–75) was highly commended, and there was some talk of nominating him for alderman," we are told in Finley Peter Dunne's sketch that introduces the Dooley pieces appearing in this collection. And if for nothing else in the way of political views, we are indebted to Dooley for his trenchant observation, "Polytics ain't bean bag."

Although it is antedated by Joseph F. Dinneen's fine novel, *Ward Eight* (1936), the best-known Irish-American political novel is Edwin

O'Connor's *Last Hurrah* (1956). As attested to by its continuing appearance in paperback, *Hurrah* is also surely the most popular such novel, perhaps because of its streak of sentimentality and great good humor as much as for what it tells us about Irish-American politics. On the other hand, it might be argued that sentimentality and good humor are precisely what are needed to tell us about Irish-American politics. However the argument might go, O'Connor seems to have distilled much of this experience into a novel that explores a crucial turning point in the fortunes of Irish-American politicians and their fictional counterparts. Appropriately, because he understands so well his Irish-American (and other) constituents, their needs, and their manner of repayment at the polling place when he has met them, protagonist Frank Skeffington calls himself a "tribal chieftain," his "tribe" being the Irish. His loss in his final campaign for mayor of a fictional Boston, his "last hurrah," signals as well the end of an old style of politics built on personal loyalties and personal services, and the beginning of modern politicking via television, surveys, and electronic images. Skeffington, like so many bosses, seldom has a grand scheme for betterment through politics but sees that politics means power and that power means the opportunity to repay voter and retinue loyalty. Replaced by social welfare programs and agencies, Skeffington's world, O'Connor seems to tell us, is a thing of the past.

Much of the Irish-American political fiction written since *Hurrah* has appeared since the Kennedy run for the White House, and much seems to have been written with elements of the Kennedy story in mind, though, unfortunately, usually without the Kennedy—and Skeffington—grace and humor. Thomas Fleming's *All Good Men* (1961), appearing just at the outset of the Kennedy era, depicts Ben O'Connor, a corrupt thirty-year ward boss under Dave Shea, boss of city hall, in a novel whose cynicism about the Irish lack of substantial achievements through politics is the antithesis of *Hurrah*'s sentimentality about the same lack. Fleming's *King of the Hill* (1965) pits Larry Donahue, idealist gone wrong and advisor to the mayor, against boyhood friend and now reformer-attorney Jake O'Connor in a novel that acknowledges, perhaps under the suasion of the Kennedy era, that a case can be made for idealism and reform.

Three novels that seem marked by some Kennedy influence are James D. Horan's *Right Image* (1967), Edward R. F. Sheehan's *Governor* (1970), and Jack Flannery's *Kell* (1977). In the first of these, Francis X. Shannon aspires to see his son, Kelly, in the White House. Sheehan's Edward Shannon is in Massachusetts politics; his brother is a radical priest—Christ and Caesar again—and Francis X. Kennedy is the machine boss. The last, also about Massachusetts politics, features junior Senator John F. X. Kane. Readers of all three might be pardoned for wondering which Massachusetts novel they are in today and for some confusion over the Shannons and the Francis X's.

Two other novels should be mentioned. Readers of the books just listed might not be willing to go ahead with Wilfred Sheed's *People Will Always Be Kind* (1973) after reading the dust-jacket's description of protagonist Brian Casey, senator from New York—"Irish to the core, he can switch from melting charmer to savage attacker at a moment's notice"—or with William Kennedy's *Billy Phelan's Greatest Game*, excerpted in this anthology, with its scrupulous rendering of low-life Albany during the Great Depression of the thirties. But both novels have something going for them. Stylistically, Sheed is a superior writer, and his Brian Casey is a sufficiently complex protagonist, combining the qualities of an old-time manipulating boss and a new idealist—suggesting, perhaps, a new version of the practical politician to sustain a reader's attention. Kennedy not only energizes *Billy Phelan* with his style, but he places the novel's politics in a context that might explain its enduring appeal to the Irish (and others). Like most else in the novel, politics is a game, a deadly serious one at times, to be sure, but always one where the fun is increased as the risk is—as a juggler increasingly amazes us by constantly adding new balls to those already at play in the air.

The exiles' commonality of a lost native land and a continuing interest in its fortunes was one thing that held Irish immigrants together. The other "glue," as more than one writer has observed, was their religion, not exclusively Catholic, to be sure, but the immigrants were largely Catholic, and it has been Catholics who have ordinarily had their stories told. In fact and in fiction, Catholicism was a major feature of unity and identity in a new and strange land, and it persisted after the nationalistic ties had been slackened.

Anything that might be said in this sketch about Irish Catholicism is doomed to superficiality and will invite rebuttal from someone somewhere; but we should run the risk others have by observing that, among other things, Irish Catholicism is more rigid—and, some would add, more rebellious[7]—than other versions of the faith. Furthermore, although the terms might not be familiar to many of them, it has been said more than once that a streak of Jansenism has led the Irish to sexual puritanism, and that a belief in Manichaeism has led to a profound sense of good and evil, of man's propensity to sin, and of the burden of guilt and the need for redemption. Thus, while points of doctrine and matters of observance counted in Catholic unity and identity, attitudes quite probably mattered as much.

With increased assimilation, doubtless the ties to the Irish brand of Catholicism loosened, though it is common knowledge that the American hierarchy was long dominated by Irish Americans; and anyone who went to a parochial school into at least the 1950s has not forgotten the famous blue-covered Baltimore Catechism, that American compendium of Roman belief. Jimmy Breslin's Dermot Davey, in *World Without End, Amen* (1973), a chapter of which appears in this collection, like thousands of other products of parochial schools, can still in manhood quote swatches, correctly recalling the emphasis on the Sixth Commandment. Still, the links were loosened by gradual and natural exposure to and involvement in the life of the larger American community and by external events and forces. World War II, for example, worked changes in the American psyche that Irish Americans of course didn't escape. Similarly, the G.I. Bill of Rights enabled millions to attend college and to encounter ideas and attitudes they otherwise might never have met. And in setting them free, often against their will, to make choices where before there had been certainty, Vatican II for many Catholics was as disorienting as arrival in America had been for their immigrant ancestors.

What relaxed in fact has been as fully portrayed in relatively recent fiction as the sterner stuff was earlier in the century. Indeed, the tensions between those who profess an older Catholicism and latitudinarians have been the source of much fictional conflict; in fact, the fiction reveals an entire spectrum of adherence and departure. Thus, while political novels are fairly simple to describe, religious belief and practice in fiction have become as protean as the actuality, and neat categories are impossible. Flannery O'Connor's "Temple of the Holy Ghost" (1954), which is included in this collection, does not fit any easy category of "Catholic fiction," yet few Irish-American readers would be puzzled by the story. Setting aside a wide range of topics that might be advanced to show what has changed and what has endured—drawn from devotionalism, the parish, and guilt, for instance—one way of seeing the range of Catholic life is to note examples of priests in fiction. At the very heart of parish life—the religious equivalent of the political ward—the priest and what he represents neatly typify much that we can learn about what has happened, from obeisance when the church was central in parishioners' lives to mockery when it has been peripheral or largely irrelevant.

Two quite different routes taken by Irish-American Catholic priests—worldly and otherworldly—can be seen by two of F. Scott Fitzgerald's works appearing in 1920, at just about the time he was ending a fairly strong flirtation with Irishness and an Irish identity. "Benediction," appearing in this collection, and *This Side of Paradise*, his first and most autobiographical and most Irish novel, offer different versions of priests. "Benediction" limns a picture of a Jesuit seminary, visited by Lois, the sister of Kieth, one of the seminarians, as she struggles with her own future relationship with a young man and how her Catholicism affects it. What we are finally meant to think of Kieth and his chosen path readers will decide for themselves; however, while the priesthood depicted is not unattractive, Lois finds herself arguing against the Church and, devastatingly, revealing how *"inconvenient* being a Catholic is." The view in *Paradise* is certainly that the traditional church is "inconvenient" and that Kieth's kind of priesthood is passé. Monsignor Thayer Darcy is attractive to protagonist Amory Blaine, Fitzgerald's fictional counterpart, precisely because he is worldly; a convert to Catholicism, he has not abandoned his dandyism and, firm enough in his adopted faith, he is still flamboyant, charming, cultivated, a raconteur, and an accomplished musician, not disqualifications for the priesthood, certainly, but not qualities, either, eagerly sought in the ordinary parish priest of the time.

Closer to the mark of what would have been acceptable are priests depicted in fiction by James T. Farrell, Joe Flaherty, and Mary Gordon, for instance, though their acceptability to parishioners was no guarantee their creators found them attractive. Two priests satirized in Farrell's Studs Lonigan trilogy are Father Gilhooley, pastor and therefore also the authoritative voice in the parish parochial school, and Father Shannon, who comes for the annual week-long retreat. Gilhooley is a certified classic bore, a man infatuated with his own voice and banality, adamant in his belief in the efficacy of a Catholic education, and adored by the women of his flock for the depth of his learning. Father Shannon is Studs's gang's idea of a great priest because he is a fine speaker and is superficially "understanding" of youth's problems—something of a forerunner of the "relevant" priests, as is Monsignor Darcy—but Farrell leaves readers remembering his anti-intellectualism. Both priests contribute to the spiritual poverty of Studs's world. Similarly suited to older—and older-minded—parishes are the priests of his youth recalled by Fogarty in Joe Flaherty's *Fogarty & Co.* (1973), excerpted in this collection, grim guardians of parish morals and ever alert in the confessional—like Breslin's Dermot Davey's boyhood confessors—for adolescents who have broken the Sixth Commandment.

At the opposite extreme are either incompetents or priests who have sold out to materialism and chic popularity, and they, too, are almost invariably satirical targets. The best and best-known satirist of American Catholicism is J. F. Powers, represented in this collection by "Bill," which contrasts a conservative, materialistic pastor with his new, laid-back curate, Bill. In Power's novel, *Morte D'Urban* (1962), Father Placidus—Hartigan in lay life—is even further removed from the traditional life of the parish priest than Fitzgerald's Thayer Darcy. As Charles F. O'Brien observes, Placidus is complacent in his role as coach of winning seminary teams, is openhanded with money, enjoys mixed company and the opera, and by his example shows novices that a priest's lot need not be an abstemious one.[8]

Joe Flaherty's Fogarty remembers the terror of his adolescent confessions, but he also remembers mod priest Father Edward Logan:

> he was one of those bridgers of the generation gap, or whatever they called that chronological chasm in those days. He was constantly organizing "youth activities"—dances, bowling nights, "open-minded" discussions of religion. . . . He was always organizing teams, circulating chance books for new uniforms, and casually "dropping around the playground" in sneakers and sweatshirt (that *Going My Way* crap) to join in the pick-me-up basketball games and talk "regular" to the guys. Real hep. . . . To be truthful, all the other kids adored Logan and called him Father Ted. Fogarty thought he was a patronizing shithead.

There may be no more savage—and comical—satire of Irish-American priests than in John Gregory Dunne's *True Confessions* (1977), where the action is located in the cloudcuckooland of Los Angeles. Monsignor Timothy J. O'Fay, nutty as a fruitcake, owns a string of useless titles and has a penchant for breaking into "My Old Kentucky Home" at the wrong time. Monsignor Mickey Gagnon dies in bed in a whorehouse. Augustus O'Dea, vicar-general, has seen *The Song of Bernadette* eleven times, a fact readers are more apt to remember than that he was "a kind, holy man." Father Des Spellacy is an "Irish Medici," exploits his wartime role as "the Parachuting Padre," fixes a raffle, golfs—perhaps the most popular sport among priests in fiction—is something of a fop, and is afflicted with hubris.

Are there no worthy clerics in all of this? Of course. Powers's Archbishop in "Prince of Darkness" (1946) is the norm against whom other priests are measured in this story, a role taken by Seamus Fargo in *True Confessions*, where he leads Des Spellacy to redemption. Edwin O'Connor's Father Hugh Kennedy in the Pulitzer Prize-winning *The Edge of Sadness* (1962) excites admiration in his too-human struggles and for his forebearance and kindliness and humor. However, given the nature of the art, the average competent priest is not usually a candidate for fictional treatment; perhaps unfortunately, we remember the extremes, the narrow-minded, the incompetent, the climbers, the sycophants by whom the Church is ill served. On the other hand, given the honorable task of the satirist, the use of extremes we have seen is not to placate but to rouse from complacency, and in this it serves well.

If we grant that different ethnic groups have different family dynamics, generalizations about the Irish-American family are even more difficult to arrive at than those about politicians or priests; the possible combinations of alliances and antagonisms are simply too many. It would be useful to have a model of the Irish-American fictional family by which to measure different depictions. We do have a very useful model of actual families in an essay written for family therapists in Monica McGoldrick's "Irish Families" in *Ethnicity and Family Therapy*, a collection which recognizes such family differences. Among other observations, McGoldrick suggests that those who deal with Irish families will be helped by recognizing the paradox of the known articulateness of the Irish and their difficulty in expressing inner feelings, a condition that leads to family hostility being dealt with by silence, a build-up of resentment, and sudden endings to relationships. When language is used, McGoldrick adds, it is likely to be marked by innuendo, obscurity, obfuscation, nonsequiturs, ridicule, and teasing. With the resultant emotional isolation, McGoldrick continues, close relationships in a family, especially between marriage partners, are often in trouble.[9] Interestingly, in remarks introducing Kate McPhelim Cleary's short story, "The Stepmother" (1901), Charles Fanning writes: "Cleary's generalization about Nebraska farmers is reinforced in twentieth-century fiction by the emergence of a similar trait among other Irish Americans— lack of communication, especially emotional, even among family members."[10]

It would be misleading to say that this failure at communication is the only or even the leading characteristic of Irish-American families, for whom, as for the population at large, normal generational conflicts are typical of family life. Thus, we find as broad a range of examples of family life as for Irish-American priests. In Finley Peter Dunne's "Shaughnessy," included in this collection, we have a heroic family man who has his antithesis in Mary Gordon's domineering father in *Final Payments* (1978). The overwhelming love of the narrator's mother in Elizabeth Cullinan's "Life After Death" (1976), appearing in this collection, is matched by the bullying mother in Mary Doyle Curran's "Mrs. Reardon's Gamble" (1966), also appearing here. Maureen Howard's *Bridgeport Bus* (1965) and *Grace Abounding* (1982) do for the mother-daughter relationship what many other works do for the father-son relationship, a matter to which we shall return briefly, and Maureen Howard's Laura Quinn in *Before My Time* (1971) strikes out on her own at forty-one as does Mary Gordon's Isabel Moore in *Final Payments* at thirty. Versions of family units range from the sentimental in Betty Smith's *Tree Grows in Brooklyn* (1947), excerpted here, to the cynical in Harry Sylvester's *Moon Gaffney* (1947), to the parodic in Tom McHale's "A Society of Friends" (1973).

Still, failure at communication does seem to loom large in Irish-American fiction of the twentieth century. While Eugene O'Neill's *Long Day's Journey into Night* (1956) is not fiction, it may be the archetypical picture of such failure, with only a few glints of light to illuminate the "night" of the title. Mary McCarthy's *Memories of a Catholic Girlhood* (1957), excerpted for this collection, confirms the McGoldrick and Fanning generalizations about the lack of communication, while distressful marital relationships may be illustrated by Jimmy Breslin's Dermot Davey and his wife in *World Without End, Amen*: "Dermot and his wife, like so many others from the same background, were unable to discuss sex. Many times they went two weeks without sex. And immediately after that, two or three more weeks. . . . Once they went for seven weeks without sex. There was no way for them to handle the subject in conversation. It always came out to be a fight over wallpaper or weak coffee."

Finally, by way of illustration of treatments of the family in Irish-American literature, there is a persistent theme that awaits fuller treatment than it has yet received. In "The Greening of America: Irish-American Writers," Joseph Browne singles out the long tradition in Irish literature of the father-son relationship/conflict, with

Joyce's *Portrait of the Artist as a Young Man* as the basic text, and notes its continuation in Irish-American literature.[11] Related to the failure of communication, this continuation suggests a primal theme. Because it tells us so many things about the Irish in America, O'Neill's *Long Day's Journey* is a primary source—a near equivalent to Joyce's *Portrait*—from which readers may draw basic ideas about the father-son theme in such works as Farrell's Studs Lonigan trilogy, his *Father and Son* (1940), Brendan Gill's "Cemetery," included in this collection, O'Connor's *Last Hurrah*, and William Gibson's *Mass for the Dead* (1968). 1973 was a banner year for fictional treatments of fathers and sons and included—all represented in this anthology—Mark Costello's *Murphy Stories*, Jimmy Breslin's *World Without End, Amen*, and Pete Hamill's *Gift*. The theme is absolutely crucial to William Kennedy's *Billy Phelan's Greatest Game* (1978), a chapter of which is included in this collection. We might note, as a kind of grand climax, that Eugene Kennedy's 1981 *Father's Day* combines family, politics, priests, and father and son into a genuinely stereotypical mélange.

In their climb from the subsistence level to material success, Irish-American families have not differed significantly in their ambitions from other immigrant groups. America, after all, has been the land of opportunity as well as of refuge, and surely all groups have pursued success and the emblems of success, and, after achieving them, have displayed them with satisfaction. On the other hand, and the Andrew Greeley who wrote "The Last of the American Irish Fade Away" would doubtless agree, there is some reason to think that many Irish Americans in the twentieth century have been preoccupied with not only distancing themselves from their proletarian roots but with concealing them and even creating appearances to the contrary. We have seen Charles Fanning citing representations of bourgeois values in late nineteenth- and earlier twentieth-century fiction. And Monica McGoldrick, in "Irish Families," notes the "Irish longing for respectability that they [immigrants] carried with them to their new country," and cites writers John Corry and Andrew Greeley's discussions of Irish-American propriety, respectability, and the fight for acceptance and concern with appearances.[12]

In June 1916, the Lonigan family of Chicago observes the graduation of fifteen-year-old William "Studs" Lonigan and his sister Frances from, as Studs puts it, "the old dump," Saint Patrick's grammar school. The evening provides the opportunity for the relatively successful senior Lonigans—Studs's father has his own painting business and owns his own home, it being part of Farrell's scheme that Studs not come from a deprived background so that readers would not automatically ascribe his failures to want of material opportunity rather than to spiritual poverty—to preen themselves on their success and respectability. Early in the evening, Patrick Lonigan is given to a long reverie in which he congratulates himself on how far he has come. Later, Patrick is smug about having done the "right thing" in sending his children to a parochial school, and Mary seconds him by her observation that "Mrs. Reilly uses awfully bad grammar, too," perhaps South Side Chicago's equivalent of retaining the stigma of the brogue. Recalling that the more successful Dennis P. Gorman now resents being called "Dinny" as inappropriate to his station, Patrick, no slouch himself, replies to Mary:

> Well, I'd rather have people use bad grammar than have 'em be smart alecks like Dinny Gorman. Why, I knew him when he didn't have a sole on his shoe; and then his stickin' up his nose and actin' like he was highbrow, lace-curtain Irish, born to the purple. And all because he's got a little booklearnin' and he bootlicked around until he became a ward committeeman. Why he was nothin' but a starvin' lawyer hangin' around until Joe O'Reilly started sendin' business his way. What is he now . . . nothin' but a shyster. Maybe he does have a little more booklearnin' than I, but what does that mean? Look here, now: Is he a better or more conscientious father? Does he pay his bills more regularly? Has he got a bigger bank account than I got?[13]

It would not do to argue for the ubiquity of this sort of thing, but a few examples from works appearing in this collection will suggest a persistence in a fair amount of Irish-American fiction. Near the end of the chapter from Betty Smith's *Tree Grows in Brooklyn*, for example, with heroine Francie's insistence on her Americanism because her parents were born in Brooklyn, and with her partial movement away from tenement life to a different kind of neighborhood, we are left with Francie's meditation on a different and better school than the one serving immigrant children which she had been attending: "It showed her that there were other worlds beside the world she had been born into and that these other worlds were attainable." The hero of Joseph Dever's "New York Girls" (1954) aspires to the publishing world and the company of New York girls but learns that his Peoria "background doesn't quite suit [him] for the publishing business." In Maureen Howard's "Three Pigs of Krishna Nuru" (1971–

72), Jimmy Cogan, aged seventeen, dog shampooer, is accepted at Fordham—the university that crops up again and again in Irish-American literature with a New York City setting—to the immeasurable pride of his parents; his mother swills gin but perhaps Jimmy's achievement will make it matter less, and immediately Jimmy plans to change the world by attacking "the problems of the day with a keen mind." Finally, in Mary Gordon's "Neighborhood" (1984), when the immigrant Irish Lynches, who have not exactly made life easy in a Long Island "neighborhood of second generation Irish," move away, the other residents are once again secure in their unified front against incursions by the lower orders.

These few examples reveal the wish to move away from an Irish-American background or, at least, to achieve higher status despite that background through education, hard work, and determination. F. Scott Fitzgerald and John O'Hara are often cited as writers who personally and in their fiction distanced themselves from their backgrounds. Fair enough, perhaps, but it could be argued that they only carried to the logical limit the quest that so many others were imposing on themselves and that they produced outcomes desired by many. In other words, even defectors can tell us something about distances travelled and why.

Fitzgerald left his briefly proclaimed brand of aristocratic Irishness—seen in some 1918 letters and also in his alter ego, the early Amory Blaine in 1920s *This Side of Paradise*—to climb socially and economically in real life and in fiction as far as he could from any Irishness, particularly the brand he knew as a boy in Saint Paul, only to return to it for important uses in his last two novels.[14] O'Hara's defection was more complete, but ironically, at least once, it enabled him to take the satiric measure of other Irish Americans who aimed to make it. In "Mort and Mary" (1931), included in this collection, Mort might have become a priest, but when his mother learns that he might make friends elsewhere "among the sons of big Tammany men or even higher-class people . . . she decides maybe the lad hadn't the true vocation, maybe he oughtn't to enter the holy priesthood. It's better to be a good man out in the world than be a priest if you haven't a true vocation. Maybe he might better go to Fordham and be a lawyer. Or a doctor"; and so Mort and his wife end the story by "slowly [getting] fat together," vacationing in Southhampton, avoiding scandal by being, we are told, "real dependable people."

Doubtless, one can infer from what has been said that the Irish on both sides of the Atlantic love a good story well told. In finding ways of telling the stories and of expressing the themes we have briefly considered—that is, in seeking styles and techniques to tell it all—Irish-American fiction has yet to produce a James Joyce or a Samuel Beckett, to name only two of modern literature's great innovators. But no matter. A literature that has given us the purity of style of F. Scott Fitzgerald, the fully realized worlds of James T. Farrell's South Side Chicago in the Studs Lonigan trilogy and William Kennedy's Albany in his Albany cycle, and the comic grotesqueries of Flannery O'Connor need not be thought of as exactly behindhand. On the whole—and at the very least—truisms about the Irish way with words have been borne out. For example, Monica McGoldrick's list of devices used by Irish Americans to hinder direct everyday communication are often turned to fictional advantage in many of the stories collected here and, ironically, imaginatively charged and rendered; they enhance the stories the writers tell. If a full analysis of devices and techniques cannot be attempted in a brief introduction, mention of a handful of features may be useful; and to begin with, the two following are representative of rather opposite styles.

An observable quality of recent years has been the New Journalistic reportorial style of Pete Hamill, Jimmy Breslin, and Joe Flaherty, all represented herein. Since all three have been successful journalists—with Breslin, for instance, ranging from copyboy to sportswriter to political commentator to nationally syndicated columnist—this is no surprise. Indeed, in having honed their skills on newspaper audiences, they have written in the tradition of Finley Peter Dunne, less the brogue and "Irishisms"; made leaner the elaborations of language of the nineteenth century; and retaining the Irish fascination with language, have moved from a belletristic, allusive style to one much closer to the ordinary "truth" of circumstances. Much of this quality, characteristic of Hamill, Breslin, and Flaherty, can be discovered in other writers as well, not reportage narrowly defined but a concern for the recall and rendition of things as they really are.

On the other hand, a number of Irish-American writers in recent years have shown an Irish penchant and talent for the nonrealistic thinking and language that, like much in Joyce and Beckett, borders on and sometimes crosses over into the surreal in both content and shifting stream of consciousness. The opposite of the style of the New Journalists, this mode organizes language differently and is more demanding of readers but is no less capable of ordering reality simply by skewing it and forcing readers to look again and yet again.

For example, although her selection in this anthology is some distance from one of her major modes, Flannery O'Connor's God-haunted novels, *Wise Blood* (1952) and *The Violent Bear It Away* (1960), are fantastic in plot, grotesque in characterization, surreal in reverie, nightmarish in metaphor, and clotted in sentence structure; but the ultimate purpose, perhaps, is to confirm orthodox religious belief through unorthodox content and form. For very different purposes, to offer a second example, the conclusion of J. P. Donleavy's *Ginger Man* (1956) underscores the continuing disorientation of protagonist Sebastian Dangerfield:

> He was walking down the slope side of the bridge past this broken building, a straight dark figure and stranger. Come here till I tell you. Where is the sea high and the winds soft and moist and warm, sometimes stained with sun, with peace so wild for wishing where all is told and telling. On a winter night I heard horses on a country road, beating sparks out of the stones. I knew they were running away and would be crossing the fields where the pounding would come into my ears. And I said they were running out to death which is with some soul and their eyes are mad and teeth out.
> God's mercy
> On the wild
> Ginger Man.[15]

Again, an illustration of disorientation—this time in the surreal world of disintegrating marriage—is taken from Mark Costello's "Murphy's Xmas," included in this anthology:

> and moving like a pale liar before his wife's bared teeth, he remembers the beginning of the end of their marriage; the masks, mirrors and carrots that began to sprout around their bed like a bitter, 2 am, Victory garden, one that Murphy had planted all by himself and was going back to pick and shake in his wife's face on the sparkling sacrosanct morning that he left for good and ever. Caught in the dowdy mosaics of their bedroom mirror, they would get down on their hands and knees and as the orange joke of the carrot disappeared between her legs, his wife would turn and ask, *who are you?* and Murphy would smile down from behind his mask and say: who are you? Then his smile would rot in his opened mouth, and Murphy *became* his impersonations. . . . now Murphy and his father are standing outside the motel window looking in at Murphy's marriage like peeping toms and his father is ordering Murphy back

into bed but Murphy resists and all his reasons are rosy and shrill like a schoolboy he screams.

Another, more pervasive, characteristic of Irish-American fiction comes as no surprise: Virtually every piece in this anthology is marked by humor of one kind or another. Special note should be taken, however, of what has ordinarily been thought of as the preserve of more avant garde writers but which in fact has long been a feature of Irish writing—macabre and grotesque humor as well as black humor. Vivian Mercier's *Irish Comic Tradition*, a pioneering work in the field, devotes a chapter to "Macabre and Grotesque Humour in the Irish Tradition."[16] And Maureen Waters's more recent *The Comic Irishman* notes that "Indeed, the Irish sense of the macabre seems directly linked to their acute consciousness of death" and makes a useful distinction between macabre humor and black humor, the latter often being "used to denote a quality that is mordant, pessimistic, and verging on the absurd," and she cites Max Schultz's use of the term "specifically to refer to American literature of the sixties in which black humor is the response to a world devoid of intrinsic values."[17]

A literature that produced Jonathan Swift's "Modest Proposal"—can there be many works more awash with macabre humor?—made room in Ireland and in America for more of the same. Flannery O'Connor's "Temple of the Holy Ghost," perhaps unclassifiable in other ways, can be subsumed under this rubric, as can Maureen Howard's "Three Pigs of Krishna Nuru," Mark Costello's "Murphy's Xmas," and the selection from Joe Flaherty's *Fogarty & Co.*, all included in this anthology, and Tom McHale's manic "A Society of Friends," mentioned earlier. The "Hades" episode at Dublin's Glasnevin Cemetery in James Joyce's *Ulysses* is marvelous in its ghoulish humor. A current near equivalent is chapter 1 of William Kennedy's *Ironweed* (1983), when protagonist Francis Phelan wanders through Albany's Saint Agnes Cemetery communing with the dead and conversing with his buried infant son, Gerald. Finally, in the present collection is J. P. Donleavy's "Fairy Tale of New York"—stylistically almost the opposite of his *Ginger Man*, cited earlier—often affectless in language about a profoundly felt death, with the tension between the protagonist's feelings and the well-meaning but endless professional chatter of an undertaker resulting in, if not black comedy, then in the distinct discomfort that such humor promotes.

Finally, often near allied to humor, indeed often inseparable from it, Irish and Irish-American satire is sometimes easygoing, sometimes diabolically mordant as it sets out to skewer inanities and follies alike. After all, someone has said of the Irish that they are an eminently fair people, never speaking well of one another—the flip side of their putative sentimentality—and they have long relished satire, Swift's "Modest Proposal" being only the best known example. Since earlier sections of this introduction have offered examples of satirical targets, these need not be repeated here, but a deliciously wicked excerpt from John Gregory Dunne's *True Confessions* is irresistible. Narrator cop Tom Spellacy remembers his mother's visit with the parish priest, when he came to take the parish census:

"Tell me about Maureen Delaney, Father. Does she still come to the Sodality Meetings ?"

"Never misses, Mrs. Spellacy."

"It's grand, as crippled as she is, with them wasted little limbs. Grand."

"You give her the Blessed Sacrament and you see her shining little face all scrubbed nice and clean to receive the sacred body and blood and she makes you feel you're doing her the grandest favor in the world."

"A living saint, Father," my mother said. I think now she was wondering if living with the old man qualified her for living sainthood.

"Not like some, Mrs. Spellacy." Then the knowing nod. "With the patent-leather shoes." Reflecting the underwear in the gleam is what he meant.

"Marie O'Connor," my mother said, with that special whisper she reserved for scarlet women.

"No names, Mrs. Spellacy." No slander from the lips of Father.

The subject was quickly changed. "Tell me, Father, Tommy's bowels are all plugged up. Would you recommend the castor oil or the milk of magnesia ?"

Father folded his hands over his stomach. His advice was sought more often on matters of purgatives and politics than it was on questions of doctrine, and he gave as much thought about what laxative to take as he did about what Protestant or Jew politician to vote against. "The castor oil, Mrs. Spellacy. Oh, yes, a grand laxative, simply grand, like a physic. That's the ticket, no doubt about it at all.

"That's high praise for the castor oil, Father, coming from a man like yourself with such a fine intellect and such grand grammar." A little more tea in Father's cup. "And tell me about Tyrone O'Keefe."[18]

In his introduction to *The Uprooted,* Oscar Handlin notes that "immigrants *were* American history," stresses his conviction "that adequately to describe the causes and effects of immigration" was a task he could not then undertake, and adds: "In this work . . . I [have] wished to regard the subject from an altogether different point of view. Immigration altered America. But it also altered the immigrants. And it is the effect upon the newcomers of their arduous transplantation that I have tried to study."[19] Telling about the Maureen Delaneys, the Marie O'Connors, the Tyrone O'Keefes, the Mrs. Spellacys, the Fathers, and the other descendants of Handlin's immigrants is what twentieth-century Irish-American writers have done and, apparently, will continue to do as the genre evolves. This anthology, which tells about them, might have been thematically or regionally arranged, but it has, instead, been ordered chronologically. There is, then, a built-in historical progression that moves the reader from past to present and unfolds those ever-changing conditions.

NOTES

1. Andrew Greeley, "The Last of the American Irish Fade Away," *New York Times Magazine,* 14 March 1971, 33.

2. Ibid., 53.

3. Peter Quinn, William Kennedy: An Interview," *Recorder* 1, no. 1 (Winter 1985): 72–73.

4. Charles Fanning, ed., *The Exiles of Erin: Nineteenth-Century Irish-American Fiction* (Notre Dame, Ind.: University of Notre Dame Press).

5. Daniel J. Casey, "When Greeley Speaks . . . ," review of *The Irish Americans: The Rise to Money and Power,* by Andrew Greeley, *National Hibernian Digest* (September-October 1981): 1.

6. Fanning, *Exiles,* 94.

7. For example, see Lawrence J. McCaffrey, *The Irish Diaspora in America* (Bloomington: Indiana University Press, 1976), 76.

8. Charles F. O'Brien, "*Morte D'Urban* and the Catholic Church in America," *Discourse* 12 (1969): 325.

9. Monica McGoldrick, John K. Pearse, and Joseph Giordano, eds., *Ethnicity and Family Therapy* (New York: Guilford Press, 1982), 315–16.

10. Fanning, *Exiles,* 232.

11. Joseph Browne, "The Greening of America: Irish-American Writers," *Journal of Ethnic Studies* (Winter 1975): 73.

12. McGoldrick, *Ethnicity,* 317.

13. James T. Farrell, *Young Lonigan* (New York: Avon, 1977), 53–54.

14. See Robert E. Rhodes, "F. Scott Fitzgerald: 'All My Fathers,' " in *Irish-*

American Fiction: Essays in Criticism, eds., Daniel J. Casey and Robert E. Rhodes (New York: AMS Press), 29–51.

15. J. P. Donleavy, *The Ginger Man* (New York: Dell, 1966), 347.

16. Vivien Mercier, *The Irish Comic Tradition* (London: Oxford University Press, 1962), 44–77.

17. Maureen Waters, *The Comic Irishman* (Albany: State University of New York Press, 1984), 177–78.

18. John Gregory Dunne, *True Confessions* (New York: E. P. Dutton, 1977), 10–11.

19. Oscar Handlin, *The Uprooted; The Epic Story of the Great Migrations That Made the American People* (New York: Grosset and Dunlap, 1951), 3–4.

2

FINLEY PETER DUNNE

(1867–1936)

Finley Peter Dunne has been associated with Chicago, though the details of his personal life remain something of an enigma. What we know is that Dunne was a journalist and later an editor at the *Chicago Evening Post,* and that, in 1893, he created, in Martin Dooley, an Irish-born bartender-philosopher. Mr. Dooley addressed habitués of his Archey Road establishment on the state of Bridgeport, an Irish ghetto on Chicago's South Side, but his saloon window became a window on the world and his pronouncements extended to national and international affairs. What started as a Saturday filler in the *Post* grew to a widely syndicated feature read by millions. Dooley's brogue echoed across the country.

The earliest sketches recall Dooley's desperation in his native Ireland, a land of hunger, eviction, and emigration, and his disillusionment in America, a land of hard labor, violent strikes, and relief lines. In short, Dooley's life becomes a chronologue of the immigrant's lot and provides a graphic sense of the squalor that accompanied transition from Old World to New. But Dooley is no malcontent. He is sensitive, generous, honest, and well informed—a classical humorist in an apron. True, he agonizes over infant mortality, unjust wars, and political corruption, but he enjoys parish fairs and *ceilis* and card playing. Like Joe Flaherty's Fogarty, Dooley is "a fan of man."

In more than seven hundred Dooley essays, Dunne offered Chicago and America a distinct Irish voice that spoke for faith and sanity. He produced more than a dozen collections: *Mr. Dooley in Peace and War* (1898), *Mr. Dooley in the Heart of His Countrymen* (1899), *Mr. Dooley's Philosophy* (1900), and *Dissertations by Mr. Dooley* (1906) among them.

Theodore Dreiser recognized Dunne as "a genuine realist," but

Dunne's realism, unlike Dreiser's, was tinged with humor. The selections that follow as "Dooley's Neighborhood"—"Archey Road," "The Bar," and "Shaughnessy"—are representative sketches that introduce Martin Dooley in his natural habitat. They ring true. Finley Peter Dunne and Martin Dooley made their marks in American literature and began a serious literary tradition that drew on the best of two worlds.

Dooley was finally put to rest in 1919. Dunne left the *Post* to write for the *New York Morning Telegraph*, became an editor at *Collier's* and eventually bought an interest in *American Magazine*. He never wrote a short story or a novel; yet, in a real sense, he fathered Irish-American fiction.

"Dooley's Neighborhood"

ARCHEY ROAD

Archey Road stretches back for many miles from the heart of an ugly city to the cabbage gardens that gave the maker of the seal his opportunity to call the city "urbs in horto." Somewhere between the two—that is to say, forninst th' gas-house and beyant Healey's slough and not far from the polis station—lives Martin Dooley, doctor of philosophy.

There was a time when Archey Road was purely Irish. But the Huns, turned back from the Adriatic and the stock-yards and overrunning Archey Road, have nearly exhausted the original population—not driven them out as they drove out less vigorous races, with thick clubs and short spears, but edged them out with the more biting weapons of modern civilization—overworked and undereaten them into more languid surroundings remote from the tanks of the gas-house and the blast furnaces of the rolling-mill.

But Mr. Dooley remains, and enough remain with him to save the Archey Road. In this community you can hear all the various accents of Ireland, from the awkward brogue of the "far-downer" to the mild and aisy Elizabethan English of the southern Irishman, and all the exquisite variations to be heard between Armagh and Bantry Bay, with the difference that would naturally arise from substituting cinders and sulphuretted hydrogen for soft misty air and peat smoke. Here also you can see the wakes and christenings, the marriages and funerals, and other fêtes of the ol' counthry somewhat modified and darkened by American usage. The Banshee has been heard many times in Archey Road. On the eve of All Saints' Day it is well known that here alone the pookies play thricks in cabbage gardens. In 1893 it was reported that Malachi Dempsey was called "by the other people," and disappeared west of the tracks, and never came back.

A simple people! "Simple, says ye!" remarked Mr. Dooley. "Simple like th' air or th' deep sea. Not complicated like a watch that stops whin th' shoot iv clothes ye got it with wears out. When Father Butler wr-rote a book he niver finished, he said simplicity was not wearin' all ye had on ye'er shirt-front, like a tin-horn gambler with his di'mon' stud. An' 'tis so."

The barbarians around them are moderately but firmly governed, encouraged to passionate votings for the ruling race, but restrained from the immoral pursuit of office.

The most generous, thoughtful, honest, and chaste people in the world are these friends of Mr. Dooley—knowing and innocent; moral, but giving no heed at all to patented political moralities.

Among them lives and prospers the traveller, archaeologist, historian, social observer, saloon-keeper, economist, and philosopher, who has not been out of the ward for twenty-five years "but twict." He reads the newspapers with solemn care, heartily hates them, and accepts all they print for the sake of drowning Hennessy's rising protests against his logic. From the cool heights of life in the Archey Road, uninterrupted by the jarring noises of crickets and cows, he observes the passing show, and meditates thereon. His impressions are transferred to the desensitized plate of Mr. Hennessey's mind, where they can do no harm.

"There's no betther place to see what's goin' on thin the Ar-rchey Road," says Mr. Dooley. "Whin th' ilicthric cars is hummin' down th' sthreet an' th' blast goin' sthrong at th' mills, th' noise is that gr-reat ye can't think."

He is opulent in good advice, as becomes a man of his station; for he has mastered most of the obstacles in a business career, and by leading a prudent and temperate life has established himself so well that he owns his own house and furniture, and is only slightly behind on his license. It would be indelicate to give statistics as to his age. Mr. Hennessey says he was a "grown up whin th' pikes was out in forty-eight, an' I was hedge-high, an' I'm near fifty-five." Mr. Dooley says Mr. Hennessy is eighty. He closes discussion on his own age with the remark, "I'm old enough to know betther." He has served his country with distinction. His conduct of the important office of captain of his precinct (1873–75) was highly commended, and there was some talk of nominating him for alderman. At the expiration of his term he was personally thanked by the Hon. M. McGee, at one time a member of the central committee. But the activity of public life was unsuited to a man of Mr. Dooley's tastes; and, while he continues to view the political situation always with interest and sometimes with alarm, he has resolutely declined to leave the bar for the forum. His early experience gave him wisdom in discussing public affairs. "Polytics," he says, "ain't bean bag. 'Tis a man's game; an' women, childher, an' prohybitionists'd do well to keep out iv it." Again he remarks, "As Shakespere says, 'Ol' men f'r th' council, young men f'r th' ward.' "

THE BAR

"It ain't ivry man that can be a bishop. An' it ain't ivry wan that can be a saloonkeeper. A saloonkeeper must be sober, he must be honest, he must be clean, an' if he's th' pastor iv a flock iv poor wurrukin'-men he must know about ivrything that's goin' on in th' wurruld or iver wint on. I on'y discuss th' light topics iv th' day with ye, Hinnissy, because ye're a frivolous charackter, but ye'd be surprised to know what an incyclopeeja a man gets to be in this profissyon. Ivry man that comes in here an' has three pans iv nicissry evil tells me, with tears, th' secrets iv his thrade an' offers to fight me if I don't look inthrested. I know injyneerin', pammistry, plumbin', Christyan Science, midicine, horseshoein', asthronomy, th' care iv th' hair, an' th' laws iv exchange, an' th' knowledge I have iv how to subjoo th' afflictions iv th' ladies wud cause manny a pang. I tell ye we ar-re a fine body iv men.

"Not that I'm proud iv me profissyon, or shud I say me art? It's wan way iv making a living'. I suppose it was me vocation. I got into it first because I didn't like to dhrive an express-wagon, an' I stayed in it because they was nawthin' else that seemed worth while. I am not a hard drinker. I find if I dhrink too much I can't meet—an' do up—th' intellechool joynts that swarm in here afther a meetin' at th' rowlin' mills. On Saturdah nights I am convivyal. On New Year's eve I thry to make th' ol' year jus' as sorry it's lavin' me as I can. But I have no more pleasure in shovin' over to ye that liquid sunstroke thin I wud if I had to dole out collars, hairdye, books, hard-biled eggs, money, or annything else that wudden't be good f'r ye. Liquor is not a nicissry evil. Hogan says it's wan way iv ra-alizin' th' ideel. Th' nex' day ye'er ashamed iv ye're ideel. Th' throuble about it is that whin ye take it ye want more. But that's th' throuble with ivrything ye take. If we get power we want more power; if we get money we want more money. Our vices r-run on f'river. Our varchues, Hinnissy, is what me frind Doc Casey calls self-limitin.'

"Th' unbenighted American wurrukin'-man likes his dhrinks—as who does not? But he wants to take it in peace. His varchues has been wrote about. But let him injye his few simple vices in his own way, says I. He goes to th' saloon an' rich men go to th' club mos'ly f'r th' same reason. He don't want to go home. He don't need anny wan to push him into a bar. He'll go there because that's a place where wan man's betther thin another, an' nobody is ra-aly on but th' bartinder. There ought to be wan place where th' poor wurrukin'-man can escape bein' patted on th' back. He ain't so bad as people think. Wurrunkin'-men don't dhrink to excess. Dhrunkenness is a vice iv th' idle. Did ye iver see a la-ad sprintin' acrost a joist two hundherd feet in th' air? D'ye think he cud do that if he were a free dhrinker? Th' on'y wurrukin'-men who dhrink too much ar-re thruckmen, an' that's because they have so much time on their hands. While they ar-re waiting' f'r a load they get wan. Even some iv thim ar-re sober. Ye can tell them be their hats.

"Somehow or another, Hinnissy, it don't seem just right that there shud be a union iv church an' saloon. These two gr-reat institutions ar-re best kept apart. They kind iv offset each other, like th' Supreem Coort an' Congress. Dhrink is a nicissry evil, nicissry to th' clargy. If they iver admit its nicissry to th' consumers they might as well close up th' churches. Ye'll never find Father Kelly openin' a saloon. He hates me business, but he likes me. He says dhrink is an evil, but I'm a nicissity. If I moved out a worse man might come in me place."

"Ye ra-aly do think dhrink is a nicissry evil?" said Mr. Hennessy.

"Well," said Mr. Dooley, "if it's an evil to a man, it's not nicissry, an' if it's nicissry it's an evil."

SHAUGHNESSY

"Jawn," said Mr. Dooley in the course of the conversation, "whin ye come to think iv it, th' heroes iv th' wurruld—an' be thim I mean th' lads that've buckled on th' gloves an' gone out to do th' best they cud—they ain't in it with th' quite people nayether you nor me hears tell iv fr'm wan end iv th' year to another."

"I believe it," said Mr. McKenna; "for my mother told me so."

"Sure," said Mr. Dooley, "I know it is an old story. Th' wurruld's been full iv it fr'm th' beginnin'; an' 'll be full iv it till, as Father Kelly says, th' pay-roll's closed. But I was thinkin' more iv it th' other night thin iver befure, whin I wint to see Shaughnessy marry off his on'y daughter. You know Shaughnessy,—a quite man that come into th' road befure the' fire. He wurruked f'r Larkin, th' conthractor, f'r near twenty years without skip or break, an' seen th' fam'ly grow up be candle-light. Th' oldest boy was intinded f'r a priest. 'Tis a poor fam'ly that hasn't some wan that's bein' iddycated f'r the priesthood while all th' rest wear thimsilves to skeletons f'r him, an' call him Father Jawn 'r Father Mike whin he comes home wanst a year, light-hearted an' free, to eat with thim.

"Shaughnessy's lad wint wrong in his lungs, an' they fought death f'r him f'r five years, sindin' him out to th' West an' havin' masses said f'r him; an', poor divvle, he kept comin' back cross an' crool, with th' fire in his cheeks, till wan day he laid down, an' says he: 'Pah,' he says, 'I'm goin' to give up,' he says. 'An' I on'y ask that ye'll have th' mass sung over me be some man besides Father Kelly,' he says. An' he wint, an' Shaughnessy come clumpin' down th' aisle like a man in a thrance.

"Well, th' nex' wan was a girl, an' she didn't die; but, th' less said, th' sooner mended. Thin they was Terrence, a big, bould, curly-headed lad that cocked his hat at anny man—or worman f'r th' matter iv that—an' that bruk th' back iv a polisman an' swum to th' crib, an' was champeen iv the' South Side at hand ball. An' he wint. Thin th' good woman passed away. An' th' twins they growed to be th' prettiest pair that wint to first communion; an' wan night they was a light in th' window of Shaughnessy's house till three in th' mornin'. I raymimber it; f'r I had quite a crowd iv Willum Joyce's men in, an' we wondhered at it, an' wint home whin th' lamp in Shaughnessy's window was blown out.

"They was th' wan girl left—Theresa, a big, clean-lookin' child that I see grow up fr'm hello to good avnin'. She thought on'y iv th' ol' man, an' he leaned on her as if she was a crutch. She was out to meet him in th' evnin'; an' in th' mornin' he, th' simple ol' man, 'd stop to blow a kiss at her an' wave his dinner-pail, lookin' up an' down th' r-road to see that no wan was watchin' him.

"I dinnaw what possessed th' young Donahue, fr'm th' Nine-teenth. I niver thought much iv him, a stuck-up, aisy-come la-ad that niver had annything but a civil wurrud, an' is prisident iv th' sodal-ity. But he came in, an' married Theresa Shaughnessy las' Thursdah night. Th' ol' man took on twinty years, but he was as brave as a gin'ral iv th' army. He cracked jokes an' he made speeches; an' he took th' pipes fr'm under th' elbow iv Hogan, th' blindman, an' played 'Th' Wind that Shakes th' Barley' till ye'd have wore ye'er leg to a smoke f'r wantin' to dance. Thin he wint to th' dure with th' two iv thim; an' says he, 'Well,' he says, 'Jim, be good to her,' he says, an' shook hands with her through th' carredge window.

"Him an' me sat a long time smokin' across th' stove. Fin'lly, says I, 'Well,' I says, 'I must be movin'.' 'What's th' hurry?' says he. 'I've got to go,' says I. 'Wait a moment,' says he. 'Theresa 'll'—He stopped right there f'r a minyit, holdin' to th' back iv th' chair. 'Well,' says he, 'if ye've got to go, ye must,' he says. 'I'll show ye out,' he says. An' he come with me to th' dure, holdin' th' lamp over his head. I looked back at him as I wint by' an' he was settin' be th' stove, with his elbows on his knees an' th' empty pipe between his teeth.'"

3

F. SCOTT FITZGERALD

(1896–1940)

Scott Fitzgerald, the most significant writer of Irish-American background in this collection, was born in Saint Paul, Minnesota, in 1896. Because his father's family had been established American landholders as early as the seventeenth century, Fitzgerald denied that he was Irish on his father's side at all. On the other hand, his mother, Mary "Mollie" McQuillan, was the daughter of a child brought to America on the wave of refugees from the Great Famine of the 1840s. His ancestry led Fitzgerald in 1933 to confess his social discomfort to John O'Hara, who shared Fitzgerald's squeamishness about his middle-class background:

> I am half black Irish and half old American stock with the usual ancestral pretensions. The black Irish half of the family had the money and looked down upon the Maryland side of the family who had, and really had, that certain series of reticences and obligations that go under the poor shattered word "breeding" (modern form "inhibitions"). So being born in that atmosphere of crack, wisecrack and countercrack I developed a two-cylinder inferiority complex. If I were elected King of Scotland tomorrow after graduating from Eton, Magdalene to Guards, with an embryonic history which tied me to the Plantagenets, I would still be a parvenu. I spent my youth in alternately crawling in front of the kitchen maids and insulting the great.
>
> I suppose this is just a confession of being a Gael though I have known many Irish who have not been inflicted by this intense social self-consciousness.

To this "intense social self-consciousness" was added Fitzgerald's self-consciousness about his mother, whose social gaffes, eccentricities, sentimentality, overindulgence, and, particularly, pietistic and moralizing Catholicism embarrassed her socially ambitious son.

Though his parents were sufficiently well-to-do to send their son to the prestigious Newman School and to Princeton University, Fitzgerald was ready at an early age to cast off his Irish-American, Catholic heritage and probably would have done so had he not come to the attention of two Irish Catholic intellectuals, Monsignor Sigourney Fay and Shane Leslie. Doubtless under their influence, from mid-May 1917 until early 1918, Fitzgerald was everywhere proclaiming himself Irish. Following military service in World War I, Fitzgerald's first novel, the semi-autobiographical *This Side of Paradise* (1920), appeared. It was dedicated to Fay, Monsignor Thayer Darcy in the novel, and traces its hero's defection from both his Irish-American roots and his Catholicism.

Thereafter, Fitzgerald published four novels, *The Beautiful and the Damned* (1922), *The Great Gatsby* (1925), *Tender is the Night* (1934), and the posthumously published *The Last Tycoon* (1941), a series that reveals their author's increasingly severe criticism of wealth and social privilege, a movement paralleled by his swing from a rejection of the Irish to a moderate acceptance of them to an Irish-American hero's victimization by wealth and power to, what may have been, in the last unfinished novel, a fuller examination of the Irish nature.

As 1920 saw the publication of *This Side of Paradise,* in which Fitzgerald's alter ego, Amory Blaine, struggles with the nature of his Catholicism, 1920 also saw the publication of "Benediction," first in *The Smart Set,* then in the first of several collections of short stories, *Flappers and Philosophers* (1920). Other short story collections followed: *Tales of the Jazz Age* (1922); *All the Sad Young Men* (1926); *Taps at Reveille* (1935); and posthumously, such collections as *The Stories of F. Scott Fitzgerald: A Selection of 28 Stories* (1951); *Afternoon of an Author, A Selection of Uncollected Stories and Essays* (1958); *The Pat Hobby Stories* (1962); *The Basil and Josephine Stories* (1973); *The Apprentice Fiction of F. Scott Fitzgerald, 1909–1917* (1965); *Bits of Paradise: 21 Uncollected Stories by F. Scott and Zelda Fitzgerald* (1973); and *The Price Was High, The Last Uncollected Stories of F. Scott Fitzgerald* (1979). The important miscellany *The Crack-Up* appeared in 1945 and the encyclopedic *F. Scott Fitzgerald, In His Own Time: A Miscellany,* in 1971. Valuable collections of letters are *The Letters of F. Scott Fitzgerald* (1963); *Scott Fitzgerald: Letters To His Daughter* (1965); *Dear Scott/Dear Max: The Fitzgerald-Perkins Correspondence* (1971); and *As Ever, Scott Fitz—: Letters Between F. Scott Fitzgerald and His Literary Agent, Harold Ober* (1972).

At his death in December 1940 in Hollywood, Fitzgerald's critical reputation was at its nadir; now, forty-odd years later, it is high and secure, a position attested to by a bibliography of Fitzgerald criticism that far surpasses that of any other Irish-American writer.

"Benediction"

The Baltimore Station was hot and crowded, so Lois was forced to stand by the telegraph desk for interminable, sticky seconds while a clerk with big front teeth counted and recounted a large lady's day message, to determine whether it contained the innocuous forty-nine words or the fatal fifty-one.

Lois, waiting, decided she wasn't quite sure of the address, so she took the letter out of her bag and ran over it again.

> "Darling": *it began*—"I understand and I'm happier than life ever meant me to be. If I could give you the things you've always been in tune with—but I can't, Lois; we can't marry and we can't lose each other and let all this glorious love end in nothing.
>
> "Until your letter came, dear, I'd been sitting here in the half dark thinking and thinking where I could go and ever forget you; abroad, perhaps, to drift through Italy or Spain and dream away the pain of having lost you where the crumbling ruins of older, mellower civilizations would mirror only the desolation of my heart— and then your letter came.
>
> "Sweetest, bravest girl, if you'll wire me I'll meet you in Wilmington—till then I'll be here just waiting and hoping for every long dream of you to come true.
>
> "Howard"

She had read the letter so many times that she knew it word by word, yet it still startled her. In it she found many faint reflections of the man who wrote it—the mingled sweetness and sadness in his dark eyes, the furtive, restless excitement she felt sometimes when he talked to her, his dreamy sensuousness that lulled her mind to sleep. Lois was nineteen and very romantic and curious and courageous.

The large lady and the clerk having compromised on fifty words, Lois took a blank and wrote her telegram. And there were no overtones to the finality of her decision.

It's just destiny—she thought—it's just the way things work out in this damn world. If cowardice is all that's been holding me back there won't be any more holding back. So we'll just let things take their course, and never be sorry.

The clerk scanned her telegram:

"Arrived Baltimore today spend day with my brother meet me Wilmington three P.M. Wednesday Love

"Lois."

"Fifty-four cents," said the clerk admiringly.

And never be sorry—thought Lois—and never be sorry—

II

Trees filtering light onto dappled grass. Trees like tall, languid ladies with feather fans coquetting airily with the ugly roof of the monastery. Trees like butlers, bending courteously over placid walks and paths. Trees, trees over the hills on either side and scattering out in clumps and lines and woods all through eastern Maryland, delicate lace on the hems of many yellow fields, dark opaque backgrounds for flowered bushes or wild climbing gardens.

Some of the trees were very gay and young, but the monastery trees were older than the monastery which, by true monastic standards, wasn't very old at all. And, as a matter of fact, it wasn't technically called a monastery, but only a seminary; nevertheless it shall be a monastery here despite its Victorian architecture or its Edward VII additions, or even its Woodrow Wilsonian, patented, last-a-century roofing.

Out behind was the farm where half a dozen lay brothers were sweating lustily as they moved with deadly efficiency around the vegetable-gardens. To the left, behind a row of elms, was an informal baseball diamond where three novices were being batted out by a fourth, amid great chasings and puffings and blowings. And in front, as a great mellow bell boomed the half-hour, a swarm of black, human leaves were blown over the checker-board of paths under the courteous trees.

Some of these black leaves were very old with cheeks furrowed like the first ripples of a splashed pool. Then there was a scattering of middle-aged leaves whose forms when viewed in profile in their revealing gowns were beginning to be faintly unsymmetrical. These carried thick volumes of Thomas Aquinas and Henry James and Cardinal Mercier and Immanuel Kant and many bulging notebooks filled with lecture data.

But most numerous were the young leaves; blond boys of nineteen with very stern, conscientious expressions; men in the late twenties with a keen self-assurance from having taught out in the world for five years—several hundreds of them, from city and town and country in Maryland and Pennsylvania and Virginia and West Virginia and Delaware.

There were many Americans and some Irish and some tough Irish and a few French, and several Italians and Poles, and they walked informally arm in arm with each other in twos and threes or in long rows, almost universally distinguished by the straight mouth and the considerable chin—for this was the Society of Jesus, founded in Spain five hundred years before by a tough-minded soldier who trained men to hold a breach or a salon, preach a sermon or write a treaty, and do it and not argue . . .

Lois got out of a bus into the sunshine down by the outer gate. She was nineteen with yellow hair and eyes that people were tactful enough not to call green. When men of talent saw her in a streetcar they often furtively produced little stub-pencils and backs of envelopes and tried to sum up that profile or the thing that the eyebrows did to her eyes. Later they looked at their results and usually tore them up with wondering sighs.

Though Lois was very jauntily attired in an expensively appropriate travelling affair, she did not linger to pat out the dust which covered her clothes, but started up the central walk with curious glances at either side. Her face was very eager and expectant, yet she hadn't at all that glorified expression that girls wear when they arrive for a Senior Prom at Princeton or New Haven; still, as there were no senior proms here, perhaps it didn't matter.

She was wondering what he would look like, whether she'd possibly know him from his picture. In the picture, which hung over her mother's bureau at home, he seemed very young and hollow-cheeked and rather pitiful, with only a well-developed mouth and an ill-fitting probationer's gown to show that he had already made a momentous decision about his life. Of course he had been only nineteen then and now he was thirty-six—didn't look like that at all; in recent snap-shots he was much broader and his hair had grown a little thin—but the impression of her brother she had always retained was that of the big picture. And so she had always been a little sorry for him. What a life for a man! Seventeen years of preparation and he wasn't even a priest yet—wouldn't be for another year.

Lois had an idea that this was all going to be rather solemn if she let it be. But she was going to give her very best imitation of undiluted sunshine, the imitation she could give even when her head was splitting or when her mother had a nervous breakdown or when she was particularly romantic and curious and courageous. This brother of hers undoubtedly needed cheering up, and he was going to be cheered up, whether he liked it or not.

As she drew near the great, homely front door she saw a man break suddenly away from a group and, pulling up the skirts of his gown, run toward her. He was smiling, she noticed, and he looked very big and—and reliable. She stopped and waited, knew that her heart was beating unusually fast.

"Lois!" he cried, and in a second she was in his arms. She was suddenly trembling.

"Lois!" he cried again, "why, this is wonderful! I can't tell you, Lois, how *much* I've looked forward to this. Why, Lois, you're beautiful!"

Lois gasped.

His voice, though restrained, was vibrant with energy and that odd sort of enveloping personality she had thought that she only of the family possessed.

"I'm mighty glad, too—Kieth."

She flushed, but not unhappily, at this first use of his name.

"Lois—Lois—Lois," he repeated in wonder. "Child, we'll go in here a minute, because I want you to meet the rector, and then we'll walk around. I have a thousand things to talk to you about."

His voice became graver. "How's mother?"

She looked at him for a moment and then said something that she had not intended to say at all, the very sort of thing she had resolved to avoid.

"Oh Kieth—she's—she's getting worse all the time, every way."

He nodded slowly as if he understood.

"Nervous, well—you can tell me about that later. Now——"

She was in a small study with a large desk, saying something to a little jovial, white-haired priest who retained her hand for some seconds.

"So this is Lois!"

He said it as if he had heard of her for years.

He entreated her to sit down.

Two other priests arrived enthusiastically and shook hands with her and addressed her as "Kieth's little sister," which she found she didn't mind a bit.

How assured they seemed; she had expected a certain shyness, reserve at least. There were several jokes unintelligible to her, which seemed to delight every one, and the little Father Rector referred to the trio of them as "dim old monks," which she appreciated, because of course they weren't monks at all. She had a lightning impression that they were especially fond of Kieth—the Father Rector had called him "Kieth" and one of the others had kept a hand on his shoulder all through the conversation. Then she was shaking hands again and promising to come back a little later for some ice-cream, and smiling and smiling and being rather absurdly happy . . . she told herself that it was because Kieth was so delighted in showing her off.

Then she and Kieth were strolling along a path, arm in arm, and he was informing her what an absolute jewel the Father Rector was.

"Lois," he broke off suddenly, "I want to tell you before we go any farther how much it means to me to have you come up here. I think it was—mighty sweet of you. I know what a gay time you've been having."

Lois gasped. She was not prepared for this. At first when she had conceived the plan of taking the hot journey down to Baltimore, staying the night with a friend and then coming out to see her brother, she had felt rather consciously virtuous, hoped he wouldn't be priggish or resentful about her not having come before—but walking here with him under the trees seemed such a little thing, and surprisingly a happy thing.

"Why, Kieth," she said quickly, "you know I couldn't have waited a day longer. I saw you when I was five, but of course I didn't remember, and how could I have gone on without practically ever having seen my only brother?"

"It was mighty sweet of you, Lois," he repeated.

Lois blushed—he *did* have personality.

"I want you to tell me all about yourself," he said after a pause. "Of course I have a general idea what you and mother did in Europe those fourteen years, and then we were all so worried, Lois, when you had pneumonia and couldn't come down with mother—let's see, that was two years ago—and then, well, I've seen your name in the papers, but it's all been so unsatisfactory. I haven't known you, Lois."

She found herself analyzing his personality as she analyzed the personality of every man she met. She wondered if the effect of—of intimacy that he gave was bred by his constant repetition of her name. He said it as if he loved the word, as if it had an inherent meaning to him.

"Then you were at school," he continued.

"Yes, at Farmington. Mother wanted me to go to a convent—but I didn't want to."

She cast a side glance at him to see if he would resent this.

But he only nodded slowly.

"Had enough convents abroad, eh?"

"Yes—and Kieth, convents are different there anyway. Here even in the nicest ones there are so many *common* girls."

He nodded again.

"Yes," he agreed, "I suppose there are, and I know how you feel about it. It grated on me here, at first, Lois, though I wouldn't say that to any one but you; we're rather sensitive, you and I, to things like this."

"You mean the men here?"

"Yes, some of them of course were fine, the sort of men I'd always been thrown with, but there were others; a man named Regan, for instance—I hated the fellow, and now he's about the best friend I have. A wonderful character, Lois; you'll meet him later. Sort of man you'd like to have with you in a fight."

Lois was thinking that Kieth was the sort of man she'd like to have with *her* in a fight.

"How did you—how did you first happen to do it?" she asked, rather shyly, "to come here, I mean. Of course mother told me the story about the Pullman car."

"Oh, that—" He looked rather annoyed.

"Tell me that. I'd like to hear you tell it."

"Oh, it's nothing, except what you probably know. It was evening and I'd been riding all day and thinking about—about a hundred things, Lois, and then suddenly I had a sense that some one was sitting across from me, felt that he'd been there for some time, and had a vague idea that he was another traveller. All at once he leaned over toward me and I heard a voice say: 'I want you to be a priest, that's what I want.' Well, I jumped up and cried out, 'Oh, my God, not that!'—made an idiot of myself before about twenty people; you see there wasn't any one sitting there at all. A week after that I went to the Jesuit College in Philadelphia and crawled up the last flight of stairs to the rector's office on my hands and knees."

There was another silence and Lois saw that her brother's eyes wore a far-away look, that he was staring unseeingly out over the sunny fields. She was stirred by the modulations of his voice and the sudden silence that seemed to flow about him when he finished speaking.

She noticed now that his eyes were of the same fibre as hers, with the green left out, and that his mouth was much gentler, really, than in the picture—or was it that the face had grown up to it lately? He was getting a little bald just on top of his head. She wondered if that was from wearing a hat so much. It seemed awful for a man to grow bald and no one to care about it.

"Were you—pious when you were young, Kieth?" she asked. "You know what I mean. Were you religious? If you don't mind these personal questions."

"Yes," he said with his eyes still far away—and she felt that his intense abstraction was as much a part of his personality as his attention. "Yes, I suppose I was, when I was—sober."

Lois thrilled slightly.

"Did you drink?"

He nodded.

"I was on the way to making a bad hash of things." He smiled and, turning his gray eyes on her, changed the subject.

"Child, tell me about mother. I know it's been awfully hard for you there, lately. I know you've had to sacrifice a lot and put up with a great deal, and I want you to know how fine of you I think it is. I feel, Lois, that you're sort of taking the place of both of us there."

Lois thought quickly how little she had sacrificed; how lately she had constantly avoided her nervous, half-invalid mother.

"Youth shouldn't be sacrificed to age, Kieth," she said steadily.

"I know," he sighed, "and you oughtn't to have the weight on your shoulders, child. I wish I were there to help you."

She saw how quickly he had turned her remark and instantly knew what this quality was that he gave off. He was *sweet*. Her thoughts went off on a side-track and then she broke the silence with an odd remark.

"Sweetness is hard," she said suddenly.

"What?"

"Nothing," she denied in confusion. "I didn't mean to speak

aloud. I was thinking of something—of a conversation with a man named Freddy Kebble."

"Maury Kebble's brother?"

"Yes," she said, rather surprised to think of him having known Maury Kebble. Still there was nothing strange about it. "Well, he and I were talking about sweetness a few weeks ago. Oh, I don't know—I said that a man named Howard—that a man I knew was sweet, and he didn't agree with me, and we began talking about what sweetness in a man was. He kept telling me I meant a sort of soppy softness, but I knew I didn't—yet I didn't know exactly how to put it. I see now. I meant just the opposite. I suppose real sweetness is a sort of hardness—and strength."

Kieth nodded.

"I see what you mean. I've known old priests who had it."

"I'm talking about young men," she said, rather defiantly.

"Oh!"

They had reached the now deserted baseball diamond and, pointing her to a wooden bench, he sprawled full length on the grass.

"Are these *young* men happy here, Kieth?"

"Don't they look happy, Lois?"

"I suppose so, but those *young* ones, those two we just passed— have they—are they——"

"Are they signed up?" he laughed. "No, but they will be next month."

"Permanently?"

"Yes—unless they break down mentally or physically. Of course in a discipline like ours a lot drop out."

"But those *boys*. Are they giving up fine chances outside—like you did?"

He nodded.

"Some of them."

"But, Kieth, they don't know what they're doing. They haven't had any experience of what they're missing."

"No, I suppose not."

"It doesn't seem fair. Life has just sort of scared them at first. Do they all come in so *young*?"

"No, some of them have knocked around, led pretty wild lives— Regan, for instance."

"I should think that sort would be better," she said meditatively, "men that had *seen* life."

"No," said Kieth earnestly, "I'm not sure that knocking about gives a man the sort of experience he can communicate to others. Some of the broadest men I've known have been absolutely rigid about themselves. And reformed libertines are a notoriously intolerant class. Don't you think so, Lois?"

She nodded, still meditative, and he continued:

"It seems to me that when one weak person goes to another, it isn't help they want; it's a sort of companionship in guilt, Lois. After you were born, when mother began to get nervous she used to go and weep with a certain Mrs. Comstock. Lord, it used to make me shiver. She said it comforted her, poor old mother. No, I don't think that to help others you've got to show yourself at all. Real help comes from a stronger person whom you respect. And their sympathy is all the bigger because it's impersonal."

"But people want human sympathy," objected Lois. "They want to feel the other person's been tempted."

"Lois, in their hearts they want to feel that the other person's been weak. That's what they mean by human."

"Here in this old monkery, Lois," he continued with a smile, "they try to get all that self-pity and pride in our own wills out of us right at the first. They put us to scrubbing floors—and other things. It's like that idea of saving your life by losing it. You see we sort of feel that the less human a man is, in your sense of human, the better servant he can be to humanity. We carry it out to the end, too. When one of us dies his family can't even have him then. He's buried here under a plain wooden cross with a thousand others."

His tone changed suddenly and he looked at her with a great brightness in his gray eyes.

"But way back in a man's heart there are some things he can't get rid of—and one of them is that I'm awfully in love with my little sister."

With a sudden impulse she knelt beside him in the grass and, leaning over, kissed his forehead.

"You're hard, Kieth," she said, "but I love you for it—and you're sweet."

III

Back in the reception-room Lois met a half-dozen more of Kieth's particular friends; there was a young man named Jarvis, rather pale and delicate-looking, who, she knew, must be a grandson of old Mrs. Jarvis at home, and she mentally compared this ascetic with a brace of his riotous uncles.

And there was Regan with a scarred face and piercing intent eyes that followed her about the room and often rested on Kieth with something very like worship. She knew then what Kieth had meant about "a good man to have with you in a fight."

He's the missionary type—she thought vaguely—China or something.

"I want Kieth's sister to show us what the shimmy is," demanded one young man with a broad grin.

Lois laughed.

"I'm afraid the Father Rector would send me shimmying out the gate. Besides, I'm not an expert."

"I'm sure it wouldn't be best for Jimmy's soul anyway," said Kieth solemnly. "He's inclined to brood about things like shimmys. They were just starting to do the—maxixe, wasn't it, Jimmy?—when he became a monk, and it haunted him his whole first year. You'd see him when he was peeling potatoes, putting his arm around the bucket and making irreligious motions with his feet."

There was a general laugh in which Lois joined.

"An old lady who comes here to Mass sent Kieth this ice-cream," whispered Jarvis under cover of the laugh, "because she'd heard you were coming. It's pretty good, isn't it?"

There were tears trembling in Lois' eyes.

IV

Then half an hour later over in the chapel things suddenly went all wrong. It was several years since Lois had been at Benediction and at first she was thrilled by the gleaming monstrance with its central spot of white, the air rich and heavy with incense, and the sun shining through the stained-glass window of St. Francis Xavier overhead and falling in warm red tracery on the cassock of the man in front of her, but at the first notes of the "O Salutaris Hostia" a heavy weight seemed to descend upon her soul. Kieth was on her right and young Jarvis on her left, and she stole uneasy glances at both of them.

What's the matter with me? she thought impatiently.

She looked again. Was there a certain coldness in both their profiles that she had not noticed before—a pallor about the mouth and a curious set expression in their eyes? She shivered slightly: they were like dead men.

She felt her soul recede suddenly from Kieth's. This was her brother—this, this unnatural person. She caught herself in the act of a little laugh.

"What is the matter with me?"

She passed her hand over her eyes and the weight increased. The incense sickened her and a stray, ragged note from one of tenors in the choir grated on her ear like the shriek of a slate-pencil. She fidgeted, and raising her hand to her hair touched her forehead, found moisture on it.

"It's hot in here, hot as the deuce."

Again she repressed a faint laugh, and then in an instant the weight upon her heart suddenly diffused into cold fear. . . . It was that candle on the altar. It was all wrong—wrong. Why didn't somebody see it? There was something *in* it. There was something coming out of it, taking form and shape above it.

She tried to fight down her rising panic, told herself it was the wick. If the wick wasn't straight, candles did something—but they didn't do this! With incalculable rapidity a force was gathering within her, a tremendous, assimilative force, drawing from every sense, every corner of her brain, and as it surged up inside her she felt an enormous, terrified repulsion. She drew her arms down close to her side, away from Kieth and Jarvis.

Something in that candle . . . she was leaning forward—in another moment she felt she would go forward toward it—didn't anyone see it? . . . anyone?

"Ugh!"

She felt a space beside her and something told her that Jarvis had gasped and sat down very suddenly . . . then she was kneeling and as the flaming monstrance slowly left the altar in the hands of the priest, she heard a great rushing noise in her ears—the crash of the bells was like hammer-blows . . . and then in a moment that seemed eternal a great torrent rolled over her heart—there was a shouting there and a lashing as of waves . . .

. . . She was calling, felt herself calling for Kieth, her lips mouthing the words that would not come:

"Kieth! Oh, my God! *Kieth!*"

Suddenly she became aware of a new presence, something external, in front of her, consummated and expressed in warm red tracery. Then she knew. It was the window of St. Francis Xavier. Her mind gripped at it, clung to it finally, and she felt herself calling again endlessly, impotently—Kieth—Kieth!

Then out of a great stillness came a voice:

"Blessed be God."

With a gradual rumble sounded the response rolling heavily through the chapel:

"Blessed be God."

The words sang instantly in her heart; the incense lay mystically and sweetly peaceful upon the air, and *the candle on the altar went out.*

"Blessed be His Holy Name."

"Blessed be His Holy Name."

Everything blurred into a swinging mist. With a sound half-gasp, half-cry she rocked on her feet and reeled backward into Kieth's suddenly outstretched arms.

V

"Lie still, child."

She closed her eyes again. She was on the grass outside, pillowed on Kieth's arm, and Regan was dabbing her head with a cold towel.

"I'm all right," she said quietly.

"I know, but just lie still a minute longer. It was too hot in there. Jarvis felt it, too."

She laughed as Regan again touched her gingerly with the towel.

"I'm all right," she repeated.

But though a warm peace was filling her mind and heart she felt oddly broken and chastened, as if some one had held her stripped soul up and laughed.

VI

Half an hour later she walked leaning on Kieth's arm down the long central path toward the gate.

"It's been such a short afternoon," he sighed, "and I'm so sorry you were sick, Lois."

"Kieth, I'm feeling fine now, really; I wish you wouldn't worry."

"Poor old child. I didn't realize that the Benediction'd be a long service for you after your hot trip out here and all."

She laughed cheerfully.

"I guess the truth is I'm not much used to Benediction. Mass is the limit of my religious exertions."

She paused and then continued quickly:

"I don't want to shock you, Kieth, but I can't tell you how—how *inconvenient* being a Catholic is. It really doesn't seem to apply any more. As far as morals go, some of the wildest boys I know are Catholics. And the brightest boys—I mean the ones who think and read a lot, don't seem to believe in much of anything any more."

"Tell me about it. The bus won't be here for another half-hour."

They sat down on a bench by the path.

"For instance, Gerald Carter, he's published a novel. He absolutely roars when people mention immortality. And then Howa— well, another man I've known well, lately, who was Phi Beta Kappa at Harvard, says that no intelligent person can believe in Supernatural Christianity. He says Christ was a great socialist, though. Am I shocking you?"

She broke off suddenly.

Kieth smiled.

"You can't shock a monk. He's a professional shock-absorber."

"Well," she continued, "that's about all. It seems so—so *narrow*. Church schools, for instance. There's more freedom about things that Catholic people can't see—like birth control."

Kieth winced, almost imperceptibly, but Lois saw it.

"Oh," she said quickly, "everybody talks about everything now."

"It's probably better that way."

"Oh, yes, much better. Well, that's all, Kieth. I just wanted to tell you why I'm a little—lukewarm, at present."

"I'm not shocked, Lois, I understand better than you think. We all go through those times. But I know it'll come out all right, child. There's that gift of faith that we have, you and I, that'll carry us past the bad spots."

He rose as he spoke and they started again down the path.

"I want you to pray for me sometimes, Lois. I think your prayers would be about what I need. Because we've come very close in these few hours, I think."

Her eyes were suddenly shining.

"Oh, we have, we have!" she cried. "I feel closer to you now than to any one in the world."

He stopped suddenly and indicated the side of the path.

"We might—just a minute——"

It was a pietà, a life-size statue of the Blessed Virgin set within a semicircle of rocks.

Feeling a little self-conscious she dropped on her knees beside him and made an unsuccessful attempt at prayer.

She was only half through when he rose. He took her arm again.

"I wanted to thank Her for letting us have this day together," he said simply.

Lois felt a sudden lump in her throat and she wanted to say something that would tell him how much it had meant to her, too. But she found no words.

"I'll always remember this," he continued, his voice trembling a little—"this summer day with you. It's been just what I expected. You're just what I expected, Lois."

"I'm awfully glad, Kieth."

"You see, when you were little they kept sending me snap-shots of you, first as a baby and then as a child in socks playing on the beach with a pail and shovel, and then suddenly as a wistful little girl with wondering, pure eyes—and I used to build dreams about you. A man has to have something living to cling to. I think, Lois, it was your little white soul I tried to keep near me—even when life was at its loudest and every intellectual idea of God seemed the sheerest mockery, and desire and love and a million things came up to me and said: 'Look here at me! See, I'm Life. You're turning your back on it!' All the way through that shadow, Lois, I could always see your baby soul flitting on ahead of me, very frail and clear and wonderful."

Lois was crying softly. They had reached the gate and she rested her elbow on it and dabbed furiously at her eyes.

"And then later, child, when you were sick I knelt all one night and asked God to spare you for me—for I knew then that I wanted more; He had taught me to want more. I wanted to know you moved and breathed in the same world with me. I saw you growing up, that white innocence of yours changing to a flame and burning to give light to other weaker souls. And then I wanted some day to take your children on my knee and hear them call the crabbed old monk Uncle Kieth."

He seemed to be laughing now as he talked.

"Oh, Lois, Lois, I was asking God for more then. I wanted the letters you'd write me and the place I'd have at your table. I wanted an awful lot, Lois, dear."

"You've got me, Kieth," she sobbed, "you know it, say you know it. Oh, I'm acting like a baby but I didn't think you'd be this way, and I—oh, Kieth—Kieth——"

He took her hand and patted it softly.

"Here's your bus. You'll come again, won't you?"

She put her hands on his cheeks, and drawing his head down, pressed her tear-wet face against his.

"Oh, Kieth, brother, some day I'll tell you something—"

He helped her in, saw her take down her handkerchief and smile bravely at him, as the driver flicked his whip and the bus rolled off. Then a thick cloud of dust rose around it and she was gone.

For a few minutes he stood there on the road, his hand on the gate-post, his lips half parted in a smile.

"Lois," he said aloud in a sort of wonder, "Lois, Lois."

Later, some probationers passing noticed him kneeling before the pietà, and coming back after a time found him still there. And he was there until twilight came down and the courteous trees grew garrulous overhead and the crickets took up their burden of song in the dusky grass.

VII

The first clerk in the telegraph booth in the Baltimore Station whistled through his buck teeth at the second clerk.

"S'matter?"

"See that girl—no, the pretty one with the big black dots on her veil. Too late—she's gone. You missed somep'n."

"What about her?"

"Nothing. 'Cept she's damn good-looking. Came in here yesterday and sent a wire to some guy to meet her somewhere. Then a minute ago she came in with a telegram all written out and was standin' there goin' to give it to me when she changed her mind or somep'n and all of a sudden tore it up."

"Hm."

The first clerk came around the counter and picking up the two pieces of paper from the floor put them together idly. The second clerk read them over his shoulder and subconsciously counted the words as he read. There were just thirteen.

> "This is in the way of a permanent goodbye. I should suggest Italy."
>
> "Lois."

"Tore it up, eh?" said the second clerk.

4

JAMES T. FARRELL
(1904–1979)

When Scott Fitzgerald left Saint Paul, Minnesota, for the Newman School and the fabled American East, it was partly to abandon his Irish-American heritage. James T. Farrell, born on Chicago's South Side in 1904, the son of James Francis and Mary Daly Farrell, left Chicago in 1931 to live in the cosmopolitan centers, in New York and Paris, and took with him the prodigiously detailed memories of a boyhood, youth, and young manhood steeped in the Chicago South Side Irish-American milieu.

The story "Studs," written in 1929, before he had published any fiction at all, is particularly appropriate as an introduction to Farrell, and not just to his most famous work, the Studs Lonigan trilogy. He wrote:

> This, one of my first stories, is the nucleus out of which the Studs Lonigan trilogy was conceived, imagined, and written. It should suggest the experience and background of these books and my own relationship to their background. But for the accident of this story, and of the impressions recorded in it, I should probably never have written the Studs Lonigan series

—and, we might reasonably speculate, that few, if any, of the subsequent fifty volumes that provide a panorama of urban Irish America in the first three-quarters of this century probably would have been written.

From the nucleus of "Studs" came Farrell's most famous trilogy, *Young Lonigan* (1932), *The Young Manhood of Studs Lonigan* (1934), and *Judgment Day* (1935). Significantly, the narrator of "Studs" is Danny O'Neill, the Farrell figure in the story. Through the eyes of

Danny, Farrell not only records an Irish-American wake but reveals the shallowness and emptiness of the dreams and fantasies that lead to Studs's death at twenty-six. In the trilogy, Studs is survived by Danny O'Neill, whose story—in many ways, Farrell's own—is set down in the O'Neill-Flaherty pentalogy: *A World I Never Made* (1936), *No Star Is Lost* (1938), *Father and Son* (1940), *My Days of Anger* (1943), and *The Face of Time* (1953).

In addition to these eight novels, which probably comprise his most significant works, Farrell published over twenty other novels, including the Bernard Clare trilogy and eight volumes of the *Universe of Time* series, dazzlingly projected to some thirty volumes. In an active writing career that spanned fifty years—decades that saw considerable political activity and writing—ending with his death in 1979, Farrell wrote two hundred and fifty or more short stories that extended his extraordinary range of types and incidents and which were collected in such volumes as *Calico Shoes and Other Stories* (1934), *Guillotine Party and Other Stories* (1935), *Can All This Grandeur Perish? and Other Stories* (1937), *$1,000 A Week and Other Stories* (1942), *To Whom It May Concern and Other Stories* (1944), *When Boyhood Dreams Come True* (1946), *The Life Adventurous and Other Stories* (1947), *An American Dream Girl* (1950), *French Girls are Vicious and Other Stories* (1955), *A Dangerous Woman and Other Stories* (1957), *Side Street and Other Stories* (1961), *Sounds of a City* (1962), *Childhood is Not Forever* (1969), and *Judith and Other Stories* (1973). In addition to his fiction, Farrell produced a body of critical essays that are acute and penetrating in their judgments of the literature of this century and in their understanding of our political and social problems.

With pardonable chagrin, Farrell felt that too many of his readers dwelt too long on the Studs Lonigan trilogy at the expense of other works and that this narrow approach kept him in a kind of critical limbo. Nevertheless, even he must have felt the staying power of the trilogy when, shortly before his death, it was given a six-hour television dramatization in March 1979.

"Studs"

It is raining outside; rain pouring like bullets from countless machine guns; rain spat-spattering on the wet earth and paving in endless silver crystals. Studs' grave out at Mount Olivet will be soaked and soppy, and fresh with the wet, clean odors of watered earth and flowers. And the members of Studs' family will be looking out of the windows of their apartment on the South Side, thinking of the cold, damp grave and the gloomy, muddy cemetery, and of their Studs lying at rest in peaceful acceptance of that wormy conclusion which is the common fate.

At Studs' wake last Monday evening everybody was mournful, sad that such a fine young fellow of twenty-six should go off so suddenly with double pneumonia; blown out of this world like a ripped leaf in a hurricane. They sighed and the women and girls cried, and everybody said that it was too bad. But they were consoled because he'd had the priest and had received Extreme Unction before he died, instead of going off like Sport Murphy who was killed in a saloon brawl. Poor Sport! He was a good fellow, and tough as hell. Poor Studs!

The undertaker (it was probably old man O'Reedy who used to be usher in the old parish church) laid Studs out handsomely. He was outfitted in a sombre black suit and a white silk tie. His hands were folded over his stomach, clasping a pair of black rosary beads. At his head, pressed against the satin bedding, was a spiritual bouquet, set in line with Studs' large nose. He looked handsome, and there were no lines of suffering on his planed face. But the spiritual bouquet (further assurance that his soul would arrive safely in Heaven) was a dirty trick. So was the administration of the last sacraments. For Studs will be miserable in Heaven, more miserable than he was on those Sunday nights when he would hang around the old poolroom at Fifty-eighth and the elevated station, waiting for something to happen. He will find the land of perpetual happiness and goodness dull and boresome, and he'll be resentful. There will be nothing to do in Heaven but to wait in timeless eternity. There will be no can houses, speakeasies, whores (unless they are reformed) and gambling joints; and neither will there be a shortage of plasterers. He will loaf up and down gold-paved streets where there is not even the suggestion of a poolroom, thinking of Paulie Haggerty, Sport Murphy, Arnold Sheehan and Hink Weber, who are possibly in Hell together because there was no priest around to play a dirty trick on them.

I thought of these things when I stood by the coffin, waiting for Tommy Doyle, Red Kelly, Les, and Joe to finish offering a few perfunctory prayers in memory of Studs. When they had showered some Hail Marys and Our Fathers on his already prayer-drenched soul, we went out into the dining room.

Years ago when I was a kid in the fifth grade in the old parish school, Studs was in the graduating class. He was one of the school leaders, a light-faced, blond kid who was able to fight like sixty and who never took any sass from Tommy Doyle, Red Kelly, or any of those fellows from the Fifty-eighth Street gang. He was quarterback on the school's football team, and liked by the girls.

My first concrete memory of him is of a rainy fall afternoon. Dick Buckford and I were fooling around in front of Helen Shires' house bumping against each other with our arms folded. We never thought of fighting but kept pushing and shoving and bumping each other. Studs, Red O'Connell, Tubby Connell, the Donoghues, and Jim Clayburn came along. Studs urged us into fighting, and I gave Dick a bloody nose. Studs congratulated me, and said that I could come along with them and play tag in Red O'Connell's basement, where there were several trick passageways.

After that day, I used to go around with Studs and his bunch. They regarded me as a sort of mascot, and they kept training me to fight other kids. But any older fellows who tried to pick on me would have a fight on their hands. Every now and then he would start boxing with me.

"Gee, you never get hurt, do you?" he would say. I would grin in answer, bearing the punishment because of the pride and the glory.

"You must be goofy. You can't be hurt."

"Well, I don't get hurt like other kids."

"You're too good for Morris and those kids. You could trim them with your eyes closed. You're good," he would say, and then he would go on training me.

I arranged for a party on one of my birthdays, and invited Studs and the fellows from his bunch. Red O'Connell, a tall, lanky, cowardly kid, went with my brother, and the two of them convinced my folks that Studs was not a fit person for me to invite. I told Studs what had happened, and he took such an insult decently. But none of the fellows he went with would accept my invitation, and most of the girls also refused. On the day of the party, with my family's permission, I again invited Studs but he never came.

I have no other concrete recollections of Studs while he was in grammar school. He went to Loyola for one year, loafed about for a similar period; and then he became a plasterer for his father. He commenced going round the poolroom. The usual commonplace story resulted. What there was of the boy disappeared in slobbish dissipation. His pleasures became compressed within a hexagonal of whores, movies, pool, alky, poker, and craps. By the time I commenced going into the poolroom (my third year in high school) this process had been completed.

Studs' attitude toward me had also changed to one of contempt. I was a goofy young punk. Often he made cracks about me. Once, when I retaliated by sarcasm, he threatened to bust me, and awed by his former reputation I shut up. We said little to each other, although Studs occasionally condescended to borrow fifty or seventy-five cents from me, or to discuss Curley, the corner imbecile.

Studs' companions were more or less small-time amateur hoodlums. He had drifted away from the Donoghues and George Gogarty, who remained bourgeois young men with such interests as formal dances and shows. Perhaps Slug Mason was his closest friend; a tall, heavy-handed, good-natured, child-minded slugger, who knew the address and telephone number of almost every prostitute on the South Side. Hink Weber, who should have been in the ring and who later committed suicide in an insane asylum, Red Kelly, who was a typical wisecracking corner habitué, Tommy Doyle, a fattening, bull-dozing, half-good-natured moron, Stan Simonsky and Joe Thomas were his other companions.

I feel sure that Studs' family, particularly his sisters, were appalled by his actions. The two sisters, one of whom I loved in an adolescently romantic and completely unsuccessful manner, were the type of middle-class girls who go in for sororities and sensibilities. One Saturday evening, when Studs got drunk earlier than usual, his older sister (who the boys always said was keen) saw him staggering around under the Fifty-eighth Street elevated station. She was with a young man in an automobile, and they stopped. Studs talked loudly to her, and finally they left. Studs reeled after the car, cursing and shaking his fists. Fellows like Johnny O'Brien (who went to the U. of C. to become a fraternity man) talked sadly of how Studs could have been more discriminating in his choice of buddies and liquor; and this, too, must have reached the ears of his two sisters.

Physical decay slowly developed. Studs, always a square-planed, broad person, began getting soft and slightly fat. He played one or two years with the corner football team. He was still an efficient quarterback, but slow. When the team finally disbanded, he gave up athletics. He fought and brawled about until one New Year's Eve he talked out of turn to Jim McGeoghan, who was boxing champ down at Notre Dame. Jim flattened Studs' nose, and gave him a wicked black eye. Studs gave up fighting.

My associations with the corner gradually dwindled. I went to college, and became an atheist. This further convinced Studs that I wasn't right, and he occasionally remarked about my insanity. I grew up contemptuous of him and the others; and some of this feeling crept into my overt actions. I drifted into other groups and forgot the corner. Then I went to New York, and stories of legendary activities became fact on the corner. I had started a new religion, written poetry, and done countless similar monstrous things. When I returned, I did not see Studs for over a year. One evening, just before the Smith-Hoover election day, I met him as he came out of the I.C. station at Randolph Street with Pat Carrigan and Ike Dugan. I talked to Pat and Ike, but not to Studs.

"Aren't you gonna say hello to me?" he asked in friendly fashion, and he offered me his hand.

I was curious but friendly for several minutes. We talked of Al Smith's chances in an uninformed, unintelligent fashion and I injected one joke about free love. Studs laughed at it; and then they went on.

The next I heard of him, he was dead.

When I went out into the dining room, I found all the old gang there, jabbering in the smoke-thick, crowded room. But I did not have any desire or intention of giving the world for having seen them. They were almost all fat and respectable. Cloddishly, they talked of the tragedy of his death, and they went about remembering the good old days. I sat in the corner and listened.

The scene seemed tragi-comical to me. All these fellows had been the bad boys of my boyhood, and many of them I had admired as proper models. Now they were all of the same kidney. Jackie Cooney (who once stole fifteen bottles of grape juice in one haul from under the eyes of a Greek proprietor over at Sixty-fifth and Stony Island), Monk McCarthy (who lived in a basement on his pool winnings and peanuts for over a year), Al Mumford (the good-natured, dumbly well-intentioned corner scapegoat), Pat Carrigan, the roly-poly fat boy from Saint Stanislaus high school—all as alike as so many cans of tomato soup.

Jim Nolan, now bald-headed, a public accountant, engaged to be married, and student in philosophy at Saint Vincent's evening school, was in one corner with Monk.

"Gee, Monk, remember the time we went to Plantation and I got drunk and went down the alley over-turning garbage cans?" he recalled.

"Yeh, that was some party," Monk said.

"Those were the days," Jim said.

Tubby Connell, whom I recalled as a moody, introspective kid, singled out the social Johnny O'Brien and listened to the latter talk with George Gogarty about Illinois U.

Al Mumford walked about making cracks, finally observing to me, "Jim, get a fiddle and you'll look like Paderwooski."

Red Kelly sat enthroned with Les, Doyle, Simonsky, Bryan, Young Floss Campbell (waiting to be like these older fellows), talking oracularly.

"Yes, sir, it's too bad. A young fellow in the prime of life going like that. It's too bad," he said.

"Poor Studs!" Les said.

"I was out with him a week ago," Bryan said.

"He was all right then," Kelly said.

"Life is a funny thing," Doyle said.

"It's a good thing he had the priest," Kelly said.

"Yeh," Les said.

"Sa-ay, last Saturday I pushed the swellest little baby at Rosy's," Doyle said.

"Was she a blonde?" Kelly said.

"Yeh," Doyle said.

"She's cute. I jazzed her, too," Kelly said.

"Yeh, that night at Plantation was a wow," Jim Nolan said.

"We ought to pull off a drunk some night," Monk said.

"Let's," Nolan said.

"Say, Curley, are you in love?" Mumford asked Curley across the room.

"Now, Duffy," Curley said with imbecilic superiority.

"Remember the time Curley went to Burnham?" Carrigan asked.

Curley blushed.

"What happened, Curley?" Duffy asked.

"Nothing, Al," Curley said, confused.

"Go on, tell him, Curley! Tell him! Don't be bashful now! Don't be bashful! Tell him about the little broad!" Carrigan said.

"Now, Pat, you know me better than that," Curley said.

"Come on, Curley, tell me," Al said.

"Some little girl sat on Curley's knee, and he shoved her off and called her a lousy whore and left the place," Carrigan said.

"Why, Curley, I'm ashamed of you," Al said.

Curley blushed.

"I got to get up at six every morning. But I don't mind it. This not workin' is the bunk. You ain't got any clothes or anything when you ain't got the sheets. I know. No, sir, this loafin' is all crap. You wait around all day for something to happen," Jackie Cooney said to Tommy Rourke.

"Gee, it was tough on Studs," Johnny O'Brien said to George Gogarty.

Gogarty said it was tough, too. Then they talked of some student from Illinois U. Phil Rolfe came in. Phil was professional major-domo of the wake; he was going with Studs' kid sister. Phil used to be a smart Jewboy, misplaced when he did not get into the furrier business. Now he was sorry with everybody, and thanking them for being sorry. He and Kelly talked importantly of pall-bearers. Then he went out. Some fellow I didn't know started telling one of Red Kelly's brothers what time he got up to go to work. Mickey Flannagan, the corner drunk, came in and he, too, said he was working.

They kept on talking, and I thought more and more that they were a bunch of slobs. All the adventurous boy that was in them years ago had been killed. Slobs, getting fat and middle-aged, bragging of their stupid brawls, reciting the commonplaces of their days.

As I left, I saw Studs' kid sister. She was crying so pitifully that she was unable to recognize me. I didn't see how she could ever have been affectionate toward Studs. He was so outside of her understanding. I knew she never mentioned him to me the few times I took her out. But she cried pitifully.

As I left, I thought that Studs looked handsome. He would have gotten a good break, too, if only they hadn't given him Extreme Unction. For life would have grown into fatter and fatter decay for him, just as it was starting to do with Kelly, Doyle, Cooney and McCarthy. He, too, was a slob; but he died without having to live countless slobbish years. If only they had not sent him to Heaven where there are no whores and poolrooms.

I walked home with Joe, who isn't like the others. We couldn't feel sorry over Studs. It didn't make any difference.

"Joe, he was a slob," I said.

Joe did not care to use the same language, but he did not disagree.

And now the rain keeps falling on Studs' new grave, and his family mournfully watches the leaden sky, and his old buddies are at work wishing that it was Saturday night, and they were just getting into bed with a naked voluptuous blonde.

5

BETTY SMITH

(1904–1972)

Betty Smith was born in the mixed German-Irish Williamsburg section of Brooklyn on December 15, 1904. She was christened Elizabeth Wehner, but underwent cultural conversion when her widowed mother married William Keogh, an Irishman.

Smith attended P.S. 23 in Greenpoint, where she, like Francie Nolan of *A Tree Grows in Brooklyn* (1943), devoured the books in her library. At fourteen, she, like Francie, was forced to leave school. She worked, then, in factories and retail and clerical jobs, until she became a reader and editor for Dramatists' Play Service. Though she had no secondary schooling, she was given special status at the University of Michigan (1927–30) and at the Yale University Drama School (1930–34), where she studied under George P. Baker.

Smith married three times: George H. E. Smith (1924–38); Joseph Piper Jones (1943–51); and Robert Finch (1957–59). The first two ended in divorce. She had two daughters by her first husband. She moved from Brooklyn to Ann Arbor to New Haven to Chapel Hill, North Carolina. Along the way she wrote articles for National Education Association syndication, columns for the *Detroit Free Press,* and a number of dramas. In Chapel Hill, with the help of a Rockefeller Dramatists' Guild Fellowship, she completed seventy-five one-act and five full-length plays.

Between 1940 and 1943, Smith added a page a day for three years to her autobiographical novel, *A Tree Grows in Brooklyn.* The book, an overnight success, has sold upward of five million copies in sixteen languages. It has since become a Broadway musical, a film, and a novel for television. On the strength of *Tree,* Smith accepted a teaching position at the University of North Carolina.

Though she originally intended a trilogy in the manner of James T. Farrell's *Studs,* Smith found that the later novels, *Tomorrow Will Be Better* (1948) and *Maggie—Now* (1958), stood well on their own. Taken together, Smith's Williamsburg fiction provides an accurate sociological view of Irish Brooklyn after the turn of the century. The selection from *Tree* (chapter 5), which follows, describes the rigors of tenement life and "melting pot" education.

Critic Orville Prescott greeted *A Tree Grows in Brooklyn* as "a first novel of uncommon skill, an almost uncontrollable vitality and zest for life, the work of a fresh, original and highly gifted talent." Diana Trilling dismissed it as a conventional little book of not much literary value. Smith mixes sentiment and realism in her fiction. She may not be quite as good as Prescott makes her, but she's certainly better than Trilling's modest estimate.

She died in Chapel Hill in 1972. In spite of her prolific work in drama, she is best remembered for her novels.

A *Tree Grows in Brooklyn*

School days went along. Some were made up of meanness, brutality and heartbreak; others were bright and beautiful because of Miss Bernstone and Mr. Morton. And always, there was the magic of learning things.

Francie was out walking one Saturday in October and she chanced on an unfamiliar neighborhood. Here were no tenements or raucous shabby stores. There were old houses that had been standing there when Washington maneuvered his troops across Long Island. They were old and decrepit but there were picket fences around them with gates on which Francie longed to swing. There were bright fall flowers in the front yard and maple trees with crimson and yellow leaves on the curb. The neighborhood stood old, quiet, and serene in the Saturday sunshine. There was a brooding quality about the neighborhood, a quiet, deep, timeless, shabby peace. Francie was as happy as though, like Alice, she had stepped through a magic mirror. She was in an enchanted land.

She walked on further and came to a little old school. Its old bricks glowed garnet in the late afternoon sun. There was no fence around the school yard and the school grounds were grass and not cement. Across from the school, it was practically open country—a meadow with goldenrod, wild asters and clover growing in it.

Francie's heart turned over. This was it! This was the school she wanted to go to. But how could she get to go there? There was a strict law about attending the school in your own district. Her parents would have to move to that neighborhood if she wanted to go to that school. Francie knew that mama wouldn't move just because *she* felt like going to another school. She walked home slowly thinking about it.

She sat up that night waiting for papa to come home from work. After Johnny had come home whistling his "Molly Malone" as he ran up the steps, after all had eaten of the lobster, caviar, and liverwurst that he brought home, mama and Neeley went to bed. Francie kept papa company while he smoked his last cigar. Francie whispered all about the school in papa's ear. He looked at her, nodded, and said, "We'll see tomorrow."

"You mean we can move near that school?"

"No, but there has to be another way. I'll go there with you tomorrow and we'll see what we can see."

Francie was so excited she couldn't sleep the rest of the night. She was up at seven but Johnny was still sleeping soundly. She waited in a perspiration of impatience. Each time he sighed in his sleep, she ran to see if he was waking up.

He woke about noon and the Nolans sat down to dinner. Francie couldn't eat. She kept looking at papa but he made her no sign. Had he forgotten? Had he forgotten? No, because while Katie was pouring the coffee, he said carelessly:

"I guess me and the prima donna will take a little walk later on."

Francie's heart jumped. He had not forgotten. He had not forgotten. She waited. Mama had to answer. Mama might object. Mama might ask why. Mama might say she guessed she'd go along too. But all mama said was, "All right."

Francie did the dishes. Then she had to go down to the candy store to get the Sunday paper; then to the cigar store to get papa a nickel Corona. Johnny had to read the paper. He had to read every column of it including the society section in which he couldn't possibly be interested. Worse than that, he had to make comments to mama on every item he read. Each time he'd put the paper aside, turn to mama and say, "Funny things in the papers nowadays. Take this case," Francie would almost cry.

Four o'clock came. The cigar had long since been smoked, the paper lay gutted on the floor, Katie had tired of having the news analyzed and had taken Neeley and gone over to visit Mary Rommely.

Francie and papa set out hand in hand. He was wearing his only suit, the tuxedo and his derby hat and he looked very grand. It was a splendid October day. There was a warm sun and a refreshing wind working together to bring the tang of the ocean around each corner. They walked a few blocks, turned a corner and were in this other neighborhood. Only in a great sprawling place like Brooklyn could there be such a sharp division. It was a neighborhood peopled by fifth and sixth generation Americans, whereas in the Nolan neighborhood, if you could prove *you* had been born in America, it was equivalent to a Mayflower standing.

Indeed, Francie was the only one in her classroom whose parents were American-born. At the beginning of the term, Teacher called the roll and asked each child her lineage. The answers were typical.

"I'm Polish-American. My father was born in Warsaw."

"Irish-American. Me fayther and mither were born in County Cork."

When Nolan was called, Francie answered proudly: "I'm an American."

"I *know* you're American," said the easily exasperated teacher. "But what's your nationality?"

"American!" insisted Francie even more proudly.

"Will you tell me what your parents are or do I have to send you to the principal?"

"My parents are American. They were born in Brooklyn."

All the children turned around to look at a little girl whose parents had *not* come from the old country. And when Teacher said, "Brooklyn? Hm. I guess that makes you American, all right," Francie was proud and happy. How wonderful was Brooklyn, she thought, when just being born there automatically made you an American!

Papa told her about this strange neighborhood: how its families had been Americans for more than a hundred years back; how they were mostly Scotch, English and Welsh extraction. The men worked as cabinet makers and fine carpenters. They worked with metals: gold, silver and copper.

He promised to take Francie to the Spanish section of Brooklyn some day. There the men worked as cigar-makers and each chipped in a few pennies a day to hire a man to read to them while they worked. And the man read fine literature.

They walked along the quiet Sunday street. Francie saw a leaf flutter from a tree and she skipped ahead to get it. It was a clear scarlet with an edging of gold. She stared at it, wondering if she'd ever see anything as beautiful again. A woman came from around the corner. She was rouged heavily and wore a feather boa. She smiled at Johnny and said,

"Lonesome, Mister?"

Johnny looked at her a moment before he answered gently, "No, Sister."

"Sure?" she inquired archly.

"Sure," he answered quietly.

She went her way. Francie skipped back and took papa's hand.

"Was that a bad lady, Papa?" she asked eagerly.

"No."

"But she *looked* bad."

"There are very few bad people. There are just a lot of people that are unlucky."

"But she was all painted and . . ."

"She was one who had seen better days." He liked the phrase. "Yes, she may have seen better days." He fell into a thoughtful mood. Francie kept skipping ahead and collecting leaves.

They came upon the school and Francie proudly showed it to papa. The late afternoon sun warmed its softly-colored bricks and the small-paned windows seemed to dance in the sunshine. Johnny looked at it a long time, then he said,

"Yes, this is the school. This is it."

Then, as whenever he was moved or stirred, he had to put it into a song. He held his worn derby over his heart, stood up straight looking up at the school house and sang:

> *School days, school days*
> *Dear old golden rule days.*
> *Readin' 'n writin' 'n 'rithmetic . . .*

To a passing stranger, it might have looked silly—Johnny standing there in his greenish tuxedo and fresh linen holding the hand of a thin ragged child and singing the banal song so un-self-consciously on the street. But to Francie it seemed right and beautiful.

They crossed the street and wandered in the meadow that folks called "lots." Francie picked a bunch of goldenrod and wild asters to take home. Johnny explained that the place had once been an Indian burying ground and how as a boy, he had often come here to hunt arrowheads. Francie suggested they hunt for some. They searched for half an hour and found none. Johnny recalled that as a boy, he hadn't found any either. This struck Francie as funny and she laughed. Papa confessed that maybe it hadn't been an Indian cemetery after all; maybe someone had made up that story. Johnny was more than right because he had made up the whole story himself.

Soon it was time to go home and tears came into Francie's eyes because papa hadn't said anything about getting her into the new school. He saw the tears and figured out a scheme immediately.

"Tell you what we'll do, Baby. We'll walk around and pick out a nice house and take down the number. I'll write a letter to your principal saying you're moving there and want to be transferred to this school."

They found a house—a one-story white one with a slanting roof and late chrysanthemums growing in the yard. He copied the address carefully.

"You know that what we are going to do is wrong?"

"Is it, Papa?"

"But it's wrong to gain a bigger good."

"Like a white lie?"

"Like a lie that helps someone out. So you must make up for the wrong by being twice as good. You must never be bad or absent or late. You must never do anything to make them send a letter home through the mails."

"I'll always be good, Papa, if I can go to that school."

"Yes. Now I'll show you a way to go to school through a little park. I know right where it is. Yes sir, I know right where it is."

He showed her the park and how she could walk through it diagonally to go to school.

"That should make you happy. You can see the seasons change as you come and go. What do you say to that?"

Francie, recalling something her mother had once read to her answered, "My cup runneth over." And she meant it.

When Katie heard of the plan, she said: "Suit yourself. But I'll have nothing to do with it. If the police come and arrest you for giving a false address, I'll say honestly that I had nothing to do with it. One school's as good or as bad as another. I don't know why she wants to change. There's homework no matter what school you go to."

"It's settled then," Johnny said. "Francie, here's a penny. Run down to the candy store and get a sheet of writing paper and an envelope."

Francie ran down and ran back. Johnny wrote a note saying Francie was going to live with relatives at such and such an address and wanted a transfer. He added that Neeley would continue living at home and wouldn't require a transfer. He signed his name and underlined it authoritatively.

Tremblingly, Francie handed the note to her principal next morning. That lady read it, grunted, made out the transfer, handed her her report card and told her to go; that the school was too crowded anyhow.

Francie presented herself and documents to the principal of the new school. He shook hands with her and said he hoped she'd be happy in the new school. A monitor took her to the classroom. The teacher stopped the work and introduced Francie to the class. Francie looked out over the rows of little girls. All were shabby but most were clean. She was given a seat to herself and happily fell into the routine of the new school.

The teachers and children here were not as brutalized as in the old school. Yes, some of the children were mean but it seemed a natural child-meanness and not a campaign. Often the teachers were impatient and cross but never naggingly cruel. There was no corporal punishment either. The parents were too American, too aware of the rights granted them by their Constitution to accept injustices meekly. They could not be bull-dozed and exploited as could the immigrants and the second generation Americans.

Francie found that the different feeling in this school came mostly from the janitor. He was a ruddy white-haired man whom even the principal addressed as *Mister* Jenson. He had many children and grandchildren of his own, all of whom he loved dearly. He was father to all children. On rainy days when children came to school soaked, he insisted that they be sent down to the furnace room to dry out. He made them take off their wet shoes and hung their wet stockings on a line to dry. The little shabby shoes stood in a row before the furnace.

It was pleasant down in the furnace room. The walls were white-washed and the big red-painted furnace was a comforting thing. The windows were high up in the walls. Francie liked to sit there and enjoy the warmth and watch the orange and blue flames dancing an inch above the bed of small black coals. (He left the furnace door open when the children were drying out.) On rainy days, she left earlier and walked to school slower so that she would be soaking wet and rate the privilege of drying in the furnace room.

It was unorthodox for Mr. Jenson to keep the children out of class to dry but everyone liked and respected him too much to protest. Francie heard stories around the school concerning Mr. Jenson. She heard that he had been to college and knew more than the principal did. They said he had married and when the children came, had decided that there was more money in being a school engineer than in being a school teacher. Whatever it was, he was liked and respected. Once Francie saw him in the principal's office. He was in his clean striped overalls sitting there with his knees crossed and talking politics. Francie heard that the principal often came down to Mr. Jenson's furnace room to sit and talk for a few moments while he smoked a pipeful of tobacco.

When a boy was bad, he wasn't sent to the principal's office for a licking; he was sent down to Mr. Jenson's room for a talking to. Mr. Jenson never scolded a bad boy. He talked to him about his own youngest son who was a pitcher on the Brooklyn team. He talked about democracy and good citizenship and about a good world where everyone did the best he could for the common good of all. After a talk with Mr. Jenson, the boy could be counted upon not to cause any more trouble.

At graduation, the children asked the principal to sign the first page of their autograph book out of respect to his position but they valued Mr. Jenson's autograph more and he always got the second page to sign. The principal signed quickly in a great sprawling hand. But not Mr. Jenson. He made a ceremony out of it. He took the book over to his big roll-top desk and lit the light over it. He sat down, carefully polished his spectacles and chose a pen. He dipped it in ink, squinted at it, wiped it off and re-dipped it. Then he signed his name in a fine steel-engraving script and blotted it carefully. His signature was always the finest in the book. If you had the nerve to ask him, he'd take the book home and ask his son, who was with the Dodgers, to sign it too. This was a wonderful thing for the boys. The girls didn't care.

Mr. Jenson's handwriting was so wonderful that he wrote out all the diplomas by request.

Mr. Morton and Miss Bernstone came to that school, too. When they were teaching, Mr. Jenson would often come in and squeeze himself into one of the back seats and enjoy the lesson too. On a cold day, he'd have Mr. Morton or Miss Bernstone come down to his furnace room for a hot cup of coffee before they went on to the next school. He had a gas plate and coffee-making equipment on a little table. He served strong, hot black coffee in thick cups and these visiting teachers blessed his good soul.

Francie was happy in this school. She was very careful about being a good girl. Each day, as she passed the house whose number she claimed, she looked at it with gratitude and affection. On windy days, when papers blew before it, she went about picking up the debris and depositing it in the gutter before the house. Mornings after the rubbish man had emptied the burlap bag and had caressy tossed the empty bag on the walk instead of in the yard, Francie picked it up and hung it on a fence paling. The people who lived in the house came to look on her as a quiet child who had a queer complex about tidiness.

Francie loved that school. It meant that she had to walk forty-eight blocks each day but she loved the walk, too. She had to leave earlier in the morning than Neeley and she got home much later. She didn't mind except that it was a little hard at lunch time. There were twelve blocks to come home and twelve to go back—all in the hour. It left little time for eating. Mama wouldn't let her carry a lunch. Her reason was:

"She'll be weaned away from her home and family soon enough the way she's growing up. But while she's still a child she has to act like a child and come home and eat the way children should. Is it my fault that she has to go so far to school? Didn't she pick it out herself?"

"But Katie," argued papa, "it's such a good school."

"Then let her take the bad along with the good."

The lunch question was settled. Francie had about five minutes for lunch—just time enough to report home for a sandwich which she ate walking back to school. She never considered herself put upon. She was so happy in the new school that she was anxious to pay in some way for this joy.

It was a good thing that she got herself into this other school. It showed her that there were other worlds besides the world she had been born into and that these other worlds were not unattainable.

6

JOHN O'HARA
(1905–1970)

John O'Hara was born in 1905 in Pottsville—the Gibbsville of so many of his works—in south-central Pennsylvania to Patrick and Katherine Delaney O'Hara. His father, one of the town's leading doctors, had sprung, in his son's words, from generations of "shanty Irish," whereas his mother was a member of a distinguished Irish-American family. O'Hara went to Saint Patrick's parochial school, was an altar boy at Saint Patrick's Church, and later attended Fordham Prep and Niagara Prep—a sufficiently Catholic background for a man who became a nonpracticing Catholic.

Because of his father's death, O'Hara could not attend Yale University. Conceivably, Yale might have wrought in him some of the changes that Princeton had worked on Fitzgerald—a sense of belonging to an upper social class and the sophistication to deal more sympathetically with his uneasy Irishness.

O'Hara worked as a journalist in Pennsylvania and New York City and wrote for *Newsweek* and *Time* and had short stories in the *New Yorker* before the publication, in 1934, of his first novel, *Appointment in Samarra*. An immediate critical and popular success, and arguably his best work, *Samarra* is set in Gibbsville and, like so much of O'Hara's other fiction, it attempts to portray not only character but the society that produced the character. Returning again and again to a terrain he knew intimately, O'Hara resembled James T. Farrell, as he resembled Farrell in his criticism of the spiritual poverty of the milieu from which he sprang. Generally, O'Hara's feelings about social class are uncertain; on the one hand, he attacks the hypocrisy and vacuity of middle-class life, on the other, he seems genuinely awed by wealth. While his social and political sympathies may be described as "liberal," the lower orders often appear as extras or, at best, as bit players in O'Hara's fiction. Of the lower orders none appears lower than the Irish-American.

In *Butterfield 8* (1935), O'Hara's second novel, Jimmy Malloy, O'Hara's mouthpiece, sets the tone for what was to become O'Hara's standard view of the Irish:

> I want to tell you something about myself that will help to explain a lot of things about me. You might as well hear it now. First of all, I am a Mick. I wear Brooks clothes and I don't eat salad with a spoon and I probably could play five-goal polo in two years, but I am still a Mick. Still a Mick. Now it's taken me a little time to find this out. . . . for the present purpose I only mention it to show that I'm pretty God damn American, and therefore my brothers and sisters are, and yet we're not Americans. We've been here, at least some of my family, since before the Revolution—and we produce the perfect gangster type! At least it's you American Americans' idea of a perfect gangster type, and I suppose you're right. Yes, I guess you are. The first real gangsters in this country were Irish. The Mollie Maguires. Anyway, do you see what I mean by all this non-assimilable stuff?

While the 1980s might have modified O'Hara's view of the Irish in America, to him they were always "Micks," outsiders. There are indeed Irish-American characters in his novels and short stories, but they never quite make it socially. They are stereotyped as maids or as social climbers or as the fat and complacent nouveau riche, like Mort in the story that follows. "Mort and Mary" first appeared in the *New Yorker* in 1931 and then in O'Hara's first collection of short stories, *The Doctor's Son and Other Stories* (1935).

In addition to *Appointment in Samarra* and *Butterfield 8*, O'Hara's best-known novels include *A Rage to Live* (1949), *The Farmer's Hotel* (1951), *Ten North Frederick* (1955), *From the Terrace* (1958), and *Ourselves to Know* (1960). Other short story collections include *Files on Parade* (1939), *Pal Joey* (1940), *Pipe Night* (1945), *Hellbox* (1947), *Assembly* (1961), *The Cape Cod Lighter* (1962), *The Hat on the Bed* (1963), *The Horse Knows the Way* (1964), *Waiting for Winter* (1966), *The Time Element and Other Stories* (1972), and *Good Samaritan, and Other Stories* (1974).

"Mort and Mary"

When Mort was quite young the neighbors in Hudson Street used to tell his mother and father what a fine, big boy he was. He was an altar boy, but so tall that people who didn't know him would say to themselves he must be at least tonsure, maybe subdeacon. He was a head taller than some of the young priests and he looked so imposing and natural there in the sanctuary that it was more or less taken for granted that he would study for the priesthood.

He would, of course, be a Jesuit, because wasn't he going to St. Francis Xavier's over in Sixteenth Street? That's a Jebby school. The only trouble with being a Jesuit is it takes so long before you say your first mass. Oftentimes a young man's father and mother have passed on before he says his first Mass, and it's always so much nicer at a first Mass if the father and mother can be there, besides all the other relations. Of course it's not really so bad if the father isn't there because then there's the mother, a widow, the centre of it all, very happy when she weeps a little because "himself would be so proud, Lord 'a' mercy on 'im."

Now it might have come to pass that Mort would have become a priest, but the real reason he didn't was that his father kept a saloon, and a very prosperous one. There is no rule in the Church that says a lad can't be a priest if his father keeps a tavern, but in Mort's case and many others like it there is the fact that a prosperous saloon-keeper can afford to give his boy an education out of his own pocket, without getting any help from the Church. And as frequently happens, when a saloonkeeper's son goes to a Jesuit school he makes friends among the sons of big Tammany men or even higher-class people. He mentions the names of these friends to his mother, and the first thing you know she decides maybe the lad hasn't a true vocation, maybe he oughtn't to enter the holy priesthood. It's better to be a good man out in the world than be a priest if you haven't a true vocation. Maybe he might better go to Fordham and be a lawyer. Or a doctor.

So Mort, who never had had any idea of becoming a priest—had, in fact, until he was fourteen, assumed that his father would get him in the cops—studied Scholastic philosophy, learned about Brooks and Frank, Marymount College, the major forks and spoons, and generally grew up to be a handsome Fordham man. When the war came he joined the Sixty-ninth Infantry.

When he came back his mother had persuaded his father to get out of the saloon business. He always had had a certain amount of political power, had been good to the poor, and had given a side altar to the Church. In a few short years he had come within striking distance of a place on the Board of Aldermen. It secretly pleased Mort, who had always thought his father, a white-haired, red-faced, quiet, abstemious man, *was* vaguely superior to the garrulous old fools and pugnacious young lads whom he served at the bar.

Mort found no unemployment problem when he got back from the war. Not so far as he was concerned. He was not too old to study law but he could not quite see himself carrying books in the subway on his way to and from the Fordham law classes in the Woolworth Building. He never expressed his thought, never was totally aware of it, but it, and not an awe of the bar examinations, was what kept him out of law school. Instead, he took a good job with an importing firm which was owned by the father of a Cuban he had known in college. He thought he was well suited to the job because he had had pretty good marks in Spanish, but he found out that he seldom needed his linguistic ability. He had a good business head and was a personable fellow, Irish and big and well dressed and good-looking. And, of course, his father always was in the background and Tammany in back of *him,* and that keeps many a man in his job in New York. Mort began to make money in sugar.

His boss' family lived in New York, and when one of the daughters got out of Manhattanville Mort suddenly became aware that she was beautiful. He figured, too, that inasmuch as he was invited to the Casablancas for dinner every now and then, it was expected of him that he pay some attention to Mercedes (you've no idea how hard it was for Mort to refrain from saying "Mersa-deeze"). He began to see her frequently, and there are many men in New York today who remember with rage the placid, almost supercilious demeanor of the giant who used to be seen with Mercedes Casablanca, whom they knew while they were at Princeton. That was only Mort's way of looking well bred.

The elder Casablanca had become Americanized—or Novum Eboracumized—and did not inquire too closely into Mort's family. Mort's father, he knew, was a man of substance, and his mother was no less presentable than many Cuban mothers. So it was a match.

The problem of whom to invite to the wedding was a delicate one because of Mort's father's Tammany connections. Mort helped to solve it: he had the more presentable of his Fordham classmates for ushers and Joe Casablanca, Mercedes' brother, as best man. The wedding took place at a nuptial Mass, and since there can be no Mass in the afternoon, most of the embarrassing voters, male and female, were at work driving their trucks, carrying their hods, washing their clothes, doing their marketing, making their beds, while Mercedes and Mort were receiving the sacrament of Matrimony. There were only about a hundred and fifty of the Hudson Street contingent in the Church of St. Ignatius Loyola when Mercedes and Mort were made one. And not more than twenty of them had been invited to go to the Plaza afterward.

Mort's father, all confusion, furnished the apartment, gave Mort a Cadillac and a cheque for two thousand dollars. The Casablancas gave them all the flat silver, and some of the best-looking Medeira linen you ever saw. Governor Smith, Mayor Walker, Surrogate Foley, and Mr. McCooey sent little trinkets. The Cuban Ambassador sent his chargé d'affaires.

There is nothing more to be said. Mort and Mercedes are slowly getting fat together. They have another Mercedes and another Morton. They go to Southampton in the summer now (only for weekends and a month, but that's something). There will never be any scandal in that family. Real, dependable people.

7

MARY McCARTHY
(b. 1912)

Born in Seattle, Washington, in 1912, Mary McCarthy lost both parents in the influenza epidemic of 1918. She and her brothers spent their childhood among relatives of different backgrounds, a factor that may have contributed to McCarthy's considerable gift for satire and irony, her acute awareness of the conflicts between appearance and reality, and her scrupulous efforts at fairness and honesty. From age six to age eleven, she lived in Minneapolis, shuttled between aunt and uncle and well-to-do Irish-Catholic paternal grandparents; then in Seattle—a period during which she lost her faith—with her maternal grandparents, a grandfather of New England stock and a Jewish grandmother.

In Minneapolis, she attended Saint Stephen's parochial school, where she won a state contest for her essay on "The Irish in American History." In Seattle, she attended the Forest Ridge Convent and an Episcopal boarding school, the Annie Wright Seminary, in Tacoma. She was graduated from Vassar College in 1933.

After Vassar, McCarthy became a book reviewer for the *Nation* and the *New Republic* and, in 1937, a drama critic for the *Partisan Review*. Her theatre pieces were collected in *Sights and Spectacles, 1937–1956* (1956) and later expanded in 1963 and published as *Mary McCarthy's Theatre Chronicles, 1937–1962*.

She taught at Bard and Sarah Lawrence colleges for a few years after her 1946 divorce from the eminent critic Edmund Wilson, whom she had married in 1938. She began publishing fiction in 1942 with the loosely connected stories of *The Company She Keeps*, followed by the novels, *The Oasis* (1949), *A Source of Embarrassment* (1950), *The Groves of Academe* (1952), and *A Charmed Life* (1955). In 1963, she published *The Group*, a best seller dealing with her own generation of

Vassar women. That novel established her as an important American author. Subsequent novels include *Winter Visitors* (1970) and *Birds of America* (1971). She also published a collection of short stories, *Cast a Cold Eye* (1950), reissued in 1981 with two additional stories and published under the title, *The Hounds of Summer and Other Stories*.

In addition to her many critical articles, McCarthy has written *On the Contrary: Articles of Belief, 1946–1961* (1961); *The Writing on the Wall, and Other Literary Essays* (1971); and *Ideas and the Novel* (1980); studies of two Italian cities, *Venice Observed* (1956) and *The Stones of Florence* (1959); and several works of nonfiction that reflect her leftist sympathies: *Vietnam* (1967); *Hanoi* (1968); *Medina* (1972); and *The Mask of State: Watergate Portraits* (1974).

Despite her name and her early background, Irish-Americans do not figure prominently in McCarthy's fiction, and when they figure, they are not portrayed sympathetically. For example, in *The Groves of Academe*, Henry Mulcahy, untenured English instructor, sometime "professional Irishman," and specialist in James Joyce, is clearly on the receiving end of McCarthy's mordantly witty satire. "Yonder Peasant, Who Is He?," first appearing in *the New Yorker*, is also the first chapter of her autobiographical *Memories of a Catholic Girlhood* (1957), a work that bears the same relationship to her own life as *A Portrait of the Artist as a Young Man* does to Joyce's. Of the autobiographical work, *How I Grew* (1987), McCarthy writes that it traces "the onset of intellectual interests" from her thirteenth year, when she was "born as a mind," to her first marriage at twenty-one. On the whole, critics have found it less satisfying than the earlier memoir, and it is less revealing of her Irish dimension than *Memories*.

"Yonder Peasant" explains McCarthy's loss of her Catholic faith and her less than intense interest in Irish-Americana. Exposed to two strains of Catholicism—that of her gentle, convert mother, a simple faith, and that of Grandmother McCarthy, "a sour, baleful doctrine in which old hates and rancors had been stewing for generations, with ignorance proudly stirring the pot"—it is not too difficult to see why McCarthy shed Catholicism. And, faced with two strains of "Irishness"—the too-brief influence of a recklessly extravagant and romantic father as opposed to the grim and tightfisted Irish-Americanism of paternal grandparents—it is perhaps understandable that she has chosen not to celebrate her "Irishness." In spite of the early years, McCarthy has emerged as one of our leading women-of-letters. She now lives in Paris with her present husband, James Raymond West.

"Yonder Peasant, Who Is He?"

Whenever we children came to stay at my grandmother's house, we were put to sleep in the sewing room, a bleak, shabby, utilitarian rectangle, more office than bedroom, more attic than office, that played to the hierarchy of chambers the role of a poor relation. It was a room seldom entered by the other members of the family, seldom swept by the maid, a room without pride; the old sewing machine, some cast-off chairs, a shadeless lamp, rolls of wrapping paper, piles of cardboard boxes that might someday come in handy, papers of pins, and remnants of material united with the iron folding cots put out for our use and the bare floor boards to give an impression of intense and ruthless temporality. Thin, white spreads, of the kind used in hospitals and charity institutions, and naked blinds at the windows reminded us of our orphaned condition and of the ephemeral character of our visit; there was nothing here to encourage us to consider this our home.

Poor Roy's children, as commiseration damply styled us, could not afford illusions, in the family opinion. Our father had put us beyond the pale by dying suddenly of influenza and taking our young mother with him, a defection that was remarked on with horror and grief commingled, as though our mother had been a pretty secretary with whom he had wantonly absconded into the irresponsible paradise of the hereafter. Our reputation was clouded by this misfortune. There was a prevailing sense, not only in the family but among storekeepers, servants, streetcar conductors, and other satellites of our circle, that my grandfather, a rich man, had behaved with extraordinary munificence in allotting a sum of money for our support and installing us with some disagreeable middle-aged relations in a dingy house two blocks distant from his own. What alternative he had was not mentioned; presumably he could have sent us to an orphan asylum and no one would have thought the worse of him. At any rate, it was felt, even by those who sympathized with us, that we led a privileged existence, privileged because we had no rights, and the very fact that at the yearly Halloween or Christmas party given at the home of an uncle we appeared so dismal, ill clad, and unhealthy, in contrast to our rosy, exquisite cousins, confirmed the judgment that had been made on us—clearly, it was a generous impulse that kept us in the family at all. Thus, the meaner our circumstances, the greater seemed our grandfather's condescension, a view in which we ourselves shared, looking softly and shyly on this old man—with his rheumatism, his pink face and white hair, set off by the rosebuds in his Pierce-Arrow and in his buttonhole—as the font of goodness and philanthropy, and the nickel he occasionally gave us to drop into the collection plate on Sunday (two cents was our ordinary contribution) filled us not with envy but with simple admiration for his potency; this indeed was princely, *this* was the way to give. It did not occur to us to judge him for the disparity of our styles of living. Whatever bitterness we felt was kept for our actual guardians, who, we believed, must be embezzling the money set aside for us, since the standard of comfort achieved in our grandparents' house—the electric heaters, the gas logs, the lap robes, the shawls wrapped tenderly about the old knees, the white meat of chicken and red meat of beef, the silver, the white tablecloths, the maids, and the solicitous chauffeur—persuaded us that prunes and rice pudding, peeling paint and patched clothes were *hors concours* with these persons and therefore could not have been willed by them. Wealth, in our minds, was equivalent to bounty, and poverty but a sign of penuriousness of spirit.

Yet even if we had been convinced of the honesty of our guardians, we would still have clung to that beneficent image of our grandfather that the family myth proposed to us. We were too poor, spiritually speaking, to question his generosity, to ask why he allowed us to live in oppressed chill and deprivation at a long arm's length from himself and hooded his genial blue eye with a bluff, millionairish grey eyebrow whenever the evidence of our suffering presented itself at his knee. The official answer we knew: our benefactors were too old to put up with four wild young children; our grandfather was preoccupied with business matters and with his rheumatism, to which he devoted himself as though to a pious duty, taking it with him on pilgrimages to Ste. Anne de Beaupré and Miami, offering it with impartial reverence to the miracle of the Northern Mother and the Southern sun. This rheumatism hallowed my grandfather with the mark of a special vocation; he lived with it in the manner of an artist or a grizzled Galahad; it set him apart from all of us, and even from my grandmother, who, lacking such an affliction, led a relatively unjustified existence and showed, in relation to us children, a sharper and more bellicose spirit. She felt, in spite of everything, that she was open to criticism, and transposing this feeling with a practiced old hand, kept peering into our characters for symptoms of ingratitude.

We, as a matter of fact, were grateful to the point of servility. We made no demands, we had no hopes. We were content if we were permitted to enjoy the refracted rays of that solar prosperity and come sometimes in the summer afternoons to sit on the shady porch or idle through a winter morning on the wicker furniture of the sun parlor, to stare at the player piano in the music room and smell the odor of whisky in the mahogany cabinet in the library, or to climb about the dark living room examining the glassed-in paintings in their huge gilt frames, the fruits of European travel: dusky Italian devotional groupings, heavy and lustrous as grapes, Neapolitan women carrying baskets to market, views of Venetian canals, and Tuscan harvest scenes—secular themes that, to the Irish-American mind, had become tinged with Catholic feeling by a regional infusion from the Pope. We asked no more from this house than the pride of being connected with it, and this was fortunate for us, since my grandmother, a great adherent of the give-them-an-inch-and-they'll-take-a-yard theory of hospitality, never, so far as I can remember, offered any caller the slightest refreshment, regarding her own conversation as sufficiently wholesome and sustaining. An ugly, severe old woman with a monstrous balcony of a bosom, she officiated over certain set topics in a colorless singsong, like a priest intoning a Mass, topics to which repetition had lent a senseless solemnity: her audience with the Holy Father; how my own father had broken with family tradition and voted the Democratic ticket; a visit to Lourdes; the Sacred Stairs in Rome, bloodstained since the first Good Friday, which she had climbed on her knees; my crooked little fingers and how they meant I was a liar; a miracle-working bone; the importance of regular bowel movements; the wickedness of Protestants; the conversion of my mother to Catholicism; and the assertion that my other grandmother must certainly dye her hair. The most trivial reminiscences (my aunt's having hysterics in a haystack) received from her delivery and from the piety of the context a strongly monitory flavor; they inspired fear and guilt, and one searched uncomfortably for the moral in them, as in a dark and riddling fable.

Luckily, I am writing a memoir and not a work of fiction, and therefore I do not have to account for my grandmother's unpleasing character and look for the Oedipal fixation or the traumatic experience which would give her that clinical authenticity that is nowadays so desirable in portraiture. I do not know how my grandmother got the way she was; I assume, from family photographs and from the inflexibility of her habits, that she was always the same, and it seems as idle to inquire into her childhood as to ask what was ailing Iago or look for the error in toilet-training that was responsible for Lady Macbeth. My grandmother's sexual history, bristling with infant mortality in the usual style of her period, was robust and decisive: three tall, handsome sons grew up, and one attentive daughter. Her husband treated her kindly. She had money, many grandchildren, and religion to sustain her. White hair, glasses, soft skin, wrinkles, needlework—all the paraphernalia of motherliness were hers; yet it was a cold grudging, disputatious old woman who sat all day in her sunroom making tapestries from a pattern, scanning religious periodicals, and setting her iron jaw against any infraction of her ways.

Combativeness was, I suppose, the dominant trait in my grandmother's nature. An aggressive churchgoer, she was quite without Christian feeling; the mercy of the Lord Jesus had never entered her heart. Her piety was an act of war against the Protestant ascendancy. The religious magazines on her table furnished her not with food for meditation but with fresh pretexts for anger; articles attacking birth control, divorce, mixed marriages, Darwin, and secular education were her favorite reading. The teachings of the Church did not interest her, except as they were a rebuke to others; "Honor thy father and thy mother," a commandment she was no longer called upon to practice, was the one most frequently on her lips. The extermination of Protestantism, rather than spiritual perfection, was the boon she prayed for. Her mind was preoccupied with conversion; the capture of a soul for God much diverted her fancy—it made one less Protestant in the world. Foreign missions, with their overtones of good will and social service, appealed to her less strongly; it was not a *harvest* of souls that my grandmother had in mind.

This pugnacity of my grandmother's did not confine itself to sectarian enthusiasm. There was the defense of her furniture and her house against the imagined encroachments of visitors. With her, this was not the gentle and tremulous protectiveness endemic in old ladies, who fear for the safety of their possessions with a truly touching anxiety, inferring the fragility of all things from the brittleness of their old bones and hearing the crash of mortality in the perilous tinkling of a tea cup. My grandmother's sentiment was more autocratic: she hated having her chairs sat in or her lawns stepped on or the water turned on in her basins, for no reasons at all except pure officiousness; she even grudged the mailman his daily promenade up her sidewalk. Her home was a center of power and she would not allow it to be derogated by easy or democratic usage. Under her jealous eye, its social properties had atrophied, and it functioned in the family structure simply as a political headquarters. Family conferences were held there, consultations with the doctor and the clergy; refractory children were brought there for a lecture or an interval of thought-taking; wills were read and loans negotiated and emissaries from the Protestant faction on state occasions received. The family had no friends, and entertaining was held to be a foolish and unnecessary courtesy as between blood relations. Holiday dinners fell, as a duty, on the lesser members of the organization: the daughters and daughters-in-law (converts from the false religion) offered up Baked Alaska on a platter, like the head of John the Baptist, while the old people sat enthroned at the table, and only their digestive processes acknowledged, with rumbling, enigmatic salvos, the festal day.

Yet on one terrible occasion my grandmother had kept open house. She had accommodated us all during those fatal weeks of the influenza epidemic, when no hospital beds were to be had and people went about with masks or stayed shut up in their houses, and the awful fear of contagion paralyzed all services and made each man an enemy to his neighbor. One by one, we had been carried off the train which had brought us from distant Puget Sound to make a new home in Minneapolis. Waving good-by in the Seattle depot, we had not known that we had carried the flu with us into our drawing rooms, along with the presents and the flowers, but, one after another, we had been struck down as the train proceeded eastward. We children did not understand whether the chattering of our teeth and Mama's lying torpid in the berth were not somehow a part of the trip (until then, serious illness, in our minds, had been associated with innovations—it had always brought home a new baby), and we began to be sure that it was all an adventure when we saw our father draw a revolver on the conductor who was trying to put us off the train at a small wooden station in the middle of the North Dakota prairie. On the platform at Minneapolis, there were stretchers, a wheel chair, redcaps, distraught officials, and, beyond them, in the crowd, my grandfather's rosy face, cigar, and cane, my grandmother's feathered hat, imparting an air of festivity to this strange and confused picture, making us children certain that our illness was the beginning of a delightful holiday.

We awoke to reality in the sewing room several weeks later, to an atmosphere of castor oil, rectal thermometers, cross nurses, and efficiency, and though we were shut out from the knowledge of what had happened so close to us, just out of our hearing—a scandal of the gravest character, a coming and going of priests and undertakers and coffins (Mama and Daddy, they assured us, had gone to get well in the hospital)—we became aware, even as we woke from our fevers, that everything, including ourselves, was different. We had shrunk, as it were, and faded, like the flannel pajamas we wore, which during these weeks had grown, doubtless from the disinfectant they were washed in, wretchedly thin and shabby. The behavior of the people around us, abrupt, careless, and preoccupied, apprised us without any ceremony of our diminished importance. Our value had paled, and a new image of ourselves—the image, if we had guessed it, of the orphan—was already forming in our minds. We had not known we were spoiled, but now this word, entering our vocabulary for the first time, served to define the change for us and to herald the new order. Before we got sick, we were spoiled; that was what was the matter now, and everything we could not understand, everything unfamiliar and displeasing, took on a certain plausibility when related to this fresh concept. We had not known what it was to have trays dumped summarily on our beds and no sugar and cream for our cereal, to take medicine in a gulp because someone could not be bothered to wait for us, to have our arms jerked into our sleeves and a comb ripped through our hair, to be bathed impatiently, to be told to sit up or lie down quick and no nonsense about it, to find our questions unanswered and our requests unheeded, to lie for hours alone and wait for the doctor's visit, but this, so it seemed, was an oversight in our training, and my grandmother and her household applied themselves with a will to remedying the deficiency.

Their motives were, no doubt, good; it was time indeed that we learned that the world was no longer our oyster. The happy life we had had—the May baskets and the valentines, the picnics in the yard, and the elaborate snowman—was a poor preparation, in truth, for the future that now opened up to us. Our new instructors could hardly be blamed for a certain impatience with our parents, who had been so lacking in foresight. It was to everyone's interest, decidedly, that we should forget the past—the quicker, the better—and a steady disparagement of our habits ("Tea and chocolate, can you imagine, and all those frosted cakes—no wonder poor Tess was always after the doctor") and praise that was rigorously comparative ("You have absolutely no idea of the improvement in those children") flattered the feelings of the speakers and prepared us to accept a loss

that was, in any case, irreparable. Like all children, we wished to
conform, and the notion that our former ways had been somehow
ridiculous and unsuitable made the memory of them falter a little,
like a child's recitation to strangers. We no longer demanded our
due, and the wish to see our parents insensibly weakened. Soon we
ceased to speak of it, and thus, without tears or tantrums, we came
to know they were dead.

Why no one, least of all our grandmother, to whose repertory the
subject seems so congenial, took the trouble to tell us, it is impossible now to know. It is easy to imagine her "breaking" the news to
those of us who were old enough to listen in one of those official
interviews in which her nature periodically tumefied, becoming
heavy and turgid, like her portentous bosom, like peonies, her favorite flower, or like the dressmaker's dummy, that bombastic image of
herself that, half swathed in a sheet for decorum's sake, lent a muse-
umlike solemnity to the sewing room and aroused our first sexual
curiosity. The mind's ear frames her sentences, but in reality she did
not speak, whether from a hygienic motive (keep the mind ignorant
and the bowels open), or from a mistaken kindness, it is difficult to
guess. Perhaps really she feared our tears, which might rain on her
like reproaches, since the family policy at the time was predicated on
the axiom of our virtual insentience, an assumption that allowed
them to proceed with us as if with pieces of furniture. Without ex-
planations or coddling, as soon as they could safely get up, my three
brothers were dispatched to the other house; they were much too
young to "feel" it, I heard the grownups murmur, and would never
know the difference "if Myers and Margaret were careful." In my
case, however, a doubt must have been experienced. I was six—old
enough to "remember"—and this entitled me, in the family's eyes, to
greater consideration, as if this memory of mine were a lawyer who
represented me in court. In deference, therefore, to my age and my
supposed powers of criticism and comparison, I was kept on for a
time, to roam palely about my grandmother's living rooms, a dan-
gling, transitional creature, a frog becoming a tadpole, while my
brothers, poor little polyps, were already well embedded in the
structure of the new life. I did not wonder what had become of
them. I believe I thought they were dead, but their fate did not
greatly concern me; my heart had grown numb. I considered myself
clever to have guessed the truth about my parents, like a child who
proudly discovers that there is no Santa Claus, but I would not speak
of that knowledge or even react to it privately, for I wished to have

nothing to do with it; I would not co-operate in this loss. Those weeks in my grandmother's house come back to me very obscurely, surrounded by blackness, like a mourning card: the dark well of the staircase, where I seem to have been endlessly loitering, waiting to see Mama when she would come home from the hospital, and then simply loitering with no purpose whatever; the winter-dim first-grade classroom of the strange academy I was sent to; the drab treatment room of the doctor's office, where every Saturday I screamed and begged on a table while electric shocks were sent through me, for what purpose I cannot conjecture. But this preferential treatment could not be accorded me forever; it was time that I found my niche. "There is someone here to see you"—the maid met me one afternoon with this announcement and a half-curious, half-knowledgeable smile. My heart bounded; I felt almost sick (who else, after all, could it be?), and she had to push me forward. But the man and woman surveying me in the sun parlor with my grandmother were strangers, two unprepossessing middle-aged people—a great-aunt and her husband, so it seemed—to whom I was now commanded to give a hand and a smile, for, as my grandmother remarked, Myers and Margaret had come to take me home that very afternoon to live with them, and I must not make a bad impression.

Once the new household was running, our parents' death was officially conceded and sentiment given its due. Concrete references to the lost ones, to their beauty, gaiety, and good manners, were naturally welcomed by our guardians, who possessed none of these qualities themselves, but the veneration of our parents' *memory* was considered an admirable exercise. Our evening prayers were lengthened to include one for our parents' souls, and we were thought to make a pretty picture, all four of us in our pajamas with feet in them, kneeling in a neat line, our hands clasped before us, reciting the prayer for the dead. "Eternal rest grant unto them, oh Lord, and let the perpetual light shine upon them," our thin little voices cried, but this remembrancing, so pleasurable to our guardians, was only a chore to us. We connected it with lights out, washing, all the bedtime coercions, and particularly with the adhesive tape that, to prevent mouth-breathing, was clapped upon our lips the moment prayer was finished, sealing us up for the night, and that was removed, very painfully, with the help of ether, in the morning. It embarrassed us to be reminded of our parents by these persons who had superseded them and who seemed to evoke their wraiths in an almost proprietary manner, as though death, the great leveler, had brought them within their province. In the same spirit, we were taken to the cemetery to view our parents' graves; this, in fact, being free of charge, was a regular Sunday pastime with us, which we grew to hate as we did all recreation enforced by our guardians—department-store demonstrations, band concerts, parades, trips to the Old Soldiers' Home, to the Botanical Gardens, to Minnehaha Park, where we watched other children ride on the ponies, to the Zoo, to the water tower— diversions that cost nothing, involved long streetcar trips or endless walking and waiting, and that had the peculiarly fatigued, dusty, proletarianized character of American municipal entertainment. The two mounds that now were our parents associated themselves in our minds with Civil War cannon balls and monuments to the doughboy dead; we contemplated them stolidly, waiting for a sensation, but these twin grass beds, with their junior-executive headstones, elicited nothing whatever; tired of this interminable staring, we would beg to be allowed to go play in some collateral mausoleum, where the dead at least were buried in drawers and offered some stimulus to fancy.

For my grandmother, the recollection of the dead became a mode of civility that she thought proper to exercise toward us whenever, for any reason, one of us came to stay at her house. The reason was almost always the same. We (that is, my brother Kevin or I) had run away from home. Independently of each other, this oldest of my brothers and I had evolved an identical project—to get ourselves placed in an orphan asylum. We had noticed the heightening of interest that mention of our parentless condition seemed always to produce in strangers, and this led us to interpret the word "asylum" in the old Greek sense and to look on a certain red brick building, seen once from a streetcar near the Mississippi River, as a haven of security. So, from time to time, when our lives became too painful, one of us would set forth, determined to find the red brick building and to press what we imagined was our legal claim to its protection. But sometimes we lost our way, and sometimes our courage, and after spending a day hanging about the streets peering into strange yards, trying to assess the kindheartedness of the owner (for we also thought of adoption), or a cold night hiding in a church confessional box or behind some statuary in the Art Institute, we would be brought by the police, by some well-meaning householder, or simply by fear and hunger, to my grandmother's door. There we would be silently received, and a family conclave would be summoned. We would be put to sleep in the sewing room for a night, or sometimes more, until our feelings had subsided and we could be sent back, grateful, at any rate, for the promise that no reprisals would be taken and that the life we had run away from would go on "as if nothing had happened."

Since we were usually running away to escape some anticipated punishment, these flights at least gained us something, but in spite of the taunts of our guardians, who congratulated us bitterly on our "cleverness," we ourselves could not feel that we came home in triumph as long as we came home at all. The cramps and dreads of those long nights made a harrowing impression on us. Our failure to run away successfully put us, so we thought, at the absolute mercy of our guardians; our last weapon was gone, for it was plain to be seen that they could always bring us back and we never understood why they did not take advantage of this situation to thrash us, as they used to put it, within an inch of our lives. What intervened to save us, we could not guess—a miracle, perhaps; we were not acquainted with any *human* motive that would prompt Omnipotence to desist. We did not suspect that these escapes brought consternation to the family circle, which had acted, so it conceived, only in our best interests, and now saw itself in danger of unmerited obloquy. What would be the Protestant reaction if something still more dreadful were to happen? Child suicides were not unknown, and quiet, asthmatic little Kevin had been caught with matches under the house. The family would not acknowledge error, but it conceded a certain mismanagement on Myers' and Margaret's part. Clearly, we might become altogether intractable if our homecoming on these occasions were not mitigated with leniency. Consequently, my grandmother kept us in a kind of neutral detention. She declined to be aware of our grievance and offered no words of comfort, but the comforts of her household acted upon us soothingly, like an automatic mother's hand. We ate and drank contentedly; with all her harsh views, my grandmother was a practical woman and would not have thought it worthwhile to unsettle her whole schedule, teach her cook to make a lumpy mush and watery boiled potatoes, and market for turnips and parsnips and all the other vegetables we hated, in order to approximate the conditions she considered suitable for our characters. Humble pie could be costly, especially when cooked to order.

Doubtless she did not guess how delightful these visits seemed to us once the fear of punishment had abated. Her knowledge of our own way of living was luxuriously remote. She did not visit our ménage or inquire into its practices, and though hypersensitive to a squint or a dental irregularity (for she was liberal indeed with glasses and braces for the teeth, disfiguring appliances that remained the sole token of our bourgeois origin and set us off from our parochial-school mates like the caste marks of some primitive tribe), she appeared not to notice the darns and patches of our clothing, our raw hands and scarecrow arms, our silence and our elderly faces. She imagined us as surrounded by certain play-things she had once bestowed on us—a sandbox, a wooden swing, a wagon, an ambulance, a toy fire engine. In my grandmother's consciousness, these objects remained always in pristine condition; years after the sand had spilled out of it and the roof had rotted away, she continued to ask tenderly after our lovely sand pile and to manifest displeasure if we declined to join in its praises. Like many egoistic people (I have noticed this trait in myself), she was capable of making a handsome outlay, but the act affected her so powerfully that her generosity was still lively in her memory when its practical effects had long vanished. In the case of a brown beaver hat, which she watched me wear for four years, she was clearly blinded to its matted nap, its shapeless brim, and ragged ribbon by the vision of the price tag it had worn when new. Yet, however her mind embroidered the bare tapestry of our lives, she could not fail to perceive that we felt, during these short stays with her, *some* difference between the two establishments, and to take our wonder and pleasure as a compliment to herself.

She smiled on us quite kindly when we exclaimed over the food and the nice, warm bathrooms, with their rugs and electric heaters. What funny little creatures, to be so impressed by things that were, after all, only the ordinary amenities of life! Seeing us content in her house, her emulative spirit warmed slowly to our admiration: she compared herself to our guardians, and though for expedient reasons she could not afford to deprecate them ("You children have been very ungrateful for all Myers and Margaret have done for you"), a sense of her own finer magnaminity disposed her subtly in our favor. In the flush of these emotions, a tenderness sprang up between us. She seemed half reluctant to part with whichever of us she had in her custody, almost as if she were experiencing a genuine pang of conscience. "Try and be good," she would advise us when the moment for leave-taking came, "and don't provoke your aunt and uncle. We might have made different arrangements if there had been only one of you to consider." These manifestations of concern, these tacit admissions of our true situation, did not make us, as one might have thought, bitter against our grandparents, for whom ignorance of the facts might have served as a justification, but, on the contrary, filled us with love for them and even a kind of sympathy—our sufferings were less terrible if someone acknowledged their existence, if someone were suffering for us, for whom we, in our turn, could suffer, and thereby absolve of guilt.

During these respites, the recollection of our parents formed a bond between us and our grandmother that deepened our mutual regard. Unlike our guardians or the whispering ladies who sometimes came to call on us, inspired, it seemed, by a pornographic curiosity as to the exact details of our feelings ("Do you suppose they remember their parents?" "Do they ever *say* anything?"), our grandmother was quite uninterested in arousing an emotion of grief in us. "She doesn't feel it at all," I used to hear her confide, of me, to visitors, but contentedly, without censure, as if I had been a spayed cat that, in her superior foresight, she had had "attended to." For my grandmother, the death of my parents had become, in retrospect, an eventful occasion upon which she looked back with pleasure and a certain self-satisfaction. Whenever we stayed with her, we were allowed, as a special treat, to look into the rooms they had died in, for the fact that, as she phrased it, "they died in separate rooms" had for her a significance both romantic and somehow self-congratulatory, as though the separation in death of two who had loved each other in life were beautiful in itself and also reflected credit on the chatelaine of the house, who had been able to furnish two master bedrooms for the emergency. The housekeeping details of the tragedy, in fact, were to her of paramount interest. "I turned my house into a hospital," she used to say, particularly when visitors were present. "Nurses were as scarce as hen's teeth, and *high*—you can hardly imagine what those girls were charging an hour." The trays and the special cooking, the laundry and the disinfectants recalled themselves fondly to her thoughts, like items on the menu of some long-ago ball-supper, the memory of which recurred to her with a strong possessive nostalgia.

My parents had, it seemed, by dying on her premises, become in a lively sense her property, and she dispensed them to us now, little by little, with a genuine sense of bounty, just as, later on, when I returned to her a grown-up young lady, she conceded me a diamond lavaliere of my mother's as if the trinket were an inheritance to which she had the prior claim. But her generosity with her memories appeared to us, as children, an act of the greatest indulgence. We begged her for more of these mortuary reminiscences as we might have begged for candy, and since ordinarily we not only had no candy but were permitted no friendships, no movies, and little reading beyond what our teachers prescribed for us, and were kept in quarantine, like carriers of social contagion, among the rhubarb plants of our neglected yard, these memories doled out by our grandmother became our secret treasures; we never spoke of them to each other but hoarded them, each against the rest, in the miserly fastnesses of our hearts. We returned, therefore, from our grandparents' house replenished in all our faculties; these crumbs from the rich man's table were a banquet indeed to us. We did not even mind going back to our guardians, for we now felt superior to them, and besides, as we well knew, we had no choice. It was only by accepting our situation as a just and unalterable arrangement that we could be allowed to transcend it and feel ourselves united to our grandparents in a love that was the more miraculous for breeding no practical results.

In this manner, our household was kept together, and my grandparents were spared the necessity of arriving at a fresh decision about it. Naturally, from time to time a new scandal would break out (for our guardians did not grow kinder in response to being run away from), yet we had come, at bottom, to despair of making any real change in our circumstances, and run away hopelessly, merely to postpone punishment. And when, after five years, our Protestant grandfather, informed at last of the fact, intervened to save us, his indignation at the family surprised us nearly as much as his action. We thought it only natural that grandparents should know and do nothing, for did not God in the mansions of Heaven look down upon human suffering and allow it to take its course?

8

BRENDAN GILL

(b. 1914)

Brendan Gill is an established critic who says that his first love is writing fiction. He has successfully authored novels, short stories, plays and essays, as well as the film and drama critiques that have been his bread and butter since he began contributing to the *New Yorker* in 1936.

Gill was born in New Haven, Connecticut, in 1914, graduated from Yale in 1935, and has become a permanent fixture in New York theater circles since the late thirties. He never suffered for his art, and he says that he disdains the tortured existence that other writers often invite. His popular *Here at the New Yorker* (1975), an amusing and informative chronologue, offers Gill's philosophical asides on writers and writing.

Gill began as a poet, with a slim volume entitled *Death in April and Other Poems* (1935). Since 1936, he has published three novels, two novellas, and nearly fifty short stories. His novel *The Trouble of One House* (1950) won the coveted National Book Award in 1951; a second, *The Day the Money Stopped* (1957) was well enough received that he rewrote it as a play. *The Malcontents (1973) also fared well critically.*

The selections from *Ways of Loving* (1974), Gill's story collection, span a generation (1938–74) and provide a fascinating study of changing Irish-American life. "The Cemetery," originally published in 1943 in the *New Yorker,* offers a sensitive portrayal of an aged doctor and his son trying to come to terms with a love that forbids tenderness. In the story, Gill shows a stylistic skill that draws the reader beneath the surface.

In addition to his fiction, Brendan Gill has, over the years, produced popular works on Cole Porter, Tallulah Bankhead, Charles Lindbergh, and others.

"The Cemetery"

The Doctor was over seventy, but he still had a big practice. Whenever Kevin came up from New York for the weekend, he found the office filled with patients waiting to see his father. They would be sitting in the wrinkled leather chairs that Kevin remembered from childhood or standing at the windows, looking down at the cemetery across the street. The cemetery had been part of the Doctor's office equipment for fifty years. The humor of its location was inescapable. "That where you bury your mistakes, is it, Doctor?" a patient would ask, and the Doctor would nod his head, his silvered reflector catching the light. He always smiled, as if he hadn't heard the question a thousand times before—hadn't heard it, indeed, a dozen times from that very patient. As a rule, the patients who asked the question were the ones who were the most afraid of being examined. With them the Doctor worked the conversation around to the point where they could spring the stale joke. "As long as you don't bury *me* there," they would add, "that's all I care." Then they would throw back their heads and laugh, never seeing the contempt and solicitude that mingled in the shadow of the old man's glasses.

The walls of the Doctor's waiting room were so thoroughly covered with pictures that there was but little space left to dust between the frames. Shutting his eyes in his law office in New York (dark burlap-covered walls, with a single brightly colored Hokusai behind his desk), or riding in the train to New Haven, Kevin could recall his favorite pictures out of all that clutter. On the north wall of the waiting room hung immense dark-brown etchings of the Castle of Chillon, the bell tower in Seville, and St. Peter's in Rome. The east wall was largely blotted out by some lithographs that the Doctor had bought on a Mediterranean cruise in the thirties. On the south and west walls, scattered between the windows and doors, hung a series of photographs of the Doctor at the various clinics he had attended fifty years earlier in London, Vienna, and Prague. The photographs showed him standing, smiling and self-confident, in the midst of bearded foreign professors two or three times his age. Except for the fact that his name was lettered in white ink under the Doctor's feet, none of the Doctors' patients would have been likely to recognize him. He was a stranger, a young Irishman with small, handsome features and a hint of the paunch that used to serve as an outward sym-

bol of a physician's success. "Oh, I was cocky enough!" the Doctor
would say. "I had the world in my pocket in those days, or thought
I had."

On a bookcase filled with early twentieth-century medical annu-
als stood a framed and faded photograph of Kevin's mother, who had
died when he was seven. Once, from the privacy of a newspaper he
was reading, he heard a woman patient explain to her husband,
"That's the Doctor's wife. She's been dead for ages. Think what a
catch he was, but he never remarried. The love of his life—they say
he can scarcely speak of her even now." Kevin was angry at the
woman for imposing her sentimental thoughts on him. Every word
she had spoken was true, but she had managed to turn them into
trash. He hated having to see his father through someone else's eyes.
As for pitying his father, nobody had the right to come as close to
him as pity implied. He kept his distance from others; they invaded
the outer kingdom of his person at their peril. Even Kevin took care
to see his father chiefly on his father's terms: an august, tireless,
expensively tailored man, who was not only the best eye specialist in
town but also a citizen of importance—a director of banks and insurance companies, a sitter on committees doing public good.

Kevin and his father had always been careful to keep their conversations centered on the office. They had never been able to talk
as Kevin and his mother might have been able to talk, for the reason
that they were too much alike to risk it. Whenever Kevin came up
for a weekend, they shared their few meals in silence, walked
through a nearby park at night if the weather was fair, and went to
bed early in the big, empty-seeming house. As Kevin had done since
childhood, he remembered to say, "Good night, Dad. Pleasant
dreams," and his father, from the adjoining room, would call out,
"Good night, boy. Pleasant dreams." That was as close to intimacy as
they ever came, and it was close enough.

Before his marriage, Kevin had spent every weekend with his
father. During the past few years, however, he had come up to New
Haven more and more infrequently. Libby disliked trains and they
had no car and, besides, the children were too young to travel—it
was exhausting for her to keep them out of mischief. And if they were
to visit his father's house, what on earth was there to do? The house,
which to Kevin was still a citadel of unexplored and unexplorable
wonders, was to Libby "that old barn." On their rare visits, the children kissed their grandfather and listened to his stories of hunting

and fishing in the Connecticut of his youth or, if they grew restless, of his encounters with murderous Indians, but Libby felt that these occasions were a great strain on everyone. Without having spoken a word, Kevin found that his agreement with this point of view was taken for granted. If, glancing up from a book or some legal home-work after dinner, he would wonder idly how his father was, Libby would say at once, "For goodness' sake, why don't you run up and spend the weekend with him?"

Kevin would say, "Maybe I will, at that. Why don't you and the children come along? Dad'd be awfully glad to see you."

Shaking her dark head, Libby would say, "You know that's out of the question, darling. Give him our love. Tell him we think about him all the time."

Kevin had not sent word to his father that he would be spending this weekend with him. He had been summoned to New Haven un-expectedly, to deal with a legal problem facing one of the firm's most important clients; by the time the conference in the client's office was over, it was nearly six o'clock and it seemed easier to walk the few blocks to his father's office than to bother telephoning him. At that hour, Dr. Downing, his father's assistant, and Miss Miles, his secretary, had already left for the day. The waiting room was empty. From the faint seesaw buzz of voices in the room beyond, Kevin guessed that his father was treating a tardy patient or someone who had insisted on being seen without an appointment. Kevin picked up a magazine and began to thumb through its pages. Unlike the doctors of legend, his father subscribed to ten or twelve magazines, none of them medical, and kept only the latest issues on the square oak table between the windows. After a few minutes his father walked to the waiting-room door with his patient, a woman with a black patch over one eye. The Doctor was making his usual speech. Its humor must have been somewhat twisted for both of them, Kevin thought, by the fact of their common old age. "Now, you've nothing to worry about," the Doctor was saying. "Come back and see me in twenty years."

As he shut the door to the hall, the Doctor caught sight of Kevin sitting in the worn leather rocker. The room was darkening, and the Doctor, cocking his head, asked uncertainly, "Kevin? Is that you?" Kevin stood up and they shook hands. He noted with pride how the Doctor's pleasure at seeing him had lightened his face, erasing the network of lines around the small, firmly compressed mouth. With a show of briskness, Kevin said, "Had a bad day?"

"Pretty bad. Come in and sit down."

They walked together into the Doctor's consulting room, which was filled, as it had always been, with the latest, most costly equipment—exquisite devices with rounded corners that glowed softly under fluorescent lights. ("I like to keep up to date," the Doctor said. "A good rule for old fogies.") The Doctor leaned back in his swivel chair, the toe of one shoe steadying him against the bottom drawer of his desk. Kevin sat on a small, straight chair beside the desk. On the wall behind him hung his college-graduation photograph, taken in a rented cap and gown. On the opposite wall hung a snapshot of him taken when he was a baby playing on the lawn at home. A hand was holding him upright, and he had hoped once that it was his mother's; his father had told him curtly that the hand belonged to Anna, his nurse—he would not yield, even to his beloved child, the least particle of his possession of his dead wife. Kevin said, "I thought you'd promised to take things easy."

"Can't be done." It was what his father had been saying for as long as Kevin could remember. "Can't refuse them if they're really in need of help."

Kevin nodded toward a couple of stout black filing cabinets. "Miss Miles told me once how many thousands of names are in those files. Fantastic. You must have the biggest practice in the state."

"Maybe. In the old days I used to love the rush. Now I hope they'll get well by themselves. I hope they'll go to the wrong office. I hope they'll forget my name."

No doubt Kevin was mistaken in thinking so, but the Doctor sounded as if he were asking for sympathy. Well, he must not. It wasn't in his character. Kevin was astonished to discover that this first sign of possible weakness in his father irritated him. He said impatiently, "You're still miles ahead of everybody else in town. As far as income goes, you make me look like a nobody."

His father glanced at him without answering. He appeared not to have heard anything Kevin said. After a moment, he asked, "How are Libby and the children?"

"Just fine. They send their love."

"And mine to them."

"The kids loved the toys you sent them."

"Silly toys. At my age, how would I know?"

Weakness again! With an asperity that he recognized as very like Libby's and perhaps learned from Libby, Kevin said, "No, they were just right. You couldn't have done better."

"They're fine children. You have a fine family." The Doctor stood up and squared his shoulders. He had always been proud of his erect posture, but now he was growing down, so he said, like a cow's tail. "Come in and let me take a look at your throat. Lots of colds around this time of year."

Kevin followed his father into a small space set off from the consulting room by frosted glass panels. In the early days, the Doctor had specialized in what was called "eyes, ears, nose, and throat," and for patients who were also old friends, he continued to fiddle with noses and throats on the trivial level of colds and laryngitis. Some of these friends were sure that the Doctor could cure colds, which he could not; but he made them feel better simply because they had been in his presence. For them he was the ideal combination of witch-doctor and priest. Kevin sat down on the familiar enameled chair and held back his head. This submission to treatment was a sacred ritual between them. It had nothing to do with his health, or the time of year. It was the Doctor's way of saying "I'm glad you're here."

The Doctor adjusted his reflector. He pressed down Kevin's tongue with a spatula. "Looks good. You've been feeling pretty well?"

"First rate."

"I'll paint it just to make sure. A little creosote won't do you any harm."

The Doctor wrapped a bit of cotton on the end of a long probe, tipped it into a dark-green glass bottle, then rubbed the cotton vigorously against the sides of Kevin's throat. Kevin gagged, as he had been gagging for thirty years. The damned probe felt as if it were halfway down into his chest.

"Fine," said his father, and handed him a piece of tissue with which to wipe the spit off his mouth.

Kevin had never seen his father perform an operation, but he had seen at the hospital the room in which they were performed—a tiled, high-domed room with batteries of lights on brackets. The Doctor had given the room in memory of his wife, and her name was engraved on a brass plate on the operating-room door. Somewhere in the hospital Kevin had been born, and somewhere in the hospital his mother had died. Ever since childhood, Kevin had been meeting people who told him, simply and abruptly, that his father had saved their lives. The fact was important to them and so was the statement;

it was not alone that their lives had been saved but that the Doctor had been the one who saved them. Learning who Kevin was, a stranger would say with something like truculence, defying Kevin to contradict him, "I'd be dead this minute if it wasn't for your dad." Kevin would answer, "I guess he must be pretty good." If, as was often the case, it was some middle-aged derelict whose life had been saved, Kevin's answer called for a protest. "Pretty good? He's the best there is. Why, all the other doctors gave me up. Wrote me off. Just walked away! And I'll tell you something else. I was a bit on my uppers at the time, and he never asked a penny from me. Never a penny. That's your dad." Then came the inevitable, triumphant lie: "I was able to pay him back later, thanks be to God." To Kevin's delight, his father never remembered the names of any of the men and women whose lives he had saved. He said only, "It's nice once in while to get a boost instead of a knock. But maybe they weren't dying at all. Maybe they only had wax in their ears."

Kevin got up from the chair. Tasting the bitter creosote, he always made the same objection. He said, "I feel a lot worse now than I did when I came in." He walked across the office to narrow, old-fashioned windows. It was impossible by now to recall how many people had told him the same story about his father and their saved lives—the number must run into scores. But surely some of the Doctor's patients had died on the operating table or shortly afterward; surely there had been hopeless cases, of which Kevin had never heard. He wondered, feeling half-unwilling to wonder, whether the Doctor had ever lost a patient through—well, through some fault of his own. Some misjudgment, some slip of a scalpel, or however it was that a surgeon lost a patient. There must have been difficult moments for the Doctor when he was trying out a new technique; there must have been even more difficult moments during those months after his wife had died and, unable to sleep, he had walked the streets all night. Had his hands shaken next morning, had his eyes blurred, his mind gone blank?

Kevin said, "Who was the old lady you just saw? Someone who sneaked in without an appointment?"

The Doctor nodded. He was getting ready to shut the office for the weekend. He switched off the overhead lights and the gleaming stainless-steel sterilizer. "Time to go home," he said.

"What was the matter with her?"

The Doctor shut the instrument cabinet, took a handful of ten-dollar bills from a drawer of his desk (though he kept up with the younger doctors in everything else, with his old friends he maintained the custom of being paid in cash), and walked out into the waiting room. Following him, Kevin repeated the question: "What was troubling the old lady? I saw the patch."

"Nothing of importance. I cut out a cataract a couple of weeks ago. Now the eye's inflamed. Of course it's inflamed. That could happen to anybody."

"You told her she had nothing to worry about."

"Quite right. She has nothing to worry about."

Kevin turned to look out over the city; the sky was filled now with a lemony dusk. It was April. The air would be sweet in the park when they took their walk that night. In the cemetery across the street, a few gray stones made light patches in the shadows. Kevin was about to say, "That where you bury your mistakes, is it, Doctor?" He had asked the question many times before, mocking the Doctor's timid patients. He glanced across the room in anticipation of the smile with which his father always acknowledged the poor little joke. His father was staring at him with his lips drawn together, head cocked to one side. In that grim darkness he looked oddly shrunken and helpless. Kevin said, "Let's go. I'm getting hungry."

The Doctor held out a fistful of bills. "Take them. Buy something for the children."

"No, no. They don't need anything."

"Neither do I."

"I won't take it," Kevin said. "Goddam it, I mean it." He had never spoken so sharply to his father, and to beg forgiveness he reached out and touched his shoulder. It was the first time in years that he had touched him. Under the cloth of his suit, his father's shoulder bone felt as thin as a pencil and as quick to break.

9

J. F. POWERS
(b. 1917)

J. F. Powers was born July 8, 1917, in Jacksonville, Illinois, but his parents migrated from Jacksonville to Rockford to Quincy to Chicago when he was young. He graduated from the Quincy Academy and attended Wright College in Chicago for a semester. Between 1938 and 1940 he enrolled in English courses at Northwestern.

Powers came of age during the Depression, so he held a variety of jobs in the thirties. He was a book store clerk, chauffeur, insurance salesman, and finally an editor of the Illinois Historical Records Survey, a WPA creation. Powers credits the Survey for his literary growth. In 1943 his first stories, "He Don't Plant Cotton" and "Lions, Harts, Leaping Does," appeared in *Accent*. His first collection, *Prince of Darkness and Other Stories,* followed in 1947.

Powers has taught creative writing at Saint John's in Minnesota, and at Marquette, Michigan, Smith, and Saint John's again since 1947. He is a writer's writer. Frank O'Connor once said that he was "among the greatest living story-tellers" and numbered him with Turgenev, Maupassant, Chekhov, and Joyce. In fact, Powers is a perfectionist, a meticulous craftsman who labors over his fiction. In 1956, he published *The Presence of Grace,* his second story collection; in 1962, *Morte d'Urban,* his only novel; and in 1975, *Look How the Fish Live,* his third story collection.

Powers has earned a reputation as a comic satirist, using modern American Catholicism as the butt of his humor. He contrasts the sacred and profane, the spiritual and mundane, and consciously works toward a moment of truth—an epiphany that reduces to a simple Christian tenet.

Powers has won major literary awards: a National Institute of Arts and Letters Grant, a Guggenheim, a *Kenyon Review* Fellowship, three

Rockefeller grants, and numerous other recognitions. In 1963 *Morte d'Urban* received a National Book Award. Powers contributes to the *New Yorker,* the *Nation, Partisan Review,* and *Kenyon Review,* among others.

His story, "Bill," which contrasts a conservative, all-business pastor with a young laid-back curate is representative of his work. It appeared in the *New Yorker* in 1969 and in *Look How the Fish Live* in 1975.

"Bill"

In January, Joe, who had the habit of gambling with himself, made it two to one against his getting a curate that year. Then, early in May, the Archbishop came out to see the new rectory and, in the office area, which was in the basement but surprisingly light and airy, paused before the doors "PASTOR" and "ASSISTANT" and said, "You're mighty sure of yourself, Father."

"I can dream, can't I, Your Excellency?"

The subject didn't come up again during the visit, and the Archbishop declined Joe's offer of a drink, which may or may not have been significant—hard to say how much the Arch knew about a man—but after he'd departed Joe made it seven to five, trusting his instinct.

Two weeks later, on the eve of the annual shape-up, trusting his instinct again though he'd heard nothing, Joe made it even money.

The next morning, the Chancery (Toohey) phoned to say that Joe had a curate: "Letter follows."

"Wait a minute. Who?"

"He'll be in touch with you." And Toohey hung up.

Maybe it hadn't been decided who would be sent out to Joe's (Church of SS. Francis and Clare, Inglenook), but probably it had, and Toohey just didn't want to say because Joe had asked. That was how Toohey, too long at the Chancery, played the game. Joe didn't think any more about it then.

He grabbed a scratch pad, rushed upstairs to the room, now bare, that would be occupied by his curate (who?), and made a list, which was his response to problems, temporal and spiritual, that required thought.

That afternoon, he visited a number of furniture stores in Inglenook, in Silverstream, the next suburb, and in the city. "Just looking," he said to the clerks. After a couple of hours, he had a pretty
good idea of the market, but he wasn't able to act, and then he had
to suspend operations in order to beat the rush-hour traffic home.

Afterward, though, he discovered what was wrong. It was his
list. Programed without reference to the *relative* importance of the
items on it, his list, instead of helping, had hindered him, had
caused him to mess around looking at lamps, rugs, and ashtrays. It
hadn't told him that everything in the room would be determined,
dictated, by the bed. Why bed? Because the room was a *bed*room.
Find the bed, the right bed, and the rest would follow. He knew
where he was now, and he was glad that time had run out that afternoon. Toward the last, he had been suffering from shopper's fatigue,
or he wouldn't have considered that knotty-pine suite, with its horse-
shoe brands and leather thongs, simply because it had a clean, mas-
culine look that bedroom furniture on the whole seemed to lack.

That evening, he sat down in the quiet of his study, in his Barcalounger chair, with some brochures and a drink, and made another
list. This one was different and should have been easy for him—with
office equipment he really knew where he was, and probably no
priest in the diocese knew so well—but for that very reason he
couldn't bring himself to furnish the curate's office as other pastors
would have done, as, in fact, he had planned to do. Why spoil a fine
office by installing inferior, economy-type equipment? Why not move
the pastor's desk and typewriter, both recent purchases, into the curate's office? Why not get the pastor one of those laminated mahogany desks, maybe Model DK 100, sleek and contemporary but warm
and friendly as only wood can be? (The pastor was tired of his unfriendly metal desk and his orthopedic chair.) Why not get the pastor
a typewriter with a different type? (What, *again?* Yes, because he
was tired of that phony script.) But keep the couch and chair in the
pastor's office, and let the new chairs—two or three, and no couch—
go straight into the curate's office.

The next morning, he drove to the city with the traffic, and
swiftly negotiated the items on his office list, including a desk,
Model DK 100, and a typewriter with different type, called "edito-
rial," and said to be used by newscasters.

"Always a pleasure to do business with you, Father," the clerk said.

The scene then changed to the fifth floor of a large department
store, which Joe had visited the day before, and there life got diffi-

cult again. What had brought him back was a fourposter bed with pineapple finials. The clerk came on a little too strong.

"The double bed's making a big comeback, Father."

"That so?"

"What I'd have, if I had the choice."

"Yes, well." Joe liked the bed, especially the pineapples, but he just couldn't see the curate (who?) in it. Get it for himself, then, and give the curate the pastor's bed—*it* was a single. And then what? The pastor's bed, of unfriendly metal and painted like a car, hospital grey, would dictate nothing about the other things for the room. Besides, it wouldn't be fair to the curate, would it?

"Lot of bed for the money, Father."

"Too much bed."

The clerk then brought out some brochures and binders with colored tabs. So Joe sat down with him on a bamboo chaise longue, and passing the literature back and forth between them, they went to work on Joe's problem. They discovered that Joe could order the traditional type of bed in a single, in several models—cannonballs, spears, spools (Jenny Lind)—but not pineapples, which, it seemed, had been discontinued by the maker. "But I wonder about that, Father. Tell you what. With your permission, I'll call North Carolina."

Joe let him go ahead, after more discussion, mostly about air freight, but when the clerk returned to the chaise longue he was shaking his head. North Carolina would call back, though, in an hour or so, after checking the warehouse. "You wouldn't take cannonballs or spears, Father? Or Jenny Lind?"

"Not Jenny Lind."

"You like cannonballs, Father?"

"Yes, but I prefer the other."

"Pineapples."

Since nothing could be done about the other items on his list until he found out about the bed—or beds, for he had decided to order two beds, singles, with matching chests, plus box springs and mattresses, eight pieces in all—Joe went home to await developments.

At six minutes to three, the phone rang. "St. Francis," Joe said.

"Earl, Father."

"*Earl?*"

"At the store, Father."

"Oh, hello, Earl."

Earl said that North Carolina *could* supply, and would air-freight to the customer's own address. So beds and chests would arrive in a couple of days, Friday at the outside, and box springs and mat-

tresses, these from stock, would be on the store's Thursday delivery
to Inglenook.

"O.K., Father?"

"O.K., Earl."

Joe didn't try to do any more that day.

The next morning, he took delivery of the office equipment
(which Mrs. P.—Mrs. Pelissier—the housekeeper must have
noticed), and so he got a late start on his shopping. He began where
he'd left off the day before. Earl, spotting him among the lamps,
came over to say hello. When he saw Joe's list, he recommended the
store's interior decorating department—"Mrs. Fox, if she's not out
on a job." With Joe's permission, Earl went to a phone, and Mrs.
Fox soon appeared among the lamps. Slightly embarrassed, Joe told
her what he thought—that the room ought to be planned around the
bed, since it was a *bed*room. Mrs. Fox smacked her lips and shrieked
(to Earl), "*He* doesn't need *me!*"

As a matter of fact, Mrs. Fox proved very helpful—steered Joe
from department to department, protected him from clerks, took
him into stockrooms and onto a freight elevator, and remembered
curtains and bedspreads (Joe bought two), which weren't on his list
but were definitely needed. Finally, Mrs. Fox had the easy chair and
other things brought down to the parking lot and put into his car.
These could have gone out on the Thursday delivery, but Joe wanted
to see how the room would look even without the big stuff—the bed,
the chest, the student's table, and the revolving bookcase. Mrs. Fox
felt the same way. Twice in the store she'd expressed a desire to see
the room, and he'd managed to change the subject, and then she did
it again, in the parking lot—was *dying* to see the room, she
shrieked, just as he was driving away. He just smiled. What else
could he do? He couldn't have Mrs. Fox coming out there.

In some ways, things were moving too fast. He still hadn't told
Mrs. P. that he was getting a curate—hadn't because he was afraid if
he did, she'd ask, as he had, "Who?" Who, indeed? He still didn't
know, and the fact that he didn't would, if admitted, make him look
foolish in Mrs. P.'s eyes. It would also put the Church—administrationwise—in a poor light.

That evening, after Mrs. P. had gone home, Joe unloaded the
car, which he'd run into the garage because the easy chair was
clearly visible in the trunk. It took him four trips to get all his purchases up to the room. Then, using a kitchen chair, listening to the
ball game and drinking beer, he put up the curtain rods. (The janitor,

if asked to, would wonder why, and if told, would tell Mrs. P., who would ask, "Who?") When Joe had the curtains up, tiebacks and all, he took a much needed bath, changed and made himself a gin-and-tonic. He carried it into the room, dark now—he had been waiting for this moment—and turned on the lamps he'd bought. O.K.—and when the student's table came, the student's lamp, now on the little bedside table, would look even better. He had chosen one with a yellow shade, rather than green, so the room would appear cheerful, and it certainly did. He tried the easy chair, the matching footstool, the gin-and-tonic. O.K. He sat there for some time, one foot going to sleep on the rose-and-blue hooked rug while he wondered why— why he hadn't heard anything from the curate.

The next day, Thursday, he gave Mrs. P. the afternoon off, saying he planned to eat out that evening, and so she wasn't present when the box springs, mattresses, student's table and revolving bookcase came, at twenty after four—the hottest time of the day. He had a lot of trouble with the mattresses—really a job for two strong men, one to pull on the mattress, one to hold on to the carton—and had to drink two bottles of beer to restore his body salts. He took a much needed bath, changed, and, feeling too tired to go out, made himself some ham sandwiches and a gin-and-tonic. He used a whole lime—it was his salad—and ate in his study while watching the news: people starving in Asia and Mississippi. He went without dessert. Suddenly he jumped up and got busy around the place, did the dishes—dish— and locked the church. When darkness came, he was back where he'd been the night before—in the room, in the chair, with a glass, wondering why he hadn't heard anything from the curate.

It was customary for the newly ordained men to take a few days off to visit and shake down their friends and relatives. Ordinations, though, had been held on Saturday. It was now Thursday, almost Friday, and still no word. What to do? He had called people at the seminary, hoping to learn the curate's name and perhaps something of his character, just in the course of conversation. ("Understand you're getting So-and-So, Joe.") But it hadn't happened—everybody he asked to speak to (the entire faculty, it seemed) had left for vacationland. He had then called the diocesan paper and, with pencil ready, asked for a complete rundown of the new appointments, but the list hadn't come over from the Chancery yet. ("They can be pretty slow over there, Father." "Toohey, you mean?" "Monsignor's pretty busy, Father, and we don't push him on a thing like this—it's not what we call hard news.")

So, really, there was nothing to do, short of calling the Chancery. Early in the week, it might have been done—that was when Joe made his mistake—but it was out of the question now. He didn't want to expose the curate to censure and run the risk of turning him against the pastor, and he also didn't want the Chancery to know what the situation was at SS. Francis and Clare's, one of the best-run parishes in the diocese, though it certainly wasn't his fault. It was the curate's fault, it was Toohey's fault. "Letter follows." If called on that, Toohey would say, "Didn't say when. Busy here," and hang up. That was how Toohey played the game. Once, when Joe had called for help and said he'd die if he didn't get away for a couple of weeks, Toohey had said, "Die," and hung up. Rough. If the Church ever got straightened out administrationwise, Toohey and his kind would have to go, but that was one of those long-term objectives. In the meantime, Joe and his kind would have to soldier on, and Joe would. It was hard, though, after years of waiting for a curate, after finally getting one, not to be able to mention it. While shopping, Joe had run into two pastors who would have been interested to hear of his good fortune, and one had even raised the subject of curates, had said that he was getting a *change,* "Thank God!" Joe hadn't thought much about it then—the "Thank God!" part—but now he did, and, swallowing the weak last inch of his drink, came face to face with the ice.

What, he thought—what if the curate, the unknown curate, *wasn't* one of those newly ordained men? What if he was one of those bad-news guys? A young man with five or six parishes behind him? Or a man as old as himself, or older, a retread, a problem priest? Or a goldbrick who figured, since he was paid by the month, he wouldn't report until the first, Sunday? Or a slob who wouldn't take care of the room? These were sobering thoughts to Joe. He got up and made another drink.

The next morning, when he returned from a trip to the dump, where he personally disposed of his empties, Mrs. P. met him at the door. "Somebody who says he's your assistant—"

"Yes, yes. Where is he?"

"Phoned. Said he'd be here tomorrow."

"*Tomorrow?*" But he didn't want Mrs. P. to get the idea that he was disappointed, or that he didn't know what was going on. "Good. Did he say what time?"

"He just asked about confessions."

"So he'll be here in time for confessions. Good."

"Said he was calling from Whipple."

"*Whipple?*"

"Said he was down there buying a car."

Joe nodded, as though he regarded Whipple, which he'd driven through once or twice, as an excellent place to buy a car. He was waiting for Mrs. P. to continue.

"That's all *I* know," she said, and shot off to the kitchen. Hurt. Not his fault. Toohey's fault. Curate's fault. Not telling her about the curate was bad, but doing it as he would have had to would have been worse. Better to think less of him than to know the truth—and think less of the Church. He took the sins of curates and administrators upon him.

That afternoon, he waited until four o'clock before he got on the phone to Earl. "Say, what is this? I thought you said Friday at the outside."

"Oh, oh," said Earl, and didn't have to be told who was calling, or what about. He said he'd put a tracer on the order, and promised to call back right away, which he did. "Hey, Father, guess what? The order's at our warehouse. North Carolina goofed."

"That so?" said Joe, but he wasn't interested in Earl's analysis of North Carolina's failure to ship to customer's own address, and cut in on it. He described his bed situation, as he hadn't before for Earl, in depth. He was going to be short a bed—no, not that night but the next, when his assistant would be there, and also a monk of advanced age who helped out on the weekends and slept in the guest room. No, the bed in the guest room, to answer Earl's question, was a single—actually, a cot. Yes, Joe could put his assistant on the box spring and mattress, but wouldn't like to do it, and didn't see why he should. He'd been promised delivery by Friday at the outside. He didn't care if Inglenook *was* in Monday and Thursday territory. In the end, he was promised delivery the next day, Saturday.

"O.K., Father?"

"O.K., Earl."

The next afternoon, a panel truck, scarred and bearing no name, pulled up in front of the rectory at seven minutes after four. Joe didn't know what to make of it. He stayed inside the rectory until the driver and his helper unloaded a carton, then rushed out, and was about to ask them to unload at the back door and save themselves a few steps when a word on the carton stopped him. "Hold everything!" And it wasn't, as he'd hoped, simply a matter of a word on a carton. Oh, no. On investigation, the beds proved to be as described on their cartons—cannonballs. "Hold everything. I have to call the store."

On the way to the telephone, passing Father Otto, the monk of advanced age, who was another who hadn't been told about the curate, and now appeared curious to know what was happening in the street, Joe wished that monks were forbidden to wear their habits away from the monastery. Flowing robes, Joe felt, had a bad effect on his parishioners, made him, in his cassock, look second-best in their eyes, and also reminded non-Catholics of the Reformation.

"Say, what is this?" he said, on the phone.

"Oh, oh," said Earl when he learned what had happened. "North Carolina goofed."

"Now, *look*," said Joe, and really opened up on Earl and the store. "I don't like the way you people do business," he said, pausing to breathe.

"Correct me if I'm wrong, Father, but didn't you say you like cannonballs?"

"Better than Jenny Lind, I said. But that's not the point. I prefer the other, and that's what I said. You know what 'prefer' means, don't you?"

"Pineapples."

"You've got me over a barrel, Earl."

In the end, despite what he'd indicated earlier, Joe said he'd take delivery. "But we're through," he told Earl, and hung up.

He returned to the street where, parked behind the panel truck, there was now a new VW beetle, and there, it seemed, standing by the opened cartons with Father Otto, the driver, and his helper, was Joe's curate—big and young, obviously one of the newly ordained men. Seeing Joe, he left the others and came smiling toward him.

"Where you been?" Joe said—like an old pastor, he thought.

The curate stopped smiling. "Whipple."

Joe put it another way. "Why didn't you give me a call?"

"I did."

"Before yesterday?"

"I did. Don't know how many times I called. You were never in."

"Didn't know what to think," Joe said, ignoring the curate's point like an old pastor, and, looking away, wished that the beetle—light brown, or dark yellow, sort of caramel—was another color, and also that it wasn't parked where it was, adding to the confusion. (The driver's helper was showing Father Otto how his dolly worked.) "Could've left your name with the housekeeper."

"I kept thinking I'd get you if I called again. You were never in."

Joe moved toward the street, saying, "Yes, well, I've been out a lot lately. Could've left your name, Father."

"I did, Father. Yesterday."

"Yes, well." Standing by the little car, viewing the books and luggage inside, Joe wished that he could start over, that he hadn't started off as he had. He had meant to welcome the curate. It wasn't his fault that he hadn't—look at the days and nights of needless anxiety, and look what time it was now—but still he wanted to make up for it. "Better drive your little car around to the back, Father, and unload," he said. "The housekeeper'll show you the room. Won't ask you to hear confessions this afternoon." And, having opened the door of the little car for the curate, he closed it for him, saying, through the window, "See you later, Father."

When he straightened up, he saw that Big Mouth, a neighbor and a parishioner, had arrived to inspect the cartons, heard him questioning Father Otto, saw, too, that Mrs. P. had decided to sweep the front walk and was working that way. Joe called her.

"I've bought a few things—besides the bed and chest here—for the curate's room," he told her, so she wouldn't be too surprised when she saw them. Then he gave her the key to the room, saying, perhaps needlessly, that she'd find it locked, and that the box springs, mattresses, and bed-spreads would be found within. The other bed—the one that should and would have been his but for the interest shown in it by Father Otto and Big Mouth—the other bed and chest, he told Mrs. P., should go into the guest room. "Fold up the cot and put it somewhere. Get the curate to help you—he's not hearing this afternoon."

Turning then to the little group around the cartons, he saw that his instructions to Mrs. P. had been overheard and understood. The little group—held together by the question "Would he ever take delivery?"—was breaking up. He thanked the driver and his helper for waiting, nodded to Big Mouth, said "Coming?" to Father Otto, since it was now time for confessions, and walked toward the church. He took the sins of curates and administrators and North Carolina upon him. He gave another his bed.

That evening, after confessions, and after Father Otto had retired to the new bed in the guest room, Joe and the curate sat on in the pastor's study. Joe, doing most of the talking, had had less than usual, the curate more, it seemed—he was yawning. "Used to be,"

Joe was saying, "we all drove black cars. I still do." Joe, while he
didn't want to hurt the curate's feelings, just couldn't understand
why a priest, even a young priest today, able to buy a new car,
should pick one the color of the curate's. "Maybe it's not important."

"Think I'll turn in, Father."

Joe hated to go to bed, and changed the subject slightly. "How's
the room? O.K.?"

"O.K."

Joe had been expecting a bit more. Had he hurt the curate's
feelings? "It's not important, what I was saying."

The curate smiled. "My uncle's the dealer in Whipple. He gave
me a good deal on the car, but that was part of it—the color."

"I see." Joe tried not to appear as interested as he suddenly was.
"What's he call his place—Whipple Volkswagon? I know a lot of 'em
do. That's what they call it here—Inglenook Volkswagon."

"He calls it by his own name."

"I see. And this is your father's brother?"

"My mother's."

"I see."

"Think I'll turn in now, Father."

"Yeah. Maybe we should. Sunday's always a tough day."

The next morning, with Joe watching from the sacristy, and later
from the rear of the church, the curate said his first Mass in the
parish. He was slow, of course, but he wasn't fancy, and he didn't fall
down. His sermon was standard, marred only by his gestures (once
or twice he looked like a bad job of dubbing), and he read the an-
nouncements well. He neglected to introduce himself to the congregation, but that might be done the following week in the parish
bulletin.

The day began to go wrong, though, when, after his second
mass, the curate mentioned an invitation he had to dine out with a
classmate. "Well, all right," Joe said, writing off the afternoon but
not the evening.

He still hadn't written off the evening, entirely, at eighteen after
eleven. The door of the pastor's study was open and the pastor was
clearly visible in his Barcalounger chair, having a nightcap, but the
curate went straight to his room, and could soon be heard running a
bath.

So Joe, despite the change from a week ago, had spent Sunday as
usual—the afternoon with the papers, TV, a nap, and Father Otto

(until it was time for his bus), and the evening almost alone. Most of
it. At seven-thirty, he'd had a surprise visit from Earl, his wife, and
two of their children.

The next morning, Joe laid an unimportant letter on the curate's
metal desk. "Answer this, will you? I've made some notes on the
margin so you'll know what to say. Keep it brief. Sign *your* name—
Assistant Pastor. But let me have a look at it before you seal it." And
that, he thought, is that.

"Does it have to be *typed?*"

"What d'ya mean?"

"Can't *type* it."

"What d'ya mean?"

"Can't *type.*"

Joe just stood there in a distressed state. "Can't type," he said.
"You mean at the sem you did everything in longhand? Term papers
and everything?"

The curate, who seemed to think that too much was being made
of his disability, nodded.

"Hard to believe," Joe said. "Why, you must've been the only
guy in your class not to use a typewriter."

"There was one other guy."

Joe was somewhat relieved—at least the gambler in him was—to
know that he hadn't been quite as unlucky as he'd supposed. "But
you must've heard guys all around you using typewriters. Didn't you
ever wonder why?"

"I never owned a typewriter. Never saw the need." The curate
sounded proud, like somebody who brushes his teeth with table salt.
"I write a good, clear hand."

Joe snorted. "*I* write a good, clear hand. But I don't do my parish correspondence by hand. And I hope *you* won't when you're
pastor."

"The hell with it, then."

Joe, who had been walking around in a distressed state, stopped
and looked at the curate, but the curate—pretty clever—wouldn't
look back. He was getting out a cigarette. Joe shook his head, and
walked around shaking it. "Father, Father," he said.

"Father, hell," said the curate, emitting smoke. "You should've
put in for a stenographer, not a priest."

Joe stopped, stood still, and sniffed. "Great," he said, nodding
his head. "Sounds great, Father. But what does it *mean?* Does it
mean you expect me to do the lion's share of the donkey work
around here? While you're out saving souls? Or sitting up in your

room? Does it mean when you're pastor you'll expect your curate to do what you never had to do? I hope not, Father. Because, you know, Father, when you're a pastor it may be years before you have a curate. You may never have one, Father. You may end up in a one-horse parish. Lots of guys do. You won't be able to afford a secretary, or public stenographers, and you won't care to trust your correspondence to nuns, to parishioners. You'll always be an embarrassment to yourself and others. Let's face it, Father. Today, a man who can't use a typewriter is as ill-equipped for parish life as a man who can't drive a car. Go ahead. Laugh. Sneer. But it's true. You don't want to be like Toohey, do you? *He* can't type and he's set this diocese back a hundred years. He writes 'No can do' on everything and returns it to the sender. For official business he uses scratch paper put out by the Universal Portland Cement Company."

Depressed by the thought of Toohey and annoyed by the curate's cool, if that was what it was, Joe retired to his office. He sat down at his new desk and made a list. Presently, he appeared in the doorway between the offices, wearing his hat. "And, Father," he continued, "when you're a pastor, what if you get a curate like yourself? Think it over. I have to go out now. Mind the store."

Joe drove to the city and bought a typing course consisting of a manual and phonograph records, and he also bought the bed—it was still there—the double, with pineapples. He was told that if he ever wished to order a matching chest or dresser there would be no trouble at all, and that the bed, along with the box spring and mattress, would be on the Thursday delivery to Inglenook.

"O.K., Father?"

"O.K., Earl."

And that afternoon Joe, in his office, had a phone call from Mrs. Fox. She just wondered if everything was O.K., she said—as if she didn't know. She was still dying to see the room. "What's it *like?*" Joe said he thought the room had turned out pretty well, thanked Mrs. Fox for helping him, and also for calling, and hung up.

Immediately, the phone rang again. "St. Francis," Joe said.

"Bill there?"

"*Bill?*"

"For *me?*" said the curate, who had been typing away, or, anyway, typing.

Joe tried to look right through the wall. (The door between the offices was open, but the angle was wrong.) "Take it over there," he said, and switched the call.

There were no further developments that day.

None the next day.

And none the next.

No more phone calls for the curate, and no mail addressed to him, and nothing in the diocesan paper, and no word from Toohey. And Mrs. P. with her "he" and "him" was no help, nor was the janitor with his "young Father," and Father Otto wouldn't be there until Saturday. But in one way or another sooner or later, perhaps in time for the next parish bulletin, though the odds were now against that, Joe hoped to learn Bill's last name.

10

MARY DOYLE CURRAN

(1917–1981)

Mary Doyle Curran was born in "the Flats," the Irish section of Holyoke, Massachusetts, on May 10, 1917. After she graduated from Massachusetts State College (University of Massachusetts) in 1940, she married George Curran, a classmate. The Currans later divorced. They had no children. Mary Doyle went on to complete her doctoral studies at Iowa, and to teach English at Wellesley, Iowa, Queens College, and finally University of Massachusetts at Boston, where she also directed the Irish Studies Program.

In 1948, Curran published her only novel, *The Parish and the Hill,* a fictional memoir set in Irish Boston. In it she compares "shanty" and "lace-curtain" Irish and contrasts both with the Yankee mill owners in their Victorian mansions on the hill. Curran's messages? In migrating, the Irish had traded one kind of serfdom for another. And, when they had pulled themselves up and established political power, they abused the less fortunate minorities on the lower rungs.

Curran also published short fiction, most of it in the *Massachusetts Review.* The following story, "Mrs. Reardon's Gamble," a wonderfully gossipy piece, appeared there in 1966.

In addition to her fiction, Mrs. Curran wrote poetry. Her collection, *Poems, Public and Private,* came out in 1965. She continued to contribute stories and poems to the *Massachusetts Review* until her death in 1981.

"Mrs. Reardon's Gamble"

Cars crept like ants over the soft tar road. The three fat women in the back seat—beginning to melt into one another—kept up a polite, desultory conversation. They tried to conceal their irritation with the slow pace, the heat, and the glaring sun that shot back from the hood, blinding them. Mrs. Reardon shifted her feet which were slowly beginning to puff over the thin straps of elegant patent leather. She felt in her big leather purse—much too hot, much too heavy—for her cologne-soaked handkerchief. Mrs. Dineen pulled the wet dress away from her neck and Mrs. Linehan fussed with her hat, tucking up strands that were escaping from her permanent. Everytime one of them moved, the others had to shift. They were like three plump birds in a tight roasting pan.

"Nevertheless," Mrs. Dineen tried, "he's a good boy, no one can say that any boy as good as he is to his mother is a bad boy, and he's put up with a lot from her. She's a cross one, I can tell you that." And Mrs. Linehan, with a moaning sigh, "God will reward him, God will reward him." Then Mrs. Reardon, irascible, harsh, New York-accented, "Well, he ought to be good to her. He'll only have her with him once." The conversation died away.

The young man in the driver's seat lit a cigarette. The smoke drifted lazily back. "How many times have I told you not to smoke when I'm in the back of this car? You want us to choke?" "All right, all right, Ma, I'll put it out." He tossed the cigarette out the window, shifted suddenly into second. "Dirty things," the mother muttered. And first Mrs. Dineen, then Mrs. Linehan, moaning, responded. "You're right, Mrs. Reardon, I'm always after my Edward to give them up." "My John, thanks be to God, has never taken them up. A sinful waste of money. Just as well take a good dollar and send it up in smoke. And so bad for you, too." The young man passed a hand over his sweating face, put on the brakes. The three fat women shot forward. Mrs. Reardon's purse fell to the floor, cascading its contents. Mrs. Dineen's rayon print split a seam, and Mrs. Linehan's hat tilted down over the dissolving permanent. Mrs. Reardon snatched up the heavy purse and—leaning forward with effort—cracked her son over the back of the head with it. "How many times have I told you to watch where you're going." All the irritation of the hot two-hour drive went into the strong second blow. The boy, waiting for it, ducked. "For Christ's sake, Ma! Lay off me. I told you what it would be like. You and your damn wheels. Why can't you sit home quietly on a Sunday and save your money?" The other two ladies exchanged significant looks. Mrs. Reardon shifted back into her seat. "You never mind your criticisms," she said. "It's my money. I work hard for it, and I don't have to ask you how to spend it. When you're bringing in as much maybe you'll have the right to talk." The car shot out of line and began passing others. "Bill, how fast are you going?" The boy concentrated on driving. Mrs. Reardon leaned over to see the speedometer, raised her bag again. "For God's sake," Mrs. Dineen said quickly, "let him be. He's not going over thirty. He's a good driver. You know what you're doing, don't you, Bill?" The car slowed and edged back into line. The other two ladies relaxed, as the mother dropped the purse into her lap. "That's all he can think about is getting back in time for some damn fool girl. No time for his mother that works like a horse all week." The others sighed and moaned in turn. "Oh let him alone, you could have a lot worse boys. He's a good son." "That's right, Mrs. Reardon, a good son, a good son." But Mrs. Reardon was not easily fooled. "It's all right for you to talk, Mrs. Dineen, you with five sons and a husband still alive and kicking. It's different when you're left a widow with an only son to bring up whatever way you can, and now he's off at the first show of a leg. It's a different thing when you see it my way."

When the car swerved into the archway decorated with flags faded by salt and sun, the mother opened her purse to hand her son the dollar for parking. The three fat women heaved themselves out and the whole car sprang up behind them. Then the mother held out her hand for the keys, dropped them in her purse and clicked it shut. "I'm going down to sit in the pavilion. It is too damn hot to go traipsing after you." Bill's tone changed, "How about a dollar, Ma? I haven't a cent in my pocket." The mother opened the purse once again, handed him two dollars. "No beer now, Bill. If I smell anything on your breath we'll sit here all night till it wears off." "I'll see you later," the boy said. The fat women stared after him. "You be back here at four," the mother called.

The women climbed up the long areaway that led to the boardwalk. The sun burned down—gay crowds shoved and pushed, an oily smell of hot dogs and pop corn rode on the salt breeze. Untidy children wormed their way through the crowd, giggling or crying, sticky with cotton candy, a little sick, a little dizzy, bumping from side to side. Mrs. Reardon pushed through the sticky mass of people, opening a way for her two friends behind. They spoke in whispers to each other. "She's heading right for the wheels." "A terrible waste, a terrible waste of hard-earned money." "You wouldn't catch me throwing away good money on those gypsters. Jim says all those wheels are fixed, but like he says, she's a sport. It's in her blood—a born gambler, and there's no stopping her." Mrs. Linehan was fixing her hat when Mrs. Reardon turned around. Mrs. Dineen, wet and red-faced, looked longingly over the crowd at the deep cool blue of the ocean. "What I wouldn't give to be sitting in the middle of that, though."

At four o'clock the fat women were back at the car—Mrs. Reardon struggling with three sleazy blankets and a heaping basket of groceries. The other two carried kewpie dolls and canes. Bill opened the trunk and unloaded each of them. The mother was excited and flushed. "Pretty good, eh? I licked them today. There wasn't a single wheel I didn't strike." "How much did you spend?" Her answer was quick, defensive. "That's not your business. How much did you?" She leaned forward, smelling his breath, but he was chewing gum. The ride home was mostly silent, and Mrs. Reardon used her handbag—with end-of-the-day satisfaction—only once, when the speedometer read thirty-five.

Mrs. Linehan, leaving Mrs. Dineen that evening, said in a sepulchral voice, "I saw her break a twenty-dollar bill. I'll bet there isn't a penny of it left, not a penny of it." Mrs. Dineen was still thinking of the cool blue water that she hadn't dipped a toe into. "Not a penny of it left." But she shook herself and said in a kindly way, "She's a good sport," and tucked one of the prize blankets under her arm. "She'll end up begging." For the first time, Mrs. Linehan's voice was crisp.

Mrs. Dineen pulled open the swinging door to the rest-room, grateful to get in out of the cold. Down the stairs, she saw the half-closed door to the matron's room swing open and Mrs. Reardon peer out. It was quiet in the rest-room at eight-thirty; a few women sat around on the benches waiting for their trolley cars; the hissing of steam from the radiators and the intermittent rise and fall of flushing water were the only sounds.

Mrs. Dineen went into the matron's room. It was dark, except for the small light on the table. Mrs. Reardon, dressed in a white starched uniform, a beaded sweater thrown over her shoulders, sat in a rocking chair by the door, her pudgy feet in the elegant high heels crossed before her. "I thought you might like an hour or so of company." Mrs. Reardon rocked back and forth and with every rock the starched skirt climbed toward her round, fatty knees, bare above the garter-rolled stockings. "Fireman's ball tonight. And there'll be plenty of those girls," she motioned upstairs, "rolling in here drunk." Mrs. Dineen settled comfortably into the other rocker.

The two old cronies rocked. This visit was a well-patterned routine. Once a week Mrs. Dineen showed up to help her friend keep the vigil over the public toilets. They passed the long slow hours in gab and gossip, rocking back and forth, talking in conspiratorial whispers. Between them on the table a few of Mrs. Reardon's things—for which she loved, righteously, to forage through the better department stores—were laid out: glycerine-and-rose-water for her hands, a handkerchief scented with *Muguet des Bois*, a green glass swan that must have been won some summer Sunday. Only rarely was there an interruption when someone came to ask for admission to the pay toilets—an area locked off from the common public. Then Mrs. Reardon, heaving herself out of the low chair, keys rattling, would go out to open the holy door. Whenever she did this she cast a quick eye around the other—the public—room. It was a cantankerous eye that denied the right of public relief.

At ten o'clock the outer door opened with a rough swing and a flood of pale-haired women came giggling down the stairs. Mrs. Reardon rose with a sigh and went into the room with the common toilets. The giggling subsided as she stood—wooden and severe—looking the girls over. Whenever one of them left a cubicle, Mrs. Reardon pushed in, first drawing on a pair of bright orange rubber gloves. She would flush the toilet again, and with her sanitary eye make clear her distaste for the excretions of the poor. When a girl had finished powdering over one of the washbowls, Mrs. Reardon brushed rudely past her and rinsed the loose powder away with efficient splashings. If any girl dared to raise a comb to her head, a loud voice would rasp over the flushing toilets, "No hair combing here. Can't you read?" They all looked at her resentfully, but she ignored them, waiting only for their exodus so that she might return to her rocker and gossip. "Common," she said, easing her folds back into the rocker. "I could tell you some things I've seen in those terlets—" She always gave toilet a New York pronunciation, she never finished the sentence, and she always added, "If I ever catch Bill with one of them—" She never finished that sentence either.

Half an hour later Mrs. Reardon began cleaning up. She locked doors and pulled curtains, deaf to the banging of people who might still want to get in. Wearing her rubber gloves, she scrubbed and cleaned until the porcelain shone. She gave special attention to the private terlets. That done she walked around the waiting room, peering under benches and into telephone booths, carefully searching every possible hiding place. At eleven-thirty she put off the last light and opened the back door that led into the City Hall. She flashed her search-light up and down and called, "Bill." His voice echoed down the long darkness. "O.K., Ma, I'm here."

On the way home she would tell Bill to stop at Louis'. "You'll come in and have a bite, won't you, Mrs. Dineen?" Mrs. Dineen's protestations were part of the ritual too. Then Bill carried the paper sack into his mother's clean modern kitchen and the two ladies followed him. "You'll kill yourself, Ma, eating that stuff at this hour." The mother, of course, ignored him and would continue opening pickled pig's feet and slicing the moist rye bread. They would all eat heartily, Mrs. Dineen included, who would have visions of her upset dreams as Bill drove her home. "It sat on my chest heavy as lead," she'd tell Mrs. Linehan the next day. "And her nearly in her sixties." "It's being born in that city," would be the moaning answer. "They go at a terrible pace, a terrible pace."

Mrs. Dineen opened the door of the sick room cautiously. All the blinds were drawn against the early dark, and at first she could make out only dimly the shape of Mrs. Reardon in bed. She moved closer and in the pale grey-yellow night light found the face. Nothing in it was recognizable. Like a wizened grey baby, Mrs. Reardon lay there, everything shrunk to the size of a child. Why, she wasn't even a good ninety pounds. Her eyes were shut, but the face was not in repose. Mrs. Reardon's stroke had pulled half her face down in a painful grimace, the other side was pulled up, seemed to be grinning. Mrs. Dineen, the tears starting to her eyes, looked around. There was not a sign of the room's former starchy, self-respecting occupant. The shiny glass, the fancy-stoppered perfumes and expensive lotions, all replaced by the dark brown smudgy bottles of the sick. No bulging leather purse ready on the night table. The shoe rack with all its shiny patent shoes, all an elegant size five, removed to make room for the night nurse's bed. And Mrs. Dineen herself had seen the practical nurse trying to squeeze a peasant foot into one of the shoes. Saying only, "Airy a use she'll have for these, with the whole side of her gone, leg, foot, and all."

Now Mrs. Dineen said a quick prayer over her friend and hurried out of the silence and sickness. There was a great laughing and talking echoing down the hall. The night nurse, thin and efficient in her uniform, was eating in the kitchen and Bill sat at the table with her—a glass of beer in his hand. Mrs. Dineen stood shocked and startled. "Bill Reardon, sitting there laughing and drinking, with your mother that's been so good to you lying in there like that." He got up then, embarrassed, but the night nurse spoke up for him in a bold hard way. "Come on now, Mrs. Dineen, none of us can help her by pulling long faces. Finish your beer, Bill," she ordered. He moved back to the table and picked up the glass, although—while Mrs. Dineen watched—he did not drink. "And I said to her," she told Mrs. Linehan leaning out her window next morning. "I said to her that I guess nursing hardened some people, and I gave her a good straight look. Imagine the lot of them sitting there eating and drinking off the fat of the land on her money. That night nurse, Casey's her name, the butcher tells me sends for nothing but the best cuts, and it's all charged to that poor woman. Bill Reardon should be spoken to, or there won't be a penny left to take care of her if she does pull through. Not that I expect it, the last I saw her." And Mrs. Linehan moaned the response, "The poor soul, the poor soul, such a good mother to that boy."

Things went on the same for four months while Mrs. Reardon fought her way back to existence. Mrs. Dineen and Mrs. Linehan shook their heads over her in admiration. "She's a good sport," said Mrs. Dineen. "A good sport." The nurses stayed on and Bill—for the first time in his life—went out and found himself a job. And the next thing the ladies knew, he had married the night nurse, named Casey. The horror-struck cries of Mrs. Linehan and Mrs. Dineen echoed from the City Hall through every precinct. And when they went to visit Mrs. Reardon, who was now definitely going to live, they clucked mysteriously before the grey distorted face until Mrs. Reardon, her one good eye watering, demanded intelligence of the disaster. Her speech was a meaningless mumble, but they finally sorted the question out of the thick gabbling, recognized a sound like "Bill." Then they told her of the marriage and watched the face crumple into grief.

At the end of the next two months, Mrs. Reardon was hoisted out of bed and into a chair. Every morning the right leg had to be laced into a high shoe and buckled into a brace. Naturally she would not let her daughter-in-law near her, and while Bill laced the shoe, she berated him—wordlessly but full of meaning—in her mumble. When he said, "But I married her, Ma, so you'd have someone to take care of you," the mother would stare at him, her one good eye watering and blinking with anger.

Mrs. Dineen and Mrs. Linehan went to see her at first every week, but their visits grew less and less frequent. The speech was too unintelligible, the anger too omnivorous; it was too depressing to sit and watch her massaging and massaging, with her good hand, the other that hung limp and heavy with paralysis. Mrs. Dineen and Mrs. Linehan had great sympathy for her. Mrs. Dineen even knew how that arm must feel hanging heavy and limp in her lap. She explained to Mrs. Linehan how she had slept with the one arm curled under her, and what an agony when she started massaging it, desperately trying to bring it back to life. "Oh, but the relief I felt when the life started coming back. I tell you I sat straight up in my bed and said a rosary for that poor woman, it was a cold night too." Mrs. Linehan sighed. "God help the poor soul, God help her. I wonder if Bill has considered taking her to Saint Anne de Beauprés." That week they went twice to see Mrs. Reardon.

So for six months Mrs. Reardon lived in the chair, massaging the hand, shuffling the leg—heavy in its brace, and trying to relearn words that would fit her anger. Then one evening at bedtime the Casey girl came and took the brace off the leg and—lifting Mrs. Reardon like a baby—carried her to bed. She undressed and arranged her comfortably, then brought her some tea. Mrs. Reardon, her eye wild with anger, pushed the tea away. The Casey girl was firm. The mother tried to articulate the question of Bill. The Casey girl, folding away clothes, seemed to understand her easily. "Bill is out," she said. "And he's out because I made him go. He's all worn out with this situation." She bent over Mrs. Reardon and looked straight into the distorted face. "Now I will tell you something. I'm going to take care of you from now on. It's too hard on Bill when he's working all day and he can't do it properly, but I can." Mrs. Reardon closed her good eye and turned away, but from that night on the Casey girl took care of her firmly and efficiently, and from that day on the leg brace disappeared. But Mrs. Reardon did not give up trying to massage the bad arm back to life, and she worked harder and harder to speak articulately.

When Mrs. Dineen and Mrs. Linehan came to see her, they commented on how much better she looked and congratulated her on her reasonableness. "What's done is done," they might say, "and it's better for Bill that the both of you should try to get along." Mrs. Reardon blinked the remarks away, but lifted up the dead weight of the hand, articulated slowly and carefully, "I think I feel life." The ladies went home still shaking their heads over her, and Mrs. Dineen said to Mrs. Linehan, "I say she's a good sport. Not many people could take it as well as she has," and Mrs. Linehan answered as usual, "God's will, Mrs. Dineen, it's God's will."

Toward the end of the year the Casey girl was pregnant, and Bill had to take over most of the care of his mother again. He lifted her in and out of the bathroom, bathed her and fed her and put her to bed at night. She relaxed in his arms and even forgot to scold him while he carried her. As the Casey girl grew rounder and rounder, Mrs. Reardon never spoke of the change, and when she heard Bill and the girl laughing and fooling in the kitchen she stared out the window, her good eye winking.

The night the Casey girl was to come home from the hospital with the new baby boy, Mrs. Linehan and Mrs. Dineen went up to visit with Mrs. Reardon. They sat in the dark living room with her, and in the darkness they could hear the continual whisper of the live hand rubbing the dead one. They did not talk much because Mrs. Reardon had not really acknowledged their presence. Finally, when she heard Bill and the Casey girl coming upstairs, she motioned to Mrs. Dineen to turn on the light. The room lit up just as the door opened. No one said anything as Bill proudly carried the squalling baby across the room and placed him in his mother's lap. Mrs. Reardon looked down at her noisy grandson and said nothing. As she stared down at the baby, he seemed—with the jerky spasms of his crying—to be slipping, even squirming from inside the circle of her good arm. She tried to clutch with the bad arm too, then, but it was Bill who rushed to grab, and caught up, his son. Mrs. Reardon sat with her good arm still stretched out, the bad one hanging limp by the side of her chair, and large round tears rolled down the distorted face. She made no sound, just sat there with the tears rolling down, and the baby, secure in its father's arms, roared loudly.

11

EDWIN O'CONNOR
(1918–1968)

The son of John and Mary Green O'Connor, Edwin O'Connor was born in 1918 in Providence, Rhode Island, where he graduated from LaSalle Academy. After finishing at Notre Dame in 1939, he became a radio announcer, and his first novel, *The Oracle* (1951), derives from his radio experiences. With the exception of *The Oracle* and *Benjy: A Ferocious Fairy Tale* (1957), however, his four other novels, a handful of short stories, and fragments of three unfinished novels are almost exclusively about Eastern, urban, Catholic Irish-Americans in the period from 1948 to 1968.

O'Connor, who was stationed in Boston with the Coast Guard during World War II, liked Boston so well that he adopted it as his home, Dublin being his next favorite city. His first published works were articles about radio and television for the *Atlantic Monthly,* and his first published story, "The Gentle, Perfect Knight," appeared in 1947; it was the beginning of a long and fruitful relationship between the writer and the periodical.

O'Connor's Irish-American world is primarily a male world, and the leading males, as often as not, are elderly survivors of the immigrant years, with their battles against poverty and discrimination already won. Again and again, O'Connor's fiction emphasizes an end to the Irishness that kept the people closely knit in ward and parish. Their sons and grandsons have already been assimilated into the American mainstream. O'Connor accepts the historical inevitability and dramatizes the father-and-son conflict.

The Last Hurrah (1956), O'Connor's most popular novel by far, and a title that has become an American catchcry, might serve as the collective title for his other Irish-American novels. Frank Skeffington, a thinly disguised Jim Curley in a thinly disguised Boston, mayor and tribal chieftain, loses an election to Kevin McCluskey—a college-educated, professional man, and the colorless tool of image-makers and media hype—but retains to the end his valor, humor, and loyalty to the old days and old ways.

The clerical counterpart to the political *The Last Hurrah* is *The Edge of Sadness* (1961; Pulitzer Prize, 1962), the story of Father Hugh Kennedy, a reformed alcoholic, posted to an ethnically mixed and decaying parish from which most of the Irish have fled. It is also the story, seen through Kennedy's eyes, of three generations of the Irish-American Carmodys—from the old-timers to, again, an almost entirely acculturated new generation—and it suggests the waning influence of the Church among Irish Americans.

O'Connor's other, less well-known novels are *I Was Dancing* (1964) and *All in the Family* (1966). Arthur Schlesinger, Jr., edited the posthumous *The Best and the Last of Edwin O'Connor* (1970), and there are a handful of uncollected short stories.

Plot, in a formal sense, often seems to matter less in O'Connor stories than character (though the writer is intensely interested in how social change affects character) and humor and language. "A Grand Day for Mr. Garvey," first published in the *Atlantic* in 1957, gives readers a good deal of O'Connor in cameo: the elderly Martin Garvey shipped off to a Catholic old people's home by his niece and the man Martin can think of only as "the husband"; Garvey's discovery that the home is a congenial place indeed; and his pleasure in having it both ways, enjoying the home and comically baiting his niece into feeling guilt when she makes her weekly duty visits.

"A Grand Day for Mr. Garvey"

At first, old Mr. Garvey had deeply resented the indignity of being shipped off to the home, and more, of being shipped there by his own flesh and blood. He was not a man in whom family feeling ran strong, but he had his pride, and the thought of being abandoned to an institution at his time of life, merely because his niece and her husband had found an old man's presence in their home a bit inconvenient, was so mortifying that he almost wept in his helplessness. As soon as he arrived at his new quarters he slumped into a chair in his neat little room and spent the day staring with miserable eyes at the holy picture above the bed, and raging at the inhuman behavior that had transferred him to this.

"Cold as stones, the pair of them," he groaned. "An old man like me, packed off like a sheep—oh, the *shame* of it!"

Yet after a week at the home, Mr. Garvey found it to be much more congenial; after a month, he admitted—though only to himself—that he had never been so well off. The house was a great shambling stone structure, built years ago as the country refuge of a celebrated dealer in narcotics, and now, in these days of burdensome taxation, the property of the Church. It was handsomely located in the Berkshire region of Massachusetts, and from his window Mr. Garvey could look down each day upon the loveliest countryside in New England.

If the beauty of the prospect affected Mr. Garvey only mildly— he had never been much of a man for what his niece liked to call The Good Green Land—the concrete fact of his personal liberty positively delighted him. Now, for the first time in years, and within certain quite comfortable limitations, he was the master of his fate.

Life with Ellen and the man whom Mr. Garvey preferred to think of simply as "the husband" had been a series of tense, unwitting violations of the little proprieties—the legitimate rumbling of the stomach after a big meal, the shoes slid off for greater ease, the discreet employment of the toothpick—and he had always been conscious of a variety of impatient reactions: Ellen's half-stifled sighs, the irritable rattling of the husband's evening paper, the silent, solid conspiracy of exasperated glances.

And now there was no more of that, for generally speaking he was left alone. When the door of his room was open he could see an occasional white-clad nun walking swiftly and noiselessly down the great immaculate hallway. Mr. Garvey liked the nuns; he found them courteous and disposed to mind their business. As they passed, sometimes they looked in and said, "Good morning, Mr. Garvey, aren't you looking well today!" And then they moved along, leaving him free to read his few books, to listen to his radio—and this had come to be the greatest of his new-found pleasures: daily he listened, fascinated, to the melancholy progress of the afternoon domestic dramas— or perhaps, in the rare intervals when he felt the need of companionship, to wander about the building, engaging in heartening snatches of acrimonious dispute with his elderly fellow residents. All in all, thought Mr. Garvey comfortably, it was a grand way to live, especially when a man was, like himself, rather close to the end of the rope.

Mr. Garvey's room faced the southwest—this was a luxury, but the husband, in his eagerness to part with Mr. Garvey, had not balked at the slight additional expense—and on the good days was filled for hours on end with the warm sunshine so welcome to old bones. But it was as an observation post that the room had its greatest advantage: from it Mr. Garvey could see every inch of gravel drive which led from the highway into the grounds. This was most important, for each Thursday afternoon his niece rode in to pay her weekly call of duty, and Mr. Garvey liked to be thoroughly prepared for her arrival. His niece was his only visitor, and he both regretted and enjoyed her coming. On the one hand, it was invariably inopportune, occurring just as he was listening to "Pepper Young"; on the other, it gave him the opportunity of playing the little game which he had spent so much time devising.

On this Thursday, his niece arrived somewhat earlier than usual; Mr. Garvey examined her dispassionately from above as she stepped briskly toward the front entrance. He thought once more that she was really quite a homely woman indeed. Then he hurried to his chair and, with a little thrill of anticipation, prepared to welcome her.

When she came in, he was sunk deep in the chair, breathing noisily, his mouth open, his eyes closed.

His niece halted and said, tentatively, "Uncle Martin?"

Mr. Garvey twisted, muttered, and blinked his eyes half open. "What is it now?" he asked wearily. "What is it this time?" Then, blinking again, he said with an air of discovery, "Ah. Ellen. It's you. I thought 'twas *them* again."

The "them" was good, a nice preliminary touch. Without being a specific complaint against authority, it was at once accusing and forlorn, and Mr. Garvey was not a little disappointed that his niece failed utterly to respond to it.

"I wasn't quite sure whether you were sleeping or not, Uncle Martin," she said, crossing the room and kissing him lightly on the forehead. "I hope I didn't wake you."

Mr. Garvey gave her a sad little smile. "I don't mind gettin' woke up," he said gently. "I get woke up a lot around here. I don't mind at all." He regarded his niece mournfully. "You look good," he said.

"I feel well, Uncle Martin, thank you."

"And the husband?"

She smiled brightly. "You mean Arthur, of course, Uncle Martin.

Yes, he's fine too; he asked me to give you his very best."

"Ah. Well well. And how are things," he asked suddenly, "out in The World?"

She laughed. "I'm sure you'd know much more about that than I would, Uncle Martin. I seldom listen to the radio these days and I don't think I've read a paper for weeks. Honestly, I just don't know where the time goes!"

Mr. Garvey was silent. Two weeks ago, the phrase "out in The World" would have done it. It would have summoned to her mind an immediate picture of his own restricted life within severe walls, so sadly contrasted to her own suburban freedom; it would have raked her conscience. And now, in deliberate misconstruction of his meaning, she had laughed! Mr. Garvey wondered grimly whether she was not becoming more adept at his little game. He resolved to try another tack. "You'll stay to supper?"

"No, I'm afraid not, Uncle Martin. I'd love to, of course, but it's such a long drive back, and Arthur is expecting me. We're having some people tonight."

"It's most likely all for the best," Mr. Garvey said. "The meals we get here are very poor. There's days I don't touch a thing."

"Why Uncle Martin!" She waggled a finger at him and her lips formed a little pout; to his horror, the old man saw that she had determined upon a course of playful reproach. "*Shame* on you, Uncle Martin. And you would never eat when you were with us, either; that's what used to worry us so. You need to eat to keep up your strength. And I'm sure you get plenty of good nourishing food up here: the menus look most attractive."

"On the menu and in the stomach: there's a difference there," Mr. Garvey observed darkly. "A man likes some taste to his food." Actually, he was quite pleased with the institutional cooking, finding it far more to his liking than the gay little neutral meals prepared by his niece. Still, there was the game to get on with, so he said doggedly, "It ain't like home cookin'."

Ellen patted his hand. "Now you're flattering me, Uncle Martin. Thank you very much, but I'm afraid I couldn't begin to feed you the way they do up here. I've never seen you looking better. And naturally your food must be agreeing with you or you wouldn't be looking so wonderfully well, would you?" She smiled briskly and with finality; it was time for a change of subject. "Now," she said, "what nice things have happened to you since I was here last week?"

Mr. Garvey's eyes gleamed; here, unlooked for, was opportunity. "They gave us a television," he said.

"A television set? Oh, how nice, Uncle Martin! That must be great fun for you!"

"And then," he said triumphantly, "they took it away!" By a great stroke of fortune, the television set had broken down the night before, and had to be removed for repairs. Everyone had been delighted; from the beginning the majority of the old gentlemen had viewed with extreme distaste the flickering antics of brash young comedians, saying things they did not understand.

"Gone for good, I s'pose," said Mr. Garvey with a sigh. He went on to tell a moving tale of aged men, huddled in the reading room, watching with disconsolate eyes as the principal vehicle of their enjoyment was trundled from the premises. As the story came to its hopeless conclusion, he watched her carefully from the corner of his eye, searching for the first sign of sympathy.

"Oh, come now, Uncle Martin, I'm sure you're exaggerating," she said, using the voice he particularly disliked: it was the assured voice with which she minimized the complaints of her small son. "They've simply taken it away to have it fixed; they'll have it back in no time. After all, they want you to be happy, don't they?"

"Aha," he said cynically, but his response lacked conviction.

There was no doubt of it, he thought, she was getting hard. Wistfully, he recalled the wonderful occasions of her first few visits when, with mounting distress and anxiety, she had listened to his mournful little fictions and had gone away troubled in heart. But now she had built up an unfeeling immunity; his little game had been destroyed. At the thought, despair surged over him; with bitter eyes he watched his niece as she walked to the window.

"Such a green place," she said, her voice trilling a little. "A cool, green place. It's so lovely here, Uncle Martin: think of all the thousands, the *millions* of people in the hot city at this time of year, and then think of yourself, up here!"

He grunted; he could not trust himself to words. It was then that he heard the tapping at the door and looked up to see old Mr. Calderone.

"A thousand pardons, my good Garvey," said Calderone in his deep, stagy voice. "I didn't know you had company. A thousand pardons. I'll return another time."

"No, no," Mr. Garvey said hastily. "Come in, Calderone. Come in, come in, man!" The warmth of the reception was without precedent, for usually when the ancient theatrical face of Mr. Calderone thrust itself through the doorway. Mr. Garvey feigned sleep or desperate illness. He considered Calderone a maniac, or worse, a nuisance; today, however, the man might have his uses. With a faint stirring of hope he said, "I want you to meet the niece, Calderone."

"Niece?" Mr. Calderone stepped jauntily into the room with a great elegance of movement. He was a tall man, only slightly bent, with long white hair and fine dark eyes. "Well, Garvey, you old rogue," he said, in fruity tones of reprimand, "why have you kept this charming creature from us until now, eh? She's charming, utterly charming!" He stood, negligently posed, smiling appreciatively at Ellen; against the worn backdrop of his features, absurdly youthful teeth gleamed.

"Aren't you nice to say such things, Mr. Calderone," Ellen said, with some awkwardness. She was not a little embarrassed by this elderly cavalier with his great young teeth.

"Calderone here was on the stage," Mr. Garvey said superfluously. "What was the name, Calderone?"

"Cardew," said Mr. Calderone. "Edwin Cardew. For the purposes of the marquee, you know. It was a name not unknown in its day, although I'll bet a button that it means next to nothing to this charming young lady. The fame of the player is all too fleeting, alas!"

"I don't believe I've actually *seen* you on the stage," Ellen said tactfully, "but of course I've heard your name." She was suddenly touched by this old man, so pathetically fishing for the rare words of recognition. Generously, she lied again. "I've heard you mentioned *many* times," she said.

"So we are remembered, after all," said Mr. Calderone, and smiled his young smile. "Well well, Garvey, fancy that. There are those who recall the brief hours, so long ago. Ah, they were good days, *great* days, and I lived them to the full. I have always had the knack of leading the full life," he said, leaning confidentially toward Ellen, "even now, here in the asylum."

"I think it's wonderful to be able to enjoy life like that. Although," she added, with a quick little laugh, "I'd hardly call this lovely place an *asylum*, would you, Mr. Calderone?"

"It's quite all right, my dear," Mr. Calderone said comfortingly. "You need have no fear: we are quite without illusion up here. We know our unhappy condition full well, eh, Garvey?"

"We do queer things now and again, I guess," said Mr. Garvey in a strange, small voice.

"Uncle Martin!" Ellen said sharply. Turning to Mr. Calderone, she said, "No, but surely you must realize that this isn't an institution in any—well, in any derogatory sense of the word. It's simply a pleasant home . . . "

"Charming!" said Mr. Calderone, with another great smile. "But it's not necessary, my dear. We may be poor crazed men up here, but we are not in the least sensitive about it, are we, Garvey?"

"Ah well," said Mr. Garvey, with a little sigh. Glancing at his niece, he had all he could do to keep from chuckling aloud. This was the stuff, he thought joyously: oh, Calderone was just the boy for the job!

"We do no harm," Mr. Calderone was saying. "We harm no living soul. We may be aged and deranged, but we bear ill will toward none, even to those who are unkind. Sometimes," he said dreamily, "as I stroll about the grounds, I go out to the wall, where I can watch the cars of normal men roll along the highway. And as I stand there watching, I can see the people pointing as they go by, and I know what they are saying, 'There is where the old madmen live.' But I bear them no ill will, I assure you. Instead, I laugh." In demonstration of this, he laughed, loudly and rather alarmingly.

"But you're very wrong!" Ellen cried, looking anxiously at her uncle. "No one says things like that, or if they do they're greatly mistaken. No one thinks that this is a place for the mentally ill, Mr. Calderone. It's simply a *retreat,* where elderly people can live more comfortably . . . "

Mr. Calderone smiled with great benignity. "She's kind, Garvey," he said. "You have a kind girl there. It warms the cockles of the heart."

"She's a grand girl," Mr. Garvey agreed, in his new weak voice. "A grand, kind girl, all right."

"Not all are so kind to people like ourselves," said Mr. Calderone. "Eh, Garvey? And yet we do not mind. For after all, we know that we have nearly run the race. We know that in a few months, or weeks, or even *days,*" he said, his fine dark eyes glowing happily, "we go to meet our Maker."

"Dust to dust," murmured Mr. Garvey helpfully.

"And not a one of us can escape, mad or sane," Mr. Calderone said, nodding sagely. "*That* I find the most consoling thought of all." Clearly, it was a thought which exhilarated as well as consoled, for one old hand tossed outward and upward in the gesture of the toast. "All dumped into the dark pit together," he said exultantly. "Eh, Garvey? Day by day we crumble."

"That's so, that's so," Mr. Garvey sighed. "We ain't what we used to be, and that's a fact." He felt like singing: his niece had sprung up from her chair and now stood by the window in rigid disapproval, her back toward them. She was pulling nervously at her gloves; with satisfaction, Mr. Garvey saw that she was on the ropes at last. He thanked the miracle that had brought Calderone to the room. Now, however, the job was done, and he was weary of this tiresome man with all his silly jabber; he said without courtesy, "Well, good-by, Calderone. Run along now."

"Yes, I must go. I have many things to attend to before the day is out," Mr. Calderone said pleasantly; in his daily rounds he had become accustomed to curt dismissal. "Good-by, Garvey, until tomorrow. And good-by to you, my dear," he said with a courtly bow. "This has been a great pleasure. I only hope we may see you again soon although, at our time of life, we make no plans, eh, Garvey?"

"Yes, yes," Mr. Garvey said impatiently. "Run along now, Calderone."

Still with her back to the room, Ellen bobbed her head stiffly; Mr. Garvey waved his hand irritably; and with a final elegant flourish, Mr. Calderone was gone.

"Ah, there goes a smart one," said Mr. Garvey in obvious admiration. "They don't fool Calderone. He's the man can tell you things."

"Uncle Martin," said his niece, turning to face him. She stood with her feet wide apart: it was the posture of Resolution, of No Nonsense. On her face, however, was hesitancy and doubt. It was the old familiar mixture that rose to the surface whenever she decided to Do Something about her uncle. Do something, yes, but what?

"Uncle Martin," she said again, and he waved a feeble hand at her and gave her a strangely sweet smile.

"Ah well," he said, his voice barely audible now, "what's to be will be, I guess. You're a grand girl, yes you are."

"Uncle Martin," she said for the third time, but more urgently now, and leaning forward, she began to talk to him. Mr. Garvey closed his eyes; his whole being was flooded with a great warm inner smile. He knew all that his niece would say, and exactly the tones in which she would say it. He knew, for example, that the mildly hectoring tone with which she now addressed him was just a bluff.

It would not last; as it went on and met no response (other than, of course, the nice little weak smile he would preserve on his lips) it would melt into the familiar wheedling manner, and when *this* got nothing (as indeed it would, for he would even keep his eyes closed tight all the while she talked, and maybe even breathe a bit on the fast side, just to help things along) then there would come, at last, the welcome rush of concern and alarm. And that, thought Mr. Garvey with satisfaction, *that* was the stuff for a selfish girl who packs her uncle off to an old folks' home way up in the hills somewheres, and then once in blue moon trots herself in to see him with her perky little step and her hard little pebble eyes and the ha ha ha on her lips and not a single blessed bit of worry in her voice! Oh yes yes, thought Mr. Garvey jubilantly, this was the stuff for her! It was indeed!

It was some time before his niece finally left the room.

"Good-by, Uncle Martin," she said loudly; in reply, she heard only small, gasping snores. She turned to go; then, at the doorway, paused once more. Mr. Garvey, observing her with some difficulty from under lowered lids, noted that she looked perplexed and worried. Then she hurried from the room, and Mr. Garvey, listening, could hear the quick anxious steps moving away from him. He knew that they were going toward the office of the sister-in-charge.

After a reasonably prudent interval, he sat up, smoothing his coat and straightening his tie. He was a neat man, he liked to keep spick-and-span, and partly because of this, partly because he had no more pressing concern at the moment, he rose, went over to the small washstand, and began to brush his teeth. He took great pride in the fact that he still had many of his own teeth; he brushed them several times each day. As he brushed, he stopped frequently, and smiled slightly into the mirror: he was thinking of the dialogue now taking place between his niece and Sister Thomasina.

He knew that, a few minutes from now, his niece would leave the building, get into her car, and hurry off down the gravel drive: she would leave, he thought, faster than she had come. He knew too that later, in an hour or so, maybe Sister Thomasina would come round to see him. She would ask questions, gently, cleverly; he would be polite, full of common sense, cheerful, convinced that long and happy years yet remained to him. He would be appreciative of everything; he would speak with fondness and gratitude of the home, of Ellen, of the husband, even. Then Sister Thomasina would go away.

After that, there would be nothing to do until supper. Then he would eat, and stop to chat a bit, maybe, with some of the other old men, and then he would come back to his room, listen a while to his radio, and then he would wash, say his prayers, and get into bed, and the day would be over for Mr. Garvey.

And then, next week, Ellen would come again. . . .

12

JOSEPH DEVER
(1919–1970)

Joseph Dever was born in Somerville, Massachusetts, a suburb of Boston, in 1919. After graduation from Boston College, he served in the Army Air Force in World War II. While in the military, he was assigned as a correspondent for *Yank* magazine and, in 1944, contributed his short story, "Fifty Missions," to an international competition sponsored by *Yank*. It won him first prize and launched his literary career.

Dever became a fiction editor at Bruce Publishing in Milwaukee in 1946, and Bruce issued his novels, *No Lasting Home* (1947) and *A Certain Widow* (1951). His third novel, *Three Priests* (1958), was published by Doubleday.

In his lifetime Dever held a wide variety of jobs; he was president of a local building service union, public relations assistant in motor vehicles, and consultant to Cardinal Cushing of Boston. He wrote a biography of Cushing in 1965.

Dever once described himself as "a family man, a registered Democrat, a devout Roman Catholic." He might have added "an unsung but talented writer of fiction." His engaging story, "The New York Girls," appeared in *Commonweal* in 1954.

"The New York Girls"

He was sitting in the reception lounge of the Zeff Publishing Company office suite when one of them walked in. This was a good place to see them, he knew, and, sure enough, a cardinal red door snapped outward and one of them came through.

"Are you Mr. Fleem?" she asked. "Mr. Hal Fleem?"

He could not answer for several moments, looking at how long and lacquered she was; the high green pumps, trim legs, the sweep and curve of her figure, and the poise, all the poise. She was one of them, all right, one of those he had thought about while reading magazines in a Texas army camp, one of those he had seen in this same lounge while on furlough several months before; she was one of the New York girls.

"Yes," he said finally, through his blushes, "I'm Hal Fleem."

She smiled sympathetically then, a full-page-ad smile.

"Very well, Mr. Fleem, Mr. Worthin will see you right away."

He followed her through the snapping red door and there were more of them sitting around desks, typing and talking, or browsing languidly through file cabinets. They were all dressed for a party, it seemed, and he trembled a little to think that this Worthin guy might give him the job.

They walked across the floor toward several glass-paneled private offices and he saw Mr. Worthin's name on one of them: Mr. Charles I. Worthin, Personnel. There were two desks in his office and at one of them he sat, prim and erect behind a Charlie Chaplin mustache.

"This is Mr. Fleem, Mr. Worthin," the exotic one said, smiling, this time a thin secretarial smile.

"Hello, hello," Mr. Worthin said with a creasy smile and a slight inclination of the head. He arose, offered a hand, limp and damp.

"Sit right down, Mr. Fleem," he said.

Fleem sat down and so did the New York girl; she, at her type-writer, glowing there behind him like a flamingo, lithe, soft and warm with multi-colors. He wondered if she hung her stockings over the bath tub to dry as he had seen them hang their stockings in a picture magazine. Maybe she wore Russian pajamas while listening, alone, to the symphony on Sunday afternoons.

Mr. Worthin picked up his application and said: "Now, let's see."

"Mmmmm," Worthin continued. "Twenty-four; unmarried; high school graduate; editor, high school magazine, *Excalibur*; recent army service as an orderly-room clerk.

"I see you're from Peoria, Mr. Fleem. Live there now?"

"My parents are there," Fleem said. "I hope to settle in New York."

I hope to settle in New York, Fleem repeated mentally, settle here forever with all the New York girls in one-room apartments. Hope to eat goulash off shaky card tables, hope to buy charcoal gray suits at Brooks Brothers, hope to meet someone for a drink at the

Biltmore between trains. Hope to see all your company's writers, Mr. Worthin, hear all the talk about their various stages of quiet desperation. Hope to work my way up in New York, Mr. Worthin, become a reader, maybe an editor, maybe eventually editor-in-chief. Read all about it in the army, Mr. Worthin, all about Perkins and Wolfe, Auden and Isherwood, Green and Waugh, Woolcott and Thompson. Hope to stay here with the New York girls in publishing houses and see what happens behind the snappy red doors.

"Well," said Mr. Worthin, "there is, as you know, a job open here for a young man."

He put one finger to his little nose-pelt, coddling it.

"It's a glorified office-boy's job—doesn't pay much for a fellow your age—thirty-three dollars a week, to be perfectly frank. Would you really be interested in that kind of money?"

Fleem nodded, restraining himself. "Yes, I would, I'd like working around a big publishing house like this."

"There really isn't much chance of advancement," the office manager said with just a hint of cruelty.

Mr. Worthin had himself been the office boy, once, with dreams of becoming a book editor. Twenty years had gone by, the New York girls had come and gone, new editors, glittery with academic degrees, heavy with literary connections in Europe and among the little magazines, had moved up and down Madison Avenue. One day Mr. Roland, Mr. Worthin's elderly predecessor as office manager, had died quietly in bed. A note had been found on the table by his bed, addressed to Worthin:

"Please tell Mr. Zeff I will not be in this morning."

"Such gentle irony!" shrewd, scholarly Mr. Zeff had said to Worthin when he read Roland's obituary note. "Well, Worthin, you'll have to carry on."

Office manager—a good position, yes. But you could be office manager in a pharmaceutical company or anywhere. It was not what Miss Curlew and he had planned.

Miss Curlew was then secretary to Mr. Zeff. Worthin had eaten goulash on her card table because of her closeness to the throne. She had done what she could: showed Mr. Zeff dull but competent book reviews Worthin had published in *The New Echelon*; she had importuned writer friends to mention Worthin to the publisher at cocktail parties. Confidential secretaries can be confidential. She had even dared, after a winey Christmas-party kiss, to alert Mr. Zeff to Worthin's eligibility for advancement.

With Roland's death, Mr. Zeff therefore felt he was pleasing both her and Worthin in making the latter office manager, or company shepherd of the New York girls.

Worthin and Miss Curlew, in their bewildered inertia, trended into wedlock and exchanged an interminable series of curious looks across the shaky card table.

"Not much chance of advancement," Hal Fleem thought. "That's what he says."

"If I meet your requirements, I'll be glad to accept the salary," Fleem replied with a certain winsome shyness.

"Very well," Worthin said. "Miss Marr, will you have Mr. Fleem take the test?"

Miss Marr rustled all her New York clothes as she leaned deep and opened a bottom desk drawer.

"Will you come with me, Mr. Fleem?"

He went, he saw, the New York girls, like Sunday paper ads come alive, conquered him again.

Miss Marr led him into an empty office and directed him to a plain metal table.

"All applicants for positions here take the psycho-semantic test," she said casually. "Even the editors."

"You've probably taken similar tests in the service. True or false, and so on."

"Oh, yes," Fleem said, sitting.

She flicked her wrist, pursed her lips and glanced at one of those starlet TV watches.

"It's two-fifteen now. You have until quarter of three. Any questions?"

"Pencil or ink?" he asked, anxious to be intelligent.

"Pencil will do. Good luck!" she concluded brightly.

"Miss Marr," he said impulsively.

"Yes?"

"May I ask you an odd question?"

"Odd?" she asked, doing something crinkly with her nose.

"Yes, I suppose so," Fleem said.

"What is it?" she asked in a throaty way, as if he were about to propose.

"Do you—do a lot of the New York girls live in one-room apartments on the East Side?"

She frowned, then sensing his Peoria earnestness, warmed into a smile.

"Yes, I suppose a lot of us do—I know I do."

"Well, frankly," Hal began, "is it true that a lot of you eat goulash off shaky card tables and dry your lingerie in the bathroom and lie around listening to the symphony on Sundays—alone?"

Then Miss Marr struck a lovely, backward-leaning stance and laughed richly out of the serpentine perfection of her body.

"Oh, no," she said laughing long and richly, "oh, no, no, no!"

She left him with gay, subsiding laughter and he, flustered, yet warmed by the sympathetic lilt of her mirth, turned to the psychosemantic test.

There were twenty-nine questions:

He matched authors with titles: *Oliver Twist*, Charles Dickens, of course; *The Fountainhead*, Ayn Rand. He numbered certain octagons as belonging within larger octagons and dared to wonder if this might signify something about his libido. Finally, after deciding whether Iran and Persia were one and the same place, as also Manchukuo and Manchuria, he came to the second to last question.

It was a long paragraph calling for punctuation and rearrangement of sentences where needed. It concerned the essence of a book editor, the sanctity and dignity of his profession. He read slowly, soberly, reflecting, and then went through it again, correcting the errors in punctuation and paragraphing.

The last question was almost querulous:

Why do you want to work for a book publisher? Answer briefly and succinctly.

A minute and a half to go. He nibbled at his lower lip and then applied his pencil and wrote rapidly as if inspired:

> "There is no frigate like a book
> to take us lands away . . . "

Below, on the street floor, he sat at a disc-like table in a subdued cocktail lounge, feeling quite dignified behind a forty-cent bottle of beer. The same beverage was probably fifteen cents a glass at the bar, but his strategic position was worth at least another quarter.

Here by the window he could watch the main entrance of the adjoining publishers' building. The waitress had informed him that many of the publishing people stopped here for a drink just after work at five. He had thought as much.

Perhaps she, too, might come in among the New York girls, chattering over their Manhattans and smoking king-sized cigarettes with knowing, graceful fury.

Miss Marr had been rather cool and officious when he handed her the completed quiz forms.

"When will I know, Miss Marr?"

"If you'll call tomorrow morning at nine-thirty . . . ," she had said with a rather wintry smile.

He was determined, however, to know tonight. So he waited in the cocktail lounge, hoping she would come in with the others, knowing she would have the answer—with one of those ready-answer charts she could evaluate the quiz in a matter of minutes.

5:00; 5:01; 5:02; 5:03.

The beer level descended. Another bottle.

They came in lilt and flutter, out of the building entrance, clock-clock-clock, into the lounge, bright and lean and lacquered.

He looked up slowly, braking his eagerness.

The laughter then, gay, lightsome, Miss Marr recalling an English novelist with popping black eyes, defiant black derby, tightly rolled umbrella.

"You can't imagine!" she said, chuckling and toying with a plastic mixer. "You simply can't imagine."

He waited until they had almost consumed their drinks. He waited, slowing the race of his pulse with a cool process of the mind. He would offer, through the waitress, to buy her and her friends a round. Nothing vulgar; a gesture of gratitude, win or lose.

He motioned for the waitress and explained softly, his boyish shyness overcoming any hint of the masher.

" . . . a sort of gesture, win or lose," he said with a shy smile. "And keep the change."

"Thank you," the waitress said, taking the currency. She did his bidding and Miss Marr looked his way a little alarmed. He smiled and nodded, serene, contained, as if to say: "It's just a job."

A tilt of chin at her three girl friends, a question, a laugh. "Yes, yes, all around." And then a decorous smile in his direction.

"I'll wander over casually," he thought. It was like a line of dialogue from a script. He savored the line mentally: "I'll wander over casually."

He did. He got up and went over there, easy and graceful.

Miss Marr thanked him and introduced her girl friends by their first names only. They regarded him with mirthful courtesy, suspicious of the first free drink, secure against a new man, haughty before the nebulous prospect of possible and even desirable involvement.

Avoiding the subject of his employment quiz, he talked of the excitement of New York, its glitter, packed streets, soaring buildings; he talked of New York with completely defenseless naiveté.

"Where are you from?" one of the girls asked him, with a slightly sly twinkle.

"Peoria," Hal said earnestly.

They tried not to smile: two drank, one fished in her handbag, one coughed, stifling a giggle behind her long gleaming talons.

Miss Marr emerged from her handbag.

"*I've* got to go," she said, running her announcement up the scale fetchingly. "Thanks again for the drink."

"Yes, thank you," the gilded creatures echoed.

"You're very welcome," Fleem said.

He'd ask her now—now or never.

"I've been wondering—I mean—could you tell me my chances?"

She looked at him directly, almost warmly, then averted her face with a shade of distress. "Well . . . ," she said reluctantly, "you didn't do too well."

The acorn of all our childhoods swelled newly in his throat.

"Not well," he said with uncontrollable chagrin.

"You received close to a passing mark, but Mr. Worthin decided your background doesn't quite suit you for the publishing business."

The acorn swelled tightly.

"Oh, I see."

"Let's go, Ann," said one of the gleaming ones.

"Why don't you take a cab with us, Ann?" another added as they gathered themselves to go.

"No cab for me," Miss Marr said, "I can go to the East Side faster by crosstown bus. Cheaper, too."

"Goodby, Mr. Fleem," she said, shaking his hand, "better luck next time."

"Goodbye and thanks," he said lamely, watching them pass in an opulent flutter through the revolving doors.

The job was gone; New York, for him, no more. One thing, at least, was true—a truth he could relate back in Peoria: You can get to the East Side by crosstown bus, faster than by cab.

13

FLANNERY O'CONNOR

(1925–1964)

Flannery O'Connor was born in 1925 in Savannah, Georgia, the daughter of Edward and Regina Cline O'Connor. After receiving her B.A. from the Women's College of Georgia (now Georgia College) in 1945, she earned an M.F.A. from the State University of Iowa in 1947. O'Connor died of lupus in 1964, at age thirty-nine, in Milledgeville, Georgia, the town most commonly associated with her work.

Two novels, *Wise Blood;* (1952) and *The Violent Bear It Away* (1960), the collection, *Three: Wise Blood, A Good Man Is Hard to Find, The Violent Bear It Away* (1964); and one short story collection, *A Good Man Is Hard to Find, and Other Stories* (1955), were published in her lifetime. Posthumously published were the short story collection, *Everything that Rises Must Converge* (1965), and *The Complete Short Stories* (1971). Her nonfictional prose was published in 1969 as *Mystery and Manners; Occasional Prose,* and her letters, *The Habit of Being,* appeared in 1979.

Despite her relatively slender output in fiction, O'Connor has achieved importance on the American literary scene. She received a Ford Foundation grant in 1959 and, posthumously, a National Book Award for *The Complete Short Stories* in 1972 and the National Book Critics award for *The Habit of Being* in 1980. Perhaps more significantly, her stature in modern American letters can be shown by the critical attention given her work—more than a dozen book-length studies and hundreds of critical essays.

Flannery O'Connor does not concern herself with Irish Americana in ways that, for example, James T. Farrell and Edwin O'Connor do. But her lack of "Irishness" is not an evasion, as it was for Scott Fitzgerald; rather, her interests lay elsewhere. O'Connor's intense preoccupation with religion—Catholicism and American Southern fundamentalist

Christianity—brings the shock of recognition to Irish Catholics, and "The Temple of the Holy Ghost," one of her most overtly Catholic stories, illustrates her theology. Although, like Graham Greene or François Mauriac, she often appears to have worked out her own version of Christianity/Catholicism, she has written of herself: "I see from the standpoint of Christian orthodoxy. This means that for me the meaning of life is centered in our redemption by Christ and that what I see in the world I see in relation to that." Readers who seek a comfortable or sentimental Christianity in her works will find instead a considerable violence in the macabre, the gothic, the grotesque, as well as a certain humor emanating from these qualities, a condition common enough in Irish writing.

Although O'Connor has staked out her claim as, in her words, "the action of grace in territory held largely by the devil," her work is firmly established in the American South, especially her native Georgia. That gives rise to the question of whether or not, pejoratively speaking, she should be considered a "regionalist." The same question has, of course, been asked of James Joyce and his Dublin and might well be asked of James T. Farrell and his Chicago. Doubtless, the short answer to such a question is that O'Connor, like other such "regionalists," successfully aspires to the universal through the particular.

"A Temple of the Holy Ghost"

All week end the two girls were calling each other Temple One and Temple Two, shaking with laughter and getting so red and hot that they were positively ugly, particularly Joanne who had spots on her face anyway. They came in the brown convent uniforms they had to wear at Mount St. Scholastica but as soon as they opened their suitcases, they took off the uniforms and put on red skirts and loud blouses. They put on lipstick and their Sunday shoes and walked around in the high heels all over the house, always passing the long mirror in the hall slowly to get a look at their legs. None of their ways were lost on the child. If only one of them had come, that one would have played with her, but since there were two of them, she was out of it and watched them suspiciously from a distance.

They were fourteen—two years older than she was—but neither of them was bright, which was why they had been sent to the convent. If they had gone to a regular school, they wouldn't have done anything but think about boys; at the convent the sisters, her mother said, would keep a grip on their necks. The child decided, after observing them for a few hours, that they were practically morons and she was glad to think that they were only second cousins and she couldn't have inherited any of their stupidity. Susan called herself Su-zan. She was very skinny but she had a pretty pointed face and red hair. Joanne had yellow hair that was naturally curly but she talked through her nose and when she laughed, she turned purple in patches. Neither one of them could say an intelligent thing and all their sentences began, "You know this boy I know well one time he . . ."

They were to stay all week end and her mother said she didn't see how she would entertain them since she didn't know any boys their age. At this, the child, struck suddenly with genius, shouted, "There's Cheat! Get Cheat to come! Ask Miss Kirby to get Cheat to come show them around!" and she nearly choked on the food she had in her mouth. She doubled over laughing and hit the table with her fist and looked at the two bewildered girls while water started in her eyes and rolled down her fat cheeks and the braces she had in her mouth glared like tin. She had never thought of anything so funny before.

Her mother laughed in a guarded way and Miss Kirby blushed and carried her fork delicately to her mouth with one pea on it. She was a long-faced blonde schoolteacher who boarded with them and Mr. Cheatam was her admirer, a rich old farmer who arrived every Saturday afternoon in a fifteen-year-old baby-blue Pontiac powdered with red clay dust and black inside with Negroes that he charged ten cents apiece to bring into town on Saturday afternoons. After he dumped them he came to see Miss Kirby, always bringing a little gift—a bag of boiled peanuts or a watermelon or a stalk of sugar cane and once a wholesale box of Baby Ruth candy bars. He was bald-headed except for a little fringe of rust-colored hair and his face was nearly the same color as the unpaved roads and washed like them with ruts and gulleys. He wore a pale green shirt with a thin black stripe in it and blue galluses and his trousers cut across a protruding stomach that he pressed tenderly from time to time with his big flat thumb. All his teeth were backed with gold and he would roll his eyes at Miss Kirby in an impish way and say, "Haw haw," sitting in their porch swing with his legs spread apart and his hightopped shoes pointing in opposite directions on the floor.

"I don't think Cheat is going to be in town this week end," Miss Kirby said, not in the least understanding that this was a joke, and the child was convulsed afresh, threw herself backward in her chair, fell out of it, rolled on the floor and lay there heaving. Her mother told her if she didn't stop this foolishness she would have to leave the table.

Yesterday her mother had arranged with Alonzo Myers to drive them the forty-five miles to Mayville, where the convent was, to get the girls for the week end and Sunday afternoon he was hired to drive them back again. He was an eighteen-year-old boy who weighed two hundred and fifty pounds and worked for the taxi company and he was all you could get to drive you anywhere. He smoked or rather chewed a short black cigar and he had a round sweaty chest that showed through the yellow nylon shirt he wore. When he drove all the windows of the car had to be open.

"Well there's Alonzo!" the child roared from the floor. "Get Alonzo to show em around! Get Alonzo!"

The two girls, who had seen Alonzo, began to scream their indignation.

Her mother thought this was funny too but she said, "That'll be about enough out of you," and changed the subject. She asked them why they called each other Temple One and Temple Two and this sent them off into gales of giggles. Finally they managed to explain. Sister Perpetua, the oldest nun at the Sisters of Mercy in Mayville, had given them a lecture on what to do if a young man should—here they laughed so hard they were not able to go on without going back to the beginning—on what to do if a young man should—they put their heads in their laps—on what to do if—they finally managed to shout it out—if he should "behave in an ungentlemanly manner with them in the back of an automobile." Sister Perpetua said they were to say, "Stop sir! I am a Temple of the Holy Ghost!" and that would put an end to it. The child sat up off the floor with a blank face. She didn't see anything so funny in this. What was really funny was the idea of Mr. Cheatam or Alonzo Myers beauing them around. That killed her.

Her mother didn't laugh at what they had said. "I think you girls are pretty silly," she said. "After all, that's what you are—Temples of the Holy Ghost."

The two of them looked up at her, politely concealing their giggles, but with astonished faces as if they were beginning to realize that she was made of the same stuff as Sister Perpetua.

Miss Kirby preserved her set expression and the child thought, it's all over her head anyhow. I am a Temple of the Holy Ghost, she said to herself, and was pleased with the phrase. It made her feel as if somebody had given her a present.

After dinner, her mother collapsed on the bed and said, "Those girls are going to drive me crazy if I don't get some entertainment for them. They're awful."

"I bet I know who you could get," the child started.

"Now listen. I don't want to hear any more about Mr. Cheatam," her mother said. "You embarrass Miss Kirby. He's her only friend. Oh my Lord," and she sat up and looked mournfully out the window, "that poor soul is so lonesome she'll even ride in that car that smells like the last circle in hell."

And she's a Temple of the Holy Ghost too, the child reflected. "I wasn't thinking of him," she said. "I was thinking of those two Wilkinses, Wendell and Cory, that visit old lady Buchell out on her farm. They're her grandsons. They work for her."

"Now that's an idea," her mother murmured and gave her an appreciative look. But then she slumped again. "They're only farm boys. These girls would turn up their noses at them."

"Huh," the child said. "They wear pants. They're sixteen and they got a car. Somebody said they were both going to be Church of God preachers because you don't have to know nothing to be one."

"They would be perfectly safe with those boys all right," her mother said and in a minute she got up and called their grandmother on the telephone and after she had talked to the old woman a half an hour, it was arranged that Wendell and Cory would come to supper and afterwards take the girls to the fair.

Susan and Joanne were so pleased that they washed their hair and rolled it up on aluminum curlers. Hah, thought the child, sitting cross-legged on the bed to watch them undo the curlers, wait'll you get a load of Wendell and Cory! "You'll like these boys," she said. "Wendell is six feet tall and got red hair. Cory is six feet six inches talls got black hair and wears a sport jacket and they gottem this car with a squirrel tail on the front."

"How does a child like you know so much about these men?" Susan asked and pushed her face up close to the mirror to watch the pupils in her eyes dilate.

The child lay back on the bed and began to count the narrow boards in the ceiling until she lost her place. I know them all right, she said to someone. We fought in the world war together. They were under me and I saved them five times from Japanese suicide divers and Wendell said I am going to marry that kid and the other said oh no you ain't I am and I said neither one of you is because I will court marshall you all before you can bat an eye. "I've seen them around is all," she said.

When they came the girls stared at them a second and then began to giggle and talk to each other about the convent. They sat in the swing together and Wendell and Cory sat on the banisters together. They sat like monkeys, their knees on a level with their shoulders and their arms hanging down between. They were short thin boys with red faces and high cheekbones and pale seed-like eyes. They had brought a harmonica and a guitar. One of them began to blow softly on the mouth organ, watching the girls over it, and the other started strumming the guitar and then began to sing, not watching them but keeping his head tilted upward as if he were only interested in hearing himself. He was singing a hillbilly song that sounded half like a love song and half like a hymn.

The child was standing on a barrel pushed into some bushes at the side of the house, her face on a level with the porch floor. The sun was going down and the sky was turning a bruised violet color that seemed to be connected with the sweet mournful sound of the music. Wendell began to smile as he sang and to look at the girls. He looked at Susan with a dog-like loving look and sang,

> "I've found a friend in Jesus,
> He's everything to me,
> He's the lily of the valley,
> He's the One who's set me free!"

Then he turned the same look on Joanne and sang,

> "A wall of fire about me,
> I've nothing now to fear,
> He's the lily of the valley,
> And I'll always have Him near!"

The girls looked at each other and held their lips stiff so as not to giggle but Susan let out one anyway and clapped her hand on her mouth. The singer frowned and for a few seconds only strummed the guitar. Then he began "The Old Rugged Cross" and they listened politely but when he had finished they said, "Let us sing one!" and before he could start another, they began to sing with their convent-trained voices,

"*Tantum ergo Sacramentum*
Veneremur Cernui:
Et antiquum documentum
Novo cedat ritui:"

The child watched the boys' solemn faces turn with perplexed frowning stares at each other as if they were uncertain whether they were being made fun of.

"*Praestet fides supplementum*
Sensuum defectui.
Genitori, Genitoque
Laus et jubilatio

Salus, honor, virtus quoque . . . "

The boys' faces were dark red in the gray-purple light. They looked fierce and startled.

"*Sit et benedictio;*
Procedenti ab utroque
Compar sit laudatio.
Amen."

The girls dragged out the Amen and then there was a silence.

"That must be Jew singing." Wendell said and began to tune the guitar.

The girls giggled idiotically but the child stamped her foot on the barrel. "You big dumb ox!" she shouted. "You big dumb Church of God ox!" she roared and fell off the barrel and scrambled up and shot around the corner of the house as they jumped from the banister to see who was shouting.

Her mother had arranged for them to have supper in the back yard and she had a table laid out there under some Japanese lanterns that she pulled out for garden parties. "I ain't eating with them," the child said and snatched her plate off the table and carried it to the kitchen and sat down with the thin blue-gummed cook and ate her supper.

"Howcome you be so ugly sometime?" the cook asked.

"Those stupid idiots," the child said.

The lanterns gilded the leaves of the trees orange on the level where they hung and above them was black-green and below them were different dim muted colors that made the girls sitting at the table look prettier than they were. From time to time, the child turned her head and glared out the kitchen window at the scene below.

"God could strike you deaf dumb and blind," the cook said, "and then you wouldn't be as smart as you is."

"I would still be smarter than some," the child said.

After supper they left for the fair. She wanted to go to the fair but not with them so even if they had asked her she wouldn't have gone. She went upstairs and paced the long bedroom with her hands locked together behind her back and her head thrust forward and an expression, fierce and dreamy both, on her face. She didn't turn on the electric light but let the darkness collect and make the room smaller and more private. At regular intervals a light crossed the open window and threw shadows on the wall. She stopped and stood looking out over the dark slopes, past where the pond glinted silver, past the wall of woods to the speckled sky where a long finger of light was revolving up and around and away, searching the air as if it were hunting for the lost sun. It was the beacon light from the fair.

She could hear the distant sound of the calliope and she saw in her head all the tents raised up in a kind of gold sawdust light and the diamond ring of the ferris wheel going around and around up in the air and down again and the screeking merry-go-round going around and around on the ground. A fair lasted five or six days and there was a special afternoon for school children and a special night for niggers. She had gone last year on the afternoon for school children and had seen the monkeys and the fat man and had ridden on the ferris wheel. Certain tents were closed then because they contained things that would be known only to grown people but she had looked with interest at the advertising on the closed tents, at the faded-looking pictures on the canvas of people in tights, with stiff stretched composed faces like the faces of the martyrs waiting to have their tongues cut out by the Roman soldier. She had imagined that what was inside these tents concerned medicine and she had made up her mind to be a doctor when she grew up.

She had since changed and decided to be an engineer but as she looked out the window and followed the revolving searchlight as it widened and shortened and wheeled in its arc, she felt that she would have to be much more than just a doctor or an engineer. She would have to be a saint because that was the occupation that included everything you could know; and yet she knew she would never be a saint. She did not steal or murder but she was a born liar and slothful and she sassed her mother and was deliberately ugly to almost everybody. She was eaten up also with the sin of Pride, the worst one. She made fun of the Baptist preacher who came to the school at commencement to give the devotional. She would pull down her mouth and hold her forehead as if she were in agony and groan, "Fawther, we thank Thee," exactly the way he did and she had been told many times not to do it. She could never be a saint, but she thought she could be a martyr if they killed her quick.

She could stand to be shot but not to be burned in oil. She didn't know if she could stand to be torn to pieces by lions or not. She began to prepare her martyrdom, seeing herself in a pair of tights in a great arena, lit by the early Christians hanging in cages of fire, making a gold dusty light that fell on her and the lions. The first lion charged forward and fell at her feet, converted. A whole series of lions did the same. The lions liked her so much she even slept with them and finally the Romans were obliged to burn her but to their astonishment she would not burn down and finding she was so hard to kill, they finally cut off her head very quickly with a sword and she went immediately to heaven. She rehearsed this several times, returning each time at the entrance of Paradise to the lions.

Finally she got up from the window and got ready for bed and got in without saying her prayers. There were two heavy double beds in the room. The girls were occupying the other one and she tried to think of something cold and clammy that she could hide in their bed but her thought was fruitless. She didn't have anything she could think of, like a chicken carcass or a piece of beef liver. The sound of the calliope coming through the window kept her awake and she remembered that she hadn't said her prayers and got up and knelt down and began them. She took a running start and went through to the other side of the Apostle's Creed and then hung by her chin on the side of the bed, empty-minded. Her prayers, when she remembered to say them, were usually perfunctory but sometimes when she had done something wrong or heard music or lost something, or sometimes for no reason at all, she would be moved to fervor and would think of Christ on the long journey to Calvary, crushed three times under the rough cross. Her mind would stay on this a while and then get empty and when something roused her, she would find that she was thinking of a different thing entirely, of some dog or some girl or something she was going to do some day. Tonight, remembering Wendell and Cory, she was filled with thanksgiving and almost weeping with delight, she said, "Lord, Lord, thank You that I'm not in the Church of God, thank You Lord, thank You!" and got back in bed and kept repeating it until she went to sleep.

The girls came in at a quarter to twelve and waked her up with their giggling. They turned on the small blue-shaded lamp to see to get undressed by and their skinny shadows climbed up the wall and broke and continued moving about softly on the ceiling. The child sat up to hear what all they had seen at the fair. Susan had a plastic pistol full of cheap candy and Joanne a pasteboard cat with red polka dots in it. "Did you see the monkeys dance?" the child asked. "Did you see that fat man and those midgets?"

"All kinds of freaks," Joanne said. And then she said to Susan, "I enjoyed it all but the you-know-what," and her face assumed a peculiar expression as if she had bit into something that she didn't know if she liked or not.

The other stood still and shook her head once and nodded slightly at the child. "Little pitchers," she said in a low voice but the child heard it and her heart began to beat very fast.

She got out of her bed and climbed onto the footboard of theirs. They turned off the light and got in but she didn't move. She sat there, looking hard at them until their faces were well defined in the dark. "I'm not as old as you all," she said, "but I'm about a million times smarter."

"There are some things," Susan said, "that a child of your age doesn't know," and they both began to giggle.

"Go back to your own bed," Joanne said.

The child didn't move. "One time," she said, her voice hollow-sounding in the dark, "I saw this rabbit have rabbits."

There was a silence. Then Susan said, "How?" in an indifferent tone and she knew that she had them. She said she wouldn't tell until they told about the you-know-what. Actually she had never seen a rabbit have rabbits but she forgot this as they began to tell what they had seen in the tent.

It had been a freak with a particular name but they couldn't remember the name. The tent where it was had been divided into two parts by a black curtain, one side for men and one for women. The freak went from one side to the other, talking first to the men and then to the women, but everyone could hear. The stage ran all the way across the front. The girls heard the freak say to the men, "I'm going to show you this and if you laugh, God may strike you the same way." The freak had a country voice, slow and nasal and neither high nor low, just flat. "God made me thisaway and if you laugh He may strike you the same way. This is the way He wanted me to be and I ain't disputing His way. I'm showing you because I got to make the best of it. I expect you to act like ladies and gentlemen. I never done it to myself nor had a thing to do with it but I'm making the best of it. I don't dispute hit." Then there was a long silence on the other side of the tent and finally the freak left the men and came over onto the women's side and said the same thing.

The child felt every muscle strained as if she were hearing the answer to a riddle that was more puzzling than the riddle itself. "You mean it had two heads?" she said.

"No," Susan said, "it was a man and woman both. It pulled up its dress and showed us. It had on a blue dress."

The child wanted to ask how it could be a man and woman both without two heads but she did not. She wanted to get back into her own bed and think it out and she began to climb down off the footboard.

"What about the rabbit?" Joanne asked.

The child stopped and only her face appeared over the footboard, abstracted, absent. "It spit them out of its mouth," she said, "six of them."

She lay in bed trying to picture the tent with the freak walking from side to side but she was too sleepy to figure it out. She was better able to see the faces of the country people watching, the men more solemn than they were in church, and the women stern and polite, with painted-looking eyes, standing as if they were waiting for the first note of the piano to begin the hymn. She could hear the freak saying, "God made me thisaway and I don't dispute hit," and the people saying, "Amen. Amen."

"God done this to me and I praise Him."

"Amen. Amen."

"He could strike you thisaway."

"Amen. Amen."

"But he has not."

"Amen."

"Raise yourself up. A temple of the Holy Ghost. You! You are God's temple, don't you know? Don't you know? God's Spirit has a dwelling in you, don't you know?"

"Amen. Amen."

"If anybody desecrates the temple of God, God will bring him to ruin and if you laugh, He may strike you thisaway. A temple of God is a holy thing. Amen. Amen."

"I am a temple of the Holy Ghost."

"Amen."

The people began to slap their hands without making a loud noise and with a regular beat between the Amens, more and more softly, as if they knew there was a child near, half asleep.

The next afternoon the girls put on their brown convent uniforms again and the child and her mother took them back to Mount St. Scholastica. "Oh glory, oh Pete!" they said. "Back to the salt mines." Alonzo Myers drove them and the child sat in front with him and her mother sat in back between the two girls, telling them such things as how pleased she was to have had them and how they must come back again and then about the good times she and their mothers had had when they were girls at the convent. The child didn't listen to any of this twaddle but kept as close to the locked door as she could get and held her head out the window. They had thought Alonzo would smell better on Sunday but he did not. With her hair blowing over her face she could look directly into the ivory sun which was framed in the middle of the blue afternoon but when she pulled it away from her eyes she had to squint.

Mount St. Scholastica was a red brick house set back in a garden in the center of town. There was a filling station on one side of it and a firehouse on the other. It had a high black grillework fence around it and narrow bricked walks between old trees and japonica bushes that were heavy with blooms. A big moon-faced nun came bustling to the door to let them in and embraced her mother and would have done the same to her but that she stuck out her hand and preserved a frigid frown, looking just past the sister's shoes at the wainscoting. They had a tendency to kiss even homely children, but the nun shook her hand vigorously and even cracked her knuckles a little and said they must come to the chapel, that benediction was just beginning. You put your foot in their door and they got you praying, the child thought as they hurried down the polished corridor.

You'd think she had to catch a train, she continued in the same ugly vein as they entered the chapel where the sisters were kneeling on one side and the girls, all in brown uniforms, on the other. The chapel smelled of incense. It was light green and gold, a series of springing arches that ended with the one over the altar where the priest was kneeling in front of the monstrance, bowed low. A small boy in a surplice was standing behind him, swinging the censer. The child knelt down between her mother and the nun and they were well into the *"Tantum Ergo"* before her ugly thoughts stopped and she began to realize that she was in the presence of God. Hep me not to be so mean, she began mechanically. Hep me not to give her so much sass. Hep me not to talk like I do. Her mind began to get quiet and then empty but when the priest raised the monstrance with the Host shining ivory-colored in the center of it, she was thinking of the tent at the fair that had the freak in it. The freak was saying, "I don't dispute hit. This is the way He wanted me to be."

As they were leaving the convent door, the big nun swooped down on her mischievously and nearly smothered her in the black habit, mashing the side of her face into the crucifix hitched onto her belt and then holding her off and looking at her with little periwinkle eyes.

On the way home she and her mother sat in the back and Alonzo drove by himself in the front. The child observed three folds of fat in the back of his neck and noted that his ears were pointed almost like a pig's. Her mother, making conversation, asked him if he had gone to the fair.

"Gone," he said, "and never missed a thing and it was good I gone when I did because they ain't going to have it next week like they said they was."

"Why?" asked her mother.

"They shut it on down," he said. "Some of the preachers from town gone out and inspected it and got the police to shut it down."

Her mother let the conversation drop and the child's round face was lost in thought. She turned it toward the window and looked out over a stretch of pasture land that rose and fell with a gathering greenness until it touched the dark woods. The sun was a huge red ball like an elevated Host drenched in blood and when it sank out of sight, it left a line in the sky like a red clay road hanging over the trees.

14

J. P. DONLEAVY
(b. 1926)

Born in Brooklyn, New York, in 1926, the son of an Irish immigrant, J. P. Donleavy was raised in the Bronx, New York. During World War II, he served in the U.S. Navy and, in 1945, attended the Naval Academy Preparatory School, where, he says, he first heard talk about good writing and James Joyce and where, through reading, he learned about Ireland. Following his stint in the Navy, he applied to Trinity College, Dublin, and was accepted.

After considerable trouble with publishers over offensive passages, his first and most famous novel, *The Ginger Man*, was published in 1955. It was followed by *A Singular Man* (1963), *The Saddest Summer of Samuel S.* (1966), *The Beastly Beatitudes of Balthazar B.* (1968), *The Onion Eaters* (1971), *The Destinies of Darcy Dancer, Gentleman* (1977), *Schultz* (1979), *Leila* (1983), a sequel to *Darcy Dancer*, and the novella *De Alfance Tennis*. His plays, based largely on his fiction, have been published as *The Plays of J. P. Donleavy; with a Preface by the Author* (1972). There is a volume of short stories and sketches, *Meet My Maker, the Mad Molecule* (1964). Many of his essays have been collected and published as *The Unexpurgated Code: A Complete Manual of Survival and Manners* (1975).

Sebastian Dangerfield, the protagonist of *The Ginger Man*, has become a cult figure. He is Donleavy's most memorable character and one of contemporary literature's first anti-heroes: an amoral and anti-establishment outsider and rebel, a boozer, womanizer, wife-beater, liar, and thief. He has reappeared as a dimmer carbon copy in subsequent works, but Donleavy is not a one-level author. He is a black humorist with an irrepressible urge to satirize modern life, and he has, as a satirist, won a large and faithful audience.

Donleavy's attitude toward America and Ireland has shifted over the years. Like Elizabeth Cullinan, represented in this anthology by "Life after Death," Donleavy's characters are frequently searching for their place in the sun or in the mist. Much of Donleavy's life and work exemplifies a conflict between the real Ireland and the Ireland of sentimental Irish-American family lore. Sebastian Dangerfield, who is more or less neutral about America, bitterly condemns the Irish. But, more recently, in the short stories, "The Romantic Life of Alphonse A" and "Wither Wigwams," and in the novel, *The Beastly Beatitudes of Balthazar B.*, America rather than Ireland becomes the object of the writer's scorn.

"An Expatriate Looks at America" first appeared in the December 1976 *Atlantic Monthly* and serves as a comment on the story, "A Fairy Tale of New York." In the essay, Donleavy contrasts the America he knew growing up, that was, despite its flaws, a serene and happy place, with modern America, characterized by "big lust, big envy, big greed," a place that is "sad and bitter," where there is no chance "to feel any love," a "land of lies . . . vulgarity, obscenity and money. A country of sick hearts and bodies." With this latter America is contrasted an imperfect Ireland but an Ireland, nevertheless, that is a "toy country. With its dazzlingly white swans sailing on glistening ponds nested in the quiet green pastures. Straight out of a fairy tale. . . . And the simplicity. In this sea fresh moist air. Here all you had to do was keep warm. And dry. To eat. To sleep. To listen. And drink in the pubs. And before you froze to death you had to start doing all these things in a hurry."

Perhaps the surest mark of Donleavy's attitude toward Ireland is that he now resides there more or less permanently on Lough Owel in County Westmeath. The 1986 *J. P. Donleavy's Ireland; In All Her Sins and in Some of Her Graces* serves as an extended gloss on both "An Expatriate Looks at America" and "A Fairy Tale of New York." Its first section sets out Donleavy's bona fides to write on Ireland and the Irish; the second and longest part traces his several consecutive years in Ireland; the last and most important section has Donleavy sorting out the tangled skein of his feelings about Ireland and America and ends with him returning to Ireland with a final eulogy compounded of sentimentality and clear-eyed astringency. Perhaps. . . .

The short story, "A Fairy Tale of New York," which first appeared in the January 1961 *Atlantic Monthly* can be read with profit in the light of Donleavy's own shifting loyalties between the land of his birth and the land of his fathers.

"A Fairy Tale of New York"

Three o'clock in February. All the sky was blue and high. Banners and bunting and people bunched up between. Greetings and sadness.

Great black box up from the deep hold, swinging in the air high over the side of the ship. Some of the stevedores taking off their caps and hoods. With quiet whisperings, swiveling it softly on a trolley and pushing it into a shed.

Cornelius Christian standing under the letter C. The customs man comes over.

"I'm sorry sir about this. I know it isn't a time you want to be annoyed by a lot of questions but if you could just come with me over to the office. I'll try to get this over as quickly as possible. It's just a formality."

Walking across the pier through the tumbling carts, perfumes, furs and tweeds, the clanging chains, and into the little warm hut with type writers pecking. Tall dark customs man, his fist with a pencil on a piece of paper.

"I understand this happened aboard ship."

"Yes."

"And you're an American and your wife was foreign."

"Yes."

"And you intend burial here."

"Yes."

"It's just that we've got to make sure of these things because it can save a lot of trouble later. Don't want to burden you with anything unnecessary. Do you have any children travelling."

"Just my wife and myself."

"I understand. And are all your other possessions your own property, all personal effects. No fine art, antiques. You're not importing anything."

"No."

"Just sign here. Won't be anything else and if you have any trouble at all don't hesitate to get in touch with me right away. Here's my name and I'll straighten out any difficulty. Just Steve Kelly, customs'll get me. Vine funeral home phoned here just a while ago. I told him everything was all right and he says you can go see them at their office, or phone any time this afternoon or tonight. You take it easy."

"Thanks very much."

Customs man giving Christian a pat on the back.

"And say, Mr. Christian, see the stevedore, guy with the fur jacket. Just tell him Steve said you'd help me with my stuff. O.K. Don't worry about anything."

"Thanks."

Out through the grinding winches, clicking high heels, the stacks of gay baggage and colored labels. The great tall side of ship. And coming out to it as it sat on the sea in Cork Harbor. A stiff cold vessel. All of us bundled up as the tender tugged us out on the choppy water. And left the pink houses on the shore twirling early morning turf smoke in the sky. Black rivets on the ship's side. And I climbed up behind her. On the stairway swaying over the water. And now through this jumble and people gathering each other in their arms. This stevedore with fur jacket, a hook tucked under his arm. Hard muscles across his jaw.

"Excuse me, Steve said you'd help me with my stuff."

"Oh yeah, sure. Sure thing. Got much."

"Three small trunks, two bags."

"O.K. You just follow me all the way. I'll put the stuff down the escalator. Meet me at the bottom of the stairs. You want a taxi?"

"Please."

Under the roof of girders and signs. No tipping. Escalator rumbling down with trunks and crates. Crashing and crushing. The treatment they give things would break open her box. And they shout, This way folks. Five bucks, Grand Central. Three fifty, Penn Station. The stevedore has scars on his face, keeps his hands on his hips. "Mr. Christian, this guy will take you wherever you want to go. Stuff's on."

"Here."

"No no. I don't want any money. I don't take money for a favor. You'll do the same for somebody. That way it goes round the world."

"Thanks."

"Forget it."

Cornelius Christian opening the door into this gleaming cab. Horns honk everywhere. This driver with a green cap turns around.

"Where to, bud."

"I don't know. Have to think of somewhere."

"Look, I haven't got all day. I want to catch another boat coming."

"Do you know where I can get a room."

"I'm no directory bud."

"Anything."

"Place is full of hotels."

"Do you know anywhere I can get a room."

"Boardinghouse for a guy like you. Just sort of dumps I know. This is some time to start looking. Everybody wants me to find a room I'd be starving. As it is I make peanuts. O.K. I know a place West Side near the museum."

Taxi twisting away. With smiles and arms laden with coats others get into cabs. The trip is over. Some made friends. And we go up a hill to the roaring highway.

"It's none of my business but what's a guy like you doing coming all the way over here with nowhere to go. You don't sound like a guy got no friends, don't look it neither. O.K. Takes all sorts of people to make a world. Keep telling my wife that, she doesn't believe me. Thinks everybody's like her. Across there long."

"Went to college."

"Good education over there. Don't you feel lonely."

"No, don't mind being alone."

"That right. Got a right to feel that way if you want. But look at this, how can you feel alone. Everything looking like it's going to explode. And I got a face looks like a monkey. Know why. Because I used to own a pet shop till a relative got the big idea to make a lot of money. So what happens, I lose the whole thing. Now I'm driving a hack. Kick in your teeth and every guy after a fast buck. What a life. Keep going, keep going till you can't stop."

Christian folding white gloved hands in his lap. Cars stream along the highway. The wail of a police car zooming by.

"Look at that, some guy murdered his mother for a dime. Guy like me got to drink milk all day, live like a baby. I tell you, it's a crime. Sweat our guts out. Something awful. Goddam place jammed with foreigners. Think they'd stay in Europe instead of coming over here and crowding us out. You foreign."

"No."

"You could pass for foreign. It's O.K. with me mister if you're foreign. My mother came from Minsk."

Clouds come grey and east. Ice down there on the edge of the river. Smoky red weak sun.

Taxi turns down off the highway. Between the pillars holding up the street above. Serve beer in there. Bar stools and sawdust. Stevedores with hooks. They say keep your mouth shut and you won't get hurt. Safe in a crowd. Close in there by the elbows, next to the sleeves where all around me are just hands to shake and squeeze.

"O.K. mister here we are. Give me five bucks."

Red grey stone. An iron fence. Where the rich lived years ago. Tall steps up. First five dollars gone.

"Mister ring the bell downstairs and I'll take your bags, never get rich this way but you look lonely. Mrs. Grotz'll take care of you. She's crazy, but who isn't."

Mrs. Grotz, cross eyed, wrapped in a black coat and a collar of silver fox, standing in the door.

"What's your business mister."

"He's all right, Ma, just back from college over in Europe. Just ain't got no friends."

"Everyone ought to have friends."

"How do you know he wants them."

"Friendship means a lot, you crazy cab driver."

"My wife thinks I'm crazy too, but my kids think I'm God."

"Go home you crazy cab driver. Follow me mister, I got a nice room."

Carrying the bags behind this large bottom shifting up the stairs. In the onion smell. And scent of dust.

"Stairs for me is work mister. Go to do everything myself. Since my husband. He drop dead right in his underwear. Right while I was watching. Such a shock. Go to turn off the lamp and drop dead right on his face. I'm nervous and shaking like this ever since. So all husbands drop dead sometime. You think they have manners and do it quiet in the hospital."

A room with red curtains high on the windows. Double bed like one I saw in Virginia where once I was walking down a street and climbed in a train standing in the hot sun. Always wishing I could save the heat for the winter.

"Four fifty dollars a night or twenty dollars a week. Look what I supply, radio, shelves, gas stove, hot water. Don't play the radio loud."

"Could I let you know in a day or two how long I'll be staying."

"Give me till Friday and you got to make up your mind. You got a funny voice, you English. Learn to speak at college."

"Just a bit."

"Was that accent you was born with."

"I don't know."

"Give me four dollars and fifty cents."

New world. Opening up the suitcase on the bed. Turn on the oven. Out into the hall past another brown door. Everything in the dark. And cars go by in the street like boats and soft bubbles.

Find the switch for the light in this bathroom. Green towel crumpled on the floor. Lift the seat. All gentlemen are requested. When little you never lift the seat and mommy tell you lift the seat. Pick up the towel. Go back. This door has a name on it under the cellophane. And now the only thing I can do is wait and wait and wait. It's got to go away. She could never pack things and her bag's a mess. I told her she was sloppy, why don't you fold things up. And I've got to go down there. To a funeral parlor. Come all the way here to a funeral parlor. Just wash my face. No one to be with her. And I was so full of dying myself. I hope I know how to get down there after all these years. How much is it going to cost. Just end up being buried among a lot of strangers.

Christian steps down into the street. Grey tweed on his back. White gloves on his hands. Street full of shadows. And dark cars parked. And straight ahead the stale stiff fingers of trees. After so much ocean. And I don't know what to say to this man. He'll be in black or something. Do I have to give him a tip or a cigar. He might think I'm not sorry enough and can't concentrate on the death.

Grey tall windows of the museum. Down these steps to the subway. Chewing gum everywhere. Turnstile reminds me of horses. Coin goes in so neatly. Click through. Could step right under a train. Just let it roar right over me. What have you got to touch to get electrocuted. How would they know to take me and put me with Helen. It would have to be written down in my wallet. In case of death take me to the Vine funeral home and bury me with Helen. So slaughtered you could put me round her in the same casket. I just can't bear for you to be cold and you said last thing of all to put you in the ground. And you always wore a green shadow around your eyes. Came near me in your silk rustling dress you sounded hollow inside. Listening with your eyes. And the first day at sea I didn't want to see you spend the two dollars for a deck chair. Now I'd let you have it. I'd let you have anything now. Helen, you could have got two deck chairs or three and I'd have said nothing. It wasn't the money, I didn't want you to get cold because you looked so ill you'd freeze up there and no one knew how sick you were. And I pulled on the towel. Pulled it right out of your hands when you said you'd spend the two dollars. It wasn't the money, I'd tear up two dollars here right on this platform. God, it was the money. I've lost you.

Head bowed. A white knuckle rubbing under an eye. A man steps near.

"'Are you all right, buddy."

"Yes I'm all right. Just a lot of dust blown up in my eyes."

"O.K., buddy, just wanted to make sure."

Roaring train in the tunnel. Sweeping into the station. Train with the tickling noise under the floor. Doors growl shut. Then up, out, crossing each avenue, when the lights turn red and the cars slide up and stop. And it's all so new around me and so old. When I was young and walking here I heard a car screech and hit a boy. Saw the white shirt on his shoulder. And I wondered if all the people would be gathering around and keep him warm and not like me running away.

Where the street slants down, further on, tall buildings and a river. Closer. There it is. Double curtained doors, two evergreens on either side. Push through. God, what a place for you. Soft carpeted hall, luxurious in here. Warm green light flowing up the walls. So soft everything. This isn't bad. This door's open. It gleams and I'll knock. Man's black shoes and gartered black socks sticking out from a desk. They move and shine. His hand in front of me.

"Good evening, you're Mr. Christian aren't you."

"Yes."

"I'm sorry that you've had to come. I'm Mr. Vine, please sit down."

"Thank you."

"Will you smoke. Cigarette. Cigar."

"No thanks."

"Go ahead, make yourself comfortable. There are only a few little things here. Customs man who dealt with you telephoned after you left the pier. Very nice of him and I'll certainly do everything I can Mr. Christian. Only these to sign."

"Thanks."

"I'm not just an ordinary man in this business. It means a great deal to me and if there is any special help I can give anyone I'm really glad to do it. So understand that."

"That's nice of you."

"We can only do our best Mr. Christian. We try to understand sorrow. I've arranged burial at Greenlawn. Do you know New York."

"Yes, I was born here."

"Then you may know Greenlawn. One of the most beautiful cemeteries in the world and it's always a pleasure to visit. My wife's buried there as well and I know it's a place of great peace. We realize sorrow Mr. Christian. I'll take care of all the immediate details for you and you can have a chat with them later on. All under my personal direction. Arranged as soon as you wish."

"Could it be arranged for tomorrow morning."

"Yes. Will it give mourners time. The notice will only be in tomorrow's Daily News, only give anybody couple of hours to get here."

"I'll be the only mourner."

"I see."

"No one knew we were coming to New York."

"I can put you in our small suite there across the hall."

"Just for a few minutes. I want to keep it very short."

"I understand. In the way of flowers."

"I'd like something simple. Perhaps a wreath with My Helen."

"Of course. Something simple. I'll see to it myself. We try to make friends with sorrow Mr. Christian. That way we come to know it. You'd like us to use glass. For permanence."

"That's all right."

"And where are you located."

"Near the Museum of Natural History."

"I'm pleased you're near there. There's much to reflect upon in that building. We'll send our car for you."

"Is that anything extra."

"Included Mr. Christian. Shall I make it nine thirty, ten, whenever you wish."

"Nine thirty is fine."

"Mr. Christian, would you like now to have a little drink before you go. Some Scotch."

"Well I would. Are you Irish, Mr. Vine."

"My mother was. My father was German."

Mr. Vine's little snap of the head and blink of the eyes, crossing his soft canary carpet. Puts a neat white hand under an illuminated picture. Sunlight filtering through mountain pines and brass name beneath says In The Winter Sun. Panels drawing apart. Shelves of bottles, glasses, and the small white door of a refrigerator. He must drink like a fish. Pick him up like a corpse every night.

"Soda, Mr. Christian."

"Please."

"Now, the way you said that. Just one word. I can tell by your voice that you're an educated man Mr. Christian. I also like your name. I never had very much in the way of education. I was a wild-catter in Texas and then became the manager of an oil field. Wouldn't think of it to look at me, would you. I left school when I was nine years old. I've always wanted to be in this business but I was thirty before I got a chance to do a high school course. Did it in the Navy, then went to morticians' school when I came out. It makes you feel closer to people. It's dignified. And art. When you see what you can do for someone who comes to you helpless. To recreate them just as they were in life. Makes you able to soften things. You're a man I can talk to, a person who's got a proper mental attitude. I can always tell. There are some of them who make you sick. Only thing I don't like about the business are the phonies and I get my share of them. Here, have another, do you good."

"Thanks."

"Some people think I'm outspoken but I've given a lot of satis-faction and people put their whole families in my hands, even in a big city like this. I opened up another branch in the West Fifties. But I like it best here where I began. My two little girls are growing up into big women now. You meet people from all walks of life. I'm a bit of a philosopher and I feel anything you've got to learn you'll learn just through what you have to do with people, in that way I never miss an education. It's a fact, I never graduated. It's especially sad when I bury those who did. But everything is how a person con-ducts themselves. That's how I know all about you, customs man said over the phone you were a real gentleman. Would you like now for me to show you the establishment. If you don't it's all right."

"I don't mind."

"You'd like to feel that she was somewhere where she's really at home. Come along, we're empty now, there's just two at my other branch although it's a busy time of the year."

Mr. Vine rising. Gently bent forward. Flicks his head and bends one shoulder up to his ear. Frown around his eyes and hair sticks straight up on his head. Holding door ajar. Smiling with his tilted face.

"I never want to have an establishment of mine get so big you lose the personal touch. It must be warm and intimate to make peo-ple feel at home. I call the other branch a home, bit of an expense to change here because parlor is in the neon sign. I feel parlor is a word that lets you down. Something poor people have. I like the word home. I don't gloom at people. I smile. Death is a reunion. And it's a pause in the life of others."

A low corridor. Mr. Vine touches Mr. Christian slowly through the soft lights, soft step by soft step.

"These are the various suites. These two have their own private restrooms. Which has been of great success. I wouldn't say it to most people but certain functions get stimulated at the passing of a cherished one. You've noticed how I've used green light and how it glows from the walls, it's a special kind of glass that makes it do that. Only kind in New York. You don't mind me showing you around."

"No it's all right."

"In a few years I'm opening a branch out in the country. For some people the country signifies peace. You saw that picture, the forest, In The Winter Sun. Looking at that gave me the idea. It's not conducive to peace to come in off the street. And you hear that elevated train out there. Thinking of tearing it down. Won't be too soon for me. Shake the teeth out of your head. And in here is our chapel. I thought I'd make it round just like the world and again green is my motif. And out here again there's the door to our work rooms. We call it the studio."

"It's all very nice."

"That makes me feel good. I'm pleased. And I hope you'll be satisfied you dealt with me. I always want people to feel that. You can trust me and know I've got reverence for my work. To love your work is happiness. It means I meet someone like you too. I'm never wrong about people. I know the real tears of death and they don't go down the cheeks. And this is my largest room, the first one I ever used. One or two personages been here. Mr. Selk the manufacturer. I had that privilege. And we light a candle behind this green glass when someone is reposing. I think it gives, or rather, let me say, lends a sacredness to the occasion."

"Yes it does."

"You go home now. Put all bother out of your head. Get a good night's sleep. And I'm here, remember that, for any kind of request. Our car will be there in the morning. Good night, Mr. Christian."

Mr. Vine and Christian shook hands. Vine gave Christian a catalogue. Pushed open the door to the cold electric light of the street. A last smile, a wave.

The windy canyon of Park Avenue. Crossing a winter city. Cold heels on the pavement. Door men rubbing hands, clicking feet, looking up, looking down the street. Beginning to snow. Like the first winter I got to Dublin. When the skies were grey for months. And I bought thick woolen blankets at the shop and they smelled like sheep.

Christian, hands plunged in pockets, takes a lonely subway west and north. Back by the shadows of the museum. And along by the stone mansions. Where I live tonight.

Music coming from the door with the name under the cellophane. Dim light in the hall, a smell of wax in the air. Dust in the nose. Door slamming. Voice yelling. Pipe down.

Must go in through this door and sleep. Pull aside the thick red curtain so tomorrow the light will wake me up. Snow streams down under the street lamp. Someone else's house is more your own if it's filled with strangers. Helen, I wouldn't have brought you to a room like this. Makes me feel I'm casting some poverty on you because this isn't the type of place you would ever be. Yours were bathrooms shining with gleaming rails and hot towels. All this plastic junk. Couldn't have been in the studio while Vine and I were talking. Couldn't talk like that. But that's the way we talked. Like pies peaches or eggs. Helen's not a pie peaches or eggs. She's mine. Taking her away. Gone already. Where is she nearest to me. Asleep on top of my brain. Came with me all over the ship when I couldn't stand them staring at me everywhere I went and whispering. Our table out in the center of the dining room. They were all thinking of the day when they had the gala occasion with the paper hats and balloons and Helen just sat there at the table and wept pink handkerchief tucked up your sleeve and pearls like tiny drops from your face and none of them ever saw you again.

They even came up to my cabin door after you were dead to listen to hear if I was crying. And the steward who said they wouldn't do your washing. He stuck his brown face in the door and closed it quietly when he saw me prostrate on the bunk. And he slammed the door in your face. Both of us utterly helpless, could do nothing could say nothing. I held the three dollars in my fist and watched his brown hand come up from his side and pull them out and leave quietly closing the door. The waiter who filled our plates with things we didn't want and came over the second day and said your wife don't eat no more and I said no. And lunchtime he came back saying he was sorry he didn't know, the wine waiter just told him and he got me a plate covered in smoked salmon. He kept as far away as he could until the last meal when hovering for his tip he asked me if I was a refugee. Went out, looked down on the strange flat shore. And in that cabin, Helen, where you left your soul and I've got to lie a night here between these sleepless sheets without you.

Sound of snow shoveling in the street. Ship's whistle from the river. Tingling and banging in the pipes along the wall. Outside the wind blows hard and shivers the window. Knocks on the door.

"Mr. Christian there's a man for you down stairs."

"Please tell him I'm coming right away."

Christian looking into the street below. A man in dark coat, green shirt, black tie. No hat over his half bald head and grey wisps of hair. A black long car. Come for me. Can't keep him waiting. Can't stop them putting you in the ground under the snow.

Mrs. Grotz at the door, hunched, breath steaming in the cold air, her hands rubbing. Watching Christian pass and meet the chauffeur halfway down the steps. A solemn soft voice and placing a black cap on his head.

"You Mr. Christian. I'm from Vine funeral home."

"Sorry to keep you waiting."

Grotz edging her slippered feet out into the snow. Straining ears to listen. Her mouth open, eyes wide. "Hey what's the matter. Who's hurt. Some trouble. You from a funeral."

Christian stopping turning. Pulling gloves tighter on his hands. Looks up the steps at Mrs. Grotz.

"It's my wife."

"What's a matter, you got a wife. Where's your wife. What's matter your wife."

"She's dead."

"Mister. Oh mister."

The park ahead, little rolling hill in velvet snow. So white and Christmas. Birds taking white baths. Plows pushing it up, conveyer belts pouring it into trucks. I've no black tie. But a green one will suit Mr. Vine. People we pass look at this expensive car.

"You comfortable, Mr. Christian."

"Yes thanks."

"They're shoveling salt. Then when the snow melts the guy's tires in front shoot it up on your windshield. Some problem. They know it's going to snow every year, you'd think they'd do something."

"Yes."

A morning sun shining in slits along the cross town streets and in shadows across the park. These tall hotels. All so slender women walk in. Where the lights glow. And everybody's scared of everybody. And maybe Vine and his personal touch.

Vine Funeral Parlor, green neon sign. Sanitation department truck stopped outside. Bedraggled men filling it with snow. Mr. Vine waves his arm. Seems red in the face.

"Good morning, Mr. Christian. Had to tell these men to get this garbage truck out of here. Come this way, Mr. Christian."

Vine pushing open the door, taking Christian's coat. A firm handshake, nodding his head and twitching. Shaking water out of his ears after swimming. Now he beckons the way.

"It's my favorite music I've chosen, Mr. Christian. She's very beautiful. She's waiting for you. And just press the button when you want me. All right."

"Yes."

The room dark. Curtains drawn across the window to the street. And the green light flickering behind the glass. Casket gleaming and black. On a pedestal, the wreath illumined in green. My Helen written with the tiny white heads of lilies of the valley. A table with a Bible. Chairs along the wall for mourners. Even has my flowers lit up. He must rake in the money. I'm glad the casket's black. I'd die if it were green. Now go and kneel. So soft and I can't look at you. See just the tips of your knuckles. You don't have to shake Vine's hand, he almost broke mine. If you'd move. Encased in glass and you can't get up. Forgive me because I haven't got the courage to look at you. Because I'd see you dead forever. What happens to all the flesh and blood. No child. You leave nothing except the pain of missing you. And I didn't want the expense because a baby cost money. I wouldn't part with a penny. Only reason I had. I knew you were begging me and I'd always say let's wait. And we waited. Your casket's so smooth. Funny I put my hand along the bottom to see if it's stuck with chewing gum. Vine would never allow that. And although he must be half crazy he's given me comfort because I don't feel you're laughed at or joked over dead. Got to keep my head down or I'll look by accident. Thought I would cry and I can't. Helen, I wish we were different from everybody else. Scream for some sort of thing that makes us you and me. Neither of us nothing. And on the ship you said you wanted to lie down in the cabin. Those first Americans you met just tired you out. And I was so proud of bringing you back to my country. I wanted you to like them. And even after you'd gone, I didn't want anyone to come and touch me on the arm and back with a pat or two and say I'm sorry about it, about your wife, have courage or something, but I did want them. I wanted someone to show something. Anything. But not a soul on that damn ship came near me except for money. And each second you get further away from me. Dig the hole with the straight sides and before it gets dark they've got you covered up. And all the times I wished you were dead. So I could be free. But they were black thoughts of anger. But I thought them. Must get up. Look out the window.

Silently crossing the room. Parting the thick curtains to the late morning light of the street. And people hunching by in the cold. Over there Murray's best for bargains. Vine said press the button when you're ready. Does he take ordinary lipstick and put it on the lips. Or take it out of a pot they use on everyone. And all sorts of lips. And make them the kind that gleam and don't have cracks, and are red and now overripe. Vine had a green handkerchief in his pocket. What has he got against the color green. Most of his life must be whispering, nodding, hand rubbing, and the five words, we'll take care of everything.

Christian turning from the window. Mr. Vine leaning over the casket wiping the glass.

"Must be a little condensation on the inside Mr. Christian. But I hate anything to mark such a lovely face. Woman's lips are one of the most beautiful parts of her body. I can always tell a woman who looks at a man's lips when he talks instead of his eyes. Are you all right."

"Yes. Do you think we could leave now."

"Yes, a few minutes. Our large reposing room is busy this morning. We never know in this business."

"Mr. Vine I think maybe you're telling me too much about your business. I don't want to say anything but it's getting me down."

"What's the matter."

"I don't want to know about the business. It's getting me down."

"Don't get sore. I forget sometimes. I try to make everyone feel at home and not treat the funeral business as something strange. People ought to know about it. My own funeral is already arranged. But don't get sore. When it happened to me and it was my wife, I found I wanted some sort of distraction and because I arranged the services myself it made me feel better. And I thought you wanted to take an interest."

"This isn't distraction."

"Take it easy son. You're not alone in this, remember that. If I shot my mouth off, I'm sorry. I don't want to do that with nobody. But getting sore isn't going to bring her back. Beauty is the only thing you can remember. Try to remember beauty. Come on, I like you, be a sport."

"My wife's dead."

"I know that."

"Well, what the hell do you mean, sport."

"If I understand you correctly Mr. Christian, you'd rather I didn't conduct this any further. I can put you in the hands of an assistant if you prefer."

"All right, all right. I'm not the kind of person who wants to start trouble. Leave everything as it is. I'm just worried about money and what I'm going to do."

"Look. Listen to me. I want to tell you straight. I don't cut cash out of nobody. I don't conduct this business on those lines. You've got as long as you want and longer. Understand me. And if that isn't long enough I'll think of something. If you hadn't come here alone from another country I wouldn't take all this trouble but you seem to be a nice guy. I even thought you were a type for this profession and that's a compliment as far as I'm concerned. You're a gentleman. And when it's over, if you want to come back and see me, I'd like that. There's a place for you here, remember that. And if you make that decision, I'd like that. Shall we close it now, Mr. Christian. You're ready."

"All right."

"You can wait with the chauffeur."

"O.K."

"We'll take care of you. Christian, remember this isn't death. All this is life."

Walking out of the hall. Through the curtained doors. Putting up coat collars. The chauffeur smoking a cigarette. One of his grey wisps of hair hangs and goes into his ear. Christian coughs. Chauffeur getting out to open the door. A flash of yellow socks with white stripes.

The car pulls across the road. The hearse draws up in front of the Vine Funeral Parlor. Three men step out, rubbing their green gloved hands, stamping their feet on the hard snow. Elevated train roaring by on its iron trestle at the end of the street. The garbage truck has taken away its pile of snow. Chauffeur blows a smoke ring. And he turns around.

"Would you like this blanket, Mr. Christian. Put it round your legs in case you get cold. Always a few degrees colder when you get out of the city."

"Thanks."

"They are coming out now, Mr. Christian."

Mr. Vine standing aside, holding back a door. Coffin on four shoulders. Like an elephant, four black legs. Vine twitches his head, bends his ear to his shoulder and rubs. Goes in again. Comes out in a black overcoat, papers in his hands, hatless, eyes bright. Crossing the street. Stepping gingerly with his gleaming black shoes over the ridges of snow. Leaning in the window to the chauffeur.

"To expedite the journey, John, we'll take the West Side drive. Go up Park and cross-town on Fifty-seventh. You all right, Mr. Christian."

"Yes."

Vine pausing, a car sweeps by. He looks upon the rest of the world as something he will bury. His gravel voiced military manoeuvres. I guess we're going. No use fighting over it. He's only trying to be nice. First time anyone ever offered me a job.

Hearse pulling out. Vine signaling with his hand. And we follow. To the end of the street. Another elevated train. Wake Helen up. Window full of refrigerators there. Say they're giving them away for nothing, almost. Just step inside for bargains beyond belief. I feel like there's nothing around me in the world. Highway on the curve of the earth. Everybody knows why I'm in this car and Helen in hers.

The two black cars swiftly moved across Fifty-seventh Street. Past the opera house on the corner where people huddle up under the marquee waiting for the bus. The sky opens up where the city ends and the Hudson flows by. Up the ramp and flowing out into the stream of cars on the smooth white highway. Towering cold bridge high up over the Harlem River. Further and the red tiled roofs of houses behind the leafless trees. Along here the rich live down to the water's edge.

Road curves up through the second woods. A lake behind in the valley, a swamp and golf course. Great chains hang from post to post. Tall iron gates. Monuments inside with stained glass windows. Some with spires. Take you in here and lay you down. This cold day. Knuckles frozen. Breasts still. Where no love can taste. Tickle or tender.

Man in soft grey uniform salutes. Mr. Vine steps out across the snow. Up the steps into a grey stone building. Thin veins of ivy. Vine's coming to speak.

"There'll be a few minutes' delay. Just a formality. John, just pull the car up in front there and wait for us."

Chauffeur turning, ice crackling under the wheels.

"It's nothing, Mr. Christian. Just identification. They have to check everybody who's buried."

Coffin on the four shoulder disappearing under the canopy and into the squat building into the side of the hill. Be looking at her again. They give us no privacy. They'd shout back at me if I object. If you own a bird and it's flown away you run out to tell the whole world. And they tell you to shut up, you're disturbing the peace.

They come out. Shift and slide it in. Engines purr and we move. All these winding roads and trees. People under the stones. So white and white. Branches frozen silver. Paths crisscrossing everywhere. Tombs on the hills. Heads in sorrow. Lightning in a sky in summer. A bronze woman melted and cold on a door. Cowled face with a hand on her cheek. Hold away the world from the rich bones inside. A white marble man and woman stand up out of their rock. Look out over a sea. Where ships die. And men slip below the cold water. And where are you nearest.

No trees here. Four men stand by the tent. They've brushed away the snow. Fake grass over the mound of earth. Norman Vine comes back to this car.

"Mr. Christian. I thought since you've got no religious preference I might read something. And I've just told John to give a few dollars to the grave diggers if that's all right, it's the average tip."

"Yes."

"We'll go then."

Gently sloping hill. Snow lies for miles. Fades below the stiff dark trees. High grey sky. Know young girls you love. Take cigarettes from lips and kiss. A dance band plays. Grow up loving memories. Die leaving none. Except the Christmas Eves. When the whole year stops. These Polish hands who shovel on the dirt sit at poker tonight and drink wine. Downtown in the city. They take away a wife who clings to railings along the side walk and she screams and they lock her up. Can't see her any more because she's crazy. Love you as much as love can be. Cooking and washing. Mending and waiting. Each thread of body till it breaks.

"If you'll just stand there, Mr. Christian, I'll read these few words I've got here."

Cornelius Christian next to Norman Vine. Who holds out his little paper. Nods his head to the diggers. Straps stiffening under the coffin. Mist in the air from his voice.

"We are gathered here as brothers and we pray for another soul. The birds, trees, and flowers are life and they are around us to give birth in spring. This interment is life and for us the living, a beauty to ennoble our lives, to give us a kiss to caress us in our living pain. We gather to see the soil give one of us peace, to all love and remember her forever. We now give her to her God. O.K. boys."

15

WILLIAM KENNEDY

(b. 1928)

William Kennedy's *O Albany! An Urban Tapestry* appeared in 1983, the same year as *Ironweed*, the third of his now famous cycle of Albany novels. The apostrophizing title, suggestive of its author's love of his native city, also points to his profound knowledge of Albany, knowledge everywhere evident in the novels. *Ironweed* brought Kennedy the Pulitzer Prize for Fiction and the National Book Critics Circle Award for Fiction, and was instrumental in his award of a MacArthur Foundation "genius" grant of a quarter of a million dollars. It was not always thus.

The only child of working-class parents, Kennedy was born in 1928 in an Irish neighborhood in North Albany. Following a stint in the Army in the late 1950s, he graduated from Albany's Siena College and went to work as a reporter for the *Albany Times-Union,* experience put to use in his first novel, *The Ink Truck* (1969), which was not part of what he later called his "cycle" of novels. At age thirty-eight, he left Albany for newspaper work in Puerto Rico and Miami, returning in 1963 to Albany, the *Times-Union,* and an extensive series on ethnic neighborhoods, his first detailed foray into the material he was to master. Though he did quit full-time journalism not many years later, the published *Ink Truck* was not a commercial success and he spent several years as a book reviewer, part-time instructor at the State University's Albany campus, and sometime journalist. In the meantime, he was also writing novels.

Legs (1975), *Billy Phelan's Greatest Game* (1978), and *Ironweed* (1983)—the last rejected by thirteen publishers before being picked up by Viking at the urging of Saul Bellow—all deal with depression era Albany and its politicians, gamblers, journalists, down-and-outers, and born losers. More than this, they are novels of the sin and guilt and redemption that are native to the Irish-Catholic community at the source of Kennedy's work. Speaking of his canon in the *Recorder*, (Winter 1985) Kennedy said: "The reason why I chose the word 'cycle' [to describe the on-going novels] is that it's an open-ended and related series of novels." And more than one reader has noted that Kennedy is a "regionalist" in the way that Joyce is of Dublin and Faulkner of the American South, writers whose characters and incidents interweave and reverberate from one work to others. Thus, for example, Marcus Garvey, Albany's best-known criminal lawyer, who narrates *Legs*—Legs Diamond, a character reminiscent of Jay Gatsby—is briefly Francis Phalen's attorney in *Billy*, and in *Ironweed*, we learn that Garvey is responsible for getting Francis the graveyard job that opens *Ironweed;* and *Billy* and *Ironweed* are complementary in their stories of Francis and his son Billy, and both adumbrate the story of the Quinns.

Indeed, the most recent novel in the cycle is *Quinn's Book* (1988), about which Kennedy said (in the same *Recorder* interview): "I'm writing a book right now about Daniel Quinn, the grandfather of the Daniel Quinn who appears in *Legs* and *Billy Phelan* and *Ironweed*. It's the same family, and all the Daughertys are going to be there, and the ancestors of Katrina. Albany is still going to be Albany, but I'm going backward now [to as early as 1849] to discover patterns that anticipate the twentieth-century present. It's a preconsciousness I'm working on right now."

Amongst Irish-American writers Kennedy has admired are James T. Farrell, F. Scott Fitzgerald, John O'Hara, Eugene O'Neill, Flannery O'Connor, and Edwin O'Connor; but he has called James Joyce the greatest writer and most important influence on his own work. While Kennedy may have meant influence in the scrupulous sense and rendition of place, he may also have meant a number of other things, for example the surreal element—which Kennedy has observed of himself—to be found in the Nighttown section of *Ulysses* and in much of *The Ink Truck* and *Ironweed*. Or he may have meant the ubiquity of the father-son theme in *Portrait* and *Ulysses* and in *Billy* and *Ironweed*. Or, more broadly, readers can observe in Kennedy a Joycean virtuosity in the sheer inventiveness of incident and sustained verbal ingenuity and energy.

The following extract is chapter 2 of *Billy Phelan's Greatest Game*, a section in which many of the novel's types and themes are suggested. Written from the viewpoint of Martin Daugherty—the novel's other point-of-view character is Billy Phelan—fifty-year-old newspaperman, short story writer who is also working on a novel and has published two books of nonfiction, one on the Irish Troubles, this chapter strongly establishes the father-son motif. There is Martin's relationship with his fourteen-year-old son Peter, who, to his father's serious disappointment, has just entered a preseminary; as Martin's surrogate son there is Billy Phelan, master of the game of life in Albany's demimonde, who himself moves towards reconciliation with his own father, Francis Phelan, in this novel and in *Ironweed*. Finally, in the precipitating event of the novel, here introduced, there are the relationships between Bindy Mc-Call and his kidnapped son, Charlie Boy, and between Morrie Berman, whom the McCalls suspect of being involved in the kidnapping, and Morrie's father, who is cast opposite McCall politics, as the early stages of the father-son relationships are seen against the broad background of the three McCall brothers and the story of their rise over seventeen years to running Albany's Irish-Democratic machine, that is, running Albany. Because of his friendly relationship with the McCalls, Martin is asked by them to find out if Billy knows anything of the kidnapping because he has been seen in the company of Morrie Berman, suspected of involvement.

Billy Phelan's Greatest Game

Martin Daugherty, wearing bathrobe and slippers, sat at his kitchen table, bleeding from sardonic wounds. In the name of the Father, in the name of the Son, who will savor the Father when the Son is gone? He salted his oatmeal and spiced it with raisins, those wrinkled and puny symbols of his own dark and shriveling years. He chewed a single raisin, thinking of Scotty dead, his own son gone to the seminary. But the boy was alive and free to change his mind in time, and the bitter-sweetness of his thought flowed on his tongue: treasure lurking among the wrinkles.

"You're mad entirely," Mary Daugherty said when she saw him smiling and chewing, grim and crazy. She broke into laughter, the lilt of Connacht, a callous response to madness in her morning kitchen.

"You can bet your sweet Irish ass I'm mad," Martin said. "I dreamed of Peter, carried through the streets by pederast priests."

That stopped her laughter, all right.

"You're at the priests again, are you? Why don't you let it alone? He may not even take to it."

"They'll see he does. Fill him full of that windy God shit, called to the front, cherub off Main Street. Give the helping hand to others, learn to talk to the birds and make a bridge to the next world. Why did God make you if it wasn't to save all those wretched bastards who aren't airy and elite enough to be penniless saviors?"

"You're worried he'll be penniless, is that it?"

"I'm worried he'll be saved entirely by priests."

The boy, Peter, had been sitting in a web of ropes, suspended beyond the edge of the flat roof of home. Billy Phelan, in another suspended web, sat beside Peter, both of them looking at Martin as they lounged in the ropes, which were all that lay between them and the earth. Martin marveled at the construction of the webs, which defied gravity. And then Peter leaped off the web, face forward, and plummeted two stories. His body hit, then his head, two separate impacts, and he lay still. Two priests in sackcloth scooped him into a wheelbarrow with their shovels and one of them pushed him off into the crowded street. Billy Phelan never moved from his web. Martin, suddenly on the street, followed the wheelbarrow through the rubble but lost it. In a vacant lot he confronted a band of children Peter's age. They jogged in an ominous circle which Martin could not escape. A small girl threw a stone which struck Martin on the head. A small boy loped toward Martin with an upraised knife, and the circle closed in. Martin rushed to meet the knife-wielding attacker and flew at the boy's chest with both feet.

He awoke and squinted toward the foot of the bed, where the figure of an adolescent, wearing a sweater of elaborate patterns, leaned back in a chair, feet propped on the bedcovers. But the figure was perhaps beyond adolescence. Its head was an animal's, with pointed snout. A fox? A fawn? A lamb? Martin sat up, resting on his elbow for a closer look. The figure remained in focus, but the head was still blurred. Martin rubbed his eyes. The figure leaned back on the legs of the chair, feet crossed at the ankles, leisurely observing Martin. And then it vanished, not as a dream fading into wakefulness, but with a filmmaker's magic: suddenly, wholly gone.

Martin, half-erect, leaning on his elbow, heard Mary say the oatmeal was on the table. He thought of the illustrated Bible he had leafed through when he'd come home after Scotty's death, compulsively searching through the Old Testament for an equivalent of the man's sudden departure. He had found nothing that satisfied him, but he'd put out the light thinking of the engraving of Abraham and the bound Isaac, with the ram breaking through the bushes, and he had equated Isaac with his son, Peter, sacrificed to someone else's faith: first communion, confirmation, thrust into the hands of nuns and priests, then smothered by the fears of a mother who still believed making love standing up damned you forever.

Had Martin's fuzzy, half-animal beside visitor been the ram that saved Isaac from the knife? In a ski sweater? What did it have to do with Peter? Martin opened the Bible to the engraving. The sweatered animal at bedside bore no resemblance to the ram of salvation. Martin re-read what he had written years ago above the engraving after his first reading of the Abraham story: We are all in conspiracy against the next man. He could not now explain what precisely he had meant by that phrase.

It had been years since the inexplicable touched Martin's life. Now, eating his oatmeal, he examined this new vision, trying to connect it to the dream of Peter falling out of the web, to Peter's face as he left home two days before, a fourteen-year-old boy about to become a high school sophomore, seduced by God's holy messengers to enter a twig-bending pre-seminary school. Peter: the centerpiece of his life, the only child he would have. He raged silently at the priests who had stolen him away, priests who would teach the boy to pile up a fortune from the coal collection, to scold the poor for their indolence. The assistant pastor of Sacred Heart Church had only recently sermonized on the folly of striving for golden brown toast and the fatuity of the lyrics of "Tea for Two." There was a suburban priest who kept a pet duck on a leash. One in Troy chased a nubile child around the parish house. Priests in their cups. Priests in their beggars' robes. Priests in their eunuch suits. There were saints among them, men of pure love, and one such had inspired Peter, given him the life of Saint Francis to read, encouraging selflessness, fanaticism, poverty, bird calls.

Months ago, when he was shaping his decision, the boy sat at this same kitchen table poking at his own raisins, extolling the goodness of priests. Do you know any good men who aren't priests? Martin asked him.

You, said the boy.

How did I make it without the priesthood?

I don't know, but maybe sometimes you aren't good. Are you always good?

By no means.

Then did you ever know any men good enough to talk to the birds?

Plenty. Neil O'Connor talked to his ducks all day long. After four pints Marty Sheehan'd have long talks with Lackey Quinlan's goose.

But did the birds talk back?

You couldn't shut them up once they got going, said Martin.

Balance: that was what he wanted to induce in Peter. Be reverent also in the presence of the absence of God.

"I just don't want them to drown him in their holy water," Martin said to Mary Daugherty. "And I don't want him to be afraid to tell them to shove their incense up their chalices if he feels like coming home. There'll be none of that failed priest business in this house the way it was with Chickie Phelan." (And Martin then sensed, unreasonably, that Chick would call him on the telephone, soon; perhaps this morning.) "His mother and sisters wanted Chick to bring a little bit of heaven into the back parlor, and when he couldn't do it, they never forgave him. And another thing. I always wanted Peter to grow up here, grow up and beget. I don't want to see the end of the Daughertys after the trouble of centuries took us this far."

"You want another Daugherty? Another son? Is that what you're saying to me?"

"It's that I hate to see the end of a line. Any line. Think of all the Daughertys back beyond Patrick. Pirates stole *him* you know, made him a slave. That's how *he* got into the saint business."

"Ah," said Mary, "you're a talky man."

"I am."

"Are you through now?"

"I am."

"Why don't you be talky like that with the boy?"

"I was."

"You told him all that?"

"I did."

"Well, then?" said the wife and mother of the family. "Well?"

"Just about right," said Martin.

The talk had calmed him, and real and present things took his attention: his wife and her behind, jiggling while she stirred the eggs. Those splendid puffs of Irish history, those sweet curves of the Western world, sloping imagistically toward him: roundaceous beneath the black and yellow kimono he'd given her for the New York vacation. The memory of coupling in their stateroom on the night boat, the memory of their most recent coupling—was it three, four days ago?—suggested to Martin that screwing your wife is like striking out the pitcher. Martin's attitude, however, was that there was little point in screwing anyone else. Was this a moralistic judgment because of his trauma with Melissa Spencer, or merely an apology for apathetic constancy? Melissa in his mind again. She would be in town now with the pseudoscandalous show. She would not call him. He would not call her. Yet he felt they would very probably meet.

The phone rang and Miss Irish Ass of 1919 callipygiated across the room and answered it. "Oh yes, yes, Chick, he's here, yes. Imagine that, and he was just talking about you."

"Well, Chickie," said Martin, "are you ready for the big move today? Is your pencil sharpened?"

"Something big, Martin, really big."

"Big enough," said Martin; for Chick had been the first to reveal to him the plan concocted by Patsy McCall, leader of the Albany Democratic Party, to take control of the American Labor Party's local wing on this, the final day of voter registration. Loyal Democrats, of which Chick was one, would register A.L.P., infiltrate the ranks, and push out the vile Bolsheviks and godless socialists who stank up the city with their radical ways. Patsy McCall and his Democrats would save the city from the red stink.

"No, Martin, it's not that," Chick said. "It's Charlie Boy. The police are next door, and Maloney too. Him and half the damn McCall family's been coming and going over here all night long. He's gone, Martin. Charlie's gone. I think they grabbed him."

"Grabbed him?"

"Kidnapped. They've been using the phone here since four-thirty this morning. A regular parade. They'll be back, I know it, but you're the one should know about this. I owe you that."

"Are you sure of this, Chickie?"

"They're on the way back now. I see Maloney coming down their stoop. Martin, they took Charlie out of his car about four o'clock this morning. His mother got up in the night and saw the car door wide open and nobody inside. A bunch of cigarettes on the running board. And he's gone. I heard them say that. Now, you don't know nothing from here, don't you know, and say a prayer for the boy, Martin, say a prayer. Oh Jesus, the things that go on."

And Chick hung up.

Martin looked at the kitchen wall, dirty tan, needing paint. Shabby wall. Shabby story. Charlie Boy taken. The loss, the theft of children. Charlie was hardly a child, yet his father, Bindy McCall, would still think of him as one.

"What was that?" Mary asked.

"Just some talk about a story."

"Who or what was grabbed? I heard you say grabbed."

"You're fond of that word, are you?"

"It's got a bit of ring to it."

"You don't have to wait for a ring to get grabbed."

"I knew that good and early, thanks be to God."

And then, Martin grabbed the queenly rump he had lived with for sixteen years, massaged it through the kimono, and walked quickly out of the kitchen to his study. He sat in the reading rocker alongside a stack of Albany newspapers taller than a small boy, and reached for the phone. Already he could see the front pages, the splash, boom, bang, the sad, sad whoopee of the headlines. The extras. The photos. These are the McCall brothers. Here a recap of their extraordinary control of Albany for seventeen years. Here their simple homes. And now this. Here Charlie Boy's car. Here the spot where. Here the running board where the cigarettes fell. Here some famous kidnappings. Wheeeeee.

Martin dialed.

"Yeah," said Patsy McCall's unmistakable sandpaper voice box after the phone rang once.

"Martin Daugherty, Patsy."

"Yeah."

"I hear there's been some trouble."

Silence.

"Is that right or wrong?"

"No trouble here."

"I hear there's a lot of activity over at your place and that maybe something bad happened."

Silence.

"Is that right or wrong, Patsy?"

"No trouble here."

"Are you going to be there a while? All right if I come down?"

"Come down if you like, Martin. Bulldogs wouldn't keep the likes of you off the stoop."

"That's right, Patsy. I'll be there in fifteen minutes. Ten."

"There's nothing going on here."

"Right, Patsy, see you in a little while."

"Don't bring nobody."

In his bedroom, moving at full speed, Martin took off his blue flannel bathrobe, spotted with egg drippings and coffee dribbles, pulled on his pants over the underwear he'd slept in and decided not to tell his wife the news. She was a remote cousin to Charlie's mother and would want to lend whatever strength she had to the troubled family, a surge of good will that would now be intrusive.

The McCalls' loss intensified Martin's own. But where his was merely doleful, theirs was potentially tragic. Trouble. People he knew, sometimes his kin, deeply in trouble, was what had often generated his inexplicable visions. Ten years without this kind of divination, now suddenly back: the certainty Chick would call; the bizarre bedside visitor heralding the unknown; the death of Scotty followed by the kidnapping of Charlie. Coincidental trouble.

The inexplicable had first appeared a quarter century ago in late October, 1913, when, fresh from a six-month journalistic foray in England and Ireland, Martin found himself in Albany, walking purposefully but against logic north on North Pearl Street, when he should have been walking west on State Street toward the Capitol, where he had an appointment to interview the new governor, a namesake, Martin H. Glynn, an Albany editor, politician, and orator interested in Ireland's troubles. But a counterimpulse was on him and he continued on Pearl Street to the Pruyn Library, where he saw his cousin, a fireman with steamer eight, sitting on the family wagon, the reins of the old horse sitting loosely on his knees. He was wearing his knitted blue watch cap, a familiar garment to Martin. As their eyes met, the cousin smiled, lifted a pistol from his lap, pointed it at the horse, then turned it to his right temple and pulled the trigger. He died without further ado, leaving the family no explanation for his act, and was smiling still when Martin caught the reins of the startled horse and reached his cousin's side.

Nothing like that happened to Martin again until 1925, the year he published his collection of short stories. But he recognized the same irrational impulse when he was drawn, without reason, to visit the lawyer handling his father's libel suit against an Albany newspaper, which had resurrected the old man's scandal with Melissa. Martin found the lawyer at home, in robust health, and they talked of Martin's father, who at that point was living in New York City. Two hours after their talk the lawyer died of a heart attack walking up Maiden Lane, and the task of finding a new lawyer for his father fell to Martin.

That same year Martin tuned in the radio at mid-morning, an

uncharacteristic move, and heard of the sinking of the excursion steamer *Sweethearts* in the Hudson River below Kingston. He later learned that a girl he once loved had gone down with the boat. He began after this to perceive also things not related to trouble. He foresaw by a week that a *Times-Union* photographer would win six thousand dollars in the Albany baseball pool. He was off by only one day in his prediction of when his father would win the libel suit. He knew a love affair would develop between his wife's niece from Galway and an Albany bartender, two months before the niece arrived in Albany. He predicted that on the day on that love's first bloom it would be raining, a thunderstorm, and so it was.

Martin's insights took the shape of crude imagery, like photographs intuited from the radio. He came to consider himself a mystical naturalist, insisting to himself and to others that he did not seriously believe in ghosts, miracles, resurrection, heaven, or hell. He seasoned any account of his beliefs and his bizarre intuition with a remark he credited to his mother: There's no Santa Claus and there's no devil. Your father's both. He dwelled on his visions and found them comforting, even when they were false and led him nowhere and revealed nothing. He felt they put him in touch with life in a way he had never experienced it before, possessor of a power which not even his famous and notorious father, in whose humiliating shadow he had lived all his years, understood. His father was possessed rather by concrete visions of the Irish in the New World, struggling to throw off the filth of poverty, oppression, and degradation, and rising to a higher plane of life, where they would be the equals of all those arrived Americans who manipulated the nations' power, wealth, and culture. Martin was bored with the yearnings of the immigrant hordes and sought something more abstract: to love oneself and one's opposite. He preferred personal insight to social justice, though he wrote of both frequently in his column, which was a confusion of radicalism, spiritual exploration, and foolery. He was a comedian who sympathized with Heywood Broun, Tom Mooney, and all Wobblies, who drank champagne with John McCormack, beer with Mencken, went to to the track with Damon Runyon, wrote public love letters to Marlene Dietrich whenever her films played Albany, and who viewed America's detachment from the Spanish Civil War as an exercise in evil by omission.

He also wrote endlessly on a novel, a work he hoped would convey his version of the meaning of his father's scandalous life. He had written twelve hundred pages, aspiring to perhaps two hundred or less, and could not finish it. At age fifty he viewed himself, after publication of two books of non-fiction, one on the war, the other a personal account of the Irish troubles, plus the short story collection and innumerable articles for national magazines, as a conundrum, a man unable to define his commitment or understand the secret of his own navel, a literary gnome. He seriously valued almost nothing he wrote, except for the unfinished novel.

He was viewed by the readers of the *Times-Union*, which carried his column five days a week, as a mundane poet, a penny-whistle philosopher, a provocative half-radical man nobody had to take seriously, for he wasn't quite serious about himself. He championed dowsing and ouija boards and sought to rehabilitate Henry James, Sr., the noted Albanian and Swendenborgian. He claimed that men of truest vision were, like James, always considered freaks, and he formed the International Brotherhood of Crackpots by way of giving them a bargaining agent and attracted two thousand members.

His column was frequently reprinted nationally, but he chose not to syndicate it, fearing he would lose his strength, which was his Albany constituency, if his subject matter went national. He never wrote of his own gift of foresight.

The true scope of that gift was known to no one, and only his family and a few friends knew it existed at all. The source of it was wondered at suspiciously by his Irish-born wife, who had been taught in the rocky wastes of Connemara that druids roamed the land, even to this day.

The gift left Martin in 1928, after his fortieth birthday debauch with Melissa, the actress, his father's erstwhile mistress, the woman who was the cause of paternal scandal. Martin returned home from the debauch, stinking of simony, and severely ill with what the family doctor simplistically diagnosed as alcoholic soak. Within a week Martin accurately sensed that his mystical talent was gone. He recuperated from the ensuing depression after a week, but rid himself of the simoniacal stink only when he acceded to his wife's suggestion, and, after a decade of considering himself not only not a Catholic but not even a Christian, he sought out the priest in the Lithuanian church who spoke and understood English only primitively, uttered a confession of absurd sins (I burned my wife's toenail parings three times) and then made his Easter Duty at Sacred Heart Church, driving out the odor of simony with ritual sacrilege.

He shoved his arms into the fresh shirt Mary Daugherty had ironed. A fresh shirt every day, Mary insisted, or you'll blow us all out the window with the B.O. Martin pushed into his black shoes, gone gray with months of scuffs and the denial of polish, threw a tie once around his neck in a loose knot, and thrust himself into his much abused suit coat. A *sughan*, Mary said. You've made a *sughan* of it. Ah well, all things come alike to all, the clean and the unclean, the pressed and the unimpressed.

In the bathroom he brushed away the taste of oatmeal, splashed his face with cold water, flattened his cowlick with the hairbrush, and then salt-stepped down the stairs, saying as he sped through the kitchen: "I've got a hell of a story, I think, Mary. I'll call you."

"What about your coffee? What about your eggs?"

But he was already gone, this aging firefly who never seemed to his wife to have grown up quite like other men, gone on another story.

Martin Daugherty had once lived in Arbor Hill, where the Mc-Calls and the Phelans lived, but fire destroyed the house of his child-hood and adolescence, and the smoke poisoned Katrina Daughtery, his mother, who escaped the flames only to die on the sidewalk of Colonie Street in her husband's arms, quoting Verlaine to him: " . . . you loved me so!" "Quite likely—I forget."

The fire began in the Christian Brothers School next door, old Brother William turned to a kneeling cinder by the hellish flames. The fire leaped across the alley and consumed the Daugherty house, claiming not only its second victim in Martin's mother, but also his father's accumulation of a lifetime of books, papers, and clippings that attested to his fame and infamy, and two unfinished plays. Edward Daugherty left Arbor Hill forever after the fire and moved into the North End of the city, politely evicting the tenants in his own father's former home on Main Street.

This was the house Edward Daugherty's parents had built on the edge of the Erie Canal the year before Martin was born, and had lived in until they died. After Edward's first stroke, Martin moved into the house also, with his wife and son, to nurse his father back to independence. But the man was never to be well again, and Martin remained in the house even until now, curator of what he had come to call the Daugherty Museum.

Martin parked his car on Colonie Street in front of the vacant lot where his former home had stood before it burned. He stepped out onto the sidewalk where he'd once pitched pennies and election cards, and the charred roots of his early life moved beneath his feet.

Chick Phelan peered out of the upstairs bay window of the house next to the empty lot. Martin did not wave. He looked fleetingly at the outline of the foundation of the old place, slowly being buried by the sod of time.

Patsy McCall's house was kitty-corner to the empty lot and Martin crossed the street and climbed the stoop. He, the Phelans, the McCalls (Bindy lived two doors above Patsy), and all the other youths of the street had spent uncountable nights on this stoop, talking, it now seemed, of three subjects: baseball, the inaccessibility of the myriad burgeoning breasts that were poking themselves into the eyeballs and fluid dreams of every boy on the street, and politics: Would you work for Billy Barnes? Never. Packy McCabe? Sure. Who's the man this election? Did you hear how the Wally-Os stole a ballot box in the Fifth Ward and Corky Ronan chased 'em and got it back and bit off one of their ears?

Martin looked at his watch: eight thirty-five. He rang the doorbell and Dick Maloney, district attorney of Albany County, a short, squat man with an argumentative mouth, answered.

"You're up early, Dick, me boy."

"Am I?"

"Are you in possession of any news?"

"There's no news I know of."

And Maloney pointed toward the dining room, where Martin found Patsy and Matt McCall, the political leaders of the city and county for seventeen years. Cronies of both brothers sat with them at the huge round table, its white tablecloth soiled with coffee stains and littered with cups, ashes, and butts. On the wall the painted fruit was ripening in the bowl and the folks were still up at Golgotha. Alongside hung framed, autographed photos of Jim Jeffries, Charlie Murphy of Tammany, Al Smith as presidential candidate, and James Oliver Plunkett who had inscribed the photo with one of his more memorable lines: "Government of the people, by the people who were elected to govern them."

"Morning, gentlemen," Martin said with somber restraint.

"We're not offering coffee," said Patsy, looking his usual, overstuffed self. With his tight haircut, rounded jowls, and steel-rimmed specs, this Irish-American chieftain looked very like a Prussian puffball out of uniform.

"Then thanks for nothing," said Martin.

The cronies, Poop Powell, and ex-hurley player and ex-cop who drove for the McCalls, and Freddie Gallagher, a childhood pal of

Matt's who found that this friendship alone was the secret of survival in the world, rose from the table and went into the parlor without a word or a nod. Martin sat in a vacated chair and said to Patsy, "There's something tough going on, I understand."

"No, nothing," said Patsy.

The McCalls' faces were abulge with uncompromising gravity. For all their power they seemed suddenly powerless confronting personal loss. But many men had passed into oblivion for misjudging the McCalls' way with power. Patsy demonstrated it first in 1919 when he campaigned in his sailor suit for the post of city assessor and won, oh wondrous victory. It was the wedge which broke the hold the dirty black Republican sons of bitches had had on the city since '99. Into the chink Patsy made in the old machine, the Democrats, two years later, drove a new machine, the Nonesuch, with the McCalls at the wheel: Patsy, the savior, the *sine qua non*, becoming the party leader and patron; Matt, the lawyer, becoming the political strategist and spokesman; and Benjamin, called Bindy, the sport, taking over as Mayor of Nighttime City.

The three brothers, in an alliance with a handful of Protestant Yankee aristocrats who ran the formal business of the city, developed a stupendous omnipotence over both county and city, which vibrated power strings even to the White House. Democratic aspirants made indispensable quadrennial pilgrimages to genuflect in the McCall cathedral and plead for support. The machine brushed the lives of every Albany citizen from diapers to dotage. George Quinn often talked of the day he leaped off the tram at Van Woert Street, coming back in uniform from France, and was asked for five dollars by John Kelleher on behalf of Patsy's campaign for the assessorship. George gave not five but fifteen and had that to brag about for the rest of his life.

"I have to say it," Martin said, looking at Patsy, his closest friend among the brothers. "There's a rumor around that Charlie was kidnapped last night."

The gravity of the faces did not change, nor did the noncommittal expressions.

"Nothing to that," said Matt, a tall, solid man, still looking like the fullback he once was, never a puffball; handsome and with a movie actor's crop of black hair. When he gained power, Matt put his college football coach on the Supreme Court bench.

"Is Charlie here?" Martin asked him.

"He went to New York," Matt said.

"When was that?"

"None of your goddamn business," said Patsy.

"Patsy, listen. I'm telling you the rumor is out. If it's fake and you don't squelch it, you'll have reporters crawling in the windows."

"Not these windows I won't. And why should I deny something that hasn't happened? What the hell do you think I am, a goddamn fool?"

The rising anger. Familiar. The man was a paragon of wrath when cornered. Unreason itself. He put Jigger Begley in tears for coming drunk to a rally, and a week later Jigger, Patsy's lifelong friend, quit his job in the soap factory, moved to Cleveland, and for all anybody knew was there yet. Power in the voice.

Martin's personal view was this: that I do not fear the McCalls; that this is my town as much as theirs and I won't leave it for any of them. Martin had committed himself to Albany in part because of the McCalls, because of the promise of a city run by his childhood friends. But he'd also come back to his native city in 1921, after two years with the A.E.F. and a year and a half in Ireland and England after that, because he sensed he would be nothing without his roots, and when, in 1922, he was certain of this truth he went back to Ireland and brought Maire Kiley out of her Gaelic wilderness in Carraroe, married her in Galway, and came to Albany forever, or at least sixteen years now seemed like forever. So to hell with Patsy and his mouth and the whole bunch of them and their power. Martin Daughtery's complacency is superior to whatever abstract whip they hold over him. But then again, old fellow, there's no need to make enemies needlessly, or to let the tone of a man's voice turn your head.

"One question then," Martin said with his mildest voice, "and then I'm done with questions."

The brothers waited solemnly.

"Is Bindy in town?"

"He's in Baltimore," said Matt. "At the races with his wife."

Martin nodded, waited, then said, "Patsy, Matt. You say there's nothing going on and I have to accept that, even though Maloney looks like he's about to have twins on the stair carpet. But very obviously something *is* happening, and you don't want it out. All right, so be it. I give you my word, and I pledge Em Jones's word, that the *Times-Union* will not print a line about this thing, whatever it is. Not the rumor, not the denial of the rumor, not any speculation. We will not mention Charlie, or Bindy, or either of you in any context other than conventional history, until you give the go-ahead. I don't break confidences without good reason and you both know that about me all my life. And I'll tell you one more thing. Emory will do anything in his power to put the newspaper behind you in any situation such as the hypothetical one we've not been discussing here. I repeat. Not discussing. Under no circumstances have we been discussing anything here this morning. But if the paper can do anything at all, then it will. I pledge that as true as I stand here talking about nothing whatsoever."

The faces remained grave. Then Patsy's mouth wrinkled sideways into the makings of a small grin.

"You're all right, Martin," he said. "For a North Ender."

Martin stood and shook Matt's hand, then Patsy's.

"If anything should come up we'll let you know," Matt said. "And thanks."

"It's what's right," Martin said, standing up, thinking: I've still got the gift of tongues. For it was as true as love that by talking a bit of gibberish he had verified, beyond doubt, that Charlie Boy McCall had, indeed, been grabbed.

"You know I saw Charlie last night down at the Downtown alleys. We were there when Scotty Streck dropped dead. I suppose you know about that one."

"We knew he was there," Patsy said. "We didn't know who else."

"We're working on that," Matt said.

"I can tell you who was there to the man," Martin said, and he ticked off names of all present except the sweeper and one bar customer, whom he identified by looks. Matt made notes on it all.

"What was Berman doing there?" Patsy asked.

"I don't know. He just turned up at the bar."

"Was he there before Charlie got there?"

"I can't be sure of that."

"Do you think he knew Charlie would be at the alleys?"

"I couldn't say."

"Do you know Berman?"

"I've been in his company, but we're not close."

"Who is close to him?"

Martin shook his head, thinking of faces but connecting no one intimately to the man. Then he said, "Billy Phelan seems to know him. Berman backed him in last night's match and did the same once before, when Billy played pool. He seems to like Billy."

"Do you trust Phelan?" Matt asked.

"No man in his right mind would trust him with his woman, but otherwise he's as good as gold, solid as they come."

"We want to keep tabs on that Berman fellow," Patsy said.

"You think he's connected to this situation?" and both Patsy and Matt shrugged without incriminating Berman, but clearly admitting there certainly was a situation.

"We're keeping tabs on a lot of people," Patsy said. "Can you ask young Phelan to hang around a while with Berman the next few days, say, and let us know where he goes and what he says?"

"Ahhhh," said Martin, "that's tricky but I guess I can ask."

"Don't you think he'll do it?"

"I wouldn't know, but it is touchy. Being an informer's not Billy's style."

"Informer?" said Patsy, bristling.

"It's how he might look at it."

"That's not how I look at it."

"I'll ask him," Martin said. "I can certainly ask him."

"We'll take good care of him if he helps us," Matt said. "He can count on that."

"I don't think he's after that either."

"Everybody's after that," Patsy said.

"Billy's headstrong," Martin said, standing up.

"So am I," said Patsy. "Keep in touch."

"Bulldogs," said Martin.

16

$\underline{\text{M}\text{AUREEN HOWARD}}$
(b. 1930)

Maureen Howard confessed in the April 25, 1982, *New York Times Book Review*, "I find too many scenes and stories that instruct me on why I've become a writer—odd encounters with language in a mixed neighborhood, mostly working class, where by the mere inflection of 'Hello' you could tell that the pert young widow had lost her beau, the Montours were coming up in the world this week, the Drews had not paid their grocery bill." Howard's talent is capturing telling moments, echoing nuances, blending humor and pathos.

She has written five successful Irish-American novels, *Not a Word about Nightingales* (1961), *Bridgeport Bus* (1966), *Before My Time* (1975), *Grace Abounding* (1982), and *Expensive Habits* (1986), and short fiction for the "little mags." "The Three Pigs of Krishna Nuru" appeared in the *Partisan Review* in the Winter issue, 1971–72.

Maureen Howard was born in Bridgeport, Connecticut, on June 28, 1930, to William L. and Loretta (Burns) Keans. She was graduated from Smith College in 1952, after which she found jobs in publishing and advertising. In 1954 she married Daniel F. Howard, by whom she had a daughter. The Howards divorced in 1967. In 1968 she married David J. Gordon, a college professor. She has taught literature, drama, and creative writing at Santa Barbara and the New School for Social Research, and edited *Seven American Women Writers of the Twentieth Century*. Among the contributors to that volume were Mary McCarthy and Flannery O'Connor.

Maureen Howard says that she writes fiction because she cannot sing or dance. She is a skillful stylist who illustrates the best in Irish-American fiction. She probably sings and dances, too.

"The Three Pigs of Krishna Nuru"

The day that Jimmy Cogan was accepted at Fordham was a happy one for his family. The notice came in the morning mail on a Saturday before he left for work. He whistled as he ran downstairs even though he missed the express that would get him to the *Chateau de Chien* by eleven o'clock. On Conner Street the cement sparkled with a thousand flickering specks of mica he had never seen before. He was not usually a cheerful boy but this morning the world was filled with promises which he never believed would be for him. His mother and father had smiled until he thought their faces would break.

At the kiosk he bought a copy of *Newsweek* determined to attack the problems of the day with a keen mind. The picture on the cover was of a young Democratic Senator, a bright hope, handsome as an actor. Jim had never heard the man's name, a fact that would never have troubled him in the past; though he had read every word from the mouth of Ché Guevara, politics had always seemed too remote and meaningless. The war was still on—his peace button thrown in a drawer with paperclips and cuff links. His peace poster over the bed had popped its tacks and now lay in a roll on the closet shelf. Today he felt that he must know something beyond his blind acceptance of a cause. Beginning now, with this magazine on the subway. There was not a moment to be lost.

For weeks he had done nothing but stare into space, thinking of the bare body of the girl he slept with—Shelly Waltz. He had tried calling her his girl but that was wrong: there was no way in which he possessed her. She was somewhat crazy, a wandering angry girl. Though she had a home she seemed more a child of the streets. Days went by when he did not see her, then she would be mysteriously available again, waiting for him outside school or sitting on a curbstone near his house. When they made love he felt drawn into *her* defiance of the world (operation total crap), so they touched and felt and were finally bound together in her fierce beliefs. Often when he thought of her nakedness it was to see her still arguing, arms thrown up in exasperation at one of his middle-class notions, breasts jiggling as she stamped her foot in protest. Only in fantasy could he have Shelly as he wanted her—naked still, but smooth, compliant, free of all the mimeographed texts that proclaimed her free. Sometimes he would dress her in his mind—in short skirts and a clean blouse like other girls wore, stockings and shoes. She looked up at him and listened for once: in this impossible vision he found that he could love Shelly Waltz.

Today, as a sacred vow, he would not think of her. He had left his family in a state of exultation. His victory was theirs. The twins were loud and high spirited for a change, asking if he could get them tickets for the Fordham basketball season now. After a powerful hug his mother had stood back against his father's chest in a conscious pose— looking as parents are supposed to look, solid and self-congratulatory. It was a happy day. "I am on the right course at last," thought Jim, ignorant as Percival and confident that there was still a quest for the chosen: "I am ready now. There is no time to be lost." The young senator, he read, often worked an eighteen-hour day, slept in his office, was capable of working all night as he had recently on his proposed amendment to a disarmament bill. When defeated in committee the next day he had started to redraft the amendment at once, dictating on his way home into a little Japanese tape recorder his children had given him for Christmas. Ten years ago as a Junior congressman he had cried openly in front of his staff upon hearing of the execution of Caryl Chessman (a footnote in the magazine identified Chessman for Jim Cogan as a convicted rapist, murderer, pervert, sentenced to death who after an arduous, inspired and inspiring battle, etc. . . .)."I cry," the young statesman said, "not for the dead, but for the terrible limits upon the minds of men. That will have me in tears for the rest of my life."

Sitting next to Jim was a Puerto Rican girl in tight pants and a white sweater cut like a man's undershirt. The top of her breasts were dark. A miraculous medal hung on a thin gold chain around her neck. She was meticulous in her movements, looking at Jim with the expert blank eyes of an experienced subway rider, opening her purse with fussy delicate fingers extracting a folded Kleenex from an orderliness that bordered on stupidity. He had gone out with a girl like that when he was fifteen, in the first throes of calling up girls and going to dances. She had gyrated as though her whole body was filled with sex, in a trance smiling her clean smile at him out of her private sensual world and like this one whose heavy thigh touched his, had turned to stone when the music stopped. *Her* little gold chain had dangled a cross, and her father's name was Jesus. That had always killed him. She had looked good out there with him in the lights and for months he was the envy of his friends. He was never

allowed to touch her—she was saving it. She carried movie magazines inside her notebook and had nothing to say to him. He was her
foreigner, some girl friend, cuento; she had quit school the day she
turned sixteen and married some guy who had probably been into
her for months.

"Hot," Jim said to the girl next to him who was carefully blotting
her upper lip. When he spoke she got up at once and moved to the
door. *Cuento,* he said to himself, one of his few Spanish words.
Shelly was something else, indifferently willing and ready at all
times. He thought about this for a while, seeing her bedraggled hair
like tangled honey, her narrow naked body, wondering when she
would show up next and in a moment the wonder turned to desire.
At Fifty-ninth Street Jim got off, full of sorrow—already his resolution had weakened. Knowing that he was late for work he stood on a
windy island facing the Coliseum and read to the end of the article:

> When faced with an audience of today's youth the Senator in-
> sisted that our history was still important, that we must take heart
> from the courageous dissenters of the past. On his desk last week
> his secretary had found this note midst the disorder of a hundred
> practical details: "Like the course of the heavenly bodies, harmony
> in national life is a resultant of the struggle between contending
> forces. In frank expression of conflicting opinion lies the greatest
> promise of wisdom in governmental action; and in suppression lies
> ordinarily the greatest peril." (Louis Brandeis, 1920)

Across the street at the Coliseum the Northeastern Gifts and
Greeting Card show was announced on the marquee: clusters of what
Jim Cogan now saw to be disgusting people were trailing in through
the big glass doors. Old ladies mostly in pale spring coats and foolish
hats, a few hopeless slopeshouldered men with their wives. He was
filled with a loathing as much for their bodies as for their purposeless
day. He marched through them swiftly, when suddenly he came to a
woman laughing uncontrollably, her cheeks like withered dumplings,
her weak eyes ringed hideously with bright jeweled glasses. Her
hand was full of dollar bills which she pressed upon her friend in
some private dispute, and turning she slapped her hand into Jim's
face and the bills fluttered away. "Cunt," he said to her in the moment before she chased her money across the broad sidewalk and
into the gutter. It was a triumph that died by the time he got to the
next corner: he would soon be at work and there lay his betrayal. At

the *Chateau de Chien* he clipped, combed, perfumed and polished the nails of quivering pedigreed poodles. He had been quick to learn. The money was good. His boss, Mimi Devereux, large bones, deep voice, wrists and hips of a tennis champ, had wanted a boy. Jimmy Cogan was a sweetheart, tall, slim, polite—crewneck sweater and sport coat. Oh, where had they gone, these college-type boys. Mimi, thirty-five and unmarriageable, fell in love with him at once. Her customers were ecstatic. If they had a son—instead of a poodle, presumably—he would be like this. The dogs were handed to him with confidence. Jim Cogan was gentle, calm—such a boy. He remembered Belinda, Amie, Serge and Watteau—and hated them all. Hated his job, and above all hated his part in the sham love of these idle, neurotic women for their pets. Their admiration showered on him like slime, a perversion of the elements.

He did it for money, for money, he said, because there was no money to educate him and he would have to do that himself. Because he had listened to the pleadings of his mother for the last time: in some way the *Chateau de Chien* touched upon a world she had seen once—an Irish secretary's view of the parlor. The job was *nice,* the big world and one step up from being a camp counselor. It was wacky. It was experience. Couldn't he look at it that way, his mother asked. For three weeks he had—grist for the mill—a fund of funny stories. And when he handed a dog back, washed, pouffed, beribboned, rhinestone collar in place, sweet as a farting rose, he smiled and always remembered the owner's name. Last week he had passed Hi-Marx Llewelyn into the loving arms of his mistress, "Looks like you're all done up too, Mrs. Schlotzer!" That was worth a five dollar tip and though he murmured the obligatory "Screw you" as she strutted out the door, it had not saved him. In three weeks he had made three hundred dollars: it was fantastic for a boy of seventeen. What did the world expect of him anyway?

He had not wanted the truth for himself: coupled with the money there was sex, the grinning American two-headed eagle. By working midtown he could easily meet Shelly, go with her on her travels in the city, appease the final obsession. Now that he was making so much money his parents had shut up about his late hours.

The minute he walked in the door he told Mimi Devereux that he was accepted at Fordham. She was relieved, thinking that something had happened to him on the way downtown. Now he could go right on working during college—"Great," she said. "that's too great!" Mimi had an accent that Jim could not place, a plain direct speech full of buoyant tones as different from anything he knew as an actress in an English movie. For reasons beyond him she was not supposed to be running a poodle parlor. "I'm something of a rebel," she told Jim. He loved that—Mimi in her neat skirts and sweaters, loafers and a man's wristwatch. Something of a rebel. As if it were a school regulation she never wore slacks, though it would have been easier with the dogs. When the shop closed she split a beer with Jim. She told him that the customers didn't know a good animal when they saw one. They cared nothing for breeding. Last year there was a standard black from Central Park West, clipped in a show cut with the confirmation of a winner, bred out of Champion Pierrot Prime, and last week when he came in he looked like a flabby, slouching child. It was criminal. Together, they made fun of the customers and Jim felt that he and Mimi were of one age, one mind. "You're a natural," she said to Jim Cogan as he swept up the clippings. High praise, indeed.

"Yes, I'm something of a rebel," Mimi said. "I've just got to work with dogs." He wondered what it was she should be doing, what she had left or put aside for the *Chateau de Chien*. Her program was to clean up on these well-heeled floozies with their pathetic ruined poodles and get hold of a kennel—Kerry Blue terriers were her passion—to breed and show real dogs. Despite her awkward size Mimi handled the dogs gracefully, with an economy of movement Jim had never quite attained even with his best shots on the basketball court. She had a singleness of purpose, a dedication that was pure and appealing. Jim found he could not belittle her to his mother or explain what seemed so right about his boss to Shelly Waltz.

"What a sell-out," Shelly said, "smiling at those dead people and that dyke."

"She's not," he said. "Mimi is something of a rebel."

Now Jim saw himself on the straight and narrow, going to college. He must look at things honestly: his mother and father had stood together this morning content and happy, like they never had through all the years. *He* was going to college. *Their* dreams were fulfilled. They had done everything in their power to defeat him: moved him from school to school, each time the neighborhood getting tougher and the teachers more like keepers patrolling the aisles. They had sold themselves into captivity—his mother for a gin bottle, his father for a stack of poker chips—and then overlaid the whole picture with a trip to Sunday Mass. All of them pulled together, washed and dressed as though this could absolve the sins of the week. Ordinary sins that they had all settled into—moody silence, dishonesty, private solace. At Mass and after when they drove over to Brooklyn to visit relatives they looked like a family instead of a bunch of small-time gangsters. This morning his brother and sister, those two delinquents, presented themselves as normal happy children— happy, happy, happy—that hollow word. *He* was going to college— the rest was a lie. Fordham because he could live at home and save money and because he had listened to them for years. Father this one and Father that one who had taught his old man—a splendid product *there* of Catholic education. His mother and father stood for nothing but the Sunday morning mock-up, nothing more than muddling through. He was infected. Already he felt their dishonesty had seeped through him—insulting an old lady on the street to set himself up, sucking up to fools with fat purses, fussing over silly animals, making it (one more time, one last time—already the lie was born) with a girl he did not love.

Jim Cogan worked hard during the afternoon. Taking in poodles from the front waiting room, following Mimi Devereaux's directions. He was allowed to do only the simplest and cheapest clips. After a shampoo he dried their ears and topknots with a little electric hair dryer meant for a person. If they nipped at his hands he put on gloves. The miniatures trembled, their hearts thumping in their tiny chests. In the late afternoon a CBS newscaster came in with a brace of gray standards for a shampoo and comb-out. The man's face was a mask of prominence, betraying nothing beyond the measured warmth with which he announced our national disasters. Jimmy Cogan stood in awe of his haircut, his fingernails, his clothes—things he did not notice on the women who came in the shop, though his mother had said, having stopped to see him work—"Those ladies! The money on their backs." He saw the customers of *Chateau de Chien* with soft bellies, tortoise like, laboring under a hump of green backs, being walked by their poodles at the curb. This was solace. At five Shelly called to say that she would be in Union Square at 9:30. After a long pause he said, all right, wanting to tell her he was accepted at college as though she were an ordinary girl friend. "What's the matter?" she asked, "You sound funny."

You bet I sound funny, Jim Cogan thought, and I'm going to sound funnier, because you are a weird sad girl and I don't need it. Hanging around street corners by yourself. It had been a month now since he'd seen any of his friends. He had not even called them this morning when he got the news. That's how far he was into Shelly's world—like he had dropped out of life. No more (just one irresolute bang tonight) and then no more. At five-thirty Mrs. Schlotzer who had no appointment showed up with Hi-Marx Llewelyn. She was hysterical. The dog would not walk for her. She took him downstairs and he would not budge. She carried him to the curb. He urinated and stood there. Up in the apartment he sat on the couch, was lifted to his meal of chopped steak for three days now. Same for Mr. Schlotzer. Same for the doorman. She knew Hi-Marx was faking—had caught him romping with his rubber porcupine in the middle of the night. What had she done to deserve this? Her couch was slubbed silk, getting a large oily spot from the one place he sat. Lifting her drained face to Jim, she pleaded, "Give him everything."

"Yes, Mrs. Schlotzer." The dog, an apricot toy, went readily to Jim.

"What have I done?" the woman cried jealously, and answering her own question, said, "I should have bred him, but I couldn't bring myself. Give him polish, cream rinse, clip and comb."

"He was clipped last week."

"*Pretend*," Mrs. Schlotzer, "make a buzzing. I never should have let you people do the utility cut. From the moment the pompoms went he's been strange."

"Yes, Mrs. Schlotzer." I hope the stones fall out of your rings. I hope your credit cards are stolen. I hope Mr. Schlotzer is making it with his secretary.

"He likes you—" she said gloomily—"Pick out something for him—a rain coat. Two weeks ago I got him one of those Italian baskets—he sits on the couch. My God—" she cried—"what have I done?"

Hi-Marx Llewelyn walked pertly into the back room with Jimmy Cogan and leapt up on the counter to be serviced, a quivering small beast, panting with excitement.

"That poor soul," Mimi said, popping a tranquilizer down his tiny throat. "This is the third dog that bitch has ruined. I don't know what she expects of them, but they feel destroyed by her, broken."

Hi-Marx Llewelyn raised his anxious face to Jim, his delicate muzzle dwarfed by a monstrous ruff of hair, his heart slowed to a heavy throb as the tranquilizer set in. He pawed Jim's sweater, he scurried around the counter, his nails clicking on the slick surface. Poor little bastard—he was having fun. Coyly dashing at Jim he had an erection: the pale pink crayon of his defeated masculinity. He was brave to sit in his oily spot on the Schlotzer silk couch, to pee and sit at the curb, not to be paraded up to the shops on Fifth Avenue in absurd costumes and a showy ruff. Jim grabbed a set of clippers and worked fast (the dog was so small he could conceal him with his body) shaving Hi-Marx Llewelyn down until he was bare as a rat. Gone the tuft at the end of his tail. Gone the ornamental rings of fur on his spindly legs. His head unnaturally exposed with the topknot gone was flat and narrow: otherwise he looked the miniature of any normal self-respecting mutt. With the dog hidden under his sweater, Jim waited for Mrs. Schlotzer to return and wrote this note:

Mimi,

I take full responsibility for my act. There comes a moment when we must stand up and be counted. Today that moment came for me.

James Cogan

P.S. I am sorry we must sever what has been one of the most meaningful relationships of my life.

Hi-Marx Llewelyn growled when he heard his mistress's voice and ran into the front room to nip at her ankles. With his rolled, tattered copy of *Newsweek* Jim waited until Mrs. Schlotzer's screams reached operatic proportions and ran past her out of the shop. Bring them down, Jim thought. Bring them down.

It was only when he was slouched in a movie seat wasting the two hours between his exit from the *Chateau de Chien* and the encounter with Shelly Waltz in Union Square that he realized he had not been paid for the week. He felt enormously proud: life had begun after all. The battle was launched. On the screen a girl with fantastic legs but a plain face made love with an artist, an older guy. They ran down the streets of a blue-hazed New York doing beautiful free things, eating ice cream cones, lying out in Central Park. Then the artist's wife showed up and it was over—he had faked it and gave this feeble speech, in a business suit and a tie now, about how much it had meant, truly. Bring them down. Bring them down. Bravely the girl rode off on her bike in the final scene, her honesty and integrity intact in the full light of day. Wearing blue jeans and a fatigue jacket she peddled off across Brooklyn Bridge.

Shelly Waltz waited at the top of the subway stairs in Union Square. Her round childish face looked less sullen than usual, more actively annoyed. This evening she wore a new Indian robe, diaphanous and white, and looked like a child who has lost its role in the Christmas play. Her first words to Jim Cogan were not encouraging: "This is all a big mistake."

Jim looked down at her filthy bare feet.

"I have to go to Clauson's place," she said defiantly.

"So?"

"I have to go there," Shelly said. "There's something on."

They argued for a while in front of May's and she started to walk east on the long block toward Third Avenue with Jim at her heels. Having seen her, he wanted her. A soft breeze billowed the white stuff of her garment and he saw, or thought he saw, that she was naked underneath. One more time to be with her in a dim back room at Clauson's or in the dirty forgotten park near her house and then no more. To impress her Jim told the story of Hi-Marx Llewelyn: in one manly act he had finished with the poodle parlor that she hated.

"You're so involved with all that," Shelly said.

"I'm *through* with it!"

"It's the same thing," she turned on him, "look at you—just look!"

It was true, he did look a sight in his chinos and sweater when he finally trailed her into Clauson's place where a crowd of squatting white-robed figures murmured in the candlelight. From a dark corner a woman with gray hair and big pearl earrings came forth clacking finger cymbals while she sang a song without words. The man next to Jim passed him a joint and they shared while Jim heard his long story, this man with orange sideburns and extremely yellow teeth, how he had done something holy that day. As participation in Creative Love he had felt the entire side of the office building he worked in with his eyes closed. He felt the oppressive regularity of the cement and the hard cold surface of the aluminum panels, the inhuman scale of the whole; the mass, the enormity of structure that made him into a mincing midget each day as he went through the great arcaded entrance. Now that he had felt, the man said, it could never frighten him again. Now that he had charged himself with negative waves from the monster he could meet the beast in battle every day and stand like a giant in his new power. He could re-create the touch of cement and glass. If you know with your body you do not fear, the guy said. After a while Jim felt obligated to say he had felt the flesh of a dog that day, the soft close curls, the nearly hairless underbelly. Some people sang together. Patrick James Clauson, their leader, sat by himself facing the group on a leather hassock, wrapped in white, of course. A plump faggy Irishman, he might have been a priest in the Archdiocese of New York. From time to time his voice rang out in maxims: "We will feel and breathe our way back into the world. The world will not change us. We will recreate the world."

Jimmy Cogan emptied his wallet into a brass box that was passed to him and began to chant. He felt again that life had truly started. He was free. His words seemed to him inspired as he told a girl with long snarled hair that he had felt the underbelly of a dog. Having experienced that soft flesh with the heart pounding he would always feel kin to the animal, feel one with its small anxious body. Girls danced, Shelly among them, rotating her head in a frenzy of relaxation. He thanked God—the old man with the beard, the God whose cross he drew on his body before each quarter in basketball, each fifty-yard dash—that he had not told Shelly Waltz he was accepted at college.

"The daughters danced in the desert, their bodies like fountains,"—P. J. Clauson rose from the hassock in glory—"and the desert was the city. With their tongues they licked the foul air and breathed forth their purity. With their hair they watered the stone and flowers grew. With their fresh bodies dancing they brought forth a garden until the city was no more."

Quiet descended as though a signal were given. All the white-robed people read in thin green books which reminded Jim Cogan of his bankbook. He alone was empty-handed, apart from their feeling. His legs were sprawled out while they, he noted, they had magically tucked their limbs neatly away like nesting birds. Trying to be one with their mood he took *Newsweek* from his pocket, his only text: "Last week," he read, "in Los Angeles Superior Court, curvaceous Sherrill Lang (39-23-35), space-wife in TV's popular *Stardust Lane*, defended herself against accusations of ex-husband Mike Dougherty that she had undergone breast surgery in El Paso, Texas, in 1962 to obtain the remarkable proportions which launched her Hollywood career. Surprising Judge Stanley Marcus, braless Sherrill bared her bosom for the jury who awarded her the five dollars plus legal fees she was seeking for defamation of character: 'Money means nothing,' said Sherrill, buttoning up her simple dress. 'I want to be a serious actress and I'm sorry if my breasts stand in the way!' " Even in this story, Jim saw the terrible deceit. It was supposed to be funny, he knew, but that was too easy. Fraud everywhere. Lies. Had Sherrill Lang *wanted* to play that scene in court? Yes. In the picture, "Space-wife with Agent," he discerned her cheap smile of victory. Priceless, this coverage in the national media. Oh, bring them down. All around him these crazies, Shelly's white-robe people, were striving for honesty and it seemed that he alone wore a sweater of dissent. What did the world expect of him? It was too hard, the pieces too various—as though there were a thousand scattered bits of glass or fool's gold and he was asked to assemble them into a mirror. The folly of Clauson's store-front temple bewildered him: incense and Indian bells you could buy in any gift shop. Yet there was no disputing fact: the room was still and full of peace. Tears streamed down Jim Cogan's face.

Shelly was beside him, holding him, begging his forgiveness. He could come with her always to Clauson's. Jim told her that his whole soul seemed to laugh and cry in torment. He was torn between visions of freedom and the dutiful years ahead. "I'm going to college," he confessed.

"You're so involved in that," Shelly said.

His mother had planned a celebration, he knew. He knew her ways—given hope once more, he knew all the little embellishments that she would foist upon his triumph to make it her own. Now she would put away an uncut cake, rejected by her wandering son. She had not boozed all the long afternoon. The children were washed and dressed. Their father was home, but now he would go out to find a card game. At Jim's own place on the kitchen table a large present gaily wrapped awaited him and he could not guess what lay inside. His tears were blotted by Shelly's hair.

"Cry," she said, "go on—cry."

It was a real breakthrough he knew, to cry with this weird girl. In her white robe, in the candlelight a beauty flared in her and in a torrent of words he confessed it—that he had wanted her one more time.

"Sex," she said, "is unimportant."

"My friends," he cried in final confusion, "I haven't seen my friends in a month."

The voice of Clauson rose as though out of Jim Cogan's emotion: "My friends, let us observe the lesson. Upon this feast day Krishna Nuru received from the Prince Dhrahman a farm which was old and in great disrepair. Thinking that the god Krishna would list the property among his dominion but would not care to see the farm, Dhrahman was well pleased with himself. Immediately Krishna Nuru rode to the place and saw that it was on the north side of the mountain where the village ends. Here lived the poor in their shacks, the farm no more than a pitiful collection of these buildings leaning one into another."

The story rang true for all the squatting figures on Clauson's floor. Holding Shelly to him Jim Cogan wondered at the man's cleverness for the last time. P. J. Clauson, pudgy, pink as an angel, was lost in his own performance: "The fields of the farm were bare as dunes and the well was dry. A few chickens and three thin pigs were the only creatures on the land. At once the god Krishna sent a letter to the prince thanking him for the tribute of this beautiful farm. The prince raged and rode out to make sure he had not given the wrong property away, but upon coming to the old farm he met Krishna Nuru sitting on the broken gate in a robe of gold cloth celebrating his good fortune with wine and song.

" 'Come see,' he said to the prince with godlike demeanor, 'come see my lovely pigs, for they are surely the wisest animals in the land.' Though Dhrahman saw three pigs who had been fed and washed but looked no better than they should, still he worried at the delight of Krishna Nuru. He returned to the palace to say that the god's powers were sorely depleted when he thought he had riches in three thin pigs. Still it troubled him and he sent spies to watch the farm. The god Krishna lavished great care upon this land. A new well was found and wheat planted. An orchard of wonderful fruit trees which had been thought dead blossomed in the spring. All the little buildings were set straight and painted. The gate was put back on its hinges and the mysterious pigs grew fat and beautiful. When Dhrahman heard these stories he was devoured with jealousy and rode out to the farm where Krishna Nuru himself was throwing grain out of a basket at the merriest chickens ever seen.

'Come see,' said the god, 'come see my lovely pigs, but be quiet for they are hard at work.' Surely, said the prince to himself, he is demented and thought with what relish he would describe the great god feeding chickens in the barnyard."

Shelly Waltz swept her arms up around Jim Cogan's neck. Lovers at last, they were enfolded in the same white robe of belief. The silence in Clauson's presence was perfect. A last shallow flame of life flickered from the candles upon the faces of his audience—his congregation.

"But strange to say the three pigs were truly busy feeding on corn that was bright as gold and when they had finished they turned to the prince that he might see their marvelous girth and it seemed to him that they smiled. Now the prince rode off in a terrible fury, humiliated by the cleverness of Krishna Nuru's pigs.

"Each day for a hundred days he returned and each day it seemed to the prince that the pigs grew more beautiful and that they mocked him, for he could not believe that they merely ate and slept and grunted in the hay and that the god Krishna had not performed some magic upon the animals. His cheek grew pale and his body wasted with envy until at last one day the prince cried out to them: 'Why are you so happy?' and Krishna smiled with his pigs.

"Why are you so happy?" cried out the prince in anguish.

"And Krishna Nuru answered: 'What your eyes see, your heart will believe.' "

Jim Cogan was enchanted by Clauson's tale and listened with full respect as the prince met his just and terrible fate. Bring them down—the empty, the deceitful of the world, the devouring parents who would feed on his heart. *He* was going to college, driven by the years of their desire. Yes, he would do their bidding, but the triumph would be his—already he could see himself in the garment of a simpler time and place they could not understand, a lamb in a murky difficult landscape. Tracings of flowers, birds, vines adorned his neck and breast in the white, white shirt he would buy tomorrow in some heavy-scented Indian shop. The Prince Dhrahman was outwitted by pigs.

Clauson stood in the dim light with arms outspread, a fat hovering Holy Ghost above them:

"Krishna Nuru has written: Dhrahman, who valued appearances, attempted to cheat the god Krishna but cheated only himself. For Krishna by honest work transfigures the commonplace into beauty. Thus he would instruct us all to live with effort and grace."

17

JIMMY BRESLIN
(b. 1930)

Jimmy Breslin is probably the best known contemporary Irish-American writer. He is a journalist, novelist, and radio-television personality. He has served his time as copyboy, sports reporter, political columnist, and feature writer for various New York papers—the *Herald Tribune, Journal American, World-Journal-Tribune, Post,* and *Daily News.*

Breslin was born in Queens (New York City) in 1930—a fertile ground for the ethnic types that populate his articles and fiction. Fat Thomas, a 450-pound bookie; Jerry the Rooster, a light-fingered shopper; and Marvin the Torch, a professional arsonist, were all born in Queens. Breslin was educated at Saint Benedict Joseph Labré Grammar School and at John Adams High School. Whether he was graduated from high school may or may not be critical, though he admits to having "done the customary five years." His mother, Frances Curtain Breslin, was an English teacher before becoming a social worker. His first wife, "the former Rosemary Dattalico" (d. 1981), was a champion of the poor and oppressed, a modern heroine whose story is yet to be told. Breslin married Ronnie Eldridge in 1984 and moved to Manhattan. Together they have nine children.

In 1962 the journalist turned biographer and produced *Sunny Jim: The Life of America's Most Beloved Horseman, James Fitz-Simmons.* In 1963 Breslin wrote *Can't Anybody Here Play This Game?, The Improbable Saga of the New York Mets' First Year.* In 1969 he entered the New York Democratic primary (with Norman Mailer) and compiled *Running Against the Machine* (ed. Peter Manso), an exposé of big-city politics. He has also published (with Dick Schaap) *The 44-Calibre Killer* (1979), the study of the "Son of Sam" murderer, and *How the Good Guys Finally Won: Notes on an Impeachment Summer* (1975), a follow-up to Watergate.

Since 1969 Breslin has written five novels: *The Gang That Couldn't Shoot Straight* (1969), a hilarious street-gang comedy; *World Without End, Amen* (1973), a reversal portrait of a bigoted New York City policeman on the wrong side in Northern Ireland; *Forsaking All Others* (1982), a story of bad times on the mean streets of the South Bronx; *Table Money* (1986), the tragedy of a returned Vietnam veteran caught between heaven and hell; and *He Got Hungry and Forgot His Manners* (1988), a black comedy that centers on the Howard Beach attacks. The selection following, taken from *World Without End, Amen,* describes the Richmond Hill section of Queens and sums up the education of Dermot Davey.

Breslin usually projects himself as "a bar-room type," "an unlettered bum," but television viewers and readers need not be deceived by appearances; he is an informed commentator, a brilliant analyst, and a sensitive writer of fiction and nonfiction. A recent winner of the coveted Meyer Berger Award, Breslin has contributed to the "New Journalism," a contribution that has yet to be weighed and credited.

World Without End, Amen

Dermot Davey comes out of St. Monica's Parish in Jamaica, in Queens, in New York City. He was living now in Holy Child Parish, in Richmond Hill, in Queens, in New York City. Richmond Hill is only twenty-five minutes away from Manhattan. But everybody in Queens always thinks of Manhattan as another place. The people say, "I'm going to the city," or, "I'm going to New York." Queens begins at the East River, directly across the water from midtown Manhattan. In Manhattan, you have the United Nations building on the water, sun exploding on the windows, sprinklers throwing water on the lawns and gardens. Directly across the river from the United Nations is the Pepsi-Cola plant in Long Island City, in Queens, its red neon sign bare and ugly in the daylight, eerie at night in the smoke rising around it.

Eddie Kieran, who lives next door to Dermot on 109th Place, was standing outside one Saturday night having a cigarette while he waited for his wife to fall asleep upstairs.

"Where'd you go?" he asked Dermot.

"Picked them up at the Maspeth Bingo," Dermot said.

"Oh, somebody says you went to the city," Eddie Kieran said.

"City? I haven't been to New York with Phyllis in, what, six months?"

"Oh, so you just went to the bingo."

"Picked them up at the Maspeth Bingo. What did you do?"

"Done nothin.' Went to her mother's."

Kieran had on a brown windbreaker with GROVER CLEVELAND HIGH lettering on the back. It is the jacket he wore on his high-school baseball team. Eddie is thirty-nine and he takes very good care of the jacket.

"Another couple of weeks," he said. He was swinging his arm in a circle.

"For what?"

"Jones Beach softball league. The start, anyway. The first meetin's and that."

"You play again this year?"

"What're you, kidding? Play every year."

Eddie took a drag on the cigarette as if he were a general. When he talks about playing ball he always is like this. Otherwise, Eddie is afraid of speaking to people. He had a job as a laborer at St. John's Cemetery. People looking for gravesites asked him too many questions. He quit and now works nights in a bakery. He puts jelly buns into paper bags and loads them onto a delivery wagon.

"I think I'm gonna play short this year," Eddie Kieran said.

"What'd you play last year? I saw you play shortstop."

"That was only the one game, against the Grumman. I played centerfield all year. I could throw, for Christ's sake, I was the only one could throw. The one game there, Mahon from the West Babylon, I threw a strike on him at the plate. What a fuckin' throw."

He took the cigarette and threw it out into the street. It made a little red arc in the darkness under the big old maple trees along the sidewalk.

"The fuckin' school is breakin' my back, too," Eddie said.

"What do they want now?"

"The same fuckin' thing. They want her to go to college. Fuck them."

"How much would it cost you?"

"She got a fuckin' scholarship to the place."

"Which place is it again?"

"The Middlebury. They give her a scholarship for speakin' fuckin' French. That ain't it. For Christ's sake. Let her go out and work and help out at home. What is this here, a fuckin' paradise I got?"

"What's the wife think now?"

"She ain't allowed to think. I'll do the thinkin'. I just wish the fuckin' schools would butt out. This here woman at the high school. Fills my daughter up with a lot of bullshit. I tell them all. I tell them, I didn't go to no college. It was good enough for me, it's good enough for my daughter. We got no money. Let her start bringin' home a coupla dollars. Bucks. That's what we need. Bucks. That's what we need. Bucks. Not some fuckin' French."

They were standing on a street of dusty wooden houses with gingerbread all over them. Small patches of lawn are in front of each house. Most of the lawns are more rutted dirt than grass. The houses are separated from each other by common driveways, so narrow a car can barely fit between the houses as it inches back to the garages in the back yard. Most men when they bring their wives home on a Saturday night open the door at the front of the house and the wives get out. The man takes fifteen minutes inching his car into the driveway. Then he comes out and stands on the sidewalk, smoking a cigarette, waiting his wife out, waiting for her to be undressed and asleep by the time he comes into the house so they will not have to as much as talk. On the blocks in Richmond Hill on a Saturday night you always can see pinpoints of cigarettes in the darkness in front of the houses.

The house Dermot Davey and his wife and three daughters live in is owned by his mother-in-law. Dermot lives on the top floor, his in-laws downstairs. The house is tan, with green trim. The house is in the middle of the block. At one end of the street is the main avenue, Jamaica Avenue. El tracks run on top of Jamaica Avenue. A throw-up-green El with rust coming out from under the ties and black pillars lining the sidewalk. At the foot of each pillar, the crevices and ledges are stuffed with cigarette and candy wrappers. The light comes through the slats in the tracks and falls on the street in wavy rectangles. The El is old and noisy. Often, as trains clatter along it, bolts loosen in the tracks and drop through to the street, two stories below.

Under the El, yellowing attached two-story buildings of Jamaica Avenue push the street into even more dreariness. As you come up

Jamaica Avenue from Lefferts Boulevard, a main cross street, you pass a wallpaper shop, a Cheap John's Bargain Store, a wedding photographer's shop, two real-estate offices with nervous young men sitting at scarred desks, a candy store with plastic toys in the window, an old A&P supermarket, several bars, Irish dungeons, with withered old men sitting in them and staring out at another day wasted. Once it becomes dark the doors to the bars are locked. The bartender lets in customers he knows by pressing a buzzer under the bar which automatically unlocks the door.

While Dermot and his next-door neighbor stood on the sidewalk, it was still early, before midnight, on a weekend night. Nearly all the houses were dark anyway. Dermot knew that day or night made little difference in the activity in the houses. In the daytime, the people were afraid to come to the door if the doorbell rang. They stayed back in the kitchens, peering down the hall. Nearly everybody in Richmond Hill has a dog. On Dermot's block, the people were buying big German shepherds. Black gums wet and flapping, yellow teeth bared, nose thrashing against the inside of the storm door, the dogs answered the doorbells for the people.

On this night, there were lights in the Laurino house in the middle of the block. On Saturday nights, the Laurinos always go to New York for plays and things like that. Laurino is an accountant. His wife, Laura, used to be a schoolteacher and now she substitute-teaches once in a while.

One time, Dermot and his wife went to a party in their house and late, while everybody was going home, Dermot was pouring himself another drink and Laura put a hand on his wrist. "You're too young to be drunk like this," she said. Ever since then, whenever she sees Dermot on the street she looks at him carefully. He turns his face from her as much as he can.

Next to Laurino, where Jackie Collins lives, is a different story. He drives a truck for Piel's Beer. His brother delivers for New Arrival Diaper Service. The two of them are always together at one of the bars on Jamaica Avenue. Jackie Collins in a zipper jacket with PIEL's stitched across the back and his name, JACKIE BOY, stitched on the front breast pocket. And his brother in a zipper jacket with NEW ARRIVAL DIAPER SERVICE stitched across the back and his name, EDDIE BOY. In the summers, Jackie works overtime. He goes to the race track as much as possible. In the winters, work is slow. He hangs out in bars. Dermot always notices his wife walking on Jamaica Avenue with her head down. She doesn't want storekeepers to notice her and come running out with one of her bad checks in their hands. The only time Dermot notices her picking up her head is when she passes the Blue Marlin or McLaughlin's or JB's, and she does this because she is looking for her husband. It is easy to spot him, in his PIEL's zipper jacket. Usually he is right alongside his brother, in his NEW ARRIVAL DIAPER SERVICE zipper jacket.

The other people on the block are older. Toner, across the street, has a good job in the Fire Department, driving a Battalion Chief. Toner has fourteen months to go on his pension, thirty years. His wife never leaves the house. She keeps sending neighborhood kids down to the corner for ice cream and stays inside with the curtains drawn, watching television. The house is a mess and the furniture torn. The wife, when you see her in a housecoat once a week or so, seems to be nearing three hundred pounds. The Taylors live next to the Toners. Taylor is a retired bank teller. The women on the block all say that they see him naked and hiding behind trees at night. The rest of the people on the block Dermot knows only by name. They all are in their sixties. One of them, Mrs. Metcalf, a shriveled woman, stopped him one day when she heard that Dermot's wife had gone to the hospital during the night to have her first baby. Mrs. Metcalf said, "Did her water break?"

"I guess so," Dermot said.

"That's bad, dry babies is very hard to have," Mrs. Metcalf said.

Dermot's mother and sister lived in Ozone Park, less than ten minutes away from his house in Richmond Hill. He had not seen or spoken to his mother in the last three years. Since the christening party for Dermot's third daughter, Tara. His mother had arrived for the party with her eyes bloodshot, her lip curled. She started an argument with Dermot's mother-in-law. The argument started for the same reason his mother's fights always start, whisky. Dermot's mother-in-law looked to him for help. He walked out of the house and went down to the avenue, to McLaughlin's. While he was there, his mother left the christening and went home. Dermot's mother-in-law came down to McLaughlin's to get him back. He said something fresh to his mother-in-law. She walked out of the bar. Dermot never went back to the christening party.

In the days following this, he first tried to call his mother and hammer at her, but he found he was always stopping short of calling her the one word, drunk, which kept running through his mind. He decided not to call her or take calls from her. Dermot still had a marriage at that time. He knew his mother was capable of keeping

two families at once living in the misery of whisky rages. He stopped
going to visit her although she lived only ten minutes away. Once in
a while over the months, Dermot's mother called his house. The
voice snapping, "Let me speak to my *son*." If he was home, Dermot
would grab the phone and hang it up. That would start her calling
every ten minutes until either she fell asleep or Dermot took the
phone off the hook. For the three years this went on, Dermot knew
that his sister, living with his mother in a four-room apartment,
was giving up her years and her nervous system so the mother would
not have to live alone. The mother continually tried to pick fights
with neighbors, who by this time did not speak to her. When his
mother would be sober, she would not understand why people ignored her. Depressed, she would start the cycle of drinking and
fighting again.

Because of age differences and because of the occupation—
policeman rarely speak to anybody but policemen, and policemen's
wives rarely speak to any other women but policemen's wives—Dermot and his wife had little to do with the people on the block. Most
of the policemen with whom Dermot works live out on Long Island.
They live in places called Deer Park and Massapequa Park, in split-
level and ranch and Cape Cod houses costing twenty thousand dollars. The houses have lawns that the policemen mow in the summer.
The houses have walks that the policemen shovel in the winter.
There are barbecue stands covered with plastic in the back yard and
a picnic table with a garden hose on it and the television set always is
on and the cop leaves the house for only three reasons. The ride to
the supermarket with his wife. The ride to the hardware store by
himself. And the hated trip, the ride on the Long Island Railroad to
the job in Queens. For eight hours a day the policeman patrols
streets he hates, watches people he despises and, if the people are
black, people who make him apprehensive or even afraid. Many of
the policemen who still live in Queens live cheaply with parents or
in-laws. The one Dermot Davey knows best in Queens is Johno
O'Donnell.

When he was straight, before he began swallowing too much
whisky, everybody always said Johno was one of the best cops they
had seen. Johno had two citations. The one Dermot knew by heart—
Johno had told it to him so many times over so many drinks—came
from a payroll holdup of a bakery plant in Long Island City. The
plant was on a dead-end street. A girl inside the plant had been able
to sneak a call. Johno was in the first car to respond. The holdup

men were coming out the metal door from the factory office. They jumped back inside. They were either going to take hostages or shoot it out from inside. Johno was out of the car and had the factory door open and was firing so quickly up the metal staircase that none of them got past the first landing. One was shot in the back, another in the leg, and the third quit.

If you saw Johno stumbling around Glendale and Ridgewood, you would have trouble believing it. But once Dermot had seen the Johno the old-timers talked about. There was a call from Schmidt's Restaurant on Myrtle Avenue. Dermot was driving Johno in the sector. When they arrived, a German waiter was standing with a group of women around a booth. The waiter was wringing his hands. In the booth, slumped against the wall, her legs on the seat, was a heavy woman with frightened eyes. They had a coat thrown over her.

Johno started the moment he came through the restaurant doorway.

"All right," he called out, almost happy, "here we are."

He put a hand on the waiter. "Excuse me, sir. That's fine. All right. Here we are."

"She's havin' a heart attack!" the waiter shouted.

The woman slumped in the booth looked even more frightened.

Johno leaned over and ran a hand over the woman's forehead.

"Well, dear, you're not having a heart attack," Johno said. "How can you have a heart attack when you don't sweat? You ought to know better than that. What did you eat? That's what's bothering you."

The frightened eyes closed. When they opened, the woman in the booth looked five years younger.

"Pain is in the chest, right?" Johno said.

She nodded yes.

He had her hand and was feeling for the pulse. "I'll tell you," Johno said, "I play horses, lady. I'm betting gall bladder. That's a four-to-five shot, dear. Relax, nobody died from gall bladder."

By the time the ambulance came, he had the woman in the booth quiet and smiling a little. The other women were calmed down. The waiters were relaxed. When the place cleared, Johno sat in a booth as if it were a broken car seat. "Hey, you," he said to the waiter, "bring me a straight VO."

Johno said to Dermot, "You see that cocksucker standin' in everybody's way when we come in? Doin' fuckin' nothin'. Scarin' the poor woman half to death. I would of done some scream job on him, but I was afraid I'd make the woman scared. What the fuck do I know what was the matter with her? She could've gone out right there on us."

"It was gall bladder," Dermot said.

"That's what you say," Johno said. "I don't know what the fuck she had. I told her she wasn't sweatin'. Chrissake, I touched her head, it was like a faucet."

Johno lives in Ozone Park, down by the race track. When Dermot and Johno and their wives go out, every fifth or sixth week, Dermot and his wife drive down to the Cross Bay Theater, on Rockaway Boulevard in Ozone Park. The wives go into the movie and Dermot and Johno walk up the block, past Shep's Army & Navy Store, Aid Auto Supplies, Chen's Chow Mein to Tommy Madden's bar. Always, in Tommy Madden's, it is the same. Dermot and Johno sit at the end of the bar, near the window, and Tommy Madden, bald, his ears lumps of skin, sits on a stool and talks about his days as a fighter.

"Al Weill managed me," Tommy Madden said one night.

"He was a hump," Johno said.

"He was a cutey," Tommy Madden said.

"A hump," Johno said. "I may be a prick, but I'm not a hump."

Nobody talked for a while. Then Johno said to Dermot, "You know, that play never worked once."

"What play?"

"What play? For Chrissake, what's the matter with you? Hump. The Long twenty-two. How many times do you think it worked?"

Dermot was trying to think. "Fuck, I don't know," he said.

"My ass you don't know. Hump. We had the Long twenty-two when I was playing and when I come to see you play, you had the same play. Don't shit me. You humps couldn't make it work either."

"Christ, I don't know," Dermot said.

"Well, I'm tellin' you again, it never worked when I played. We couldn't even make it work against Flushing the year we beat them thirty-seven points. We used to make it out of a double wing. Second and short yardage. Or right after you recover a fumble and you're lookin' to—boom!—hump 'em. The ends go way down and cross over. You throw the fuckin' thing as far as you can. What are you tellin' me you can't remember. Chrissake. You had the same thing. I seen you try it against Stuyvesant. Out of the T, but the same thing. Long twenty-two. You humps couldn't make it work, either."

When the movies got out, the wives came to the sidewalk in front of the bar. Johno and Dermot came outside and took them to the pizzeria two doors down. They ordered pies. Johno swallowed wine. His wife, Emily, kept her cloth coat on. She was so fat that she wore the same smocks, faded and worn, that she used when she was pregnant.

"We don't have long to go," Emily said.

"Twenty-three months," Johno said. "Then right to Fort Lauderdale. No geese there. People down there know what to do with the niggers. They're not humps, the people in Fort Lauderdale."

"Maybe someday we all could be livin' in Fort Lauderdale," his wife said.

• • •

Dermot's parents were born in Queens. His father in Woodside, his mother in Jamaica. His father played the piano in taverns in Sunnyside and Woodside, and in the summer at Long Beach, out on Long Island. All the saloons in the west end of Long Beach, the Irish end, had piano players on Sunday afternoons.

Dermot can remember only two scenes involving his father, both of them during the winter.

He came home one day and said to Dermot's mother, "I saw Carmen Cavallaro today."

"Did you?"

"He was having a cup of coffee in the Automat."

"Really? What did he look like?"

"Looked like a million dollars."

And Dermot remembers the afternoon in the winter. He was in second grade then, and he and his sister, who wasn't in school yet, were running toy cars over the linoleum on the floor of the apartment in Sunnyside. Dermot and his sister kept asking the father if they could go downstairs and play out on the street. All the father did was stand at the window with his hands in his pockets. The day was cold and became dark early. Dermot and his sister sat on the couch and the sister began picking on him and he pushed her and she began crying. The father kept looking down at the street and not seeming to hear them. Finally, his mother came in from work. She had a city job with the Department of Purchase. His mother did not talk. She put on a light, stood there with her coat still on, and glared at Dermot's father. Dermot remembers his mother going into the kitchen and his father walking into the bedroom. In the kitchen, dishes still were on the table and sink. Dermot heard his mother taking ice out of the refrigerator. When the father went in to see her, she had her back to him.

"Just stay out of here now," she said.

He and his sister were on the couch, pushing each other, when Dermot's mother came out of the kitchen and walked into the bedroom. She slammed the door behind her. First, there was whispering. Then his mother shouted, "You!"

There was a big noise now, and his father was shouting and his mother shrieking. One shriek after the other. Dermot opened the bedroom door. His father, standing nearest to Dermot, was trying to ram the bed against Dermot's mother and pin her to the wall. Dermot grabbed at his father's arm. His sister came into the room crying. His mother threw herself onto the bed. She was half sitting, half kneeling, grabbing for her husband's face. The father shoved Dermot away and walked out of the apartment. The mother sat on the bed crying with her mouth open. His sister had her arms wrapped around her mother. Dermot went into the kitchen and got a can of Campbell's tomato soup. The same red-and-white label they have today. He put the can of soup against the apartment door. This made him feel like he was protecting his mother and sister and he stood by the door, watching his can of soup that kept the door shut. He heard his father come back to the door. The lock turned. He still can see the apartment door swinging in, the can of soup rolling into the dimness in one of the corners of the living room.

Dermot does not remember ever seeing his father after that day. His mother took his sister and him to his grandmother's house, her mother's house, in Jamaica. The grandmother was a widow. Dermot's two uncles lived in the house. The grandmother's other child, an aunt, was married and lived in White Plains, up in Westchester. Nobody ever mentioned his father's name in the house. Whenever somebody in school asked Dermot about him, Dermot said his father was dead. Dermot was terrified that one of the kids would find out that his father was really alive and not living in Dermot's house.

One day when he came home from school, Dermot found his grandmother in the kitchen talking to an older woman and the older woman made a fuss over Dermot.

"Looks just like his mother," Dermot remembers his grandmother saying.

"And he's got a lot of somebody else in that face too," the other woman said.

The grandmother held a finger to her lips and Dermot remembers her saying, "Shhhhhsh now," and the words went through him and he ran out of the kitchen.

One day, Dermot was in the bedroom he shared with one of his uncles, and his sister was trying to get in and Dermot tried to keep her out. He slammed the door on his sister's hand, cracking one fingernail badly, and she ran downstairs screaming. His mother stood in the hallway looking at the finger, and Dermot remembers hanging over the banister and his mother looking up at him and saying to him, "You're no good. You're just like him. He's no good and you're no good."

At home, all Dermot ever heard from his uncles was police talk. Early one morning when he was about nine, he came downstairs, it was about six-thirty, and he found his Uncle Tom had his pistol and blackjack on the table and he was drinking beer out of a Kraft-cheese glass that had blue flowers on it. Uncle Tom took a quart bottle of Piel's beer and poured it like ketchup. The beer splashed and foam ran up over the sides of the glass. Uncle Tom's head dropped like an elevator and he began sucking up foam. "The people dyin' in the desert!" he said. Dermot went over to the refrigerator to get milk for his Rice Krispies. On the wall alongside the refrigerator was the Proclamation of Irish Independence of 1916. Everybody in the family, the uncles first of all, had Dermot memorize it. "Irishmen and Irishwomen: In the name of God and of the dead generations from which she receives her old tradition of nationhood, Ireland, through us, summons her children to the flag and strikes for her freedom. . . . "

Dermot remembers sitting over his cereal on the opposite side of the table from Uncle Tom. Tom patted the blackjack. "Ah, your Uncle Tom got plenty use out of this last night," he said.

"Where?" Dermot asked.

"Bedford-Stuyvesant."

"Bedford-Stuyvesant?"

"Niggers," Uncle Tom said.

He produced some whisky to slop into the beer and he threw one big drink down, this one so quickly that it splashed against his bottom lip and brown drops fell on his undershirt. He took the pistol out of the holster. He released the cylinder, dropped bullets onto the table, pushed the cylinder back, and held out the gun. "Listen to

your Uncle Tom now. Good boy! Go upstairs and poke your Uncle
Jack with this. Just poke him and say, 'Post time!' Do that now. Good
boy!"

Dermot took the gun and ran upstairs. The grip and the ridges of
metal felt nice in his hand. The finger on the trigger gave him the
same feeling he has had every time he ever holds a gun. It starts
between the legs.

Uncle Jack was asleep on his face. Dermot shouted, "Post time!"
and poked the gun into his ear. He moved his head and his face
rolled out on the pillow and Dermot held the gun steady so that
when his Uncle Jack opened his eyes for the first time he was looking
into the barrel of the pistol. His mouth popped open. In one motion
he grabbed the pistol and gave Dermot a clout on top of the head.

He remembers his Uncle Jack walked into the kitchen, opened
the cylinder, poked it with a finger, and a bullet fell onto the kitchen
table. Gray and brass rolling around in the spilled beer, the sun from
the kitchen windows shining on the wet metal. Dermot reached to
grab the bullet. Uncle Jack hit him on top of the head again, this
time so hard that everything went black.

When Dermot came home from school that day, Uncle Jack was
still in his pajamas at the kitchen table. He was sitting across from
Dermot's grandmother and they both were drinking from a quart
bottle of Piel's beer.

"You really saw it?" the grandmother said.

"I saw my whole life," Uncle Jack said.

Uncle Tom was back on the living-room couch. He was snoring
loudly. He smelled so badly from his breath, armpits, and socks with
caked soles that Dermot could not stay in the room with him.

• • •

Dermot Davey came out of St. Monica's grammar school with the
same grounding in life as so many other policemen in New York. The
girls in his class were told by the nuns never to wear patent-leather
shoes. The nuns said, "They give you headaches." In the higher
grades, in the boys' room, Dermot learned that the nuns were
against patent leather because a man could look down at a girl's
shoes and see up her dress.

The rest of the education which stuck, the religious education,
came out of the Baltimore Catechism. The name "Baltimore" comes
from the Council of American Bishops, which first approved the

book. The Baltimore book used by Dermot had a blue cover, which he still remembers, and it taught him the basics of the Roman Catholic belief, which he, like everybody else, still can recite with no preparation.

Q   Who made the world?
A   God made the world.
Q   Who is God?
A   God is the creator of heaven and earth, and of all things.
Q   What is man?
A   Man is a creature composed of body and soul, and made to the image and likeness of God.
Q   Why did God make you?
A   God made me to know Him, to love Him, and to serve Him in this world, and to be happy with Him forever in heaven.
Q   Are the three Divine Persons one and the same God?
A   The Three Divine Persons are one and the same God, having one and the same Divine nature.
Q   How do we know this to be true?
A   It is a mystery.
Q   What is the Sixth Commandment?
A   The Sixth Commandment is: Thou shalt not commit adultery.
Q   What are we commanded by the Sixth Commandment?
A   We are commanded by the Sixth Commandment to be pure in thought and modest in all our looks, words and actions.
Q   What is forbidden by the Sixth Commandment?
A   The Sixth Commandment forbids all unchaste freedom with another's wife or husband; also all immodesty with ourselves or others in looks, dress, words or actions.

The last one always sticks. Dermot and his wife had their first two children in the first two and one-half years of marriage. They spoke of not having any more children for some time. Dermot came home one night after working a four-to-midnight and having a couple of drinks on the way home. Phyllis was sleeping with her back to him. He reached over her shoulder and ran a hand over her. She shook her shoulder. He began kissing her neck. She moved away. "Come on now, it's a very bad time," she said. Dermot said he would be careful. He put a hand onto her breast. She shrugged her shoulder to get his hand away and pulled the cover up over her. "Come on now," she said. "I'm telling you it's a bad time."

Dermot went to sleep irritated with her. In bed, Phyllis always took the last look to be sure the bedroom door was closed. She never wanted sex in the daytime, and Dermot worked many nights, and when they were having sex she seemed to be trying to control her breathing. She was now going even beyond this.

When they got up the next morning, Dermot was even more irritated with her. Phyllis acted as if nothing had happened. Phyllis's mother had agreed to take care of the kids for the day, and they were going to take a drive out to Long Island. Dermot gave Phyllis the car keys. He sat in the front seat with his eyes closed. When Phyllis got in next to him, his left side, the side touching her, squirmed. Phyllis drove on the Northern State Parkway.

It was the last week of October and the trees were changing colors. As they got farther out on Long Island, the trees had brighter reds and yellow. Dermot said nothing during the drive. For an hour and a half he sat in the car and looked out the window and he did not speak to his wife and she did not speak to him. Finally, when they were out at the end of the parkway and were going onto Montauk Highway, Dermot turned on the car radio. It made a loud static and nothing else. They were going down an incline at Eastport, with a pond in the incline covered with red and yellow leaves on one side, and on the other side the sun glinting off the bay that leads to the ocean. And Dermot said the only words he was to say all day. "Just take me home."

She pulled into an old gas station with thick trees and a portico hanging out over the gas pumps, turned around, and started back for Queens.

They were almost home when she said, "That's why you're mad."

Dermot didn't answer.

"You're mad because of that," she said.

He still didn't answer.

"You don't understand," she said.

• • •

Sometimes, Dermot felt that if he and Phyllis had been born a little later, just a couple of years later, they might be like so many of the young Catholic couples of today. Dermot always noticed that younger people do not seem to become embarrassed or to lapse into Queens words at the subject of sex. He and Phyllis received the old Diocese of Brooklyn schooling. She was taught that sex is solely for having children who will become good Catholics. And never to wear patent-leather shoes. Dermot was taught that it is perfectly natural for a young man to have severe temptations, but there is no temptation which cannot be overcome by an Our Father and ten Hail Marys. The one line that stayed with Dermot the most during his life was said to him late one Saturday afternoon by a priest in confession. Dermot was in his first year in high school. Eyes closed, highly nervous, he told a priest that he had committed a sin of touch.

"How?" the priest said.

"I touched a girl with my hand," Dermot said.

"Externally or internally," the priest said.

"Internally."

"Would you like somebody doing that to your sister?" the priest said.

Dermot and his wife, like so many others from the same background, were unable to discuss sex. Many times they went two weeks without sex. And immediately after that, two or three more weeks. It seemed to Dermot that his wife was always heaving herself onto her side, her back to him. It would make him angry and he would move out onto the edge of the bed on his side. And then he would not come near her for weeks. Once, they went seven weeks without sex. There was no way for them to handle the subject in conversation. It always came out to be a fight over wallpaper or weak coffee.

Phyllis had light-brown hair that she had brushed the same way for so long that it was almost unnoticeable to Dermot. Her face was still thin and together enough to be acceptable for a twenty-eight-year-old. The extra years were in the eyes. A greeting would produce some reaction. A conversation with her about anything would produce almost no movement, no brightening or dimming, no coupling of her eyes with anybody else's to show interest. Always, no matter what was going on, she was a woman staring at the stove waiting for coffee water to boil.

Her body fell apart at the hips. Three children had weakened the muscles, and the weight spread her hips and went down through the tops of her thighs. From behind she began to look like a bell buoy. What saved her was her legs from the knees down. They had the form and spring of youth. When she walked through the house quickly, she made Dermot remember Sunday afternoons, walking in Forest Park, before they were married.

The afternoon Dermot was taken in by the Internal Affairs Division, two detectives from the IAD came to the house to talk to Phyllis. One of them had a briefcase. He put his hand inside it, but never took any papers out. They asked Phyllis if she had noticed anything abnormal about Dermot's sexual instincts. They asked her if Dermot had undergone any psychiatric treatment.

When Dermot finally was allowed to leave the IAD office on Poplar Street that night, he came home and found Phyllis in the kitchen in silence. The next afternoon they started an argument about newspapers on the floor. During the argument, Phyllis did not look at Dermot. Through the weeks that followed she rarely looked at him the few times they talked while they were alone.

• • •

The catechisms in the higher grades began to intermingle conservative religion, patriotism, and obedience and produced the special doctrine of Diocese of Brooklyn Roman Catholic American.

Essay question:

> Giles is murdered by a Communist just as he leaves the church after his confession. Giles has been away from the church for 28 years. He just about satisfied the requirements for a good confession, having only imperfect contrition, aroused during this week's mission. The Communist demanded to know if Giles was a Catholic, threatening to kill him if he was. Fearlessly, Giles said, "Yes, thank God!" The Communist murdered Giles. Did Giles go immediately to Heaven, or did he go to Purgatory for a while? Give a reason for your answer.

Nobody in Dermot's class ever considered Giles as anything but a martyr who ascended to heaven immediately. All people killed while resisting Communists essentially were Catholic saints and needed only the publicity drive to force Rome to recognize them as such, according to the priests and nuns in charge of schools when Dermot attended.

Giles is murdered by a Communist.

Other questions had their own answers underneath.

243
Q Does the Fourth Commandment oblige us to respect and obey others besides our parents?
A Besides our parents, the Fourth Commandment obliges us to re-

spect and to obey all our lawful superiors. All are obliged to respect and to obey legitimate civil and ecclesiastical authorities
when they discharge lawfully their official duties.

Q   Name three moral virtues under the Fourth Commandment.

A   Obedience, which disposes us to do the will of our superiors.
Liberality, which disposes us rightly to use worldy goods.
Chastity, or purity, which disposes us to be pure in mind and
body.

252

Q   What are we commanded by the Fifth Commandment?

A   By the Fifth Commandment we are commanded to take proper
care of our own spiritual and bodily well-being and that of our
neighbor.

(a) Man does not have supreme dominion over his own life; he
was not the cause of its beginning nor may he be the deliberate
cause of its end. Man must use the ordinary means to preserve
life. He is not, however, obliged to use extraordinary means
which would involve relatively great expense or intolerable pain
or shame.

(b) The life of another person may lawfully be taken:

first, in order to protect one's own life or that of a neighbor, or a
serious amount of possessions from an unjust aggressor, provided
no other means of protection is effective;

second, by a soldier fighting a just war;

third, by a duly appointed executioner of the state when he
metes out a just punishment for a crime.

• • •

The rest of Dermot's education, the nonreligious topics, prepared
him for nothing but a badge.

Dermot Davey's grandmother, who owned the house he grew up
in, was a widow. She died when he was ten. One of his uncles' wives
came running into the hospital room, Mary Immaculate in Jamaica,
hysterical. She had an enormous black crucifix in her hands as a gift.
She thrust the crucifix at the grandmother. The grandmother thought
the crucifix meant she was dying, and she fainted and died later that
night. At the funeral, they began to talk of the grandfather. Dermot
didn't remember him. He had worked as a messenger for a big Wall
Street lawyer named Dufficey. The lawyer used to help support Irish

actors and poets. When Yeats came to New York, the lawyer subsidized him. Dermot's grandfather had the job of delivering the envelopes to Yeats. In an album they were showing around during the wake, there was one newspaper clipping which mentioned Dermot's grandfather. That got Dermot's mother excited about Yeats. Then when some old relative from Brooklyn said that somebody else on the grandfather's side had been the editor of a weekly newspaper in Brooklyn, Dermot's mother began talking of her family as if she were a Pulitzer.

She took Dermot into the living room on a few Saturday mornings and had him read from a book of Yeats poems. She wanted him to read out loud so he would memorize it. She was always tense in the morning. Tense and snappish. Dermot would have his thoughts on playing ball in a lot down by the railroad tracks and his mother would be snapping at him and making herself nervous and her son nervous and trying to learn "Cathleen Ni Hoolihan." It was, Dermot remembers, a fuck of a way to learn and of course he never did.

In St. Monica's school one day in June, in the last week of school when Dermot was in the seventh grade, the nun was trying to spend the day collecting books and putting them away for the summer and she had to keep the class busy so she had them write a composition on anything they wanted. Dermot put down his "JMJ" heading, which means Jesus, Mary, and Joseph bless this work. He started doing something he never had done before in school. In St. Monica's all the composition topics were mandatory. They were all of the "My Trip to the Planetarium" type. Dermot started to write about an old man who worked at the stables at Jamaica Race Track. The track is gone now. When he was growing up all the kids used to play baseball in an empty lot in the stable area. There was an old man who used to stomp around on a wooden leg. He used to have a big tub of boiling water. The lower part of a race horse's legs are so thin that almost no blood circulates. A race horse can have something bad the matter with his ankle and never feel it and keep walking on it until he starts dying of gangrene. So the old man used this boiling water on leg injuries, and it was fine except his stable was right by the fence. Just outside the fence was a bus stop. All the people looking out the windows of the bus would see an old man torturing a horse with boiling water. People bombarded the ASPCA with phone calls. Finally, the ASPCA sent inspectors to the stable. The old man started fighting with them. All the kids came over from the baseball lot and watched. In the middle of the argument, the old man said, Here, I'll show you the water doesn't hurt anybody. He walked over to the tub and put his leg into it. The people from the ASPCA, particularly this one woman, got hysterical. They didn't know it was a wooden leg the old man was sticking into the water. All the kids were jumping up and down.

So on this one day in St. Monica's school Dermot began to write a composition about the old man. He couldn't write fast enough to keep up with the things he wanted to put down. After a while his hand started to hurt because he was gripping the pen so hard. When he finished, he took the composition up and put it on the Sister's desk. He slid it right in front of her and stood waiting.

"Well," she said. She began reading. When she finished the second side, she told Dermot to take it to Sister Rita, the eighth-grade teacher. He ran it down the hall to Sister Rita's room. Usually he was nervous about opening the door and walking into another class, the whole room always looked at you, but this time he couldn't wait to get the composition onto Sister Rita's desk.

She took it and read the one side so quickly he couldn't understand how anybody could be that fast, and when she turned it over and only glanced at the second side, and when he saw she wasn't reading, the bottom fell out of him.

"Well," she said.

"Yes, Sister."

"Do you know why Sister had you bring this up to me?"

"No, Sister."

"Well, come over here. Look at this handwriting. Just look at this handwriting. Do you call this penmanship?"

"No, Sister."

"Well. Neither do I. And neither does Sister. Do you know why she sent this up to show me? Because she was so ashamed of such a sloppy piece of work. She wanted to know just what kind of sloppy boy I am getting in my class next fall. Now let me warn you about something. The summer goes very fast. And then you are going to be sitting right here in this class with *me*. So you better not embarrass Sister and arrive here next fall from her class and not have better penmanship than what you have just shown us here with this."

18

ELIZABETH CULLINAN
(b. 1933)

Elizabeth Cullinan was born in New York City in 1933 to Cornelius and Irene O'Connell Cullinan. She received her B.A. in 1954 from Marymount College, Manhattan, and between 1955 and 1964, she was intermittently a secretary and typist for the *New Yorker*. She lived in Dublin during 1961–1962; after returning to New York for several months, she went back to Dublin for two more years, finally returning to America to continue her work as a free-lancer, sometime faculty member of the University of Iowa's Writers' Workshop and the University of Massachusetts-Amherst, and at present, teacher of creative writing at Fordham University.

Her stories of Irish-American life—and of the lives of Irish Americans in Ireland—began appearing in 1960 in the *New Yorker*, which has published virtually all of her short fiction since then. Most of her stories have been republished in two collections, *The Time of Adam* (1971) and *Yellow Roses* (1977). Two novels—*House of Gold* (1970), for which she was awarded a Hougton-Mifflin Literary Fellowship and a New Writers Award, and *A Change of Scene* (1982)—have also received wide critical acclaim.

Beginning with "The Voices of the Dead," in the *New Yorker* in 1960, Cullinan has focused on urban Irish-American Catholics who undergo a generational conflict. "The Voices of the Dead" anticipates the prize-winning *House of Gold* in several ways, including a psychological exploration of older Irish Americans trying to control the young. In the novel, an old-style Catholic Irish-American family, the Devlins, gather on the death-day of the domineering matriarch, Julia Devlin, and attempt to settle past, present, and future.

Cullinan also explores the weight of the past on younger Irish-American women caught in extramarital affairs. Three of the stories in

The Time of Adam take place in Dublin and two of them, "A Swim" and "A Sunday Like the Others," explore the relationships of Irish-American young women with Irish men, a theme repeated in the uncollected "Good Loser," which appeared in the *New Yorker* in 1977. Three of the pieces in *Yellow Roses,* the title story, "An Accident," and "A Foregone Conclusion," are linked by the affair between Louise Gallagher and an unhappily married man. From the same volume, and first appearing in the *New Yorker* in 1976, "Life after Death" is the story of an affair between Constance and the married Francis Hughes, which dramatizes generational relationships and the burdens of the past on the present.

Cullinan's latest work, *A Change of Scene,* meshes several of her preoccupations and develops themes appearing in the earlier stories. Beginning and ending in New York City, the novel recalls Anne's ten-month stay in Dublin where, at twenty-six, she fell in love with an Irish journalist. He was the first of several men who introduced her to Irish society, a process that sorely tested her hyphenate identity.

Cullinan is an Irish-American woman writer who is Irish in ways that others in this volume—Flannery O'Connor, Mary McCarthy, and Mary Gordon—are not. She has moved beyond the position of her early life as she described it in 1977: "You were given a context to grow up in and that was supposed to be your identity. That's where you were. You were fortunate. You didn't need anything else." Cullinan is a first-rate stylist, a storyteller of no mean talent.

"Life After Death"

Yesterday evening I passed one of President Kennedy's sisters in the street again. They must live in New York—and in this neighborhood—the sister I saw and one of the others. They're good-looking women with a subdued, possibly unconscious air of importance that catches your attention. Then you recognize them. I react to them in the flesh the way I've reacted over the years to their pictures in the papers. I feel called on to account for what they do with their time, as if it were my business as well as theirs. I find myself captioning these moments when our paths cross. *Sister of the late President looks in shop window. Sister of slain leader buys magazine. Kennedy kin hails taxi on Madison Avenue.* And yesterday: *Kennedy sister and friend wait for light to change at Sixty-eighth and Lexington.* That was the new picture I added to the spread that opens out in my mind under the headline "LIFE AFTER DEATH."

It was beautifully cold and clear yesterday, and sunny and windless, so you could enjoy the cold without having to fight it, but I was dressed for the worst, thanks to my mother. At three o'clock she called to tell me it was bitter out, and though her idea of bitter and mine aren't the same, when I went outside I wore boots and put on a heavy sweater under my coat. I used to be overwhelmed by my mother's love; now it fills me with admiration. I've learned what it means to keep on loving in the face of resistance, though the resistance my two sisters and I offered wasn't to the love itself but to its superabundance, too much for our reasonable natures to cope with. My mother should have had simple, good-hearted daughters, girls who'd tell her everything, seated at the kitchen table, walking arm in arm with her in and out of department stores. But Grace and Rosemary and I aren't like that, not simple at all, and what goodness of heart we possess is qualified by the disposition we inherited from our father. We have a sense of irony that my mother with the purity of instinct and the passion of innocence sees as a threat to our happiness and thus to hers. Not one of us is someone she has complete confidence in.

Grace, the oldest of us, is married and has six children and lives in another city. Grace is a vivid person—vivid-looking, with her black hair and high color, vivid in her strong opinions, her definite tastes. And Grace is a perfectionist who day after day must face the facts—that her son, Jimmy, never opens a book unless he has to and not always then; that her daughter Carolyn has plenty of boyfriends but no close girlfriends; that just when she gets a new refrigerator the washing machine will break down, then the dryer, then the house will need to be painted. My mother tells Grace that what can't be cured must be endured, but any such attitude would be a betrayal of Grace's ideals.

My middle sister, Rosemary, is about to marry a man of another religion. Rosemary is forty and has lived in Brussels and Stuttgart and Rome and had a wonderful time everywhere. No one thought she'd ever settle down, and my mother is torn between relief at the coming marriage and a new anxiety—just as she's torn, when Rosemary cooks Christmas dinner, between pleasure and irritation. Rosemary rubs the turkey with butter, she whips the potatoes with heavy cream; before Rosemary is through, every pot in the kitchen will have been used. This is virtue carried to extremes and no virtue at all in the eyes of my mother, whose knowledge of life springs from the same homely frame of reference as my sister's but has led to a different sort of conclusion: Rubbed with margarine the turkey will brown perfectly well; to bring the unbeliever into the fold, you needn't go so far as to marry him.

Every so often I have a certain kind of dream about Mother—a dream that's like a work of art in the way it reveals character and throws light on situations. In one of these dreams she's just died— within minutes. We're in the house where I grew up, which was my grandmother's house. There are things to be done, and Grace and Rosemary and I are doing them, but the scene is one of lethargy, of a reluctance to get moving that belongs to adolescence, though in the dream, as in reality, my sisters and I are grown women. Suddenly I realize that Mother, though still dead, has got up and taken charge. There's immense weariness but no reproach in this act. It's simply that she's been through it all before, has helped bury her own mother and father and three of her brothers. She knows what has to be done but she's kept this grim knowledge from Grace and Rose- mary and me. She's always tried to spare the three of us, with the result that we lack her sheer competence, her strength, her powers of endurance, her devotedness. In another dream Mother is being held captive in a house the rest of us have escaped from and can't get back into. We stand in the street, helpless, while inside she's being beaten for no reason. The anguish I feel, the tears that wake me are not so much for the pain she's suffering as for the fact that this should be happening to her of all people, someone so ill-equipped to make sense of it. Harshness of various kinds and degrees has been a continuing presence and yet a continuing mystery to her, the enemy she's fought blindly all her life. "I don't think that gray coat of yours is warm enough," she said to me yesterday.

"Sure it is," I said.

"It isn't roomy enough," As she spoke, she'd have been throwing her shoulders back in some great imaginary blanket of a coat she was picturing on me.

"It fits so close, the wind can't get in," I explained. "That's its great virtue."

"Let me give you a new coat," she said.

When I was four years old I had nephrosis, a kidney disease that was almost unheard of and nearly always fatal then. It singled me out. I became a drama, then a miracle, then my mother's special cause in life. From this it of course follows that I should be living the life she'd have liked for herself—a life of comfort—but desire has always struck me as closer to the truth of things than comfort could ever be. "I don't really want a new coat," I told her yesterday. "I like my gray one."

"Dress warmly when you go out," she said. "It's bitter cold."

As I was hanging up there was an explosion—down the street from me, half a block on either side of Lexington Avenue is being reconstructed. The School for the Deaf and the local Social Services Office were torn down, and now in place of those old, ugly buildings battered into likenesses of the trouble they'd tried to mend, there are two huge pits where men drill and break rocks and drain water, yelling to each other like industrious children in some innovative playground. And all day long there are these explosions. There was another; then the phone rang again. It was Francis, for the second time that day. "Constance," he said. "What a halfwit I am." I said, "You are?"

He gave the flat, quick, automatic laugh I hate, knowing it to be false. When Francis truly finds something funny, he silently shakes his head. "Yes, I am," he said. "I'm a halfwit. Here I made an appointment with you for tomorrow afternoon and I just turned the page of my calendar and found I've got some sort of affair to go to."

"What sort of affair?" I asked. It could have been anything from a school play to a war. Francis produces documentaries for television. He's also married and has four sons, two of them grown. He's a popular man, a man everyone loves, and when I think of why, I think of his face, his expression, which is of someone whose prevailing mood is both buoyant and sorrowful. He has bright brown eyes. His mouth is practically a straight line, bold and pessimistic. He has a long nose and a high forehead and these give his face severity, but his thick, curly, untidy gray-blond hair softens the effect.

"I'm down for some sort of cocktail party," he said. "This stupid, busy life of mine," he added.

This life of his, in which I figure only marginally, is an epic of obligation and entertainment. Work, eat, drink, and be merry is one way of putting it. It could also be put, as Francis might, this way: Talent, beauty, charm, taste, money, art, love—these are the real good in life, and each of these goods borrows from the others. Beauty is the talent of the body. Charm and taste must sooner or later come down to money. Art is an aspect of love, and love is a variable. And all this being, to Francis's way of thinking, so—our gifts being contingents—we can do nothing better than pool them. Use me, use each other, he all but demands. I say, no—we're none of us unique, but neither are we interchangeable. "Well, if you've got something else to do, Francis," I said to him yesterday, "I guess you'd better do it."

He said, "Why don't I come by the day after tomorrow instead?"

I said, "I'm not sure."

"Not sure you're free or not sure you want to?"

"Both." I wasn't exactly angry or hurt. I have no designs on Francis Hughes, no claim on him. It would be laughable if I thought I did.

"Ah," he said. "Inconstance."

I said, "No, indefinite."

He said, "Well, I'm going to put Thursday down on my calendar and I'll call you in the morning and see how you feel about it."

"All right," I said, but on Thursday morning I won't be here—if people aren't interchangeable, how much less so are people and events.

"Tell me you love me," said Francis.

I said. "I do."

He said, "I'll talk to you Thursday."

"Goodbye, Francis," I said, and I hung up and put on my boots and my heavy sweater and my gray coat and went out.

The college I went to is a few blocks from this brownstone where I have an apartment. It's a nice school, and I was happy there and I can feel that happiness still, as though these well-kept streets, these beautiful houses are an account that was held open for me here. But New York has closed out certain other accounts of mine, such as the one over in the West Fifties. Down one of those streets is the building where I used to work and where I first knew Francis. His office was across the hall from mine. His life was an open book, a big, busy novel in several different styles—part French romance, part character study, part stylish avant-garde, part nineteenth-century storytelling, all plot and manners, part Russian blockbuster, crammed with characters. His phone rang constantly. He had streams of visitors. People sent him presents—plants, books, cheeses, bottles of wine, boxes of English crackers. I was twenty-two or three at the time, but I saw quite clearly that the man didn't need more love, that he needed to spend some of what he'd accumulated, and being twenty-two or three I saw no reason why I shouldn't be the one to make that point. Or rather, what should have put me off struck me as reason for going ahead—for the truth is I'm not Francis's type. The girls who came to see him were more or less voluptuous, more or less blonde, girls who looked as if they were ready to run any risk, whereas I'm thin, and my hair is brown, and the risks I run with Francis are calculated, based on the fact that the love of someone like me can matter to someone like him only by virtue of its being in doubt. And having, as I say, no designs, I find myself able to be as hard on him as if he meant very little to me when, in fact, he means the world. I try now to avoid the West Fifties. Whenever I'm in that part of the city, the present seems lifeless, drained of all intensity in relation to that lost time when my days were full of Francis, when for hours on end he was close by.

I also try to avoid Thirty-fourth Street, where my father's brother-in-law used to own a restaurant, over toward Third Avenue. Flynn's was the name of it, and when I was twelve my father left the insurance business to become manager of Flynn's. He's an intelligent man, a man who again and again redeems himself with a word, the right word he's hit on effortlessly. His new raincoat, he told me the other day, "creaks." I asked if there was much snow left after a recent storm, and he said only a "batch" here and there. Sometimes he hits on the wrong word and only partly accidentally. "Pompadour," he was always calling French Premier Pompidou. He also has a perfect ear and a loathing for the current cliché. He likes to speak, with cheery sarcasm, of his "life-style." He also likes to throw out the vapid "Have a good day!" "No way" is an expression that simply drives him crazy.

The other night I dreamed a work of art about my father. He was in prison, about to be executed for some crime having to do with money. Rosemary and my mother and I had tried everything, but we failed to save him. At the end we were allowed—or obliged—to sit with him in his cell, sharing his terror and his misery and his amazing pluck. For it turned out that he'd arranged to have his last meal not at night but in the morning—so he'd have it to look forward to, he said. I woke up in despair. My father's spirit is something I love, as I love his sense of language, but common sense is more to the point in fathers, and mine has hardly any. As for business sense— after eight months at Flynn's, it was found that he'd been tampering with the books; six thousand dollars was unaccounted for. No charges were pressed, but my father went back to the insurance business, and from then on we didn't meet his family at Christmas and

Easter, they didn't come to any more graduations or to Grace's wedding, Rosemary no longer got a birthday check from Aunt Kay Flynn, her godmother. You could say those people disappeared from our lives except that they didn't, at least not from mine. Once, when I was shopping with some friends in a department store, I spotted my Aunt Dorothy, another of my father's sisters. She was looking at skirts with my cousins Joan and Patricia, who are Grace's age— I must have been about sixteen at the time. A couple of summers later I had a job at an advertising agency where my cousin Bobby Norris turned out to be a copywriter. He was a tall, skinny, good-natured fellow, and he used to come and talk to me, and once or twice he took me out to lunch. He never showed any hard feelings toward our family, and neither did he seem to suspect how ashamed of us I was. Around this time I began running into my cousin Paul Halloran, who was my own age. At school dances and at the Biltmore, where everybody used to meet, he'd turn up with his friends and I with mine. Then one Christmas I got a part-time job as a salesgirl at Altman's. A boy I knew worked in the stockroom, and sometimes we went for coffee after work, and once he asked me to have a drink. We were walking down Thirty-fourth Street when he told me where we were going—a bar that he passed every day and that he wanted me to inspect with him. Too late to back out, I realized he was taking me to Flynn's. As soon as I walked in, I saw my father's brother-in-law sitting at a table, talking to one of the waiters. He didn't recognize me, but I couldn't believe he wouldn't. I'm the image of my mother and I was convinced this would have to dawn on him, and that he'd come over and demand to know if I was who he thought I was, and so I drank my whiskey sour sitting sideways in the booth, one hand shielding my face, like a fugitive from justice. Or like the character in a movie who, when shot, will keep on going, finish the business at hand, and then keel over, dead.

It's three blocks north and three blocks east from the house where I live to the building where I went to college. Sometimes, of an afternoon, I work there now, in the Admissions Office, and yesterday I had to pick up a check that was due me. The Admissions Office is in a brownstone. The school has expanded. Times have changed. On the way in I met Sister Catherine, who once taught me a little biology. "Is it going to snow?" she asked.

I said, "It doesn't look like snow to me."

In the old days these nuns wore habits with diamond-shaped headpieces that made them resemble figures on playing cards, always looking askance. Yesterday Sister Catherine had on a pants suit and an imitation-fur jacket with a matching hat on her short, curly gray hair, and it was I who gave the sidelong glance, abashed in the face of this flowering of self where self had for so long been denied.

"It's cold enough for snow," Sister Catherine said.

I said, "It certainly is," and fled inside.

The house was adapted rather than converted into offices, which is to say the job was only half done. Outside Admissions there's a pullman kitchen—stove, sink, cabinets, refrigerator, dishes draining on a rack. Food plays an important part in the life of this office, probably because the clerical staff is made up of students who, at any given moment, may get the urge for a carton of yogurt, or a cup of soup, or an apple, or a can of diet soda. I went and stood in the doorway of the room where they sit: Delia, Yeshi, Eileen, Maggie. They knew someone was there, but no one looked up. They always wait to make a move until they must, and then they wait to see who'll take the initiative. One reason they like it when I'm in the office is that I can be counted on to reach for the phone on the first ring, to ask at once if I can help the visitor. But the routine of Admissions is complicated; every applicant seems to be a special case, and I work there on such an irregular basis that I can also be counted on not to be able to answer the simplest questions, and this makes the students laugh, which is another reason they like having me around. That someone like me, someone who's past their own inherently subordinate phase of life, should come in and stuff promotional material into envelopes, take down telephone requests for information, type up lists and labels—and do none of this particularly well—cheers them. I stepped into the office and said, "Hello, everybody." They stopped everything. I said, "Guess what I want."

"You want your check," said Yeshi, who comes from Ethiopia—the cradle of mankind. Lately I've been studying history. A friend of mine who's an Egyptologist lent me the text of a survey course, and now there are these facts lodged in my mind among the heaps of miscellaneous information accumulating there. "Where is Constance's check?" asked Yeshi. She speaks with a quaver of a French accent. Her hands are tiny, her deft brown fingers as thin as pencils. She has enormous eyes. "Who made out Constance's time sheet?" she asked.

Maggie said, "I did." She wheeled her chair over to the file cabinet where the checks are kept. "It should be here. I'm sure I saw it this morning with the others." Maggie is Haitian. Her hair is cut close and to the shape of her head. She has a quick temper, a need to be listened to, and a need, every bit as great, to receive inspiration. "Uh-oh," she said.

"Not there?" I asked.

"It's got to be. I made out that time sheet myself," said Maggie. "I remember it was on Thursday—I'm not in on Wednesday, and Friday would have been too late."

I said, "Well, I don't suppose anyone ran off with it. It was only for a few dollars."

"Money is money around here." This came from Delia, a premed student and the brightest of the girls. Her wavy light-brown hair hangs below her waist. She has prominent features—large hazel eyes, an almost exaggeratedly curved mouth, and a nose that manages to be both thin and full; but there's a black-haired, black-eyed sister, the beauty of the family, and so Delia must make fun of her own looks. She's Puerto Rican and must also make fun of that. She speaks in sagas of self-deprecation that now and again register, with perfect pitch, some truth of her existence. "There's no poor like the student poor," she said yesterday.

"That's a fact, Delia," I said. "But I don't plan on contributing my wages to the relief of the Student Poor."

Maggie began pounding the file cabinet. "I made out that time sheet *myself*. I brought it in *myself* and had Mrs. Keene sign it; then I took it right over to the business office and handed it to feeble-minded Freddy. He gave me a hard time because it wasn't with the others. I hate that guy." She pounded the cabinet again.

Yeshi said, "Maybe Mrs. Keene has it."

"Is she in her office?" I could see for myself by stepping back; Olivia was at her desk.

"Come on in," she called.

I said to the students, "I'll be back," and I went to talk to my friend.

"You're just in time for tea and strumpets," she said.

Olivia was in school with me here, but her name then was McGrath. She's been married and divorced and has two sons, and I say to myself, almost seriously, that the troubled course of her life must be the right course since it's given her the name Keene, which describes her perfectly. She's clever, capable, resilient, dresses well, wears good jewelry, leads a busy life. Except for the divorce, Olivia is an example of what my mother would like me to be, though her own mother continually finds fault. "I wonder what it's like to be proud of your children," Mrs. McGrath will say.

Olivia reached for the teapot on her desk and said, "Have a cup."

"No thanks," I said. "I only came by to pick up my check, but it doesn't seem to be outside."

She opened her desk drawer, fished around, and came up with a brown envelope. "Someone must have put it here for safest keeping." She handed me the envelope and said, "Come on, sit down for a minute. Hear the latest outrage."

I sat down in the blue canvas chair beside the desk. I love offices and in particular that office, where the person I am has very little fault to find with the person I was. I begin to wonder, when I'm there, whether the movement of all things isn't toward reconciliation, not division. I'm half convinced that time is on our side, that nothing is ever lost, that we need only have a little more faith, we need only believe a little more and the endings will be happy. Grace's children will be a credit to her. Rosemary will find herself living in a style in keeping with her generous nature. My mother will come to trust the three of us. Olivia's mother will learn to appreciate Olivia. Francis will see how truly I love him. I'll be able to walk down Thirty-fourth Street and not give it a thought. "All right," I said to Olivia, "let's hear the latest outrage."

"Yesterday was High School Day."

"How many came?" I asked.

"A record hundred and seventy, of whom one had her gloves stolen, five got stuck in the elevator, and twelve sat in on a psychology class where the visiting lecturer was a transsexual."

"Oh God," I said.

"Tomorrow I get twelve letters from twelve mothers and dads."

"Maybe they won't tell their parents." I never told mine about seeing Aunt Dorothy shopping for skirts, or about the time I went to Flynn's for a drink, or how my first boyfriend, Gene Kirk, tried to get me to go to bed with him. To this day, I tell people nothing. No one knows about Francis.

Olivia said, "Nowadays kids tell all. Last week Barney came home and announced that his teacher doesn't wear a bra."

I looked at the two little boys in the picture on Olivia's desk, "How old is Barney?" I asked.

"Ten."

He has blond hair that covers his ears, and light-brown eyes with a faraway look. He calls the office and says, "Can I speak to Mrs.

Keene? It's me." His brother, Bartholomew, is a couple of years older. Like Olivia, Bart has small, neat features and an astute expression. He sometimes does the grocery shopping after school. He'll call the office and discuss steaks and lamb chops with his mother, and I remember how when I was a little older than he I used to have to cook supper most evenings. The job fell to me because Grace wasn't at home—she'd won a board-and-tuition scholarship to college—and Rosemary was studying piano, which kept her late most evenings, practicing or at her lessons. And after my father's trouble at Flynn's my mother had to go back to teaching music herself. She's a good—a born—musician, but the circumstances that made her take it up again also made her resent it. I resented it, too, because of what it did to my life. After school, I'd hang around till the last minute at the coffee shop where everyone went; then I'd rush home and peel the potatoes, shove the leftover roast in the oven or make the ground beef into hamburgers, heat the gravy, set the table—all grudgingly. But Bartholomew Keene takes pride in his shopping and so does Olivia. In our time, people have made trouble manageable. I sat forward and said, "I'd better get going."

"Think of it," said Olivia. "A transsexual."

I said, "Put it out of your mind."

In the main office, the students were in a semi-demoralized state. Their feelings are in constant flux; anything can set them up or down, and though they work hard, they work in spurts. My turning up was an excuse to come to a halt. I showed them my pay envelope. Maggie pounded the desk and said, "I *knew* it had to be around here somewhere."

"And I believed in you, Maggie," I said.

" 'I be-lieve for ev-ry drop of rain that falls,' " sang Delia, " 'a flow-er grows.' " They love to sing—when they're tired, when they're fresh, when they're bored or happy or upset.

" 'I be-lieve in mu-sic!' " Maggie snapped her fingers, switching to the rock beat that comes naturally to them. Eileen got up and went into her dance—she's a thin, pretty blonde with a sweet disposition and the soul of a stripper.

" 'I be-lieve in mu-sic!'" they all yelled—all except Yeshi, who only smiled. Yeshi is as quiet as the others are noisy but she loves their noise. Noise gives me eyestrain. I began backing off.

"When are you coming in again?" asked Delia.

I said, "Next week, I think."

Yeshi laughed. Her full name is Yeshimebet. Her sisters are named Astair, Neghist, Azeb, Selamawit, and Etsegenet. Ethiopia lies between Somalia and the Sudan on the Red Sea, whose parting for Moses may have been the effect of winds on its shallow waters.

After I left the office yesterday, I went to evening Mass. I often do. I love that calm at the end of the day. I love the routine, the prayers, the ranks of monks in their white habits, who sit in choir stalls on the altar—I go to a Dominican church, all gray stone and vaulting and blue stained glass. Since it's a city parish, my companions at Mass are diverse—businessmen and students and women in beautiful fur coats side by side with nuns and pious old people, the backbone of congregations. I identify myself among them as someone who must be hard to place—sometimes properly dressed, sometimes in jeans, not so much devout as serious, good-looking but in some undefined way. It's a true picture of me but not, of course, the whole truth. There's no such thing as the whole truth with respect to the living, which is why history appeals to me. I like the finality. Whatever new finds the archeologists may make for scholars to dispute, the facts stand. Battles have been won or lost, civilizations born or laid waste, and the labor and sacrifice entailed are over, can perhaps even be viewed as necessary or at least inevitable. The reasons I love the Mass are somewhat the same. During those twenty or so minutes, I feel my own past to be not quite coherent but capable of eventually proving to be that. And if my life, like every other, contains elements of the outrageous, that ceremony of death and transfiguration is a means of reckoning with the outrageousness, as work and study are means of reckoning with time.

Yesterday Father Henshaw said the five-o'clock Mass. He doesn't linger over the prayers—out of consideration, you can tell, for these people who've come to church at the end of a day's work—but he's a conscientious priest and he places his voice firmly on each syllable of each word as he addresses God on behalf of us all, begging for pardon, mercy, pity, understanding, protection, love. By the time Mass was over yesterday, the sun had set, and as I stepped onto the sidewalk I had the feeling I was leaving one of the side chapels for the body of the church. The buildings were like huge, lighted altars. The sky was streaked with color—a magnificent fresco, too distant for the figures to be identified. The rush hour had started. The street was crowded with people—flesh-and-blood images, living tableaux representing virtue and temptation: greed on one face, faith on another, on another charity, or sloth, fortitude, or purity. And there, straight out of Ecclesiastes, I thought—vanity of vanities, all is vanity. Then I realized I was looking at President Kennedy's sister. She was with a dark-haired man in a navy-blue overcoat. I had the impression at first that he was one of the Irish cousins, but I changed my mind as she smiled at him. It was a full and formal smile, too full and formal for a cousin and for that drab stretch of Lexington Avenue. It was a smile better given at official receptions to heads of state, and I got a sense, as I walked behind the couple, of how events leave people stranded, how from a certain point in our lives on—a different point for each life—we seem only to be passing time. I thought of the Kennedys in Washington, the Kennedys in London, the Kennedys in Boston and Hyannis Port. Which were the important days? The days in the White House? The days at the Court of St. James's? Or had everything that mattered taken place long before, on the beaches of Cape Cod where we saw them sailing and swimming and playing games with one another?

We reached the corner of Sixty-eighth and had to wait for the light to change. It's a busy corner, with a subway station, a newsstand, a hot-dog stand, and a flower stand operated by a man and his wife. The flower sellers are relative newcomers to the corner. I began noticing them last summer, when they were there all day, but when winter came they took to setting up shop in late afternoon. For the cold they dress alike in parkas, and boots, and trousers, and gloves with the fingers cut out. They have the dark features of the Mediterranean countries and they speak to each other in a foreign language. They have a little boy who's almost always with them. I'd guess he's about five, though he's big for five, but at the same time, he also seems young for whatever age he may be, possibly because he appears to be so contented on that street corner. A more sophisticated child might sulk or whine or get into trouble, but not that little boy. Sometimes he has a toy with him—a truck or an airplane or a jump rope. He also has a tricycle that he rides when the weather is good. If it's very cold he may shelter in the warmth of the garage a few doors down from the corner, or he'll sit in his parents' old car, surrounded by flowers that will replenish the stock as it runs out. In hot weather, he sometimes stretches out on the sidewalk, but that's the closest I've ever seen him come to being at loose ends. He's a resourceful little boy, and he's independent like his parents, who work hard and for the most part silently. I've never seen them talking with the owner of the hot-dog stand or the newsdealer. Business is business on that corner, and not much of it comes from me. I never buy hot dogs, flowers only once in a blue moon, and newspapers not as a rule but on impulse. Yesterday, I put my hand in my pocket and found a dollar bill there and I decided to get a paper. I picked up a *Post* and put my money in the dealer's hand. As he felt through his pockets full of coins, the flower sellers' little boy suddenly appeared, dashed over to his parents' cart, seized a daisy, and put his nose to the yellow center. The newsdealer gave me three quarters back. The traffic lights changed. President Kennedy's sister started across the street. The flower seller's wife grabbed the daisy from her son, and he ran off. I put the quarters in my pocket and moved on.

Yesterday's headlines told of trouble in the Middle East—Israel of the two kingdoms, Israel and Judah; Iran that was Alexander's Persia; Egypt of the Pharaohs and the Ptolemies. I love those ancient peoples. I know them. They form a frieze, a band of images carved in thought across my mind—emperors, princesses, slaves, scribes, farmers, soldiers, musicians, priests. I see them hunting, harvesting, dancing, embracing, fighting, eating, praying. The attitudes are all familiar. The figures are noble and beautiful and still.

19

MARK COSTELLO

(b. 1933)

Mark Costello's contribution to American literature rests on an acclaimed series of short stories about the breakup of a marriage. *The Murphy Stories,* collected in 1973, appeared individually in the *Chicago Review, Epoch, North American Review,* and *Transatlantic Review.* As a chronicle of one man's tortured reaction to a marriage on the rocks, the episodes are brilliantly conceived and developed.

"Murphy's Xmas," reprinted here, probes the psyche of a young academic desperately trying to make sense of a surreal world and surreal relationships. It is Christmas and his pregnant wife, Irish-Catholic parents, and small son are conspiring to keep him trapped in a loveless marriage. In desperation he clings to Annie, a nymphet music student, for love and reassurance.

Costello's use of elisions in shifting streams of consciousness, his terse but vivid dialogue, his use of imagery and allusions, mark him as a serious literary stylist. "Murphy's Xmas" is a modern classic.

Costello sets his fiction in Decatur, Illinois, where he was born in 1933. He has received degrees from the University of Iowa and the University of Illinois, and he has taught creative writing at various workshops. Costello is married and the father of three children. He is working on a novel.

"Murphy's Xmas"

I

Murphy's drunk on the bright verge of still another Christmas and a car door slams. Then he's out in the headlights and in bed waking up the next afternoon with Annie kissing his crucified right fist. It's blue and swollen, and when he tries to move it, it tingles, it chimes and Annie says, How did you hurt your hand? Did you hit somebody?

Murphy waits while that question fades on her mouth, then the room glitters and he sniffs the old fractured acid of remorse asking: Was I sick?

Yes.

Where?

On the floor. And you fell out of bed twice. It was so terrible I don't think I could stand it if it happened again promise me you won't get drunk anymore, Glover had to teach both of your classes this morning you frighten me when you're this way and you've lost so much weight you should have seen yourself last night laying naked on the floor like something from a concentration camp in your own vomit you were so white you were blue.

is the color of Annie's eyes as Murphy sinks into the stars and splinters of the sheets with her, making love to her and begging her forgiveness which she gives and gives until Murphy can feel her shy skeleton waltzing away with his in a fit of ribbons, the bursting bouquets of a Christmas they are going to spend apart and

bright the next morning they rise in sweet sorrow to part for Christmas; she to her parents' home in Missouri, he to haunted Illinois.

Murphy holds her head in his hands with whispers: I can't leave you. I won't be able to sleep. I know I won't. I'll get sick. I need you Annie.

She squeezes his shoulders, kisses his cheeks and tells him he can do it. It's only for two weeks. Goodbye. And be careful. Driving.

The door slams, the windows rattle, and Annie walking through the snow is no bigger than her cello which she holds to her shoulder, a suitcase bangs against her left knee and the door opens and there's Glover jangling the keys of his Volkswagen, offering again to drive Murphy's family into Illinois for him.

Stricken by swerving visions of his son strewn across the wet December roadside, his toys and intestines glistening under the wheels of semi-trucks, Murphy says no, he will drive and as he takes the proffered keys, Glover says: Is Annie gone already? I was supposed to give her a cello lesson before she left

then he leaves, the door slams and Murphy hates him, his Byronesque limp through the snow, his cello and his Volkswagen and sobriety. Rubbing his right fist, Murphy goes to the kitchen and drains a can of beer. Then he packs his bag and lights out for his abandoned home.

II

Now the trunks are tied down and the Volkswagen is overladen and they roll out of Kansas into Missouri with the big wind knocking them all over the road while vigilant Murphy fights the wheel and grins at the feather touches of his five year old son who kisses his neck and romps in the back seat, ready for Christmas.

In Mexico, Missouri, his ex-wife looks at his swollen right fist and says: Tsk-tsk. You haven't grown up yet have you. Who did you hit this time?

Into the face of her challenge, Murphy blows blue cigarette smoke.

When they cross the mighty Mississippi at Hannibal, she looks up at the old, well-kept houses, pats her swollen stomach and says: Maybe I could come here to live, to have my baby.

Murphy's son rushes into the crack of her voice. And he doesn't stop asking him to come back and be his daddy again until Murphy takes dexamyl to keep awake and it is dark and his son is asleep and the Volkswagen hops and shutters over the flat mauve stretches of Illinois.

At Springfield, where they stop to take on gas, the florescent light of the filling station is like the clap of a blue hand across the face. Murphy's son wakes and his wife says: This is where President Lincoln lived and is buried.

Where?

In a tomb. Out there.

She points a finger past his nose and Murphy makes a promise he knows he can't keep: I know what. Do you want to hear a poem, Michael?

With his son at the back of his neck all snug in a car that he

should never have presumed to borrow, he drives through Springfield trying to remember "When Lilacs Last In The Dooryard
Bloom'd." But he can't get passed the first stanza. 3 times he repeats
"O powerful western fallen star," and then goes on in prose about the
coffin moving across the country with the pomp of the inloop'd flags,
through cities draped in black until his son is asleep again and

that coffin becomes his wife's womb and from deep in its copious
satin Murphy hears the shy warble of the foetus: *you are my father,*
you are my father, the throat bleeds, the song bubbles, Murphy is
afraid enough to fight. He looks at his wife and remembers the wily
sunlight of conception, the last time he made love to her amid the
lace iron and miniature American flags of the Veteran's Cemetery
(it's the quietest place I know to talk, she said) while the crows
slipped across the sun like blue razor blades and the chatter of their
divorce sprung up around them.

stone and pine, lilac and star, the cedars dusk and dim: *well it's*
final then, we're definitely going to get a divorce? Murphy said *yes,*
for good? *yes* and his wife caught him by the hip as he turned away
well it's almost dark now so why don't we just lay down and fuck
once more for old time's sake here on the grass come on there are
pine needles and they're soft

Did you take your pill?

Yes

Ok, but no strings attached and

three and half months later Murphy is informed that he is going
to be a father again and again, hurray, whoopee now

Murphy drives across slippery Illinois hearing a carol of death
until the singer so shy becomes a child he will never hold or know,
and the sweet chant of its breath gets caught in the whine of the tires
as he imagines holding the child and naming it and kissing it, until it
falls asleep on his shoulder—*how could you have tricked me this*
way? how could you have done it?

That question keeps exploding behind Murphy's eyes, and when
they hit his wife's hometown, he stops the car in front of a tavern and
says: I can't do it.

What?

Face your parents.

He gets out: I'll wait here. Come back when you're unloaded.

His wife says *wait a minute,* and Murphy slams the door. He
walks under the glittering *Budweiser* sign and she screams: I can't
drive. I don't even know how to get this thing in reverse . . .

Push down.

Child!

Murphy hovers over the car: *I'm not a child!* and the motor roars, and the gears grind, and the Volkswagen hops and is dead. A red light flashes on in the middle of the speedometer and Murphy turns to the wakening face of five year old Michael: Are we at grandma's yet daddy?

He slams his swollen right fist into his left palm: Yes we are!

Then he gets in and takes the wheel. And he drives them all the way home.

But he doesn't stop there. Murphy roars northwest out of Illinois into Iowa in search of friends and gin he can't find. Then he bangs back across the Mississippi, cuts down the heart of Illinois, and holes up in the YMCA in his wife's hometown, within visiting distance of his son.

Whom he loves and doesn't see. He keeps telling himself: *I think I'll surprise Michael and take him to the park this afternoon*, then he races down to the gym to run in circles and spit against the walls. He sits in the steam room, watches the clock and slaps his stomach, which is flat, but on the blink. To ease his pain, he drinks milk and eats cottage cheese and yogurt and calls Annie long distance in Missouri: God I love you and miss your body Annie I haven't slept for two days

and she says: Guess what?

What?

Glover was through town and gave me a cello lesson, he's a great guy

his gifts are stunning and relentless, he limps off to take your classes when you're too drunk to stand up in the morning—his hair is scrubbed, his skin cherubic, his wrists are opal and delicate; right now Murphy would like to seize them and break them off. Instead he says: Is he still in town?

Who?

Glover.

Heavens no, he just stopped through for about two hours are you all right?

Yes. Listen Annie I love you

Murphy slams the phone down and bounds back upstairs to his room in the YMCA to sit alone while his cottage cheese and yogurt cartons fill up with snow on the window ledge and he imagines Annie back in their rooms in Kansas. When she walks across the floor her heels ring against the walls and every morning Murphy hears her before he sees her standing at the stove, her hair dark, her earrings silver, her robe wine, her thighs so cool and the pearl flick of her tongue is like a beak when she kisses him

Murphy tastes unbelievable mint and blood and

imagines Glover limping across the floor of the living room with two glasses of gin in his hands. The betrayal is dazzling and quick. Bending under Glover's tongue, Annie whispers *no, no,* and as she goes down in their bed, her fingers make star-shaped wrinkles in the sheets.

Murphy slams his fist down on his YMCA window sill. Then popping them like white bullwhips over his head, he stuffs his towels and clothes into his bag, and lights out of there on lustrous Highway 47. The night is prodigal, the inane angels of the radio squawk out there 1000 songs of Christmas and return. Bearing down on the wheel, Murphy murders the memory of Annie and Glover with the memory of his father, whom he has betrayed to old age, the stars and stripes of the U.S. MAIL.

Composing them on the back of his American Legion 40 *and* 8 stationery, Murphy's father sends quick notes *BY AIR* to his grandson saying: I was feeling pretty low x until I got the pictures you drew for me Michael boy x then I bucked up x God bless you x I miss you x give my love to your daddy x who

unblessed and rocking in the slick crescents of dexamyl and fatigue, is on his way home for still another Christmas. Now as he drives, he notes the dim absence of birds in the telephone lines, and thinking of the happy crows that Michael draws with smiles in their beaks, Murphy sees his father stumbling under the sign of the cross, crossing himself again and again on the forehead and lips, crossing himself on his tie clasp, wandering in a listless daze across the front lawn with a rake in his hands, not knowing whether to clean the gutter along the street or pray for his own son who has sunk so low out in Kansas.

It is just dawning when Murphy breaks into the mauve and white outskirts of his dear dirty Decatur where billboards and *Newport* girls in turquoise are crowned by the bursting golden crosses of Murphy's high school then

he's home. Pulled up and stopped in his own driveway. And sitting there with his hands crossed in his lap he feels agog like a buddhistic time bomb about to go off, about to splinter and explode inside the dry sleep of his parents, the tears will smoulder, the braying angels of insomnia will shatter around the childless Christmas tree, there will be a fire, it will sputter and run up the walls and be Murphy's fault. Sitting there he feels hearts beginning to pump in the palms of his hands and he doesn't want to let anybody die

as he knocks on the dry oaken door of his parents' home and is welcomed with open arms and the sun rising behind his back.

Inside the sockets of his mother's eyes, there are mauve circles and they have had the living room walls painted turquoise. Murphy blinks, shakes his father's hand, and his mother leads him into the kitchen.

There he drinks milk, eats cottage cheese and kisses his mother's hands. She cries and wants him to eat a big breakfast. With tears in her eyes, she offers him bacon, eggs, cornbread, coffee, butter chunk sweet rolls and Brazil nuts. When Murphy shakes his head she says: I think you're making the biggest mistake of your life, I think you'll live to regret it. Patricia is a lovely girl, you have a wonderful son and another child on the way. Isn't there any hope of you getting back together? I pray night and day and can't get little Michael off my mind. What's ever going to happen to him and the new child? Oh I wish I were twenty years younger

After breakfast they go shopping, and for his Christmas present Murphy picks out three packs of stainless steel razor blades and a pair of black oxford basketball shoes. Then he slips off for a workout at his high school gym. The basketball team is practicing and Murphy runs in wide circles around them, not bothering a soul.

Left to himself that afternoon, he drinks rum and egg nog and plays with the remote controls of the color television set. Then he roams the house and neighborhood and everything has changed. The sheets of his bed are blue. On the walls, where once there were newspaper photographs of himself in high school basketball uniform, there are now purple paintings of Jesus Christ kneeling on rocks in the Garden of Gethsemane. Every place he looks, in corniced frames of diminishing size, there are color photographs of Murphy in tight collared military attire. As he looks, the photographs get smaller and smaller and there is always a snub-nosed statue of St. Francis of Assisi standing there, to measure himself by.

Up and down the block, birds bang in and out of bird-feeders. The withering neighbors have put up fences within fences within fences. Half-drunk, Murphy keeps hitting the wrong switches and floodlights glare from the roof of the garage and light up the whole back yard. All night long his father keeps paying the encroaching Negro carolers not to sing. Finally Murphy gets up from the sofa, and smiling, announces that he's going out. Taking his rum and egg nog with him, he sits in the Volkswagen and drinks until 3 o'clock in the morning. Then he gets out, vomits on the curb, and goes back inside

Where his mother is awake in a nightgown of shriveled violet, with yellow spears of wheat sewn into the shoulders like cross-staves of static lightning about to go off and how

will Murphy hold her when she stops him on the carpet outside his bedroom door to tell him that she loves him, that he will always be her son no matter what happens she is so sorry that he had to leave his wife and children for

a mere girl, it is unbelievable that

in his hands her small skull buzzes and even before she mentions the fact of Annie, Murphy is holding Annie's skull in his hands and the sinking wings of mother's sweet shoulders are Annie's shoulders in his mother's nightgown sinking: What are you talking about?

That girl you're living with. She called tonight

on Christmas Eve

Murphy hears the old familiar bells of his father's fury gonging

Your father answered, he was furious

Mother I'm not living with anyone

Michael I know you are

then the small lightning of her nightgown begins to strike across her shoulders and she is sobbing against his throat and Murphy is in bed holding his lie like a sheet up to his chin: Mother I told you I'm not living with anyone

Stroking his leg through the blankets, she disregards the crocked insomnia of his eyes, and makes him promise to try to sleep. Do you promise now?

Yes mother, I promise

and she leaves him sleepless between the blue sheets with Christ kneeling on the wall, the scent of his mother's handcream on the back of his neck and he hears her alone in her room coughing like a wife he has lost at last and picking at her rosary beads all night long

There is no sleep
or peace on earth. But with the muzzy dawn Murphy rises and
goes to church with his parents. In the choir loft, the organs shutter;
in his pew, Murphy shivers and sniffs the contrition of Christmas-
tide. All around him the faithful kneel in candle smoke and pray; all
day long Murphy kneels and shuffles around trying to get Annie *long
distance*, trying to tell her *never to call him at home again*. Then at
7 p.m. the phone rings and Murphy's simmering 70 year old father
answers it hissing: Long distance, for you

By the time Murphy hangs up, his father is dizzy. He staggers
through the rooms slamming doors while Murphy's mother follows
him whispering: Mike your blood pressure, your blood pressure

Then in the living room they face each other: The bitch! Calling
here on Christmas Day! The little bitch!

Murphy turns to his mother and says, *I'm leaving* and his father
spins him by the shoulder: You're not leaving, *I* am!

They both leave. Murphy by the back, his father by the front.
Storm doors slam, crucifixes rattle on the walls. Murphy's father
rounds the corner and screams: Come back here!

His voice is higher than Murphy has ever heard it, and the wind
pulls at their clothes while they walk toward each other, his father in
a slanting stagger, his overcoat too big for him, his eyes filled with
tears.

I'm an old man. I'm dying. You won't see me again. Go back to
your family, don't abandon your son.

Murphy reaches for his shoulder and says *Dad I can't* and his
father slaps his hand away

Michael Murphy. You have a son named *Michael Murphy* and
you tell me you can't go back to him?

Murphy lifts his hand and starts to speak, but his father screams:
Phony! You're a phon*eee*, do you hear me?

They are at the door and Murphy's mother, in grief and her
nightgown, pulls them in. His father stumbles to the wall and hits it:
You phony. You ought to be in Viet Nam!

Murphy's laughter is curdled and relieved. He slaps his hands
together and screams: That's it, that's it!

Then he spins and bolts toward the back door, with his mother
screaming: Michael! Where are you going?

To Viet Nam, god damn it! To Viet Nam

Which isn't far. 150 miles north. From a motel room deep in her own home town, Murphy calls his wife and when he asks her to come over she says: Why *should* I come over?

You know why. I am going out of my mind.

Be my guest.

Click

She opens the door during half-time of a T.V. football game and neither of them say a word as their clothes fly in slurred arcs onto the bed. Then standing naked in front of her, Murphy hunches up with holy quietude and smiles and breathes as he holds a glass of gin and tonic to her lips and she drinks and smiles as the lime-skin nudges her teeth and she nods when she's had enough. While her mouth is still cool, Murphy kisses her tongue and gums and wants to push the bed against the wall and then to drive all the other guests to insomniac rack and ruin by humping and banging the bed with wet good health against the wall all afternoon but

his wife is sunk in an older despair. She runs her fingers up the vapid stack of Murphy's spine and says: You *are* handsome. I love to touch you.

Bare-chested Murphy turns on it, and the quick trick of her flattery gets them into bed, where to the pelvic thud of the inter-spring, she sucks on the spare skin of his collar bone and says: Tell me that you love me. You don't have to mean it. Just say it . . .

Murphy would like to, but he can't. Both memory and flesh legislate against him. He looks down, and like painted furniture, his wife's ribs now seem chipped by a 1000 kicks; when he takes them in his mouth, her nipples taste tight and deprived as walnuts; within the pregnant strop of her stomach against his, Murphy can feel the delicate strophes of Annie's waist, and moving like a pale liar before his wife's bared teeth, he remembers the beginning of the end of their marriage; the masks, mirrors and carrots that began to sprout around their bed like a bitter, 2 am, Victory garden, one that Murphy had planted all by himself and was going to pick and shake in his wife's face on the sparkling, sacrosanct morning that he left for good and ever. Caught in the dowdy mosaics of their bedroom mirror, they would get down on their hands and knees and as the orange joke of a carrot disappeared between her legs, his wife would turn and ask, *who are you?* and Murphy would smile down from behind his mask and say: *who are you?* Then his smile would rot in his opened mouth, and Murphy *became* his impersonations; he played and moaned within an adultery so hypothetical it stunk and smoked the

bedroom ceiling up like the induced death of love between them *HARDER, OH HARDER* now Murphy and his father are standing outside the motel room window looking in at Murphy's marriage like peeping toms and his father is ordering Murphy back into the bed but Murphy resists and all of his reasons are rosy and shrill like a schoolboy he screams: *I wouldn't swap Annie for anybody, do you hear me, not anybody* and his father, in tears and death screams: *Not for your son? Not for Michael Murphy?* I'M
COMING
and Murphy opens his eyes to endure his wife's orgasm like a slap across the face *OH THANK YOU GOD, OH THANK YOU*

Thanking her with whispers and pecks about the neck and ears, Murphy sweeps his wife out into the brittle December afternoon and bright the next morning he picks up his son to take him home, 150 miles south, to his grandmother. Michael's raucous teeth glitter in the rear view mirror of the VW, and as they rattle into Decatur, Murphy loves him so much, he can't stop or share him with anybody just yet: I know what Michael. Do you want to go to the zoo before we go to grandma's? Yes

he does. Right now. And Murphy, full of grins and flapdoodle, takes him there. He buys Michael a bag of popcorn, and as he goes back to the car to flick off the headlights, he turns to see the popcorn falling in white, jerky sprays among the ducks and geese.

The whole pause at the zoo is that way: spendthrift, inaugural and loving. Murphy squats and shows Michael how to feed the steaming billy goat with his bare hands. He flinches and giggles at the pink pluck of his lips, then they race over to look through the windows at the pacing leopards. Bare-handed and standing there, Murphy wonders how he would defend his son against a leopard. He can feel his fists and forearms being ripped away, but also he can feel his son escaping into the dusk and dim of the elm trees that surround the zoo.

Then he gets zany and amid giggles and protests, Murphy drives the borrowed VW up over the curb and through the park to grandmother's house they go with the radio blaring: help I need somebody's help then

suddenly it's darker and cooler and their smiles are whiter when the subject changes like a slap across the face to

Michael's dreams. 5 years old in a fatherless house, he sleeps alone and dreams of snow. Murphy pulls him into the front seat, sets him on his lap and turns off the radio. Holding him too tight, he says: what kind of snow Michael?

You know. The kind that falls.

What do you dream?

That it's covering me up.

Then Michael begins to cry and says: I want somebody to sleep with me tonight and tomorrow night. I want *you* to sleep with me daddy.

Murphy does. Three nights they stay in his parents' house and Murphy sleeps between the blue sheets while Michael sucks his thumb and urinates the first night against Murphy's leg, giving him the chance to be patient father loving his son

he carries him to the bathroom with sure avowals and tender kisses. That's all right Michael boy, dad will take care of you

Always?

Always

and Murphy's mother is there in her nightgown in the stark light of the bedroom changing the sheets, putting down towels, kissing her grandson, wishing she were twenty years younger

In the lilac morning, quick with clouds and sunlight, Murphy and his mother and son go up town. Standing in front of laughing mirrors in the Buster Brown Shoe Store, Murphy and Michael grow fat and skinny and tall and short together, then go to see Pinnochio not in the belly of a whale

but in the outer space of sure death and forgiveness, they eat silver sno-cones and Murphy is finally able to eat steak while his father roams through the rooms presenting his grandson with a plastic pistol on the barrel of which an assassin's scope has been mounted.

Compounding that armament with love, he displays, on the last afternoon, Murphy's basketball clippings. Spreading them out for his grandson on the bed, he whispers, smiles and gloats until 5 year old Michael can't help himself. He walks over to Murphy and says: Grandpa says your were a great basketball player and played on T.V.

is that right daddy?

That's right Michael, then they

are leaving. Clasping his toys to him, Michael cries pained and formal tears. Murphy stands on the curb, the wind in his eyes, and the apologies are yet to be made. Overhead the street light clangs and they are standing on the same corner where Murphy used to sit under the streetlight at night on the orange fire hydrant twirling his rosary beads like a black propeller over his head waiting for his parents to come home and light up the dark rooms with their voices and cigarettes then

he would see their headlights coming up the street and he would rise and put away his rosary beads to greet them now

he takes off his gloves and puts out his right hand to his father and says: Dad, I'm sorry.

When his apology cracks the air, his mother begins to cry. Grateful for that cue, his father takes his hand and says Goodbye, good luck, God bless you.

III

Out there in Kansas the next afternoon, under a sere and benedictory sun, Murphy's Christmas comes to an end. He tools west away from home and the holidays, southwest toward the snaggled conclusion of still another New Year. His family rides in a swarm of shredded Kleenex, Cracker Jack and terror referred

is terror refined: like the crucial envoy of his grandfather, Michael, sweet assassin, holds his plastic pistol to the base of Murphy's skull and says: Daddy? Why don't you come back and be my daddy?

Terse and perspirate, Murphy's wife takes a swipe at the pistol, but Michael moves out of her reach, and keeping it trained on the back of his father's skull, he repeats his question: Why don't you come back daddy?

Before he can think or excuse himself, Murphy says, *Because*

Because why?

Because mommy and I fight

You're not fighting now.

In tears and on her knees, Murphy's wife lunges into the back seat and disarms her son. But he begins to cry and find his ultimatum: Daddy

I'm too shy to have a new daddy, I want you to be my daddy, and if you won't come back and be my daddy

I'm going to kill you.

The moment of his threat is considered. And then it is foregone.

Out of his fist and index finger, Michael makes a pistol and a patri-
cide: Bang, bang, bang
you're dead daddy
you're dead

Coffin that passes through lanes and streets, Volkswagen that
blows and rattles under the new snow's perpetual clang, here, Murphy hands over his sprig of lilac and return, his modicum of rage and
disbelief.
Certain that his son's aim was shy and hypothetical, he stops the
Volkswagen in front of his apartment, flicks off the headlights, slams
the door and hears the
dual squawk of tuned and funereal cellos
their notes curdle the snow, splinter the windows with a welcome so baroque and sepulchral, Murphy can't stand it. Roaring toward the door, he imagines Annie and Glover sitting on stiff-backed
chairs, their cellos between their legs, their innocence arranged by
Bach, certified by
the diagonal churn of their bows on string, the spiney octagons of
their music stands, the opal bone and nylon of Annie's knees. Murphy rattles the door with his fist, and for a moment their music needles his rage, then squeaks to a stop. In turquoise slacks and sweater,
with a smile brimful of tears and teeth so bright, Annie throws open
the door and how
will Murphy return her kiss, while blurred in the corner of his
eye, Glover scurries, gathering up his cello and his music: *Happy
New Year did the car run all right* he takes the proffered keys and
guilty of nothing but his embarrassment
he says *don't mention it* as he leaves, slams the door and
left in the rattled vacuum of that departure, Murphy has no one
to beat up or murder, no one on whom to avenge his Christmas; he is
left with only the echo of the music, a suspicion founded on nothing
but a cherub's limp and hustle through the chiming snow.

In bed. Annie is a sweet new anatomy of hope and extinction.
She kisses him, the *Newport* flood of her hair gets in his eyes, and
Murphy cracks an elegiac and necessary joke; *Annie you'll never
leave me for Glover will you?* She tells him not to be silly then
Murphy kisses her, and in a rush of flesh and new avowals, he
puts everything in to his love-making but his
heart

which hangs unbelievable and dead in his ribs, all shot to smithereens by Michael.

Outside the new snow falls and inside it is over. Annie is asleep in his arms and Murphy lies sleepless on a numb and chiming cross of his own making. On the walls there are no praying Christs, the turquoise Gethsemanes of Decatur are gone forever. The clock drones, the womb whirrs, the shy trill of his wife's gestation comes to Murphy through the pines like Michael calling to him: *Sleep with me tonight and tomorrow night daddy* the cradle's eloquence depends on pain, it is sewn in lilacs and shocks of wheat. Shy charlatan, Murphy sneaks up to it and in a room full of white, white sunlight, he looks in at his newborn child, and cannot look away or kid himself, his fatherhood is the fatherhood

of cottage cheese, the retreating footprints of snow and yogurt up his father's spine, the borrowed Volkswagen that will never run out of gas or plastic pistols. Then the dry bells of the furnace begin to hiss against Murphy's ankles and he hears the whistling pines, the clangorous tombstones of the Veteran's Cemetery. Flapping their arms like downed angels in the middle of winter, Murphy and Annie make love and forgive each other until their ears and eyesockets fill up with snow

    then Michael stands over them, takes aim at Murphy and

    makes his final declaration: Bang

    bang, bang

    you're dead daddy

    you're dead

IV

And for the first time in his life, Murphy lies there and knows it.

20

PETE HAMILL

(b. 1935)

Pete Hamill was born on June 24, 1935, in the Park Slope section of Brooklyn, the son of immigrant parents from Belfast. He attended Holy Name Grammar School in Brooklyn and Regis High School in New York City. But at 16, Hamill left school for the Brooklyn Navy Yard, where he was a sheet-metal worker for a year. In 1952 he enlisted in the U.S. Navy.

After service, Hamill continued his education in design at Pratt Institute and at Mexico City College from 1955 to 1958. He worked for a time as an advertising designer in New York City, but joined the *New York Post* as a reporter in 1960. He has since been on staff at the *Saturday Evening Post*, the *New York Post*, *Newsday*, and the *New York Daily News*. He has also contributed features and political commentary to major periodicals—the *New York Times Magazine*, *Playboy*, *Cosmopolitan*, *Life*, *Ramparts* and many others.

Hamill has received the Meyer Berger Award from Columbia University for an exposé on urban slums and the Newspaper Reporters Association Special Award for an investigative series on police corruption. His on-the-scene coverage of the Vietnam War and commentary on the Kent State massacre influenced public opinion against continued U.S. involvement in Southeast Asia. His 1972 *Post* series on the British occupation of Belfast brought him further professional recognition. Hamill's best journalism has been collected in *Irrational Ravings* (1971)

In spite of his productivity as a journalist, Hamill has found time to write film and television scripts and occasional fiction. In 1968 he published *A Killing for Christ*, a Vatican murder mystery; in 1973, *The Gift*, a sensitive autobiographical novella; in 1977, *Flesh and Blood*, a sordid novel on the boxing game. More recently, he has turned to the detective story.

The Gift, Hamill's most successful fiction to date, offers a critical insight into the Irish psyche, especially the father-son relationship. Pete, the narrator, has come home to Brooklyn on a Christmas furlough from the Navy. The selection that follows is rites-of-passage fiction in which the young man closes the gap without ever puncturing the myth of fatherhood.

In the end, he understands that, despite emotional barriers, his father genuinely loves him. *The Gift* was serialized for television two years after publication.

The Gift

I awoke to a room flooded with an oblique winter sun. The blanket was pink wool, and itchy, except on the edges, where it was trimmed with sateen. I was used to the broad ceiling beams of barracks, open rows of bunk beds, the wide chill murmur of boot-camp mornings. Now I was in a room that had once been large and suddenly had shrunk, and my eyes played on the lone picture, two snow-white parrots in a Brazilian jungle.

The jungle had to be Brazil; I had figured that out one time in geography class, and I was probably wrong. But I knew that parrots had to mean South America, because they didn't have them in Africa. And lying there, gradually becoming familiar with the molding around the ceiling trimming the green walls, feeling safe, I thought of Bomba. *A jagged streak of lighting shot athwart the sky, followed by a deafening crash of thunder. The lurid glare revealed Bomba, the jungle boy, crouched in a hollow beneath the roots of an overturned tree.* It was from "Bomba the Jungle Boy in the Swamp of Death, or The Sacred Alligators of Abarago" by Roy Rockwood, and I had memorized those opening lines, sitting alone at the top of the stairs one summer, next to the roof door. Bomba lived in a South American jungle with a naturalist named Cody Casson; he didn't know his mother or father, and reading about him, about how old Casson had been injured in an accident, and how Bomba became the provider, how at fourteen he was as strong as men twice his age, I would inhabit that distant jungle, alone, fighting pumas, jaguars, snakes, storms and cannibals. I copied pictures out of the books, which were published by Cupples and Leon, and which my brother Tommy and I would buy in the used-book store on Pearl Street, and once, with a flat sheet of cork stolen from a factory, I carved a whole river system, marked with jungles, native villages, and the massive headwaters of the Giant Cataract. At the end of every book, Bomba got closer to discovering the secret of his vanished parents, whose names were Andrew and Laura Bartow, and I wandered the used-book shops trying to find the missing volumes in the series, the volumes that would tell the whole story about this white boy lost in the South American jungle. Each book would end with Bomba wondering about his mother, longing for her, crying alone in the jungle. I never did find the missing volumes.

I looked up and my brother Denis was staring at me. He was only two, a kid with square shoulders and huge wet brown eyes. He was standing beside a chair, tentative and puzzled.

"Hello, Denis."

He said nothing.

"Don't you remember me?"

Wordless, he turned and started to run, waddling as he went, heading for the kitchen. Everybody else was gone, including my father. I got up and went to my father's closet. An old pair of light-blue civilian trousers was hanging next to a zipper jacket. I pulled them on, then took a shirt out of his drawer. Above the bureau, brown and fading, was an old photograph of an Irish soccer team. There were fifteen players and two coaches, and there was a banner before them that said *St. Mary's*. One of the players was my father.

The year before, after dropping out of high school, I had worked for a year in the sheet-metal shop of the Brooklyn Navy Yard, and men there had told me how good my father had been, when he was young and playing soccer in the immigrant leagues. He was fierce and quick, they said, possessed of a magic leg, moving down those Sunday playing fields as if driven by the engines of anger and exile, playing hardest against English and Scottish teams, the legs pumping and cutting and stealing the ball; hearing the long deep roar of strangers, the women on the sidelines, the hard-packed earth, the ice frozen in small pools, the needle beer in metal containers, and the speak-easies later, drinking until the small hours, singing the songs they had learned across an ocean. Until one day, in one hard-played game, a German forward had come out of nowhere and kicked, and the magic leg had splintered and my father fell as if shot, and someone came off the bench and broke the German's jaw with a punch, and then they were pulling slats off the wooden fence to tie against the ruined leg and waiting for an hour and a half for the ambulance to come from Kings County Hospital while they played out the rest of the game. The players and the spectators were poor; not one of them owned a car. And then at the hospital, he was dropped in a bed, twenty-eight years old and far from home, and there were no doctors because it was the weekend. Across the room, detectives were questioning a black man whose stomach had been razored open in a fight; and the ceiling reeled and turned, his face felt swollen and choked, he remembered his father's white beard and lifting bricks in the mason's yard; remembered all that, and the trip down the hill that day with the clothes in the bag, dodging the British soldiers, heading for a certain place where a certain man would get him on the boat to Liverpool and then to America; remembered that, he said later, and remembered how the razored man died in silence, and there was no feeling in the magic leg. When the doctors finally showed up the next morning, the leg was bursting with gangrene, and they had to slice the soccer boot off with a knife, and in the afternoon they took the leg off above the knee. When he talked about it later, he never mentioned the pain. What he remembered most clearly was the sound of the saw.

"Fried, Peter, or scrambled?"

I went into the kitchen. My mother was at the stove. Denis stood in silence in a corner, staring at me. I went into the L-shaped bathroom, with the swan decals on the walls, and the pull-chain box up high near the ceiling. I closed the door and felt tight and comfortable as I started to shave. And I knew that he shaved there too, every morning, shaved, and washed his face hard with very hot water so that his skin was shiny and gleaming, and then combed his hair very tightly, so that it was slick, black, glossy. And I wondered if he ever stood there and thought about me.

I wondered whether he cursed the vanished leg, the terrible Sunday at Wanderers' Oval, and whether he was sorry because he never could do the things with me and Tommy that fathers were expected to do in America. He had never played baseball with us, or thrown us a pass with a football. We had never gone fishing, or wandered around Brooklyn on long walks, or gone on rides to the country, because he never learned to drive a car. He was a stranger to me, though we shaved at the same mirror, often with the same razor, and I had come to love him from a distance. I loved him when he would come home with his friends and sit in the kitchen drinking cardboard containers of beer, talking about fights, illustrating Willie Pep's jab on the light cord or throwing Ray Robinson's hooks into the wash on the kitchen line. I loved the hard defiance of the Irish songs, and I would lie awake in the next room listening to them, as they brought up the old tales of British malignance and murders committed by the Black and Tans and what the men in the trench coats did in the hours after midnight. But I didn't really know him, and I was certain he didn't know me. I had some bald facts: he had left school at twelve to work as a stonemason's apprentice, because there were eleven children in the family; he had been in Sinn Fein, and a policeman had been murdered, and he came on the run to America; for a while he struggled with night school at Brooklyn Tech, with my mother helping him with spelling. But I was seventeen and a half, and I still didn't know when they had married, whether my mother was pregnant with me at the time, whether they had been married at all. There were no anniversary parties, and no wedding pictures on the walls. I tried not to care. But he didn't know really how to deal with me, didn't know what to do when I asked for help, and in many ways he was still Irish and I was an American. But I loved the way he talked and the way he stood on a corner with a fedora and raincoat on Sunday mornings, the face shiny, the hair slick under the hat, an Irish dude waiting for the bars to open, and I loved the way he once hit a guy with a ball-bat because he had insulted my mother. I just never knew if he loved me back.

I sat down to eat, and then heard him coming up the stairs. He worked across the street in the Globe Lighting Company, which took most of the third floor of the Ansonia Clock Building, once the largest factory in Brooklyn, to us a dirty red-brick pile. He was a wirer, a member of Local 3 of the International Brotherhood of Electrical Workers; but basically he was just another pair of hands on the assembly line, and sometimes in the night he would come home, after working all day on those concrete floors, and he would take off the wooden leg, and the stump sock, and lie back on the bed, the flesh of the stump raw and blistered; I never heard him complain; he would just lie there, hurting, his hands touching the bedsheets as if afraid to touch the ruin of the leg, as if admitting pain would be some ultimate admission that the leg was gone forever and he was mortal and growing old. Before the war he worked at the Roulston's plant, down on Smith Street, a clerk, because the Irish came to America with good handwriting, as they called it; he would bring home mysterious bundles, sometimes wrapped in newspapers and tied with twine, containing canned food or packaged spaghetti, and he would hand them to my mother, always in silence, explaining nothing. He left Roulston's for the war plant, and then there were a couple of years after the war, made up of uncertainty, idleness, Rattigan's, the attempt to make something of the apartment on Seventh Avenue, where we had all moved in 1943; everything was always being painted, because the rumor was that fresh coats of paint would kill the eggs of the cockroaches; the kitchen table and the chairs were painted with Red Devil red, a coat a year, with newspapers spread out on the linoleum floors, and the walls were painted, and the closets; but the roaches still came, long and sleek and heavy with eggs, chocolate-brown, dark blond, plump and long and sometimes wedge-shaped, invincible, insidious, silent; and there is a dream I still have about a cockroach that moves into my ear at night, and gnaws its way to my brain, chewing, silent, its feelers humming and tentative, moving around in the crevices, an inhabitant of my skull.

"Hello, Magee."

He was in the door, with the familiar rolling limp, wearing a lumberjack's coat and a flannel shirt, hatless, the hair slicked back, and I got up and went over to him, and he shook my hand. My mother was behind us, making American cheese sandwiches while tomato soup heated in a saucepan.

"Hey, you look good," he said, and he stepped back.

"They feed you pretty good there," I said.

"They must," he said. He had the jacket off now, and was sitting down, reaching for a steaming cup of tea. Denis put his head on my father's lap, and he rubbed the boy's head.

"You hear about O'Malley?"

"No, what?"

"The son of a bitch is taking the Dodgers out of Brooklyn."

"Billy," my mother said. "The language . . . "

"They're goin' to California," he said. "Him and the other son of a bitch, Stoneham. In a couple of years . . . "

"I don't believe it."

"Tommy Holmes had it in the *Eagle*."

"What for? I mean, why are they goin' out there?"

"Because O'Malley is a greedy son of a bitch, that's why."

My mother had sliced the sandwich in quarters and placed it before him, and he started to eat. Denis wandered into the other room.

"The players oughtta go on strike," he said. "Just say they're staying, and to hell with O'Malley. Never would've happened with Branch Rickey. He was a man, Rickey. Loved baseball, too. Put together the best bloody farm system in history."

"Yeah."

"Archie Moore's fighting Maxim this week, title fight."

"Moore should flatten him."

"I don't know," he said. "Maxim's a clever guinea. And Jack Kearns doesn't take any chances. Some manager, that Kearns. He managed Dempsey, you know. And Mickey Walker."

"But he can't break an egg with a punch, Maxim."

"He holds, and grabs ya, and it's hard to bang him. It's no cinch for Moore. He hasn't made the weight in two years."

"What did you think of the election?"

"I didn't like Stevenson."

"You mean you voted for a Republican?"

"Ike was a hell of a general," he said flatly. "Even if he looks like someone's aunt."

"He sounded pretty dumb, compared to Stevenson."

"He was a hell of a general," he said. There was a note of finality in the statement; I remember it as a moment when I realized he was changing, because there wasn't a general who ever lived that Billy Hamill could admire. He was an enlisted man for life. I picked up the light zipper jacket.

"Well, I'll see you later," I said.

"Right," he said, without looking up.

I went out, moving quickly down the stairs, trembling.

21

JOE FLAHERTY
(1936–1983)

Joe Flaherty was born in 1936 in Brooklyn, New York, of Irish immigrant parents. He attended Catholic grammar school and various high schools until he was 16, when he went to work as a longshoreman on the New York City docks.

While on the waterfront, Flaherty wrote a piece on Mayor John Lindsay's fight to secure a civilian review board to oversee the New York City Police Department. It was a witty and colorful account that won him, in 1966, a contributor's seat on the *Village Voice*. He contributed for the next eleven years.

Flaherty published four books: *Managing Mailer* (1970), a riotous campaign diary of the Mailer-Breslin mayorality run in 1969; *Fogarty & Co.*, a masterpiece of black comedy (1973); *The Tin Wife* (posthumously—1984); and *Chez Joey*, a collection of journalistic gems. Flaherty's work appeared in *Penthouse*, the *Nation*, the *Saturday Review*, the *New York Times*, the *N.Y. Daily News*, the *New York Post*, *Esquire*, *New York*, *Inside Sports*, the *Chicago Tribune*, the *Los Angeles Times*, the *Boston Globe*, and many other publications.

Flaherty had an encyclopedic knowledge of politics, sports, and New York neighborhoods. The following selection from *Fogarty & Co.*, though irreverent, demonstrates the writer's verbal dexterity—he is an acknowledged master of the one-liner.

Flaherty lived in Greenwich Village until his death in October 1983.

Fogarty & Co.

He couldn't bring himself to stop trying to solve the eternal riddle. He prayed he might become vacuous and cease thinking, since other men always seemed happier than he. But he knew this was a lie: Some men just disguised their despair better.

Fogarty was a fan of man. He admired man's courage and his ability to make laughter, though in the social sense of things many of them bored him. He thought of suicide a lot these days, not so much from anguish as curiosity. This, too, he knew, was not his exclusive franchise. How many millions, he wondered, were sick and tired of being forced to dance to a tune they hadn't requested? He suspected the world would end, not from the holocaust of war but because of some secret, unspoken cabal among people to stop reproducing.

He had an inkling this was taking place already, through the rise of the pill, the adulation of abortion as social progress, and the rampant homosexuality skipping across the land. The signs were there. One encountered murderous assaults on family life in every publication. And there were those gymnastic charts on experimental sex that swung the sperm from every angle, never allowing it to land on its feet in the womb. Loads in the mouth, loads in the rectum—at the nihilistic mercy of the spit or the shit. Against his will Fogarty began to believe humanity was calling God's hand.

He hated such thoughts and tried to overcome them the way Houdini shed his chains, always looking for another escape route from death. Since Fogarty was given to boredom, he granted God the same condition and concluded that man's morality was what made him interesting, not only to himself but to the Deity. If one took death out of the human experience, would there ever have been a book written, a canvas painted, a rock sculpted? He doubted it.

If men could walk the earth forever, wouldn't Freud's theories be merely graffiti on some bathroom wall? He tried to believe mortality was the stage mother to art who dictated the show must go on for the entertainment of the Lord.

Of course, it all could be absurd, as the French intellectuals pointed out, but Fogarty believed someone had to be responsible for drying millions of years of tears. Anyway, how could he take the life-is-absurd school seriously, he reasoned, when that claque was the same one that repeatedly despaired about its seating at the Cannes

Film Festival? Fogarty, even in his present condition, could distinguish tragedy from farce.

Mustering courage, Fogarty took a walk into no-man's-land, stopping at the church steps. He sat down and lit a cigarette. The steps were where he and his friends had gathered as boys, the jump-off area from which they plotted their assault on the confessional box. Endless strategies were plotted there, the foremost concerning how they could confess, in delicate English, that randy preoccupation of boys and avoid having the priest bellow at them or give them penance so severe they would have to spend hours (as though chained) at the altar rail.

Masturbation was no mean stunt to explain. The favorite maneuver was to innocently tuck the dastardly deed in the middle of a host of innocuous ones. "Bless me, Father, for I have sinned. It has been two weeks since my last confession. I disobeyed my mother four times I used bad language eleven times I fought with my brother three times I committed impure acts three times (pick up the tempo here) I-stole-a-Hershey-bar-from-the-A-&-P-and I-talked-in-class-four-times."

All this was delivered in a marvelous verbal wind sprint, like a spy passing information on the Orient Express. Of course, it had never worked. The priest in question would shout: Whoa, hold your hellish horses, and demand that you cover the middle ground again more slowly.

In retrospect, Fogarty couldn't blame the priests for this. (They probably spent most of their days listening to dried-up scones lament the ingratitude of their children.) And here was some punk who had spent a fortnight cannonading sperm all over the place, even if all of it landed on inanimate objects, trying to hustle the good father out of an interlude of excitement!

But not all the church step conversations were geared toward machination. Philosophy and theology were banked about like an eight ball. Since a good confession required "a firm resolution not to sin again," what would one do, the argument went, if—on exiting from the confessional with a bleached soul—one was approached by Ava Gardner (no picayune occasion of sin) with a proposition to roll in squalid sheets? (As he dragged on his cigarette, this meaty metaphysic even now gave Fogarty pause.)

He remembered that all his friends were confounded by the complexity—except Jay Gilliam. "I'd throw her a bounce right on the church steps," Jay cavalierly announced.

But then Jay was a Promethean figure among them: the only wearer of electric blue pants with gray pistol pockets and a peg so tight his Italian featherweight shoes had to be removed before he could put them on, a smoker of raunchy Chesterfields which he could inhale indoors or after a glass of milk without getting dizzy. He was their sexual pathfinder with a giant-size organ, who bragged he could ejaculate a wad of sperm over his head and turn around and catch it. This image was reincarnated years later, when Fogarty watched Willie Mays execute the basket catch, and gave him an eerie feeling.

But the statement that enshrined Jay forever in street legend was delivered at yet another tactical session on the steps. "Tell him what I tell him," Jay offered, "that you flogged the bishop." When the heavens didn't open and strike the blasphemer dead, Fogarty knew he was privy to someone who had clout in the stratosphere.

Fogarty decided to give it a go. The church door yawned open under his apprehensive push, and he slid through the opening—a cagey sinner sneaking up on the Lord. It was in here that, as so many previous times in his life, Fogarty was overcome by the smell. The sheet of his past was being pulled over his head, and he was smothered in memories. The more he thrashed about, trying to punch the phantoms, the more they engulfed him, opening up his subconscious.

Damn smell. He cursed the nose for the torment it dredged up. Pity Cyrano, who must have been able to inhale man's history. Odd, he thought, how that damn, clownish appendage, more than anything else, convinced him he was alive. Why, he wondered, wasn't the sensitive eye granted such powers? Or the magnificient machinery of the brain? Why the nose? The vulgarian's thesaurus: honker, schnoze, horn, beak, snotbox. Another one of God's jokes maybe?

His damnable nose and, he mused in embarrassment, rehearing popular music from his past evoked more of his history, opened more floodgates of old miseries, than loftier senses and more profound philosophies. The mockery of it: Wafting and crooning were the touchstones of his life.

The church seemed the same to him. Nice thought that—like Peter's Rock. The flames of the altar candles alternately dimmed and brightened, playing the game of existence and extinction. Flowers surrounded the tabernacle, the field headquarters of the Supreme Commander. He wondered if the flowers still were placed there by the same three women. The thought came to him because he knew women had to be granted special permission to enter beyond the altar rail. Some kind of purity screening, he had heard.

He remembered that he had once fainted on the altar at a high mass, and no one would pick him up (after all, he *did* ruin the ceremony), till a panicky female parishioner rushed through the open rail to his aid. The poor woman was bodily ushered from the holy ground, like a domestic who has tried to infiltrate a DAR convention, and Fogarty was later admonished, as if he were one of the Queen's Royal Guards who had let the sun get the better of him.

The memory stoked up his old hatred of priests, though "old" wasn't precise, since the current-day crop, like the Berrigan brothers, gave him a pain in the ass, too. Pious revolutionaries he couldn't endure. He could not imagine trying to kidnap Henry Kissinger and naming Jesus as an accomplice. Even the use of Christ was trendy these days.

Looking at his formidable surroundings—the altar, the statues, the stations of the cross, Fogarty thought possibly his judgment on the clergy was too harsh. After all, who could live up to these surroundings? What mere actors could bring grace to a setting that dwarfed them? There was just too much grandiloquence for a human to contend with. It was like being asked to play *Aida* on a harmonica.

It was his nose again, he decided. He had never liked priests or nuns, because of the way they smelled. They smelled dead, like the lilies on the altar. There was an aroma of phony purity about them, the three of them: priests, nuns, lilies. In Fogarty's head this trinity opted for a plasticized permanence—there wasn't a whiff of pollen in any of them. They had deliberately murdered their sting: They would never reproduce, and they thought they were superior for it. Fogarty had more respect for the earthly stink of sweat, because it smacked of exertion in life, not embalmment. What a bogus halo: I am, because I don't.

Most ludicrous to Fogarty were the nuns, who wore wedding rings and proclaimed they were brides of God. Didn't they know (at least in the earthbound scheme of things) that they were proclaiming the Lord had a harem the likes of which Farouk never envisioned? He cursed his blasphemy, but nonetheless, he could not get the idea of heavenly groupies out of his head.

This kind of thinking was getting him nowhere. In desperation he walked to a confessional box, pulled back the maroon drape, and stepped inside. After much shuffling and coughing (which was the penitent's standard calling card), no one pulled back the confessional partition. He thought of knocking on the partition but was afraid that the Holy Ghost would appear in fiery livery and tell him to use the delivery entrance. Much to his relief, he realized it was Saturday, and confessions were not heard till three o'clock, a time by Fogarty's estimate that was hours away.

He left the box, deciding to make a call on the rectory in search of absolution. This wrinkle bothered Fogarty, since for years he had been a loyal union man, and working hours were working hours. Besides, he knew his soul did not have the muscle to press God's agents into overtime.

The rectory was a three-story building of red brick with an ornate carved wooden door. The brick was dusted with a white powder to diminish its blush. Fogarty wondered if the same biddy of a housekeeper would answer the door. That couldn't be possible, he calculated, since she had been ancient when he was a boy—a shriveled slice of bacon, bent and burnt, in a black housedress. That was by design, of course. A young, meaty maiden might have conjured up visions of those hanky-panky Popes of the past among the more cynical of parishioners.

He pressed the buzzer and heard the chimes ring inside the priests' house. Chimes to be sure. Not the harsh summons of a bell, but the fey ding-dong of bareass angels. He knew it. A crumpled wad (one of God's discarded memos?) answered the door. Was it Agnes? Bridget? Nellie? Or were they all one, the withered women who had been answering the doors of rectories since he could remember?

He was about to say something, but she beat him to the draw. "What do you want at this hour? It's noontime."

The volume of her voice stunned him. It was a cannon roar coming from a derringer. "I would like to see a priest," he said mealy-mouthedly.

"I would like to see a priest," she mimicked back at him. "Well, it's noon, and the fathers have a busy afternoon with confession, and unless you're dying, which I doubt looking at the lummox size of you, you'll have to wait to see one of the fathers this evening."

Fogarty couldn't believe it. This sexless collection of old rags, a housedress with sweater upon sweater piled on, with her feet stuck into a pair of knitted slippers (shanty shits, he thought, they could never accustom themselves to shoes), was mocking him.

"In the evening. Is that clear?"

Fogarty had one ploy open, and he tried it. "Madame, I am in need of a priest." The key word was "need," and he waited till it sank in.

"Need, you said?"

"Need," he affirmed. (That ought to bring Barry Fitzgerald running, he thought).

"Anyone in particular?" she asked.

Sensing he had turned the current of the battle, he countered: "Who do you have on tap? I'm afraid I've been away a long time."

"Oh, a long time," she crooned, reminding Fogarty of Arthur Godfrey when he had a hot discovery on his *Talent Scout* show. "Well, there is Father Patton, Father Genovese, Pastor O'Brien—but he already left for the racetrack. And Father Logan."

Fogarty opted for the Italian, rationalizing that he would be more sympathetic to his tale. "Father Genovese will be fine."

"Oh, I'm sorry, He's out on a sick call."

"Logan then."

"He had a late mass and is about to have his breakfast, but I'll ask if he'll see you." She ushered Fogarty into the foyer, and she mounted the flight of stairs.

Logan, as Fogarty remembered him, was insufferable. He had come to the parish when Fogarty was about eleven years old and beginning to have some grievous doubts about what he had learned his first ten years on earth. Worse, Logan was a convert. His mother was Catholic and his father Lutheran, and one day Logan had decided to tell his father his God was bogus. When one thinks about that, it's a pretty pompous thing to do—to inform your father he has made a bum choice for eternity.

But what was really contemptible about Logan, as far as Fogarty was concerned, was that he was one of those bridgers of the generation gap, or whatever they called that chronological chasm in those days. He was constantly organizing "youth activities"—dances, bowling nights, "open-minded" discussions of religion. He also was a sports buff and had the reputation of having been a big gun in basketball during his high school days.

He was always organizing teams, circulating chance books for new uniforms, and casually "dropping around the playground" in sneakers and a sweat shirt (that *Going My Way* crap) to join in the pick-me-up basketball games and talk "regular" to the guys. Real hep. A little joke about how Marie Beretta's sweater must be starched; chiding Johnny Cashman about his pimples and how he'd got them, advising that he take a basketball to bed with him to hold in his hands. Then someone would shout that Johnny was already a great ball handler, and everyone would break up.

Except Fogarty. To be truthful, all the other kids adored Logan and called him Father Ted. Fogarty thought he was a patronizing shithead. Besides, Logan had a habit of standing behind a boy, with his hand around the kid's neck, rocking back and forth while he asked him some question about sports. After Fogarty received that treatment one day, he wondered to which sport Logan was referring.

Logan, the whole six feet five of him, descended the stairway solemnly, book in hand—Hamlet interrupted at his vespers. The skirts of his cassock swept across the floor like a majestic broom. He milked every step, the way Gene Kelly used to when he was playing to the last row in the balcony. What hams priests are, Fogarty thought. They are such puppets to their paraphernalia. Put a priest in pants, and he's just another guy with a bum tailor.

Logan paused and stared at Fogarty. "My eyes deceive me! Surely not Shamus?"

"Hello, Father. How have you been?"

"Fine, Shamus. But the question is, how have you been? As if we didn't know. Our ex-altar boy being written up gloriously in *Time* magazine for his . . . what do you call it, Shamus—sculpturing?"

"Dollmaking, Father."

"Yes, how roughshod of you. But you always were a bit of a diamond in that way."

"If you say so, Father."

"Oh, but I do. Remember the time you. . . . "

"Look, Father, I'm not here to talk about my press clippings or my artistic stance. I came here because I wanted to talk to a priest. In a priestly way."

"Now, don't tell me our man of the world has troubles that can be solved by a humble Catholic priest?"

"I didn't come here for ballbreaking either, Logan."

"Perhaps you're out of your milieu, Shamus. That kind of language will get you little around here."

"Look, I just came in here asking to talk to someone."

"Oh, how I love your kind! Nobody sees hide nor hair of you for years, and suddenly you come barging in here at high noon asking for a priest, as if he was a butler."

"Father, remember the prodigal son."

"I don't need the likes of you to teach me my catechism, Fogarty."

"So what do we do, Father, stand here in the hall and shout at each other?"

"What's your problem then, Shamus? Let's hear it."

"It's private and painful, Father, and I don't believe it's a story you swap standing up in a hallway."

"What then? Confession?"

"If that's the way they still do it, yes."

"Some things endure, Shamus. Come to my room. I'll hear you there."

Logan's room was decorated in early country priest: a desk, a bed, endless volumes on religious subjects, and a crucifix on the wall. No statues or religious paintings, just the crucifix. It was so contrived Fogarty swore it had been done by a decorator: "Look, Sweety, we're going to do it in humble. Provincial Humble."

"Kneel down, Shamus."

"What!" Fogarty asked, incredulous.

"I presume you want your confession heard. It's not like a bar, Shamus, where one tells his stories standing up."

"Where?"

"The other side of my desk will be fine. I'll sit on this side. That should give you a degree of privacy under the circumstances."

"Couldn't we go to the church?"

"Look, Fogarty, I don't start hearing confessions until three o'clock. I am not going to the church now. Even if we went to the church, I'd still know it was you."

That last part made sense to Fogarty, and he sank to his knees. Just then the door burst open, and the housekeeper entered with a breakfast tray. Spotting Fogarty on his knees, she inquired, "Did you lose something, sir?"

"Oh, my God," Fogarty moaned.

The housekeeper was beside him. She set the tray on the desk, then dropped on all fours next to Fogarty.

"What was it, sir? I'll give you a hand looking for it."

Fogarty hugged his body in anguish and moaned, "Sweet Jesus, sweet Jesus."

"Oh, my God, Father," she moaned in unison, "I think it's his heart. I'll run and get a priest."

"THERESA!" Logan shouted. "Leave this room immediately. Everything is under control."

Fogarty got to his feet, wanting to flee.

"Look at him, Father. He's fine. Immaculate Mother, you're a miracle worker." She kissed Logan's hand.

"Goddammit, Theresa, get out of this room."

"I just didn't want your breakfast to get cold."

"That was kind of you, Theresa, but please leave."

Realizing she hadn't witnessed a mini-Lourdes after all, Theresa contritely backed out of the room.

"I'm sorry about that, Shamus. Shall we begin again?"

"What about your breakfast?"

"That can wait. There are more important things at hand."

Fogarty looked at the tray. It held a half grapefruit, bacon, eggs, toast, coffee, silverware, and napkin rolled in a silver ring. He remembered coming to the rectory as an altar boy and being so impressed by this simple posh display, posh, that is, compared to the way he ate at home.

"Shall we begin?"

Fogarty knelt again. "Father, I've left my wife and child."

"Hmm."

"Hmm what?"

"What do you mean 'what,' Fogarty? Do you want me to make your confession for you?"

"No, I don't, Father. But what the hell does 'hm-m' mean?"

"It means continue, or are you hoping for some instant absolution?"

"I'm not hoping for a thing. I just want to talk—I'm miserable about the boy."

"What about your wife?"

"I don't love her anymore, Father."

"One doesn't enter marriage, Fogarty, as one approaches the seasons. Marriage is a constant—we accept the hot with the cold."

"I can't, Father. It's the hot memories that make the cold unendurable."

"Well, it was doomed from the start anyway, wasn't it?"

"What do you mean?"

"You weren't married in the church, were you?"

"You know I wasn't."

"Yes, I do know. I cautioned your mother this would end in disaster."

"What the hell does my mother have to do with it?"

"This is a confession, Fogarty. So speak accordingly."

"All right, all right, but what's the sense of dredging up my mother?"

"At the time I hoped she could exercise some control."

"Look, Father. It's a fact of life that sons savage their mothers."

"I hardly think you're in a position to teach me the facts of life."

"That's debatable, but let's get off it. The current fact is that everything seems lost, and I don't give a good damn if I'm alive or dead."

"Oh, I would, if I were you. I don't think your soul is in any shape to be contemplating eternity."

"Father, I don't want to argue. It's the boy." Dammit, Logan had won. Fogarty heard the sound of his own weeping, ungraceful snorts—a dumb, clumsy animal choking on its own mucus.

"Is the boy baptized?"

"No."

"Just how many souls do you intend to start on the road to hell, Fogarty?"

"Oh, for Christ sake."

"Never mind invoking strangers. What chance does the child have, relegated to limbo by your heretical beliefs?"

"If it's any solace to you, the kid has probably been baptized fifty times behind my back by my fanatical relatives. He's probably waterlogged."

"You impudent son of a bitch—God forgive me. Don't mock the sacraments in this house, in my presence."

"Then don't imply I'm destroying my son."

"Enough. I'll try to be the Christian here. You certainly call up my darker impulses. Is anyone else involved in this?"

"Yes, another woman. I'm in love with her." Fogarty heard a squish and wondered what Logan was doing on the other side of the desk.

"Immaculate Mary, the predictability of it. Do you live in sin with her?"

"Meaning what?"

"Are you adulterous?"

"Yes, but I prefer not to call it that."

"How long has this been going on and how often?"

"Let's skip the numbers, Logan. Besides, I don't keep count."

"Do you perform acts other than copulation?"

Fogarty heard the squish again and swore Logan had shifted in anticipation. He wondered where his hand was. "You know what you should have been, Logan? A cop. That's how they grill people 'When he exposed himself, my dear, were you doing anything unconsciously that might have titillated him? Just how prominent was his organ, my child?' A horny, squirming cop, Logan—Bless me, Father, my ass— you couldn't father a wet dream. Go get your rocks off over someone else's life."

Logan let out a low wail, like a banshee's, leaped up, and began smashing at Fogarty with his fists. Fogarty struggled to his feet, pushing the priest off more in disgust than anger.

But when he looked over at the desk, Fogarty was driven to fury. The sound of the squish was now clear to him. Logan's grapefruit was half-eaten. He couldn't believe it. Eating a fucking grapefruit while he, Fogarty, Shamus, knelt blubbering on his knees!

Fogarty reached for the tray and picked up the grapefruit. He grabbed Logan by the back of the neck. "Why you, you. . . . " He couldn't find the proper word.

So, with his lips still pursued, he jammed the grapefruit into Logan's face. Terrified, the priest cowered in what he hoped was a neutral corner.

Fogarty gave his pants a couple of hitches with his elbows. Strutting out of the room, he did a jaunty dance step down the stairs, whistling. "Yankee Doodle Dandy."

The incident with Logan pleased Fogarty only momentarily; as he walked away from the rectory, his despair fell in step behind him. So he had won one over a pious creep. Little difference. It wasn't what he wanted. That sad ass was at sea, too. He disliked priests, because they didn't live up to their billing. That was his Catholic dilemma. If Fogarty had decided to become a priest, he would have made a workmanlike job of it; he wouldn't have squished when a soul came searching. Squish, went his soul. God, was that a sign?

22

MARY GORDON
(b. 1949)

Mary Gordon, the youngest of the writers represented in this collection, was born on Long Island in 1949. Her father, a convert to Catholicism, was a writer and a publisher; her mother, a legal secretary. She received her B.A. from Barnard College in 1971 and her M.A. from Syracuse University in 1973, after which she taught English at Dutchess Community College in Poughkeepsie, New York, and at Amherst College in Massachusetts.

Gordon has written poetry and has published several short stories; but it is on the strength of her first two novels, particularly the first, *Final Payments* (1978), and *The Company of Women* (1981), that she has gained stature as an interpreter of modern Catholic life in America. Given her parental background, which is Catholic but not Irish, it is all the more interesting that *Final Payments* is so perceptive and so detailed a portrait of Irish-American Catholic life in Queens, New York, and suburbia. In it, Isabel Moore's life has been dominated by the powerful Irish-Catholic presence of her recently deceased father. Now Isabel, who nursed her father for eleven years through a series of strokes, sets out at age thirty to make a life of her own. She finds herself a job, establishes new relationships, and becomes involved with married men, for which "self-indulgence" she is guilt-ridden and moved to take on terrible penances in the kind of Catholic "ghetto" she had left by devoting herself once again to another, in this case a woman she despises, her father's former housekeeper, Margaret Casey.

The Company of Women adds to Gordon's gallery of Catholic parochialism by presenting Felicitas Taylor, fourteen at the novel's opening, as the hope of "the company of women" whose life centers on Father Cyprian because he "detests the permissiveness of the contemporary church." Felicitas's constricted existence continues when she

265

goes to a Catholic college; but as Isabel Moore had broken out with the death of her father, Felicitas breaks out by entering Columbia University, embarking on an affair with a professor and becoming pregnant, then returning, as does Isabel, to her source, here the group of women for whom Felicitas's daughter becomes the new hope for the future.

In *Men and Angels* (1985) Gordon extends her range beyond the earlier parochialism—though retaining the earlier strain of intense religiosity—by creating Laura Post, fanatically religious, who takes care of the children of Anne Foster, who is researching the life of a woman painter while her professor husband is on sabbatical. *Temporary Shelter* (1987) is Gordon's first collection of short stories, several previously published in periodicals; three of the stories, "Eileen," "Agnes," and "Delia" are about Irish immigrants to America.

"The Neighborhood," first appearing in the July 1984 *Ms.*, presents an Irish immigrant family, the Lynches, displaced by moving into a Long Island "neighborhood of second generation Irish." Seen sometimes as "exotics," sometimes as "shanty Irish," after seven years the Lynches leave under dubious circumstances, and the neighborhood is relieved that the new occupants of the Lynches' house are like themselves and that they know what to expect of them.

"The Neighborhood"

My mother has moved from her house now; it was her family's for sixty years. As she was leaving, neighbors came in shyly, family by family, to say good-bye. There weren't many words; my mother hadn't been close to them; she suspected neighborly connections as the third-rate PR of Protestant churches and the Republican Party, the substitute of the weak, the rootless, the disloyal, for parish or for family ties. Yet everyone wept; the men she'd never spoken to, the women she'd rather despised, the teenagers who'd gained her favor by taking her garbage from the side of the house to the street for a dollar and a half a week in the bad weather. As we drove out, they arranged themselves formally on either side of the driveway, as if the car were a hearse. Through the rearview mirror, I saw the house across the street and thought of the Lynches, who'd left almost under cover, telling nobody, saying good-bye to no one, although they'd lived there seven years and when they'd first arrived the neighborhood had been quite glad.

The Lynches were Irish, Ireland Irish, people in the neighborhood said proudly, their move from the city to Long Island having given them the luxury of bestowing romance on a past their own parents might have downplayed or tried to hide. Nearly everybody on the block except my family and the Freeman sisters had moved in just after the War. The War, which the men had fought in, gave them a new feeling of legitimate habitation: they had as much right to own houses on Long Island as the Methodists, if not, perhaps, the old Episcopalians. And the Lynches' presence only made their sense of seigneury stronger: they could look upon them as exotics, or as foreigners and tell themselves that after all now there was nothing they had left behind in Brooklyn that they need feel as a lack.

Each of the four Lynch children had been born in Ireland, although only the parents had an accent. Mr. Lynch was hairless, spry, and silent: the kind of Irishman who seems preternaturally clean and who produces, possibly without his understanding, child after child, whom he then leaves to their mother. I don't know why I wasn't frightened of Mrs. Lynch; I was the sort of child to whom the slightest sign of irregularity might seem a menace. Now I can place her, having seen drawings by Hogarth, having learned words like *harridan* and *slattern*, which almost rhyme, having recorded, in the necessary course of feminist research, all those hateful descriptions of women gone to seed, or worse than seed, gone to some rank uncontrollable state where things sprouted and hung from them in a damp, lightless anarchy. But I liked Mrs. Lynch; could it have been that I didn't notice her wild hair, her missing teeth, her swelling ankles, her ripped clothes, her bare feet when she came to the door, her pendulous ungirded breasts? Perhaps it was that she was different and my fastidiousness was overrun by my romanticism. Or perhaps it was that she could give me faith in transformation. If, in the evenings, on the weekends, she could appear barefoot and unkempt, on Monday morning she walked out in her nurse's aide's uniform, white-stockinged and white-shod, her hair pinned under a starched cap, almost like any of my aunts.

But I am still surprised that I allowed her to be kind to me. I never liked going into the house; it was the first dirty house that I had ever seen, and when I had to go in and wait for Eileen, a year younger than I, with whom I played emotionlessly from the sheer demand of her geographical nearness and the sense that playing was the duty of our state in life, I tried not to look at anything and I tried not to breathe. When, piously, I described the mechanisms of my forbearance to my mother, she surprised me by being harsh. "God help Mrs. Lynch," she said, "four children and slaving all day in that filthy city hospital, then driving home through all that miserable traffic. She must live her life dead on her feet. And the oldest are no help."

Perhaps my mother's toleration of the Lynches pointed the response of the whole neighborhood, who otherwise would not have put up with the rundown condition of the Lynches' house and yard. The neighbors had for so long looked upon our family as the moral arbiters of the street that it would have been inconceivable for them to shun anyone of whom my mother approved. Her approvals, they all knew, were formal and dispensed *de haut en bas*. Despising gossip, defining herself as a working woman who had no time to sit on the front steps and chatter, she signaled her approbation by beeping her horn and waving from her car. I wonder now if my mother liked Mrs. Lynch because she too had no time to sit and drink coffee with the other women; if she saw a kinship between them, both of them bringing home money for their families, both of them in a kind of widowhood, for Mr. Lynch worked two jobs every day, one as a bank guard, one as a night watchman, and on Saturdays he drove a local cab. What he did inside the house was impossible to speculate upon; clearly, he barely inhabited it.

My father died when I was seven and from then on I believed the world was dangerous. Almost no one treated me sensibly after his death. Adults fell into two categories: they hugged me and pressed my hand, their eyes brimming over with unshed tears, or they slapped me on the back and urged me to get out in the sunshine, play with other children, stop brooding, stop reading, stop sitting in the dark. What they would not do was leave me alone, which was the only thing I wanted. The children understood that, or perhaps they had no patience; they got tired of my rejecting their advances, and left me to myself. That year I developed a new friendship with Laurie Sorrento, whom I never in the ordinary run of things would have spoken to since she had very nearly been left back in the first grade. But her father had died too. Like mine, he had had a heart attack, but his happened when he was driving his truck over the Fifty-ninth Street Bridge, at five o'clock, causing a traffic jam of monumental stature. My father had a heart attack in

the Forty-second Street Library. He died a month later in Bellevue.
Each evening during that month my mother drove into the city after
work, through the Midtown Tunnel. I had supper with a different
family on the block each evening, and each night some mother put
me to bed and waited in my house until my mother drove into the
driveway at eleven. Then, suddenly, it was over, that unreal time; the
midnight call came, he was dead. It was as though the light went out
in my life and I stumbled through the next few years trying to recognize familiar objects which I had known but could not seem to
name.

I didn't know if Laurie lived that way, as I did, in half-darkness,
but I enjoyed her company. I only remember our talking about our
fathers once, and the experience prevented its own repetition. It was
a summer evening, nearly dark. We stood in her backyard and
started running in circles shouting, "My father is dead, my father is
dead." At first it was the shock value, I think, that pleased us, the
parody of adult expectation of our grief, but then the thing itself took
over and we began running faster and faster and shouting louder and
louder. We made ourselves dizzy and we fell on our backs in the
grass, still shouting "My father is dead, my father is dead, " and in
our dizziness the grass toppled the sky and the rooftops slanted dangerously over the new moon, almost visible. We looked at each other,
silent, terrified, and walked into the house, afraid we might have
made it disappear. No one was in the house, and silently, Laurie fed
me Saltine crackers, which I ate in silence till I heard my mother's
horn honk at the front of the house, and we both ran out, grateful for
the rescue.

But that Christmas, Laurie's mother remarried, a nice man who
worked for Con Edison, anxious to become the father of an orphaned
little girl. She moved away and I was glad. She had accepted normal
life and I no longer found her interesting. This meant, however, that
I had no friends. I would never have called Eileen Lynch my friend;
our sullen, silent games of hopscotch or jump rope could not have
been less intimate, her life inside her filthy house remained a mystery to me, as I hoped my life in the house where death had come
must be to her. There was no illusion of our liking one another; we
were simply there.

Although I had no friends, I was constantly invited to birthday
parties, my tragedy giving me great cachet among local mothers.
These I dreaded as I did the day of judgment (real to me; the wrong
verdict might mean that I would never see my father), but my

mother would never let me refuse. I hated the party games and had become phobic about the brick of vanilla, chocolate, and strawberry ice cream always set before me and the prized bakery cake with its sugar roses. At every party I would run into the bathroom as the candles were being blown out and be sick. Resentful, the mothers would try to be kind, but I knew they'd felt I spoiled the party. I always spent the last hour in the birthday child's room, alone, huddled under a blanket. When my mother came the incident would be reported, and I would see her stiffen as she thanked the particular mother for her kindness. She never said anything to me, though, and when the next invitation came and I would remind and warn her, she would stiffen once again and say only, "I won't be around forever, you know."

But even I could see there was no point trying to get out of Eileen Lynch's party. I didn't say anything as I miserably dressed and miserably walked across the street, my present underneath my arm, a pair of pedal pushers I was sure Eileen wouldn't like.

Superficially, the Lynches' house was cleaner, though the smell was there, the one that always made me suspect there was something rotting, dead, or dying behind the stove or the refrigerator. Eileen's older sisters, whose beauty I then felt was diminished by its clear sexual source, were dressed in starched, high dresses; their shoes shone and the seams in their stockings were perfect. For the first time, I felt I had to admire them, although I'd preferred their habitual mode of treatment—the adolescent's appraisal of young children as deriving from a low and altogether needless caste—to their false condescending warmth as they offered me a party hat and a balloon. Eileen seemed unimpressed by all the trouble that had been gone to for her; her distant walk-through of Blind Man's Bluff and Pin the Tail on the Donkey I recognized as springing from a heart as joyless as my own.

Throughout the party, Mrs. Lynch had stayed in the kitchen. After the presents had been opened, she appeared, wearing her nurse's uniform and her white hose, but not her cap, and said to all of us, "Will ye come in and have some cake, then?"

It was the cake and ice cream I had known from all the other birthday parties and I closed my eyes and tried to think of other things—the ocean, as my mother had suggested, the smell of new-mown grass. But it was no good. I felt the salty rising behind my throat: I ran for the bathroom. Eileen's guests were not from my class, they were a year younger than I, so I was spared the humiliation of knowing they'd seen all this a dozen times before. But I was wretched as I bent above the open toilet, convinced that there was nowhere in the world that I belonged, wishing only that I could be dead like my father in a universe which had, besides much else to recommend it, incorporeality for its nature. There was the expected knock on the door. I hoped it would be Mrs. Lynch instead of one of Eileen's sisters whose contempt I would have found difficult to bear.

"Come and lay down, ye'll need a rest," she said, turning her back to me the way the other mothers did. I followed, as I always had, into the indicated room, not letting my glance fall toward the eating children, trying not to hear their voices.

I was surprised that Mrs. Lynch had led me, not into the child's room but into the bedroom that she shared with Mr. Lynch. It was a dark room, I don't think it could have had a window. There were two high dressers and the walls were covered with brown, indistinguishable holy images. Mrs. Lynch moved the rose satinish coverlet and indicated I should lie on top of it. The other mothers always turned the bed down for me, and with irritation, smoothed the sheets. Mrs. Lynch went into the closet and took out a rough brown blanket. She covered me with it and seemed as though she were going to leave the room. She sat down on the bed, though, and put her hand on my forehead, as if she were checking for fever. She turned the light out and sat in the chair across the room in the fashion, I now see, of the paid nurse. Nothing was said between us. But for the first time, I understood what all those adults were trying to do for me. I understood what was meant by comfort. Perhaps I was able to accept it from Mrs. Lynch as I had from no other because there was no self-love in what she did, nothing showed me she had one eye on some mirror checking her posture as the comforter of a grief-stricken child. She was not congratulating herself for her tact, her understanding, her tough-mindedness. And she had no suggestions for me; no sense that things could change if simply I could see things right, could cry, or run around the yard with other children. It was her sense of the inevitability of what had happened, and its permanence, its falling into the category of natural affliction, that I received as such a gift. I slept, not long I know—ten minutes, perhaps, or twenty—but it was one of those afternoon sleeps one awakes from as if one has walked out of the ocean. I heard the record player playing and sat up. It was the time of the party for musical chairs.

"Ye'd like to join the others then?" she asked me, turning on the light.

I realized that I did. I waited till the first round of the game was over, then joined in. It was the first child's game I can remember enjoying.

My mother didn't come for me in the car, of course. I walked across the street so she and Mrs. Lynch never exchanged words about what had happened. "I had a good time," I said to my mother, showing her the ring I'd won.

"The Lynches are good people," my mother said.

I'd like to say that my friendship with Eileen developed or that I acknowledged a strong bond with her mother and allowed her to become my confidante. But it wasn't like that; after that time my contacts with the Lynches dwindled, partly because I was making friends outside the neighborhood and partly because of the older Lynch children and what happened to their lives.

It was the middle fifties and we were, after all, a neighborhood of second-generation Irish. Adolescence was barely recognized as a distinct state; it was impossible to imagine that adolescent rebellion would be seen as anything but the grossest breach of the social contract, an incomprehensible one at that. "Rebel Without a Cause" was on the Legion of Decency condemned list; even Elvis Presley was preached against on the Sunday mornings before he was to appear on the "Ed Sullivan Show." So how could my neighborhood absorb the eldest Lynch kids: Charlie, who left school at sixteen and had no job, who spent his afternoons in the driveway, souping up his car. Or Kathy, who'd got in trouble in tenth grade and then married, bringing her baby several times a week, assuming that Eileen, at ten, would be enchanted to take care of it. She wasn't of course, she viewed the child with the resentful gaze she cast on everything in life and refused to change its diapers. Rita, the third daughter, had gone to beautician school and seemed on her way to a good life except that she spent all her evening parked with different young men in different cars—we all could see that they were different, even in the darkness—in front of the Lynch house.

I was shocked by the way the Lynches talked to their parents. In the summer everyone could hear them, "Ma, you stupid asshole," "Pop, you're completely full of shit." "For Christ sake, this is America, not fucking Ireland." Once in the winter, Charlie and Mrs. Lynch picked Eileen and me up from school when it was raining a gray, dense, lacerating winter rain. In the backseat, I heard Mrs. Lynch and Charlie talking.

"Ye'll drop me at the supermarket, then."

"I said I'd pick these kids up. That was all."

"I just need a few things, Charlie. And I remember asking ye this morning and ye saying yes."

He slammed the brakes on and looked dangerously at his mother. "Cut the crap out, Ma. I said I have things to do and I have them. I mean it now."

Mrs. Lynch looked out the window, and Charlie left us off at the Lynch house, then drove away.

People said it was terrible the way the Lynches sat back, staring helplessly at their children like Frankenstein staring at his monster. My mother's interpretation was that the Lynches were so exhausted simply making ends meet that they didn't have the strength left to control their children, and it was a shame that children could take such advantage of their parents' efforts and hard lot. The closest she would come to criticizing them was to say that it might have been easier for them in the city where they didn't have the responsibility of a house and property. And such a long commute. But it was probably the kids they did it for, she said. Knowing how she felt, nobody said "shanty Irish" in front of my mother, although I heard it often on the street, each time with a pang of treachery in my heart as I listened in silence and never opened my mouth to defend.

Everyone for so long had predicted disaster for the Lynches that no one was surprised when it happened; their only surprise was that it happened on such a limited scale. It was a summer night; Charlie was drunk. His father had taken the keys to the car and hidden them so Charlie couldn't drive. We could hear him shouting at his father, "Give them to me, you fucking son of a bitch." We couldn't hear a word from Mr. Lynch. Finally, there was a shot, and then the police siren and the ambulance. Charlie was taken off by the police, and Mr. Lynch wheeled out on a stretcher. We later found out from Joe Flynn, a cop who lived down the street, that Mr Lynch was all right; Charlie'd only shot him in the foot. But Charlie was on his way to jail. His parents had pressed charges.

Then the Lynches were gone; no one knew how they'd sold the house; there was never a sign in front. It was guessed that Mr. Lynch had mentioned wanting to sell to someone in the cab company. Only the U-Haul truck driven by Kathy's husband and the new family, the Sullivans, arriving to work on the house, told us what had happened. Jack Sullivan was young and from town and worked for the phone company; he said he didn't mind doing the repairs because he'd got the house for a song. His father helped him on weekends, and they fixed the house up so it looked like all the others on the street. His wife loudly complained, though, about the filth inside; she'd never seen anything like it; it took her a week to get through the kitchen grease, she said, and they'd had to have the exterminator.

Everyone was awfully glad when they were finally moved in. It was a relief to have your own kind, everybody said. That way you knew what to expect.

IRISH STUDIES

Irish Studies presents a wide range of books interpreting important aspects of Irish life and culture to scholarly and general audiences. The richness and complexity of the Irish experience, past and present, deserves broad understanding and careful analysis. For this reason an important purpose of the series is to offer a forum to scholars interested in Ireland, its history, and culture. Irish literature is a special concern in the series, but works from the perspectives of the fine arts, history, and the social sciences are also welcome, as are studies which take multidisciplinary approaches.

Irish Studies is a continuing project of Syracuse University Press and is under the general editorship of Richard Fallis, associate professor of English at Syracuse University.

An Anglo-Irish Dialect Glossary for Joyce's Works. Richard Wall
Beckett and Myth: An Archetypal Approach. Mary A. Doll
Caught in the Crossfire: Children and the Northern Ireland Conflict. Ed Cairns
Children's Lore in "Finnegans Wake." Grace Eckley
Cinema and Ireland. Kevin Rockett, Luke Gibbons, and John Hill
The Decline of the Union: British Government in Ireland, 1892–1920. Eunan O'Halpin
The Drama of J. M. Synge. Mary C. King
Dreamscheme: Narrative and Voice in "Finnegans Wake." Michael Begnal
Fictions of the Irish Literary Revival: A Changeling Art. John Wilson Foster
Finnegans Wake: A Plot Summary. John Gordon
Fionn mac Cumhaill: Celtic Myth in English Literature. James MacKillop
Great Hatred, Little Room: The Irish Historical Novel. James M. Cahalan
Hanna Sheehy-Skeffington: Irish Feminist. Leah Levenson and Jerry H. Natterstad
In Minor Keys: The Uncollected Short Stories of George Moore. David B. Eakin and Helmut E. Gerber, eds.
Intimidation and the Control of Conflict in Northern Ireland. John Darby
Irish Life and Traditions. Sharon Gmelch, ed.
Irish Literature: A Reader. Maureen O'Rourke Murphy and James MacKillop, eds.
'Ireland Sober, Ireland Free': Drink and Temperance in Nineteenth-Century Ireland. Elizabeth Malcolm
The Irish Renaissance. Richard Fallis
James Joyce: The Augmented Ninth. Bernard Benstock, ed.
The Literary Vision of Liam O'Flaherty. John N. Zneimer
Northern Ireland: The Background to the Conflict. John Darby, ed.
Old Days, Old Ways: An Illustrated Folk History of Ireland. Olive Sharkey
Peig: The Autobiography of Peig Sayers of the Great Blasket Island. Bryan MacMahon, trans.
Selected Plays of Padraic Colum. Sanford Sternlicht, ed.
Selected Poems of Padraic Colum. Sanford Sternlicht, ed.
Selected Short Stories of Padraic Colum. Sanford Sternlicht, ed.
Shadowy Heroes: Irish Literature of the 1890s. Wayne E. Hall
Ulster's Uncertain Defenders: Protestant Political, Paramilitary, and Community Groups and the Northern Ireland Conflict. Sarah Nelson
Yeats. Douglas Archibald
Yeats and the Beginning of the Irish Renaissance. Phillip L. Marcus

MODERN IRISH-AMERICAN FICTION

was composed in 10 on 12 Caledonia and Optima on a Linotron 202
by BookMasters;
printed by sheet-fed offset on 50-pound, acid-free Glatfelter Natural Hi Bulk,
Smyth-sewn and bound over binder's boards in Holliston Roxite B,
and notch bound with paper covers
by Braun-Brumfield, Inc.;
with paper covers printed in 2 colors
by Braun-Brumfield, Inc.;
and published by
SYRACUSE UNIVERSITY PRESS
SYRACUSE, NEW YORK 13244-5160